A Cold Wind Blows

~

R J Barron

Content compiled for publication by Richard Mayers
of *Burton Mayers Books*.

First published by Burton Mayers Books 2025.

A CIP catalogue record for this book is available from the British Library

ISBN-13: **9781917224116**

Typeset in **Garamond**

www.BurtonMayersBooks.com

DEDICATION

To Juliet, Rosa and Daniel, with love always.

ACKNOWLEDGMENTS

With many thanks to The Creative Writing Programme, Kemptown Books, Brighton and The South East London Writers group, in New Cross, for all the encouragement and constructive criticism. Writing does not have to be a solitary experience.

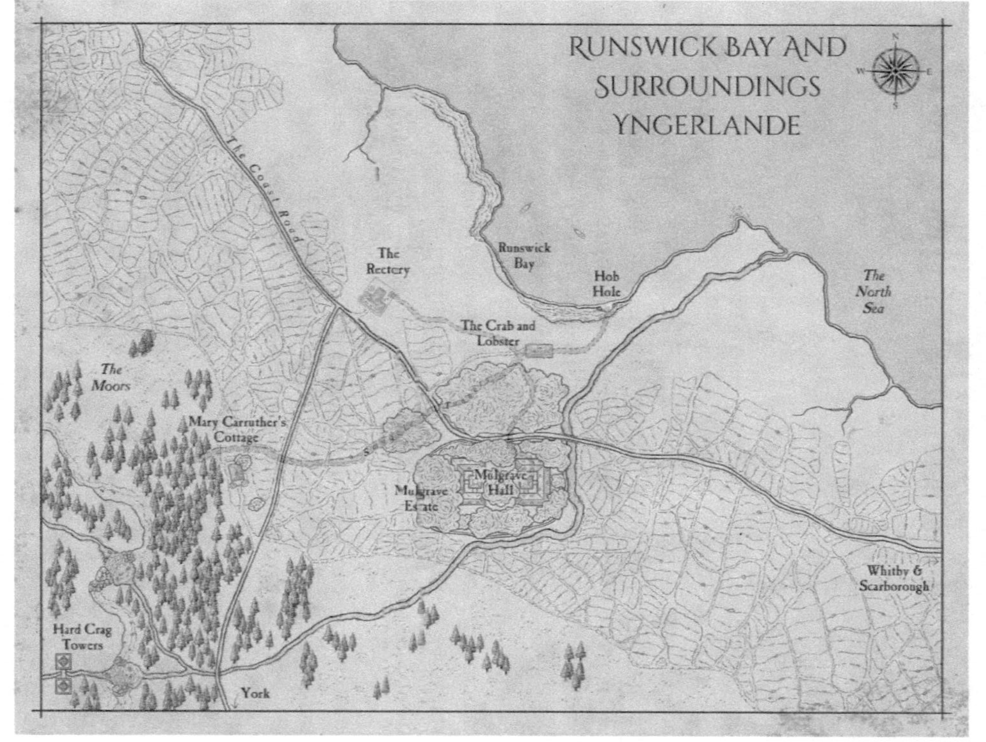
RUNSWICK BAY AND
SURROUNDINGS
YNGERLANDE
N
W
E
S
The Coast Road
The Rectory
Runswick Bay
Hob Hole
The North Sea
The Crab and Lobster
The Moors
Mary Carruther's Cottage
Mulgrave Hall
Mulgrave Estate
Whitby & Scarborough
Hard Crag Towers
York

In "The Watcher and The Friend", the first book in the trilogy, thirteen-year-old Thomas Trelawney is spending Christmas at an old Rectory on the North Yorkshire coast. It is the family's first holiday since the death of Tom's sister Grace. Here, Tom discovers a portal to another world and travels through it to Yngerlande, in 1795, with his cousin, Dan. Yngerlande is a parallel world to England, but is a much more diverse, equal society. He meets Silas Cummerbund, who is The Watcher, the mysterious character who guards the portal between the two worlds. He tells Tom that he is the new Friend, the person whose role is to act as the link between the two worlds. Tom has been summoned to help Silas and his allies defeat the relatives of the old King, Oliver and Jacob, who want to overthrow Queen Matilda and take the country back to a time when racism and discrimination were ever present. His task is made more complicated by the fact that he discovers that his sister, Grace, is alive and well in Yngerlande and is living there as a reward for her service when she was the Friend of Yngerlande. After many adventures and dangerous scrapes, they succeed, and Queen Matilda maintains her rule of peace, love and equality.

"A Cold Wind Blows" begins eight months later.

PROLOGUE: ENGLAND, THE PRESENT DAY

As soon as he turned the corner out of the main playground, Thomas Trelawney realised his mistake. His eyes darted left and right, weighing up whether he could just turn round or make it to the side entrance. But it was too late. Already, a couple of the casually posted lookouts had closed off his return to the playground. They bunched together, swaggering towards him, eyes sparkling with the prospect of confrontation. Behind them, the distant noise of hundreds of kids swirling round rose to taunt him with the stupidity of his lack of care. The first day of the new school year, early, in the last week of August, had made him forget.

Up ahead, more lookouts, posted on the corner of the tennis court, grinned and pointed in his direction, eagerly anticipating some fun before the bell and the whistle summoned them back inside. Tom's heart sank when he saw Harris, the King of all he surveyed, surrounded by his followers and henchmen, in a loose gaggle on the steps below. The tell-tale clouds of vape smoke drifted above their heads. How could he have been so stupid? Every kid in the school knew this was where Harris and his gang always hung out at break and lunchtime. The ground was thick with disposable vapes, and occasionally one of the teachers on duty was early enough to stop them gathering. Once in a blue moon, teachers were clever enough to catch some of them in the act and a temporary exclusion would result, but it was never frequent enough to constitute a threat and so they returned every day to take up their position.

As a result, all the kids (and some of the more timid staff) knew to avoid going anywhere near this part of the school. And so did Tom, but today, engrossed in his phone, he had forgotten and had sleep-walked into danger. And now he would inevitably have to pay the price. He put his head down and tried to nonchalantly walk past, as if nothing was wrong. On another day he might have got away with it, but on this particular day, there was no other victim in range, and Harris was bored.

As Tom passed in front of the group, his head down and eyes averted, he felt them all nervously looking to their leader to give them a sign. Harris stirred.

"Oi!" he bellowed. "Oi, you, you big girl. You're trespassing."

The crowd around him all whooped and jeered, their anticipation growing.

Tom kept going, his eyes firmly on his shoes.

Harris winked at the nearest hanger on.

"Oh dear, oh dear… I think our little trespasser needs to learn some manners, don't he?"

Not waiting for a reply, he looked back to where Tom was walking. Just as he got to the outer reaches of Harris' empire, he bawled, "Don't just stand there, you muppets, bring 'im here. Jimmy, Mo, go on!"

Two boys, hard faced, grabbed him and hauled him back the way he'd come. As he approached, Harris' eyes narrowed in recognition.

"Oh yeah, you're the kid with the sister, incha?" he sneered.

Tom's fists clenched and unclenched, his face just on the right side of a belligerent scowl.

"Or rather," Harris continued, his eyes raking the audience for their acclaim, "the kid without a sister."

His eyes gleamed and he lapped up the raucous laughter that spread through the crowd, delighted with his own cruel wit.

Tom's hands balled into fists, and his hardened face crossed the line into rage. He yanked himself free from his minders and launched himself at Harris.

This time his fists did not unclench.

I

KING'S MANOR

The room waited and waited. A gust of wind creaked the joists. Somewhere, deep in the structure of the building, rafters groaned, timbers shivered, plaster shifted. The clock ticked on. And then a new noise. Barely perceptible at first, a scratch perhaps, and then a scrape. The jug rose uncertainly from the table and moved towards one of the goblets, tipped slightly and poured a thin stream of golden liquid, filling it perfectly to just below the rim. Then, the jug moved again, more smoothly this time and repeated the procedure with the second goblet. As soon as the goblet was full, the jug lowered itself to the table. Just as it reached the surface, the jug wobbled and a splash left a puddle sparkling its accusations in the middle of the table.

"Hell's teeth, will I never learn to do this properly?"

"Now now, Mistress. Don't be hard on yourself. That was nearly perfect."

The disembodied words broke the spell, and two figures materialised in front of the fire.

"Nearly perfect, Silas? Nearly? We both know that that's not good enough," complained the slight young woman, frowning.

Silas put his hand on her shoulder.

"Come now, Princess Gaia, it's much better than it was last week and 'twill be twice as good again next week."

He smiled at her, his eyes sparkling, his grey hair framing an ageless face, pulled back into a pigtail that hung down his back like the pendulum of a clock.

The young woman attempted to maintain her glower,

but Silas' twinkle disarmed her, and her face broke into a wide smile.

"Words of wisdom, as ever, Silas. But less of the Gaia, if you please. And absolutely none of the Princess. To you I am Clara, and always will be. Clara from Coram's Fields Orphanage in London town, no less."

Silas bowed.

"But, your Highness, it would be impolite to address you as such. Your mother, the Queen, would not like it."

Clara scoffed. "Silas, my mother thinks the world of you since you found me and rescued me last year. You can do no wrong in her eyes. That's why she's so happy for me to stay up here, while she is back holding court in London. In fact, I think she's glad I'm here, safe and out of the way. She doesn't have to worry, you see."

Her face clouded for a second as she thought back to the events of the previous Christmas. Everything that had seemed so certain, everything she loved about Yngerlande had suddenly been put at risk and what had seemed solid and permanent had been exposed as being very precarious indeed.

"Come now, Clara, let's not be glum. We all survived and the Kingdom too, so let's look on the bright side, eh? And mothers will always worry – it's what they do best."

Clara cut across him. "But are we safe, Silas? Really safe, I mean. The Kingdom, our way of life, everything that is precious to us. Will they not come for us all again?"

"Oliver and Jacob, you mean?"

"Yes, and all of those other old men who want to take over again. Surely they will try again."

"Clara, my dear, that is precisely why we are spending the summer doing all of this."

He gestured around the candlelit room towards the two goblets on the table. "So that, when the time comes, you are ready."

Clara suddenly reached out and grabbed Silas' arm.

"But what if we were just lucky last time? Things would

have been very different if you hadn't been there. What if…"

"But it wasn't just me. There were a few others involved as well."

A faint blush spread across Clara's face.

"Yes, I know it very well. And we have all become great friends as a result. Friends! Who would have thought that this time last year? I thought I was alone in the world with no-one who understood me. I thought I was some kind of freak of nature, with strange powers that would have got me burned for witchcraft if I had been discovered."

She paused, as if deciding whether to carry on. Silas filled the gap for her.

"And you played as big a part as anyone, remember. If you had not summoned the Steedwings to get you all to York in time, the game would have been up. And, of course, Thomas and Daniel were there as well."

Clara smiled at the memory before another cloud passed across her face.

"Thomas and Daniel! I had forgotten about them."

They both knew that was not true. Clara had thought of Tom every day since she had last seen him on Christmas Eve, holding on for dear life as the Steedwing soared into the frosty air above York Minster. They had held each other's eyes until the Steedwing became a far distant dot in the sky, with a trail of stars that only they could see, linking them together like a rope. She had never felt so close to anyone, even now when they were separated by, well, by what exactly? The universe?

"I don't suppose you have been in contact with them, Silas? Have you?"

"The Watcher and The Friend only meet when there is a need. But I can see him, in his own world. And you must not worry. He is safe and well. Before too long, he will return, of that there is no doubt. And when he does, you will see him."

"Is it really true, Silas, what Grace told me? That they are both from another world, like ours, but in the future? Even saying it aloud sounds strange."

"Are Steedwings strange? And ghosts? What about moving goblets of wine around the table without touching them, eh? For someone with your powers, nothing should surprise you. There are more things in this world, and others, than just what we can see and touch. So, yes, it is true. That and much more. But enough of all of that. You have had a successful day, but you can't do everything that needs to be done in one day, you know. You need to rest before we have dinner. We can start again tomorrow."

"And we'll go back to The Rectory in a few days? You promised, Silas. It would be nice to see everyone again. I did tell Tom I would keep an eye on his sister, remember."

"Yes, of course. We'll spend another day here and then we'll travel back to Runswick Bay for the weekend. It will be good for you to see your friends. But we must carry on with our lessons after that. You only have a month at most before you have to rejoin your mother back at court in St James' Palace. That was the agreement, and even The Watcher must be careful about doing what his Queen demands."

Clara laughed. "Yes, Silas. Not even your powers could protect you from my Mother's anger."

"Off you go, my child, and I will join you for dinner later. I have a few more things to do here."

He watched as Clara left the room. As the great oak door closed, his expression changed, the benign smile replaced by a frown. He quickly glanced around the room, his eyes scanning all four corners, and then fumbled in the pocket of his frock coat. He pulled out a pebble, the size of a hen's egg, and laying it on the palm of his hand, raised his hand high into the air. As he did so, the pebble began to glow, casting a bright luminous blue light that stained Silas' hand and seeped into the air that surrounded it. After half a minute, the pebble cast a brilliant blue light on to the walls of the room, and Silas, holding the pebble high in the air, turned slowly in a full circle, like a lighthouse, so that the blue beam passed over every nook and cranny of the ancient walls. When he had completed one circuit around the room he stopped and waited, his ears pricked, his eyes alert to the merest hint of movement. But there was nothing.

He covered the stone with his other hand, the blue light spilling out from between his fingers and then brought it up to his lips, kissing it lightly. The light seemed to be sucked away from the stone and there, on the palm of his hand, was a perfectly ordinary looking pebble, which he popped back into his pocket. The frown reappeared on his face and he shook his head.

"Nothing," he muttered, "nothing at all. And I was so sure. Oh well, let's not go looking for bad news, eh, Silas? If it's there, it will come soon enough of its own accord."

He turned back to the table, gathered together a sheaf of papers he had left on one of the chairs, and strode towards the door. At the threshold he turned and looked back into the room, still dimly lit with candles. One of the servants would come along shortly to put them out. The room looked back at him, and he listened to the moaning gusts of wind, the ticking of the clock, and the creaking of the ancient walls and floor. Satisfied, he turned and shut the door.

Behind the closed door, the room waited as the gathered air pulsed gently, like some great animal breathing regularly in sleep. And then came another movement, another sound, as the door of the grandfather clock opened a tiny crack. There was a pause, and then the door was carefully pushed open an inch or two. First a bony hand and then a leg eased themselves through the impossibly narrow gap, and then the whole figure, slight and wiry, squeezed through.

It was a young man, barely seventeen, with a shock of spiky red hair, atop a face the colour of raw dough, and piercing green eyes that darted around the room. He was wearing a grubby smock, spattered with grease, patched brown britches, and thin leather ankle boots. A piece of rope served as a rough belt around his middle and held a huge kitchen chopping knife, its blade sparkling from the reflected light of the candles. Once he was sure that the room was empty, a smirk played across his face and he nodded to himself, the smirk widening to a smug smile.

"So," he muttered. "It's back to Runswick Bay at the weekend. And she's already getting better. Who knows what she'll be able to do with the old man's help in a year's time. And with the boy, Thomas, from another world."

He paused and considered. "Another world? That's dark, powerful magic, that. We're all in trouble if the boy returns. We'll have to act, sooner rather than later. I must get a message to my masters, before it's too late."

SHRIKE

He moved quickly across the floor, ready to slip out of the door into the corridor outside. Without warning, the door burst open, and a tall, imposing man strode into the room, his boots ringing on the oak floorboards. The boy froze, an expression of horror momentarily etched on his features. In a split second, he wiped the shock from his face and calmly reached for one of the goblets on the table.

The man, catching sight of him, stopped dead in his tracks, his hand still holding on to the door handle.

"Shrike, you good for nothing layabout. What the devil do you think you're doing in here, lad?"

There was a pause.

"Well?" he bellowed, his face turning an alarming shade of red.

The boy lowered his eyes respectfully, his voice calm with just the right hint of panic in it. "Sorry, Mr Saddleworth, I was just clearing away the glasses, Sir.'

He proffered the goblet in his hand as proof of this claim.

Saddleworth seemed a little disappointed and his fury subsided to mere annoyance.

"Well, what are you waiting for, lad? Take them out. You're wanted in the kitchen downstairs. Mrs Harris has been cursing you to the high heavens. Hasn't set eyes on you for an hour, she says."

Shrike shrank and began to ease himself past Saddleworth, holding the two goblets, one in each hand.

Saddleworth grabbed his collar as he passed and yanked him to a halt. He bent down and looked Shrike in the eye.

"So what the hell have you been doing for the past hour, eh? Doesn't take more than a minute to get a couple of glasses, does it, lad? Have you been skulking in corners, snooping around and up to no good, as usual?"

"No, Sir, honestly. I just had five minutes. I was in the stables and I lost track o' time."

Saddleworth paused, searching for more reasons to berate the boy. Ever since he had arrived in the kitchens at Kings Manor a month ago, Saddleworth had had his doubts about him. He was polite enough and did his work well enough, there were no causes for complaint there, but there was just something about him that he couldn't quite put his finger on. He sometimes seemed to disappear and couldn't be found anywhere when he was wanted. And then, you would suddenly come across him in the most unexpected of places, where he had no right to be. Normal kitchen boys didn't stray too far from the warmth of the kitchen in the winter, making it as far as the outside yard in the heat of the summer. But not Shrike. He seemed to turn up everywhere. Occasionally, Saddleworth had caught him with a strange, twisted expression on his face, as if he held everyone at The Manor in contempt, even Princess Gaia and the old man, Reverend Cummerbund, who everyone spoke highly of. But then it would disappear and Shrike would present his usual innocent face to the world, as if he were perfectly happy with his job and his position in the world.

Saddleworth shook his head and admitted defeat. He let go of his collar and gave him a push that propelled him into the corridor.

"Go on then, lad, get yourself down to the kitchens."

"Yes, Sir," Shrike replied meekly. He scurried away with downcast eyes, the light from the candles gleaming in the silver blade of his enormous knife.

Saddleworth shouted at the retreating back as it

disappeared down the passage, "And thank your lucky stars I caught you when I was in a good mood, lad."

He was not able to see Shrike's angelic countenance disappear to be replaced by a twisted smirk, full of venom against Saddleworth and the rest of the world.

"Yes, Sir," he called back. "Thank you, Sir."

He stroked the flat blade of the knife lovingly as he walked along the corridor, muttering to himself.

"And you'd better hope I'm in a good mood when I catch you, Mr Saddleworth."

AT THE PALACE

The Queen paced up and down her private apartment at St James' Palace. From the window at one end she could see the garden, bathed in warm, late August sunshine, the heady scent of roses masking the stink of the River Thames that was a feature of summer in London, even for the rich and privileged. She would normally be in her castle at Windsor at this time of year, away from the bustle, but she was worried about her daughter. In September, Princess Gaia would return from the North, and be safely ensconced at home where she could keep a motherly eye on her, free from that worry.

She smiled to herself and shook her head a little. No, not free from worry, that was too much to hope for, for any parent, let alone the mother of the future Queen, but at least she would know that she was safe. Whereas now, every waking moment, and many moments in her sleep, she was troubled by the wildest fears of all manner of tragedies and calamities that might have befallen her.

On the table by the window was a miniature portrait of Gaia, painted a year before. Matilda picked it up and examined it. Even in a picture, Gaia's character shone through. Black eyes sparkling, a determined line of a mouth, dark, flawless skin and tightly cropped hair, this was a portrait of someone who was spiky, difficult and ill at ease in the world. It had been painted a few months before she had disappeared and even now it pained Matilda to remember that she had had no inkling of the troubles that had been going through Gaia's mind back then. Gaia had managed to keep from her mother her confusion over the strange powers she evidently possessed, powers which thrilled and frightened her in equal measure.

And those powers, which had saved the Kingdom at Christmas, had to be managed carefully. Matilda was a singularly popular Queen, with all sections of Yngerlande society showing her and the crown love, admiration and respect. This was, in part, because Matilda was at heart a fair-minded and generous person but also because she was clever and knew that it would not go amiss to show concern for the people. She was determined that, during her reign, no-one would go hungry and that the rule of law would apply to everyone, no matter what their station in life. At some point in the future, she may have to rely on the people's support and goodwill. She was, if truth be told, still shaken by the plot to bring her down, and the realisation that the society that had been established in Yngerlande for the last hundred years or so was less secure than they had all thought. Clearly, there were some people who were appalled that a black woman was on the throne of Yngerlande and that something close to true equality and diversity had been established.

It had been with this in mind that Matilda had sought the help of The Reverend Silas Cummerbund, the strange, elderly vicar from Runswick Bay in the far north of the country. It was he who had done the most to protect her and the kingdom of Yngerlande from harm. And it was he who understood the most about Gaia's strange powers. Matilda had had the distinct impression that Silas Cummerbund had powers that would make Gaia's seem insignificant and that he knew of other worlds and beings that could not be spoken of. She had immediately been confident enough to ask him to take charge of helping Gaia come to terms with her special gift, not least because Silas seemed to know all about these powers and how to harness them for good. But ever since she had waved Gaia away in June to spend the Summer in the north under the Reverend Cummerbund's supervision, her doubts had begun to grow.

She returned the portrait to the table and from the drawer underneath it she brought out a tightly folded sheet of parchment, the red wax seal already cracked from repeated readings of the letter. She glanced around the room. Just one footman was there, silent in the shadows in the corner, waiting patiently for any royal command. Satisfied, she opened the letter and read it again. She skipped the usual polite greetings due to a monarch, and went straight to the business end of the letter.

"I regret to inform Your Majesty that my fears over Princess Gaia's safety grow every day. The spies I have installed around the Reverend Cummerbund and his household report that his intentions are much darker towards your daughter than we had thought and that your Majesty's trusting nature has been taken advantage of by the scheming of your enemies. My spies have overheard secret conversations that confirm this. The so-called training that Cummerbund proposed is nothing more than a cover to keep her in an isolated part of the north of the kingdom, away from Your Majesty's loyal troops. It is not yet clear whether this is the work of the plotters that were foiled last Christmas when they tried to blow Your Majesty and half of your court to kingdom come. It may be that they have regrouped and are plotting another attempt on your life before taking the throne. Either they have convinced Cummerbund to join them or his heroics in saving Your Majesty in York was a double bluff.

Rest assured that all of my spies are working to uncover proof of his guilt. I will report any new developments as soon as I can. In the meantime, I beg Your Majesty to entrust this news to Frobisher, Captain of the Queen's Guard, and Lord Pembroke, your personal advisor. Between them they will take the necessary steps to keep Your Majesty safe. You must speak of this to no-one else - you are in great danger.

I remain your most obedient servant,

Frederick Marlborough"

She had already read the letter many times over and each time it had left her close to despair. If only she could be certain! She could not bring herself to believe that Silas Cummerbund was plotting against her, not after his heroics at Christmas, and certainly not that he was prepared to use Gaia as a bargaining chip. But neither could she think that her most trusted servant, Marlborough, who had been in her service since the beginning of her reign, was wrong.

She carefully refolded the letter, replaced it in the drawer, and locked it. Once again she looked around the room. The silent servant was still there in the shadows, as blank as a statue. Matilda struggled to hold back the tears that were only ever a moment away. She was alone in the world and who could she trust? Marlborough, who she had known for years? Or Cummerbund, who she knew not at all, but who had saved her daughter? If only her dear husband were still alive, he would at least be…

She got no further with this train of thought for there was a sudden, urgent hammering on the door. It burst open and a man strode into the room, brandishing a letter in his hand. He got no further than a couple of paces before the servant in the shadows sprang out from the corner and blocked his passage, a sword at his throat.

"Not another step," he growled, the tip of his sword resting lightly on the intruder's throat. The man took a step backwards, a grimace of irritation on his face. He called out, over the sword, in Matilda's general direction, "Your Majesty, if you could perhaps bring this pup to heel. I have an urgent communication."

Matilda sighed. "Yes, thank you, Pargeter. As efficient as usual. Though where you keep that sword of yours, heaven only knows."

The sword was sheathed, the man nodded and slipped back into the shadows.

Matilda turned her attention to the newcomer. "Pembroke, you really do need to knock and wait, you know. One day, the guard will not have such good reactions, and you will lie bleeding out on the royal floor. Think of the mess."

The man bowed. "My humble apologies, Your Majesty, but this message really could not wait. And I'd have thought that Pargeter there," - he nodded towards the shadows where the guard had retreated - "might have recognised me as your Chief Advisor, not a common assassin."

"Hmm," Matilda replied, "I'd much rather he acted first and thought later. It's the kind of thing that will keep me safe and well for a while longer. And Chief Advisors can be replaced, you know."

Pembroke's face fell.

"Oh come now, Pembroke, you're not going to sulk are you? You're marvellous, you really are. Is that better now? Now the letter, if you please."

She held out her hand and Pembroke sprang forward and laid it down in her palm with the faintest of bows. She ripped it open and quickly scanned the contents. Her face clouded over and she gasped, holding a hand to her mouth. Her legs suddenly gave way, and she sank down into her chair. For a moment, she looked utterly lost. Then she summoned all of her authority and forced herself into action. She looked back at Pembroke, her mouth a steely line, her eyes blazing.

"Prepare the carriage and my personal cavalry guard. We must travel north to York immediately."

SOMETHING OF THE NIGHT

Shrike had been in the shadows of one of the lanes leading down to the river for the last five minutes, his eyes flicking this way and that, scanning the waterfront. In front of him, the bulk of Ouse Bridge loomed and on the other side of the river, a string of lights could be seen, their reflections dappled in the gently undulating river. The occasional boat came into view, some crossing between the two banks while others were headed for destinations further downstream, oars dipping rhythmically into the inky black surface of the water.

The night was still, the air heavy and warm. Shrike shifted from one foot to the other, a bead of sweat icing its way down his neck and back, sending a shiver down his spine. Then the quiet was broken by the sudden sound of hooves and iron clad wheels on the cobbles. Shrike froze and took a step back deeper into the shadows under the overhanging roof of the building at the end of the lane. He narrowed his eyes as a carriage pulled up in front of the Kings Arms. There was the muffled sound of conversation as the fare was settled, before the door swung open and two men quietly slipped out of the carriage and into the street.

Shrike smiled to himself in the darkness. "Yes, here they are, my fine two gentlemen. And on time as well. Time to play the game."

The two men dusted themselves down from the journey, exchanged a brief word, opened the door to the inn and stepped briskly inside. For a moment, yellow light and chatter spilled out onto the cobbled street, before the door swung closed, leaving the riverside bathed once again in quiet darkness.

Shrike counted a couple of minutes, checked the coast was clear in the streets, and then gathering his wits, followed them into the inn.

Inside was well lit with candles and lamps blazing, and even with many of the windows wide open, there was a sticky warmth that lay on the scattered groups of drinkers. Shrike slipped in through the open door, closing it carefully behind him. He had an uncanny ability to almost slide over the ground silently, like a ghost, and prided himself that he could enter and leave any room without drawing attention to himself.

Amongst the huddled conversations and dice players, he spotted a corner booth tucked away at the side, with a clear view of the door he'd just come through and close to the rear exit leading to the back yard. He made a beeline for it and slipped into the corner, all the while keeping his eyes on the two gentlemen who were at the bar, ordering refreshment and scanning the room. Shrike locked his eyes onto the first, a tall older man with an impassive expression, and a scar down one side of his face. Their eyes met, as if Shrike had somehow forced him to look his way. A momentary flash of annoyance passed across his face and he turned and squeezed his companion's elbow. He, a younger man with short cropped blond hair, turned to listen to his partner's urgent whisper. They were both well dressed with heavy cloaks, fine leather boots and silk shirts, but all in plain colours so as not to draw attention to themselves.

They walked over to Shrike's booth, and without a word, eased themselves into two of the seats on the other side of the table. In a low voice, the older of the two began.

"Young Master Shrike, good evening. I trust you have something for us, to summon us to this den of thieves so urgently."

Shrike bowed to both of them in turn.

"Masters both, good evening. 'Tis not for the likes of me to summon my elders and betters anywhere. But this is not a den of thieves. 'Tis beneath your excellencies for sure, but for common folk such as myself, it is a house of good repute. Fine ale and food, comfortable beds, honestly priced. A place where business can be transacted in some privacy."

He stopped as a serving girl approached their table with a pitcher of wine and waited in silence as she set down three beakers and began to pour. When she got to his beaker, he covered it with his hand and shook his head at the girl. She placed the pitcher on the table and with a small bow withdrew. The blond younger man turned to watch her go, a smile growing on his face. His companion scowled and laid a hand on his arm. "Concentrate on the matter at hand, Oliver."

Oliver roughly cast off his hand and returned his scowl. Then he turned to Shrike, his easy smile back in place. "Not drinking, Shrike? We don't share our table with just anyone, you know. Some people might be offended by your refusal."

Shrike bowed again and with a smirk on his face, said, "I am honoured and flattered, Sir, but I must respectfully decline. I like to have my wits about me when I am at work, and drink tends to scramble them."

"Wise words for one so young," interjected the older man. "But enough of these pleasantries. If you are at work, let us see what you have for us. We have little time to waste and our work requires us to be out of the public eye as much as possible. This had better be worth it for us to take the risk to be here. Why could you not meet with our man as usual?"

Shrike leaned forward, his voice lowered. "This is for your eyes and ears only, my Lords."

He paused, expectantly.

The older man snapped back at him.

"Don't delay us, Shrike. You shall have your payment as usual, when we have heard your information. Out with it."

Shrike continued. "The girl progresses in her work with Cummerbund. Everyday they practise, and every day I watch them."

Oliver interrupted. "They have no knowledge of you? You have been careful?"

Shrike smiled. "My Lord, they have no idea who I am. I am invisible when I go about my work."

"Good. Carry on, Shrike. You must have more, surely. We did not think the girl was here to see the sights of York. What are the girl's powers, exactly?"

Shrike's looked cautiously around the tables of drinkers. "They are growing every day. She can move objects from afar without touching them. She can be in two places at once. I saw her, in their practice room at Kings Manor. I swear, she …"

He hesitated and took a quick look around the room, as if Clara might be lurking in the shadows somewhere in this very pub.

"She what, Shrike? Spit it out, lad. We haven't all night."

"There were two of her, my Lords, one at each end of the room, like peas in a pod. Walking and talking like twins."

Oliver's face drained of colour. "Hell's teeth! What witchcraft is this?"

Shrike was enjoying himself now. His two masters, who had up until now called all the shots, were hanging onto his every word.

"There's more. She can move between rooms instantly. I saw her. It took a few goes for her to get it right, but one day, she just disappeared! Vanished completely and then, a second later, she appeared again at the other end of the room. The longer it goes on, the more she can do. Like today, they were working on shape shifting. She is able to transform herself into other forms, animals or people. She does not have the gift perfectly as yet, but from what I've seen so far, 'tis only a matter of time."

Oliver reached for his glass of wine and took a deep drink. Shrike's news had evidently shaken his confidence. His voice had a faint tremble as he spoke.

"Shape shifting. Invisibly moving. This is bad news, Jacob. We must act quickly, before she gets any more powerful. If we delay, it will get harder to move against them."

"Hold your tongue!" Jacob spat back angrily. "No-one else need know of this. Least of all Shrike here, who would slit his own mother's throat for a purse of gold coins."

"Now, now, that's not very friendly, is it? And you will have more need of my services shortly, so let us be civil to each other."

Jacob narrowed his eyes and looked at Shrike curiously. "Why do you say that? Is there more? Come now, Shrike, out with it, before I lose my patience."

Shrike paused for effect before leaning forward and beginning again. "Your Lordships asked me to keep a look out for a boy."

Jacob spoke as if he had been stung. "What? The Trelawney boy? Is he here? Where? Speak, you guttersnipe, speak!"

He rose from his chair and was about to grab Shrike by his smock before he thought better of it and sank slowly back into his chair. Oliver, meanwhile, had turned a greenish colour. He took another gulp of his wine.

"Not yet," Shrike resumed. "But soon. They were talking about his return at the end of their session yesterday. And Masters, they spoke of the boy coming from another world. This is dark and powerful magic. As you well know, by the look of you. They plan to go back to the Reverend's house in Runswick Bay this weekend. The girl wants to see some of her friends again, she said."

Oliver roused himself. "Friends! Pah! That will be the coach driver woman and that pretty young vixen of a doctor. We still owe them for what they did to us in York last Christmas."

Jacob interrupted him.

"Oliver, they are nothing in this. 'Tis the boy, the Princess and the old man that stand in our way. We heard the stories of what they did last time" He turned back to Shrike. "And will the Trelawney boy be there as well? At Runswick Bay, I mean."

Shrike shrugged. "They did not say, my Lord."

Jacob thought for a moment, chewing his lip. Oliver shifted uneasily in his chair, waiting, the knuckles on his clenched fists white with tension.

At last, he had decided.

"You must go there, Shrike, with all haste. You are sure they will not recognise you from Kings Manor? You do have a distinctive appearance after all."

"They will not, my Lord. I know my business. None better. But what will you have me do there?"

"Go to Mulgrave Hall and speak with Lord Mulgrave. I will furnish you with a letter to explain all to him, so that you will be granted an audience. The letter will be in code in case it falls into enemy hands. The Rectory is several miles to the north on the coast at Runswick. You must find a way of gaining their confidence. Get access to The Rectory and watch and listen. It is vital that we know how the girl progresses, whether the boy will return, and what their movements are going to be before their return to London. If there is anything urgent, ride like the wind over the Moors back to York. You know how to get a message to us, if need be."

"Of course"

"Make your preparations and be at Clifton Green at midnight. There will be a horse and the letter waiting for you. Make haste. There is no time to lose."

Shrike hesitated. "There is one more thing, Masters,"

he said, his voice a smooth, oily river of charm.

Oliver finally exploded. "For God's sake, Shrike, you oik, what the devil is it? I grow tired of your reptilian face, you dog. The sooner your business with us is done, the better."

Jacob raised an eyebrow. "Oliver, calm please. Calm." Turning to Shrike, he continued. "Well? What is it?"

"Money, my Lords, money. Expenses and fees, this will be an expensive trip. And a dangerous one, so I expect proper remuneration."

Jacob laughed quietly and reached inside his cloak. He drew out a small leather pouch and passed it onto Shrike, who weighed it in the palm of his hand and nodded his approval. He slipped it quickly in an inside pocket and stood up in one smooth flowing movement.

He bowed slightly towards them. "Midnight, my Lords." And then was gone. It seemed as if he had never been there, so quickly, smoothly and unobtrusively had he moved. Oliver and Jacob stared after him. None of the other drinkers seemed to have noticed either his entrance or his departure.

Oliver turned back to Jacob, an expression of extreme distaste on his face.

"Thank goodness he has gone. That young man sends shivers down my spine, Jacob. There is something of the night about him."

"Patience, Oliver, patience. He is very useful to us now. When he no longer has a purpose, we will dispose of him. We need his ears and eyes to find out what the girl and the old man are scheming. From what he has already told us, it seems likely we will have to move sooner than we planned."

"The sooner the better and then I can reclaim what is rightfully mine," muttered Oliver bitterly. "But we must deal with the boy, Jacob. He thwarted us once before, remember. But is he really from another world? Can such things be?"

"You remember Dredge's account of what happened in the cellars at The Assembly Rooms? People dying and coming back to life without a scratch on them? That was no human rescue. The boy could be from the moon for all we know, but he is a dark power, that's for sure."

"And what of the first part of our plan, Jacob? Has that woman received Shrike's letter?" He pronounced the words "that woman" with disdain, a look of contempt on his face.

Jacob smiled, the scar on his face crinkling unevenly. "The Queen has received it. And believed it, more importantly."

He reached underneath his cloak and pulled out a silver pocket watch in a chain. He flicked it open and consulted the time. Satisfied, he closed it with a snap. "I imagine that she is well on the way now. No doubt with a considerable troop of men guarding her. But they will be powerless to protect her, if all goes to plan."

He stood up suddenly and drained his beaker of wine. "Come now, Oliver. Drink up and let us go. The carriage is outside and we have much to do." He looked around the room at the tables of drinkers and gossipers. "And the less time we are out in society the better. For all we know, any one of these villains might be spying on us. We need to slip back into the shadows, Oliver."

A flash of anger passed over the younger man's face.

"I've had enough of skulking in the shadows, Jacob," he hissed. "When will I get what is rightfully mine?"

"Patience, Oliver. We will wait in the shadows until it is our time. And rest assured, our time is coming. Yes, our time is coming, Thomas Trelawney or no Thomas Trelawney."

*

Shrike had not had enough of skulking in the shadows. On the contrary, it was where he felt most at home. There were still a few people out on the streets, so Shrike took extra care to slip along back alleys, his collar upturned, his hat jammed down on his head. Finally, he reached his destination, a shabby door with blistered black paint at the end of a row of butchers' shops in The Shambles. A permanent smell of blood and guts hung in the air, and the cobbled street was littered with the remnants of the day's meat trade. He looked around before approaching the door and then gave a cautious rap. He was observed only by the rats and cats that fought a permanent battle there every night when the sun went down. Shrike stepped back from the door and waited. Above him the towers of York Minster loomed, eerily lit up in the moonlight, and the sign over the door creaked in the breeze. It read: "John Talbot, Apothecary"

The door opened a crack, and Shrike squeezed his way inside. Five minutes later, he emerged, his saddle bag over his shoulder carried with deliberate care. He glanced both ways along The Shambles and then slipped back into the shadows, moving like a ghost in the direction of Clifton Green.

A SPY IN THE SHADOWS

Silas leant back in his chair and sighed and stretched. He surveyed the company with some satisfaction: Della sitting next to Amelia, deep in animated conversation, their eyes sparkling. Then came Grace and Clara, a little more serious, still picking at the remnants of the hunk of cheese in the middle of the table. Finally, there was Elizabeth, Silas' housekeeper, the previous Friend of Yngerlande, contemplating whether to begin clearing the table. The Friend was the link between Yngerlande and England, the person chosen to work with Silas, The Watcher, to keep the portal between the two lands open.

"My friends," Silas announced, "what a treat to have you all here together. And a rare treat, given this beautiful weather, to be eating and talking outside in the warm summer night's air. For this, indeed, is the coast of North Yorkshire, not some far flung exotic location. So, clearly, we are blessed."

Della looked up from her conversation with Amelia, her long, wavy black hair framing her dark skin. The sparkle in her eyes was matched by the moonlight glittering on her silver and jet jewellery that fell from her ears, wrists and throat. There was a small crescent shaped scar above her right eye, a legacy of the events of the previous Christmas, when somehow she had got herself mixed up in the fight to prevent the old King's grandson from deposing Queen Matilda and taking back the throne by force. Amelia, never far from her side, was almost a mirror image in negative, with her fair complexion and long blonde ringlets. The other contrast was their clothes. Amelia wore a blue silk dress, while Della had a more practical outfit of breeches, leather riding boots, white linen shirt and waistcoat.

"We are blessed indeed, Silas," she said, laying her hand on top of Amelia's and smiling. "And, well fed too. That was a marvellous feast you gave us, Elizabeth."

"Oh, hush now, child. It is a pleasure to have you all here again," Elizabeth replied, blushing faintly. "It has been too long."

"Yes, it has been," Clara interjected. "I can hardly believe we have not been together since Christmas Eve. The last time I was in Runswick Bay, things were very different. As I recall, Della, we spent a long time hiding in cellars and tunnels, fearing for our lives."

Della nodded. "And a long time wondering where our next meal would come from. We dreamed of a feast as good as this. We were lucky to escape with our lives."

"As were Grace and I," said Amelia, casting a hesitant look at Grace, directly opposite her. "I still have nightmares about our time in York dungeons. And as for the cellar under The Assembly Rooms, well, we were seconds away from being blown to kingdom come."

Grace shivered and a shadow passed over her face, as she remembered the confrontation with Dredge. "And yet, I remember it as a happy time."

There was a silence, as everyone left Grace to her memories. They all knew how cruel it was that death had separated Grace from her family back in England, particularly her brother Thomas. They knew as well that the consolation of new life in Yngerlande was bittersweet, and that Grace was beset with a sadness that only ever seemed to lift for brief periods of time before descending on her again like a black cloud.

It was Silas who broke the spell.

"Come now, Grace. It was a wonderful thing for you to see Master Thomas last Christmas, and you will see him again. But life goes on here as well without him, and you must grasp it and take the love offered to you here."

Grace looked around the faces at the table, shining in the moonlight of a beautiful warm summer's evening. She nodded. "Of course, Silas. I am with the best of people here and I am grateful. So grateful. But still, I remember the life I had."

She trailed off. Clara took up the conversation, speaking lightly as if it was of no concern to her at all.

"So, Thomas will return, will he? Is that definite, Silas? And when might that be? Soon, perhaps? And what of his cousin Dan?"

"To answer your first question, Thomas is The Friend. He will return, but when, exactly, is less predictable. The only thing that is sure is that The Friend will always appear when there is trouble in Yngerlande. As for Daniel, the King of the ghosts, well that is less certain. If you remember, he was not invited to enter our world, he was a trespasser. He may come back or he may not."

The silence that followed seemed to indicate that the after dinner conversation had run its course. Elizabeth broke the spell by standing up and announcing, "Well, Thomas or Daniel won't help us get the clearing up done."

Amelia sprang up after her. "I'll help you. We can make quick work of it together." Della and Clara began to get to their feet to lend a hand.

"No, no," interjected Amelia, "You all sit down. Elizabeth and I can manage."

They did not need telling twice, and the table was cleared in double quick time. Shortly afterwards, the sounds of running water from the kitchen suggested that Elizabeth and Amelia were also making a start on the washing up.

The heat of the night showed little sign of easing, and the air was still and sticky with moisture. From far away came the distant, regular sound of the North Sea, and the sucking and pulling of the waves onto the beaches below the cliffs. Silas, Della, Grace and Clara sat around the newly-cleared table, their faces beaming out of the darkness in the pools of thin, warm light cast by the candle lamps.

"So, Silas," Della began, "I take it from what you said that we won't see Tom again soon. The Friend appears when Yngerlande is in trouble - isn't that what you said? And, surely, all is well, isn't it? There has been no sign of the heir to the old mad King. All of those in the uprising were caught and imprisoned. Even Lord Mulgrave is lying low and saying nothing out of place. They were defeated at Christmas and there is no sign of them coming back. Isn't that so?"

Silas considered the question. Eventually he spoke.

"There has been nothing so far. The Sisterhood, as you know, have their ears and eyes everywhere, and they have not heard of anything to worry about. Oliver and Jacob have disappeared completely. There have been no sightings of them since January, when our spies tracked them to Paris, where they were lying low. So, yes, it seems as if Yngerlande is safe. For the time being."

"You don't sound very convinced," said Grace. "What aren't you telling us?"

Silas stroked the pigtail that hung loosely over one shoulder as he considered his reply. Finally, he spoke. "Oliver thinks he is the rightful King and that Matilda and her line are usurpers. Everyday he is in exile, his bitterness will grow. He will have been plotting every day since then to have his revenge. One day he will try again. And he will be determined not to make any mistakes next time. To put it bluntly, as long as he remains hidden, Clara and her mother, the Queen, are in grave danger."

"It's not just my mother and me, though, is it, Silas?" said Clara. "We know all about Oliver and what he and his supporters believe. They want to turn back the clock and go back to the old days. People of colour, women, people who go where their love takes them - they are all at risk from those old, mad ideas."

Silas nodded. "I'm afraid you're right, my dear. Which is precisely why we are spending so much time developing your powers. Because one day, and I hope it will be a long time from now, you will have to use them to keep Yngerlande safe."

"Then, surely, we should go back to King's Manor and carry on with my lessons," Clara spoke with a note of urgency in her voice. "It's wonderful to see everyone again, but we can't afford to waste any more time, from what you've just said."

"I think for the moment it is better if we stay where we are. I'm not sure how safe King's Manor is at present." Silas replied.

"What do you mean? Were we in danger?"

"No, not exactly, my dear. You were safe, but there were too many people coming and going. I think it is wiser if we finish your training here and then go back to London in the next couple of weeks, as we planned. I will write to your mother to ask her permission."

Grace smiled broadly. "It will be wonderful to have you staying at The Rectory for a few more weeks," she said, laying her hand on Clara's arm.

Clara returned her smile. She would certainly welcome the opportunity to talk more with Clara about Tom and their life in England. And, if truth be told, she was enjoying the company of someone closer to her in age, as well as having Della and Amelia there. Her life as a Princess had been terribly lonely. True friends were worth more to her than all the riches and privilege of her position.

They talked for a little while longer in the warm evening air, but finally, tiredness called them into the house and to bed for the night. When the lamps had been extinguished and taken back inside the house, and the door closed, the table was surrounded by darkness as the garden once again was left to nature and the night.

There was not a breath of wind to stir the branches of the trees that crowded in on The Rectory garden. The trees and bushes seemed to hold their breath in the sticky, still air. The woods crowded in on the garden, from the land that rose up to the bleak moorlands above. A silence settled on the house, the garden and the moors, with the distant shingle roll of the sea in the background.

Then the silence loosened its grip. First came the hoot of an owl from the trees to the left of the house, returned by another in the copse opposite. Then came the snuffling of creatures hidden in the undergrowth. One broke cover from under a laurel bush bathed in moonlight. A fox stepped tentatively onto the lawn and began to trot across it towards the table, drawn by the scent of crumbs of food that had fallen there. Suddenly, it stopped stock still and raised its head, sniffing the air cautiously. From the thicket of bushes came the sound of a twig snapping. The fox shot back to the cover of the undergrowth, a red flash against the moonlit green lawn.

Shrike cursed his carelessness. He must be losing his touch, stepping on a stray twig like that. Still, it seemed as if he had gotten away with it.

"So, they're going to stay here, are they?" he muttered under his breath. "Perfect."

No-one stirred in the house: no doors opened, no lights came on, no one on guard, just to check. A sly smile passed across Shrike's face. Perhaps this was going to be easier than he had first thought.

Carefully avoiding twigs and branches, he pulled up his hood and eased his way to the back of the shrubbery, to the old brick wall that surrounded the garden. He reached up to a hand hold in the wall and hauled himself up to the parapet that was covered in clinging, dusty ivy. From the top, he dropped silently to the ground below to find himself on a rough track that led to the woods. Just inside the line of trees, out of sight of prying eyes, was his horse, still tied up where he had left it a couple of hours before.

Shrike untied the reins, stroked the horse's head and whispered gently to it, bowing his head towards it.

"Well, my lad, you've done very well tonight. As have I. Yes, very well indeed. And what will our reward be, eh?" He stroked the horse's ears in the darkness. "Well, for you, how about this?"

He rummaged in his shoulder bag and produced an apple. The horse, expecting the treat, nuzzled against the palm of his hand and began to munch contentedly. Shrike watched him eat, stroking its flank.

"And for me? Perhaps I'll have more than an apple, eh?"

He sniggered quietly as a plan began to form in his mind.

Holding the reins, he led the horse quietly down the track towards the road.

THE QUEEN RIDES NORTH

It was stiflingly hot inside the coach, even with the windows open. Matilda fanned herself furiously before falling back against her seat, gasping for air. Pembroke had tried to dissuade her from making the journey on the grounds that it was too dangerous to travel unannounced, even in the company of an armed guard, but Matilda would not be moved. She was determined to make sure that Princess Gaia was safe. There may even have to be arrests. Pembroke could see why, when she had shown the letter to him, but even so, he was a cautious man and had felt very uneasy about her making the journey. Much of the road north went through wild and lonely countryside, where it would be a simple matter to hold up a coach at gunpoint.

She got up from her seat and poked her head out of the open window into the darkness to get a cooling breath of air. From there, she could see the coach surrounded by redcoats on horseback, cantering beside it in formation, her personal guard against any sign of possible attack. It was a reassuring sight.

Refreshed, she sank back into her seat, taking the tightly folded letter from the purse she wore around her neck. It was the third time she had done so since they had set off. She unfolded the sheet of parchment and scanned it again in the light of the candle lamp embedded in the carriage wall above her head.

"I imagine it says exactly the same thing it did when you read it last time. Your Majesty."

The voice came from the shadows opposite her. It had a strange, playful tone, and the Queen's title was added very much as an afterthought.

Matilda looked up from the parchment, her face a mixture of fury and anxiety.

"That does not help, you know, Pembroke," she said. "I'm worried. You might try sympathy, or reassurance. Or anything except being clever."

"Forgive me, Your Majesty, I spoke out of turn. Of course, I am sympathetic. I understand that this must be a terrible worry for you. But, Madam, was it really necessary for us to come on this journey north, so far from the safety of St James' Palace? Can you be sure of the contents of that letter? Or of the person who sent it?"

"Of course I can. I wouldn't take such a risk of coming all this way if there had been any doubt about it. Marlborough is completely loyal, completely trustworthy. From what he says it's only a matter of days before they try to kidnap Princess Gaia. And once they have her, they can demand anything. They can force me to step down so that they can take back the throne."

Her eyes glittered with tears that sparkled in the lamplight as they rolled down her cheeks.

"I will do anything to keep my daughter safe. Anything. And they know that."

She dropped her head and dabbed at her eyes with a handkerchief, composing herself.

"But I also know that, if they take her, she will never be safe, no matter what I promise to do. Once the time is right, they will kill her. "

"Your Majesty, I hardly think–" Pembroke began.

"Enough!" Matilda snapped back. "I am not a child to be told fairy stories. She will be killed."

With every word of this last sentence, she rapped her knuckles on the wall of the carriage for emphasis.

She began again, but this time her voice was quiet, and had a steely quality to it.

"So, I must make sure they do not take her. Not now, not ever."

*

The Rectory was dark and quiet. All the doors and windows had been secured, even though it was a sticky, uncomfortable night. Silas had insisted on this, and although they exchanged glances, they all knew him well enough not to question his instructions. Despite the heat, everyone was sleeping soundly in their beds, exhausted by the events of the day just gone. Only one light shone from the house into the hot dark night. Not everyone was asleep. Silas sat in his study, a single lamp on his desk, deep in thought.

A thick silence weighed heavily on the house, broken in his study only by Silas' occasional muttering, and by the comforting tick of the grandfather clock in the corner. After spending some moments like this he seemed to have finally made up his mind about something, something that had been troubling him for some days now. He reached down into the desk drawer and brought out a small leather pouch. Fiddling with the drawstring, he opened it up and pulled out a smooth pebble about the size of an egg. It fitted snugly in the palm of his hand where it nestled with a comforting weight. His face was etched with concentration as he brought all his attention to bear on the stone. Slowly, the stone began to grow warm in his hand and a thin blue light began to seep from it, adding to the lamplight in the study. It grew steadily until it was a brilliant, luminous sapphire blue, a light that penetrated every corner of the room. When the light reached a pitch of intensity, he began to speak.

"Mary? Mary, are you there? Speak if you can."

Silas stopped and waited, listening intently. There was no answer, and no sound in the room, except for the ever-present ticking of the clock. Silas hardly dared breathe in case he missed a sign of life. His thoughts raced. Where was she? Why hadn't she contacted him, as they had agreed? For the first time, Silas was genuinely fearful of what might have happened to her.

He was just about to have one last try before stowing the Sounding Stone back in the drawer, when the sapphire light flickered like a guttering candle. He cursed and slumped back, sure that there would be no communication with Mary Carruthers that night. Suddenly, the light flared, coming back again even stronger than before. Silas sat forward in his chair, straining for any sign of Mary's voice.

"Mary, can you hear me? It's Silas, are you there?" he whispered hoarsely.

And then, at last, it came, a faraway thin sound at first, as if from the end of a long tunnel, growing steadily stronger.

"Silas, at last! I've been trying to get through to you for days."

"Mary, are you alright? Are you safe? Speak, if you can."

The voice at the other end faltered. "Listen to me, Silas, there is no time to waste. They may come for me at any minute."

"Mary, wherever you are you must get out at once. Keep yourself safe, and come back to us. We can–"

"No, Silas, no!"

Mary interrupted him with renewed urgency.

"Listen to me. They are here, Silas. And they have already started. They know more about us than we thought. They have planned terrible things for the Queen and Princess Gaia. Matilda's man has been captured and she is receiving false messages…"

There was a pause, and the faint sound of footsteps and Mary's coughing. She sounded terribly weak. Then she started to speak again, her voice cracking in between faint coughs.

"Silas, they are coming for you. You must beware Mulgrave Hall - it is a nest of vipers. There is only one thing left to do, Silas. You must summon The Friend, from England. You must summon Tom, or all is lost…"

There was a crackle in the air, and then silence, a silence so immediate and total that it was like a thick blanket hung over the world. The blue light drained away, and Silas was left in his study alone. The lamp glowed on his desk and the grandfather clock ticked as he sat deep in thought. After a moment, he reached for a sheet of parchment and his quill. He dipped the quill in his silver inkwell and began to write, the quill scratching away on the parchment, leaving a spidery trail of black ink.

"Dear Thomas,

All your friends in Yngerlande are in grave peril. You will have received this letter from someone at The Rectory. After you have read it, spend some time discussing what is to be done with those who are left. I have complete faith in you, Thomas, and whatever you decide to do, but this is what you need to know before you make any decisions."

He continued to write at breakneck speed, stopping only to dip his quill into the inkwell once again. Once he had finished the first letter, he dried the ink with some sand, sealed it, and immediately began a second sheet. It would be some time before Silas would have any sleep that night.

*

Mulgrave Hall stood in stately isolation, sweltering under the dark clouds of a sticky midsummer night. The bulk of the estate was shrouded in darkness, lit only by a thumbnail moon, which cast jagged shadows around the trees, shrubs and statuary. The Hall itself stood out like a stage set, with flaming torches illuminating the towers and crenelations of the ancient building. The torches burned through the evening, even though effectively the great Hall was asleep. Occasionally, the sounds of stamping, quietly snorting horses could be heard from the stables, or the muffled footsteps of the night servants, who plodded along gloomy corridors to ensure all was ready for his Lordship's breakfast. Unseen in the shadows of every wing of the house, were discreetly stationed soldiers, each with a view of every possible approach to the Hall, alert and well-supplied with weapons. They were never called into action, but all were encouraged to be on their guard by the fate of the last man who had fallen asleep while on duty. He had been whipped for disobedience, and then dismissed in disgrace.

Suspicion still clung to Lord Mulgrave after the events of the previous Christmas, but he had played a patient game, keeping a low profile apart from those occasions when he could show his loyalty to the Queen: attendance at society balls, involvement in her favourite charitable works, public speeches singing her praises. He comforted himself with the thought that the time was soon coming when he could abandon these pretences and show his true colours.

But that was for the future. Now, he was snoring gently, burrowed under the mound of silken perfumed sheets and the velvet coverlets of his four-poster bed. Far below him, far below even the grand entrance to Mulgrave Hall on the ground floor, someone else lay on their bed, someone who was finding it more difficult to get to sleep. In a dark, damp, windowless dungeon, a long, thin figure shifted their weight to try and find some relief from the stabbing pains that made every muscle scream. His wrists and ankles were bound with heavy iron shackles that cut into his skin with every turn on his filthy mattress. His face was spotted with patches of dirt and congealed blood, and his open mouth, now ungagged, revealed a row of broken teeth. The removal of the gag, that had been tied so tightly it had cut into both corners of his mouth, had not been an act of mercy, but was done simply to save his jailer time and effort. He could scream at the top of his voice and no-one would hear him. The dungeon was sunk into thick rock, many metres below the ground, and no sound could penetrate, either out or in. No friend knew he was here and no-one was coming for him.

Frederick Marlborough, alone in the darkness, was utterly lost to the world, with only his guilt for company.

BELTON HOUSE

Matilda dozed lightly in her seat. The coach had trundled along the Great North Road for several hours now, and every bump and rut on the road had jolted her, making sleep difficult and wakefulness painful. Normally, when the Queen travelled this distance by road, comfort was the priority, not speed. She would be accompanied by maids and footmen, and there would already have been several stops for the Queen to meet local dignitaries and eat celebration meals laid on by her loyal subjects who would be honoured to have her as a guest. But this journey had been different to all of the others. No-one knew about it, apart from a handful of trusted advisors and servants. Even Matilda's clothes were different. On Marlborough's advice, she had dispensed with her usual crown, her fine gowns of silk and velvet and her jewellery, and was instead wearing sensible, plain travelling clothing, so as not to draw attention to herself when they finally had to stop.

And on this journey, there was no greater priority than speed. She must get to York as quickly as possible to confront Cummerbund, before he could carry out his plan to imprison Princess Gaia, and before anyone knew she was on her way. She would put up with any amount of discomfort to protect her daughter.

A sudden bump in the road jolted her completely awake. She blinked, taking in the darkened coach, and as she stretched, she realised she had a raging thirst.

"Drat this infernal heat," she muttered. "I do not like being poached, like an egg."

From the shadows opposite her, Pembroke replied, "The weather will break soon enough, Your Majesty. A storm is coming, I fear."

"The sooner the better. A storm would clear the air and make it easier to think. I hope we reach our destination before it arrives, though. Getting drenched would be the last straw. We must be getting close now, surely?"

"Another twenty minutes or so, Your Majesty. It will be a relief for you to rest in comfort this evening."

"Indeed. Marlborough's letter said we were to go to Belton Hall. It is close to the Great North Road, near Grantham. He has made the arrangements and Sir John Brownlow is expecting us. He also knows that it must be a discreet stay. No one must know we are on our way to York, or Cummerbund will get wind of it."

"Hard to keep it a secret when we are accompanied by a dozen redcoats on horseback, your Majesty. Has Marlborough done anything about that?"

"I don't know. He has thought of everything else, so I assume there will be a plan for my men to make themselves scarce. I…"

She did not finish her sentence. From outside the carriage came a commanding shout, followed by a commotion of activity and noise. The carriage came to a screeching stop, the metal wheel rims scraping against the dirt and pebbles of the road surface. There was a cacophony of harsh cries and the snorting of horses, their hooves clattering against the road to bring the carriage to a halt. Matilda fell forward and only just prevented herself from falling into the lap of her travelling companion. She quickly sat back in her seat and regained her composure.

"What is all this? Well?" she demanded. "Go and check, man, quickly."

Pembroke bowed his head slightly, and jumped down from the carriage. As he did so, the first rumble of thunder erupted from the lowering skies. Matilda shivered at the sound and peered through the open window to see what was going on. A sudden flash of distant lightning froze the scene in front of her for a split second. Half of her redcoats surrounded the carriage while the others had trotted forward to confront another man on horseback. Behind him, set back from the road, Matilda could make out a splendid gatehouse that was clearly the entrance to an estate, judging by the lines of trees and well clipped lawns that surrounded it. She watched as her companion, shouting at the horsemen to let him through, went up to the lone rider who bent down to speak to him. After a short conversation, the mounted man handed over a letter, which her man brought to the door of the carriage.

"Well?" demanded Matilda. "What is going on?"

"We are at Belton Hall, Your Majesty," Pembroke explained. "Sir John Brownlow has instructed his servant, the man on the horse here, to meet us with a letter from Marlborough. Evidently, your Redcoats are to be billeted on the far side of the Estate, so that they are not obvious to the servants and tradespeople who visit. As you know, Your Majesty, those sorts of common people are worse than the gentry for gossiping. We are to proceed without the guards directly to the Hall, where we will be met by Sir John and further letters from Marlborough. Letters that cannot leave the Hall. I have the letter here, Your Majesty."

He bowed, and handed her the letter. It was on thick parchment, folded and sealed with a shiny crimson blob of wax, imprinted with a coat of arms. Matilda examined it closely. "Yes, that is Marlborough's seal, alright."

She pulled at the parchment breaking the seal and then unfolded the letter and scanned it quickly.

"And he says everything you have just confirmed. Almost word for word, in fact. Good - it seems as if Marlborough has managed all of this very well. We will spend the night here and leave at dawn tomorrow. I can hear Marlborough's latest news when we eat."

She looked up from the letter, and called through the

window of the carriage. "Captain! A word, if you please."

One of the redcoats dismounted and walked over to the window. He bowed and waited.

"All of this is in order, Captain. Take your men with the messenger. He will have your men and the horses fed and watered and rested. We leave at dawn tomorrow, so have them ready."

The captain of the Guard looked hesitant. "Yes, of course, Your Majesty, but I am not sure we should leave you unguarded. My orders were to not let you out of my sight."

Matilda sighed. "Captain, your orders come from me. No-one else. Your concern does you credit, but all is well. Now go."

He bowed and backed away to his horse. One of the men who had stopped the carriage waited for him to mount and then he led all of the Queen's guard on horseback through the gateway. Matilda watched them go until they had faded completely into the darkness. Then the darkness was temporarily obliterated as another jagged bolt of lightning snaked down from the skies to the far woods, followed by a violent crack of thunder. The horses reared in fear, and the driver struggled to maintain control.

"And now, Your Majesty, we must proceed to the house. If we're lucky, we'll get there before the heavens open."

Matilda nodded and from the shadows, he rapped on the roof, raising his voice.

"Driver! Take us to the Hall. Follow the main path and we'll be there in a minute or two."

He was right. The carriage drew to a halt in front of a grand set of stone stairs that led to an imposing front door, with two great pillars on guard at either side. Just as they descended, another bolt of lightning, directly above this time, split the night sky with a jagged tear. The crack of thunder was like an explosion, such was its power, and before the sound had rolled away, the first fat raindrops splashed around them, heavy as water bombs. By the time they had rushed to the shelter of the doorway, the rain was coming in sheets like a waterfall, in a deafening torrent. The door opened on to a warmly lit entrance hall and they tumbled inside, drenched even in the few seconds it had taken them to reach the door. Matilda felt the relief of shelter in the midst of a rising annoyance about the undignified nature of her reception, more befitting a serving woman than a Queen. Pembroke would regret this shoddy treatment, she would make sure of that. The door shut behind them, and a key turned in the lock. Outside, the rain, turning now to giant hailstones, hammered down.

THE QUEEN IN CHECK

It took a moment or two for Matilda to catch her breath and take in her surroundings. Her clothes were sodden and her hair was plastered to her face, streams of water trailing down her cheeks and the back of her neck. She blinked, expecting to see a warmly lit, spacious entrance hall, lined with servants, and a bowing figure of Sir John, proud to welcome the Queen, to his family seat. She did not feel very regal at that precise moment, instead she was more than a little embarrassed that she had had to rush in, in such a bedraggled state. She waited for the polite greetings and the servants rushing around to make sure she was taken care of. No-one came. No-one spoke.

Confused, she pushed her hair out of her eyes and peered towards the end of the dark corridor that led away from the doorway she had just come through. It was quite empty, with just one lamp lit at the far end. She turned, about to ask Pembroke what on earth was going on and her confusion deepened. There was no-one there! But he had rushed into the house out of the storm with her. Hadn't he? A sudden chill of fear iced through her veins. She was entirely alone in a dark and empty house.

Her heart hammered against her chest as she called out, "Hello? Is anyone here?" The words echoed down the corridor and then drifted away into silence. She turned and tried the handle, but the door would not move. With a rising tide of panic, she fumbled with the handle, rattling it in desperation. It must be stuck. She must be doing it wrong. It can't be, surely…

And then a dread calm descended upon her as she finally realised that she had been stupid. Oh so very stupid. Collecting herself, she took a deep breath and began to walk down the shadowy corridor towards the distant lamp. With every step she forced herself to remain calm and to prepare. Whatever was waiting for her at the end of the corridor she would greet it as The Queen of Yngerlande, not as a frightened woman.

Her footsteps echoed as she passed a series of gloomy looking oil paintings and an old suit of armour that caught the beams from the lamp and glittered in the darkness. The corridor had a musty smell, as if it hadn't been aired or cleaned for several months, and out of the gloom, the pale bulk of white sheets covering items of furniture loomed like icebergs. This was a house, it occurred to her, that had not been used for some time.

She stopped outside the door at the end of the corridor and took a moment to compose herself. Taking a deep breath she reached for the handle, when without warning the handle turned itself and the door swung open to reveal the dazzling lights of the room within. She gasped in shock and screwed up her eyes. Strong hands grasped either arm and she was ushered into the room.

"A thousand apologies, Your Majesty, for all of this mystery, but as you will see, it was necessary. For your own benefit, you understand."

Summoning all of her courage, she asserted herself, raising her voice.

"Take your hands off me! How dare you manhandle your Queen. What on earth is going on here? I could have you all clapped in irons and sent to the Tower for this."

She only just managed to keep the quiver of fear out of her voice, which resonated with icy fury combined with dignity. It worked on the two men who had pulled her forward into the room. They dropped their hands from her immediately and stepped back, their faces a picture of guilt.

Matilda scanned the room, looking in vain for a friendly face, for someone who could explain all of this mystery. But there was no-one. Just the two men who had ushered her in, and the owner of the oily, polite voice that greeted her. He was a middle-aged man, with short greying hair. His clothes were of the finest quality, all silks and velvets, in dazzling blues and gold. He had a brilliant white lace ruff at his throat and he was bedecked in jewellery.

"Who on earth are you?" she demanded imperiously. "And why aren't you on your knees to your Queen?"

The man smiled at her. "My name is of no importance, Your Majesty. And I'm afraid no-one will be going down on their knees to you here. Probably never again, actually."

Matilda was furious.

"How dare you talk to me like that, you guttersnipe? You'll be wishing you had kept a civil tongue in your head when you're chained up in the Tower. Where on earth is Pembroke, my man?"

The man's smile faltered, and his irritation broke through.

"Oh, for goodness sake, enough of all of this nonsense. It will be you wishing for that, unless you change your tune. The only reason I'm calling you "Your Majesty" is because I'm a reasonable man. You're not a Queen, you never have been, so don't put on all of these airs and graces with me. You've been squatting on the throne of Yngerlande for long enough, but all of that is coming to an end. And as for Pembroke, your man, well, let's just say he isn't your man anymore. He's ours. For a time, at least."

Matilda looked dumbstruck. She went to speak but the man held up his hand to silence her.

"Don't waste your breath. Just listen to me and do exactly what I say, if you want to see your precious daughter again."

Matilda crumpled. "Gaia? Where is she? What have you done with her? Is she safe?"

The man sighed theatrically. "Ah, questions, questions!

You're very demanding, aren't you?"

He smiled at her and paused. His smile was at the same time threatening and mocking. "As I said, before you so rudely interrupted me, just listen to me and do exactly what I say. Understand?"

Matilda was silent. She looked afraid and utterly defeated. The man in front of her sneered and took a step towards her. He was just a few inches away from her now, his face almost touching hers.

"Understand?" he repeated in a near whisper.

She nodded. "Yes." She knew she was powerless and her only chance to help Princess Gaia was to be quiet and compliant.

"Good. That's much better. Now come this way."

He turned on his heels and strolled out of the door that Matilda had come through a minute earlier.

On the other side of the door, he stopped and turned to face her again.

"And don't make me clap you in irons, will you? That would be very foolish, because my men here like nothing more than a bit of torture."

Matilda nodded, bit her lip and bowed her head. He continued on his way and she followed him, the two guards at her side. They walked in silence, turning in the dark corridor to mount a wide imposing staircase. They went up three flights of stairs, with each landing lit by a solitary ghostly lamp, before coming to another doorway. They entered, and her captor indicated a chair in front of the fireplace where she should sit. He sat in a matching chair opposite her.

There were two glasses of wine, already poured, waiting for them on the table. He passed one to Matilda and took a sip of his own.

"So, let us begin. Please don't interrupt me until I've finished. Once I have explained the situation to you, it is reasonable to answer any questions you may have."

"Reasonable?" spluttered Matilda.

He frowned at her and Matilda reluctantly pursed her lips. There was nothing she could do but listen and it did not seem a good idea to provoke this man, whoever he was.

"These are your apartments. There are several rooms as well as this. Through there" - he nodded behind her - "is your bedchamber and a room where you may bathe. You will take meals in here and they will be provided at your usual times. You will be locked in here at all times."

He stopped as he noticed that Matilda's eyes had strayed to the windows.

"Yes, the windows are all securely barred and the door will be locked at all times. The door is the only way in and out. Please do not waste time thinking of escape, because that is impossible. If you waste our time with escape attempts, your stay will become less and less comfortable."

Matilda moved to speak but the raised hand kept her quiet.

"Now let us move to the reason you are here. In the next few days, Princess Gaia will be captured. She will be denounced as a witch. We have damning evidence of her unnatural powers. You will be accused of plotting with her to take over the crown and to set up Yngerlande as a kingdom of witches. Once this is known, the people will take to the streets and storm the Palace. If they find you, they will burn you at the stake in the street. The common herd loves nothing more than a gory execution, the more painful and horrific the better.

"And then, King Oliver will be invited by a committee of Yngerlande's oldest and richest families. He will bring peace and stability to the country, saving it from the chaos you and your kind have brought. He will be advised by his Uncle Jacob and, at last, the old ways will be restored and Yngerlande can be great again."

Matilda felt suddenly faint. The room began to spin and her knuckles tightened on the edge of the chair. Everything they had worked for was slipping out of her grasp. And she had let it happen. The events at The Christmas Ball in York had been a warning, but she had ignored it, or got hold of the wrong end of the stick. What had she been thinking? And where were all of her advisors and allies and guards. How could they all be so defenceless? These people were ruthless, she knew that. And what's more, they felt that they were in the right, that they were the natural rulers of Yngerlande and always would be regardless of the law and what the people wanted. And now her beautiful daughter would be killed in the most horrific of ways. She broke down and began to sob quietly, tears trickling down her cheeks

"Of course, it doesn't have to be like that."

The oily, smooth voice was quieter now. It floated on the air and settled on the room like a comfort blanket, until, finally, it penetrated Matilda's despair.

"What?" she stammered. "What do you mean? Is my daughter safe or not? What do I have to do to protect her?"

He smiled. "There, there, that's better, isn't it? A little bit of hope feels so much better when you have contemplated the very worst that might happen. And there is another way. All you have to do, to keep yourself and your daughter safe, is to step down from the throne on the grounds of Princess Gaia's illness. You, the devoted mother, will sacrifice the throne to look after your daughter in her time of need. And you will, at the same time, out of your love for Yngerlande, hand the crown to Oliver. The rumour of witchcraft will be spread around quietly, but because of your sacrifice, the people's reaction will be one of sympathy, not fear or hatred. It's rather a neat solution, don't you think?"

Matilda wiped her face and took a deep breath. In the cloud of despair that enveloped her, there was a flickering glimmer of hope. She was determined she would keep it alive at all costs. She was not to be killed, or at least not yet. Now, she just had to keep her mind clear and concentrate until it was time to act. She would play the part of the cooperative prisoner, smiling and nodding and not causing any trouble. And then, when the time came, she would strike, for her daughter, and they would not know what had hit them.

THE DAWN CHORUS

When dawn broke over The Rectory, the pale light cresting the waves of the North Sea, Silas had already been up for some time. He had wanted to quietly make coffee and finalise his plan, but any noise in the kitchen would send Elizabeth down to check on the heart of her empire at The Rectory. Sure enough, she appeared at the kitchen door minutes after Silas.

"Goodness, Silas, you are an early bird today. Let me get you some breakfast. Sit yourself down."

Her first look at the grim set of his face told her that, as usual, he was up early for a reason. It was confirmed by his response.

"Thank you, Elizabeth. I have a lot to do today and I need your help."

There was a creak on the stairs and a moment later Della and Amelia came into the kitchen, bleary eyed and a little dishevelled. They came in stretching and yawning before they caught sight of Silas with Elizabeth.

"Oh," said Della, puzzled, "it must be later than we thought. We thought we were the only ones getting up so early. I have to get to Whitby this morning. I'm driving the York coach today."

"No, my dear, it is early - only just after dawn in fact. But it's as well the two of you are here, because you need to know what's going on. Sit down, sit down."

They could tell something was afoot. All signs of tiredness disappeared and they were alert and ready to hear Silas' news.

"I wasn't quite truthful with you all last night over

dinner," Silas began. "It appears that we are all in danger now. Oliver and Jacob are back and they are plotting to take the throne again."

"What?" gasped Amelia. "What has happened? How do you know of this, Grandfather?"

"After dinner, I heard from Mary at last. I had been worried about her, expecting her to use the Sounding Stone to make contact days ago. She has found out that the Queen's man, Frederick Marlborough, has been taken prisoner and forced to send false messages to the Queen. This is all coming from Mulgrave Hall again. Both Mary and Marlborough are being held there and are in terrible danger. She managed to tell me that they are planning to capture the Queen and Princess Gaia, Clara, I mean. But then the Stone faded and I heard no more."

"But what will you do, Silas? And how can we help?" Della's voice was a mixture of anxiety and excitement. Although she feared what might have happened to Mary Carruthers, she did not always like the quiet life they had been living since Christmas. Part of her longed for adventures, when the small world of Runswick Bay and coach driving closed in on her and was not enough.

"I will go on to Mulgrave Hall to see if Mary is actually there. And to set her free if I can. I need to talk to her to find out exactly what she has discovered and what Oliver and Jacob are planning. Above all, I need to know where they are. They may be at Mulgrave Hall as well, but somehow, I doubt it. We also need to know where the Queen is."

"But surely, Grandfather, she will be at St James' Palace, won't she? Why would she have left the safety of London where she is protected by her redcoats? That doesn't make sense," said Amelia.

"Until I spoke to Mary last night, that's what I thought as well. But I think she will have been convinced to leave to protect the Princess."

"You mean Clara. Is she in danger?"

"I fear so. The Queen has received forged letters telling her Clara is in danger. They must have been authentic to make her doubt her own judgement. But I think it was all a scheme to make her take to the road where she could be intercepted and taken prisoner."

"So, what can we do? We must be able to help in some way."

"I do not want to place you all in danger. You did more than enough last Christmas."

"Silas, if anything, that should tell you that you can trust us and that you don't have to worry. Just tell us what we have to do and we will do it."

The light outside the kitchen was growing stronger now. Soon, all of Runswick and North Yorkshire would be awake and going about their business. Silas knew that time was against them.

"You must stay here and watch and wait," he said finally.

Della was scornful. "Watch and wait, Silas? Come on, there must be more for us to do than that."

Silas insisted. "Watch and wait here, Della. Keep a close eye on Clara. Remember, she is the one they want, the one they need. Look out for any strange people, any strange goings on. At the first sign of danger…no , not even danger, at the first sign of something you cannot explain, take to the tunnels under the moors."

Della smiled. "The tunnels! Yes, Silas, that's more like it."

The tunnels were where they had escaped last Christmas when they were trapped in the cellars under the Crab and Lobster in Runswick village. They had got them out of a sticky situation then and Della had a good feeling about them again.

"Remember! They will take you either to the woods high up on the moors near Mary's Cottage, or to Mulgrave Hall. You will know which direction to take, if the need arises."

"Alright," said Amelia, "that seems quite straightforward. And, presumably, we will hear from you, whichever way we go."

Silas hesitated. "Well, that's the idea. But of course, it may not be possible. And there's more."

"What do you mean more? That is never good in my experience," said Della.

"Before I leave this morning, I just have time to do one last lesson with Clara. Her powers have developed remarkably quickly, and you will be able to rely on her to defend you all in most circumstances, but not all. I must teach her the secrets of the Sounding Stone before I go. I think it very likely that she will have to summon The Friend to help us once again."

Della, Amelia and Elizabeth exchanged glances and smiled.

"Thomas! Thomas is coming back. How wonderful it will be to see him again," said Della.

"And will his annoying cousin, what was his name, Dan, was it, will he be coming too?" Elizabeth attempted to look severe, but her smile broke through as she remembered Dan's mischief last time.

"That is possible, although it will be altogether more dangerous than last time. He is not The Friend and that makes it harder for him. But listen to me, all of you, because time runs short and there is much to do. Think about what I have said. All being well, I will see you soon. I will leave immediately after Clara's lesson, so no time for goodbyes. Trust in each other, and all will be well."

He stood up and strode to the door.

"Grandfather - be careful, won't you?" Amelia called after him.

He turned. "My dear, my safety is the least of your worries. Remember what I have said, all of you."

There was no time for any questions, he had made that much clear. The door closed and the three women looked at each other in turn, their faces a picture of fear. The safe world of their dinner party the night before suddenly seemed a long, long way away. Each of them knew that it may never return.

BREAKING AND ENTERING

In the shadows, Shrike moved with his customary silence until he appeared at the spy hole to the dungeon. He peered through, and in the dim light of a solitary candle, saw two figures at a rough table, chewing the meagre hunk of bread that had been delivered to them minutes before. He had deliberately followed one of Mulgrave's servants, lurking in one of the recesses, so that when he checked on the prisoners, they would have some light in their cell. The servant would return in twenty minutes and remove whatever was left of the food, and the lamp.

In the gloom, he could make out Marlborough. Gone were the fine silks and perfume. He was dressed in filthy rags and his face bore all the hallmarks of rough treatment at the hands of Mulgrave's thugs. He ate ravenously, unlike his companion, who nibbled the bread cautiously, and sipped the water they had been given.

Either she had only just joined him and was still not broken, or she was made of stern stuff, Shrike calculated. He was surprised. She was an old lady, as far as he could make out, and looked as if she was more used to knitting and reading books, but no-one knew better than he that appearances could be deceptive.

She finished her piece of bread, brushed the crumbs away and wiped her mouth delicately with her hand. Shrike smirked to himself. My word, the old goose thinks she's in a fine hotel with the gentry of North Yorkshire. Silly old fool! Then, after carefully looking around the filthy cell, she quietly rummaged around deep inside of her clothes and pulled out a small pebble.

Shrike froze and all of his senses moved into a different gear. What was she up to? She brought the pebble to her lips and kissed it lightly. Gradually, the gloomy dungeon began to fill with a sapphire light that banished the shadows to the far corners. Marlborough finally stirred from his silence, intrigued by what she was doing. He made to speak but Mary silenced him with a single finger raised to her mouth.

She turned her attention back to the sounding stone, its intense blue light staining her face.

"Silas! Silas!" she hissed. She waited and tried again. Outside the cell, Shrike held his breath as he watched what was unfolding before him. Then the blue light flickered and a different sound crackled from the stone.

"Mary, listen to me, we don't have much time. I've warned Clara and the others at The Rectory. They are to send for Thomas if I do not return there. I have left letters for Clara and for Thomas to be read when he arrives, so they know what to do. I will come for you soon and you can tell me all you know. But for now, Mary, tell me, are you well? Have they harmed you?"

"I am fine, Silas. As you know, I'm a tough old boot. But Frederick Marlborough is here with me, and that is a different story. They have tortured him terribly and he is very weak. I think he has tried to protect the Queen at great cost to himself. He has been very brave. You need to come soon because he needs a doctor urgently, I think. They will try the same thing with me, Silas. I don't know what time it is. We are deep underground and there is no light. We are in the darkness in every way."

Mary's voice began to wobble as she carried on.

"I am afraid, Silas. I don't know how long I can hold out here."

Silas' crackly voice interjected. "Be brave, Mary. I will be with you very soon. But now, I must go."

His voice faded, the light from the stone receded, and

the cell was once again submerged in darkness.

Outside, Shrike racked his brains. He would have to move fast, that much was clear. He turned over what he had just heard in his mind. "That pebble, the Sounding Stone she called it, is a powerful weapon and no mistake. I think it would be better all round if she didn't have it and I did. And the Reverend is coming to rescue the old biddy, is he? I don't think I want to show myself when he's around, not just yet anyway. There'll be plenty of time for that later. So, I'd better get on with it."

He moved back from the door of the cell and slipped away down the corridor into the shadows. Up ahead, light flickered on to the walls of the passage from a candle-lit side room. He knew that was where the guard sat with his feet up, resting until he had to make another trip to the cell. He also knew that the guard was aware that no-one ever bothered to come down here, deep into the bowels of The Hall. It was too far, too dark, and too damp to bother. The guard was left alone to do his job, and so he began to cut corners. He forgot to lock his own room. He left a candle burning. The keys to the dungeons were often idly thrown onto his table because if no one was coming down here, why bother?

Shrike slid to the doorway and craned his neck around the door jamb until he could see inside. As he suspected, the guard was snoring, dozing in a chair by the table, and Shrike could see the keys lying on the table in front of him. A broad smile broke out on his face. This was child's play for him, something he had learned to do when he was an urchin, ducking and diving in the filthy back streets of York. He almost floated into the room and, keeping his eyes on the snoring guard at all times, picked up the keys, taking care not to make a sound.

Once he had pocketed them, he stood in front of the guard, watching how his snoring rattled the room with his mouth wide open. He took a small glass bottle from his inside pocket and unscrewed the top that had a rubber bulb attached to it. He held it over the guard's open mouth and gently squeezed until a few drops of liquid fell into his open mouth. The guard spluttered a little but then resumed his snoring. Shrike repeated this another couple of times and then screwed the stopper back on the bottle. He looked at the label and a grin spread widely across his narrow pale face.

"Tincture of Laudanum - it never fails to hit the spot. That should keep our eagle-eyed guard here nice and quiet for an hour or so. I knew my visit to the apothecary would be worth it."

He slipped out of the guard's room and carefully locked the door, leaving him to his opium-drenched sleep. Then he made his way back down to the dungeon. With a quick check of the inky black corridors, he opened the door of the cell and locked it behind him. Mary Carruthers sat bolt upright, immediately alert. Marlborough was more sluggish, but when he finally became aware of the presence of another man in the dungeon, he scrambled away from the table, knocking his chair to the stone floor in the process. He whimpered and moaned, holding his hands up in front of his face in terror. A man in the dungeon clearly meant more unspeakable torture as far as he was concerned.

"Who are you?" demanded Mary, as coolly as she could. "You're not the usual guard. What do you want?" She narrowed her eyes as she thought. "Who sent you here?" She was hoping against hope that this was part of Silas' plan.

Shrike read her mind. "I'm very sorry, Grandma, I'm not the knight on the white horse come to rescue you, sent by old Silas. This is not a fairy tale, you know."

"What do you know of Silas? Who are you?" Mary's brain was working overtime now, desperately trying to work out who this strange newcomer was.

Shrike grinned at her. "You really should be more careful to make sure that no-one is listening when you gabble on into that pebble you've got."

Mary's face fell. "The Sounding Stone..." she whispered in shock.

"Yes, that's right, dear, the Sounding Stone. Very useful, I reckon. So, be a good girl and hand it over and then I can go about my business."

Mary gulped. "I don't know what you're talking about, young man."

Shrike sighed. "Well, if you're sure that's the way you want to play this."

He marched across to the trembling figure of Marlborough in the corner. In the light of the one candle in the cell, the blade of his kitchen knife sparkled, as he slid it from its sheath. He grabbed Marlborough by the collar, hauled him to his knees, and held the knife at his throat. Marlborough whimpered, not able to move an inch without the blade drawing blood.

He looked across to Mary, who was powerless to intervene.

"Please, don't hurt him. He has been through enough." Her voice was quiet and calming. The last thing she wanted to do was to provoke this man. She had no idea who he was and how he was likely to react if he was crossed.

"If you are concerned about him, you can easily help. Put the Sounding Stone on the table and step away."

Mary hesitated, her eyes flicking from the knife to the door and back.

"Please don't waste time. I know very well you are more dangerous than you look. But you also should have worked out that I won't hesitate to slit his throat if you don't do what I ask. And then I'll slit yours and I'll get the stone anyway. It shouldn't take you too long to work out what is the best thing to do here."

Mary seemed to deflate in front of him, as she realised she truly had no choice. She pulled the stone from her dress and placed it on the table.

"You know you won't be able to do anything with it. To you, it will always be just a pebble," she said defiantly.

Shrike smiled. "You'd be surprised just exactly what I can do, in time. And, if the worst comes to the worst, at the very least you won't have the stone to use either."

He let go of Marlborough, who slid to the floor moaning, and reached across and held the pebble in the palm of his hand. It was just an ordinary greyish, speckled stone that could have come from the beach at Runswick Bay. He slipped it inside his coat where it nestled with the bottle of laudanum and turned towards the cell door.

"Just exactly who are you working for?" Mary called as he reached for the door handle. "It can't be Lord Mulgrave and Oliver and Jacob, otherwise you wouldn't be skulking around in the dark on your own. The guard would have just let you in. I'm willing to bet that no-one knows you are down here. Why is that then? Are you too common for the high ups?"

Shrike, still with his back to them, winced. He turned to face them.

"You're very clever for a little old lady, aren't you? So let's see. You know about Lord Mulgrave and King Oliver and his uncle Jacob. So, you must also know that they are essentially useless individuals, who would kill their own grandmothers for power and gold. As would I, of course, there's nothing wrong with that, obviously. It's just a question of who does it first. Once I've done my work for them, I have no illusions that I will be fairly rewarded. I'll be got rid of, because I know too much. So I have to be a little bit cleverer than them, that's all. Thankfully that's not too difficult." He gestured to the side of the room. "Even that table is a bit cleverer than them.

"Now, I'd love to stay and chat some more, but I'm a busy man with a lot to do and I'll have to make a move. I imagine from the conversation you were having with old Silas earlier that he will show up before too long. I've seen him work with the Princess and I know he's not your average vicar, but you're going to have to pray he gets here soon, otherwise you're finished.

"No, change that. It doesn't matter when he arrives. You're finished anyway. Toodle-oo."

He slipped through the narrowest crack in the door and locked it behind him. It took him a minute to retrace his steps to the guards' room. Standing stock still outside the door, he could hear the guard's rhythmic snores, still deep in his drugged sleep. Shrike bent down and pushed the key to the door through the gap at the bottom. As he walked away along the pitch-black passage, he thought of the guard waking up later, without any memory at all of the laudanum, to find himself locked into his own room, looking at the key on the floor in front of him, utterly perplexed by how that could possibly have happened. He bounced along, a little spring in his step, and his bark of laughter echoed along the damp walls.

THE LAST LESSON

The light outside Silas' study had grown stronger. It was time to finish the lesson and get on with his plan while he could still do something to help. He looked across to Clara, who was standing opposite him, a Sounding Stone in the palm of her hand. The blue light was fading and the stone beginning to cool.

"So, you see, Clara, the stone is not just for communicating across great distances, though that is incredibly useful. It has other, even more mysterious uses, for someone with the gift. We have gone through many of them this morning, and you may need to use them before this is over. I am sorry we do not have more time for you to practise, but I must leave as soon as possible. I've already delayed too long. You must keep the stone safe, hidden about your person, and then forget about it. You will know how and when to use it when the time comes."

Clara frowned. She rolled the stone, now an ordinary looking pebble, in her hand and considered what to say. Finally, she decided.

"But, Silas," she began, "how will I know what to do and when to do it?"

"If I have not returned by this evening, you are to contact Master Thomas. You know what it is you must say to him. As for the rest, have faith. When the time comes, you will know what to do. But remember, it is you they want, and you and Tom who they fear the most. They know everything you both did last Christmas, so they know they have to be wary of challenging you. Now, Della,

Amelia, Elizabeth and Grace will remain here with you. They will keep you safe for a while, but there may come a time when you will have to do the same for them. For they will be easier for Oliver's men to take than you. You will be faced with difficult decisions very soon. Hopefully, I will be back by then, with Mary."

Clara bit her lip. "And if you're not? Back, I mean. What will I do then?" Her eyes began to glitter and Silas saw that she was crying. Behind all of her confidence and all of her powers, she was a young girl still not sure of her place in the world, desperately worried about her mother.

Silas went towards her, taking her in his arms and planting a feather kiss on the top of her head. He held her for a moment and then took a step back with his arms resting on her shoulders.

"My dear girl, you are ready. Listen to your heart, remember your lessons and all will be well. Now, dry your eyes and go back to the house. You must be confident for the others if no one else."

Clara managed the ghost of a smile and made her way to the door of the study. As she opened it, she turned.

"If I am to be careful, Silas, then so must you. Make sure you return."

With that, she slipped out into the corridor, closing the door behind her.

Silas watched her go, and sat staring at the closed door for a moment. Then he reached down into the drawer of his desk and pulled out two folded sheets of parchment, both bearing his red wax seal. One was addressed to Thomas, the other to Princess Gaia. Although Silas thought of her as Clara, the formality of writing made him use her regal title on the letter. He placed them in the centre of his desk top and then went back to the drawer and drew out a leather pouch, closed at the top with a leather drawstring.

He stood up, walked to the centre of the room and then emptied the contents of the pouch into his hand.

Three brightly coloured balls hovered in the air above his palm. Green, yellow and red, the balls began to glow and spin the second they were released from their bag. After a second, the colours and the balls blended into one blurred whole and Silas walked forward until he had been enveloped by this spinning kaleidoscope of colour. There was a soft popping sound and then nothing. Silas had vanished.

*

From the window, the stone tower atop a green mound of grassy earth dominated the view. Jacob's face exuded anxiety as he gazed upon the monument that had been part of the old castle. It was now a prison and try as he might, he could not help but be reminded of the Tower in London, a place where for centuries, traitors had been held and tortured before meeting their death. As an example to other would-be traitors, the end was always bloody and brutal in an attempt to make them think twice in the future before they plotted against the monarch and the country. If caught, he and Oliver too would die a horrible death, after agonising torture had been carried out to find out the other names behind their plot.

He shivered before turning away from the window to face Oliver.

"I don't know why we had to take this house, fine though it is, in full view of that Tower. It's a bad omen, if you ask me."

Oliver was sitting at a table on the far side of the room, picking at various delicacies that were laid out on porcelain plates. It was an elegant, beautifully furnished room, full of fine pictures, tapestries, and ornaments, with a heavy Persian rug on polished wooden floorboards.

"The house suits me well enough at present, Uncle. A little small, perhaps, but certainly better than the hovel we had to endure in Paris. But for a King? No, it is very modest, but I will put up with it for a time. It was good of Mulgrave to arrange it for us."

"Good? You think he was doing it because he's a nice fellow? Hell's teeth, Oliver, you are like a child at times. He has arranged it, as you put it, because he wants something in return when you are back on the throne."

"I'm not a complete idiot, Jacob. Of course he wants something. And when we're in St James' Palace, he'll get his reward. For heaven's sake, man. Come away from the window and sit down for a moment, you're making me nervous. And if you're worried about being spotted, staring out of the window for all to see is not very clever, is it?"

Jacob snorted in reply and, taking a last look at the Tower and the sparkle of the River Foss that wound round to one side of it, crossed the room to join Oliver at the table. There were a handful of opened letters to the side of the remains of Oliver's snacking. Jacob scooped them up and quickly flicked through them.

"All of these reports are encouraging. Matilda is under lock and key at Belton Hall and Marlborough will probably not survive his ordeal in Mulgrave's dungeon. His men are particularly ruthless when it comes to winkling information out of people. That old hag Carruthers has also been caught, which is a bonus, and is sharing a cell with him."

Oliver guffawed. "My goodness, I almost feel sorry for the man. I'd rather be tortured than to have to share a prison cell with that ghastly old woman. It was bad enough sharing the coach from York to Whitby with her last Christmas."

Jacob was thoughtful. "She completely played us last time, Oliver, and don't forget it. The silly old woman routine was an act and we fell for it. She may be in a cell, but we would do well not to think she wasn't still dangerous. Particularly if she is in communication with Cummerbund."

"How could she be, Uncle Jacob? The dungeon at Mulgrave Hall is under many feet of thick rock and earth. No-one has ever escaped from it, and hardly anyone knows that it exists. There is no way she could get a message to anyone from there. No, she will cause us no more trouble, Uncle, you can put your mind to rest about that."

"Are you forgetting the things they all did at Christmas? Things that no earthly person should be able to do? And after what Shrike told us about the Princess' lessons with the old man, we can't take anything for granted."

"What are you suggesting, Uncle?"

"We will not be safe until we have neutralised Cummerbund and Princess Gaia. Matilda will only go along with our plan if that is the only way to save her daughter, so we must get hold of her before she gets wind that anything is wrong. As soon as she does, she will disappear and Matilda will hold out forever. We can't harm Matilda if you want to be accepted by the people as the rightful King. If we spread the story that the daughter Gaia is unnatural, with devilish powers, that will encourage Matilda to step down from the throne because she has to look after her poor unfortunate daughter in some remote, secure religious house. Unless Matilda agrees to do that she knows that the people will want Gaia to burn at the stake like a witch."

"Well, what are we waiting for? We have Matilda in Belton Hall, Marlborough and the old woman in the dungeons at Mulgrave Hall and a spy in The Rectory. Everything is coming along nicely, isn't it?"

Jacob grimaced and his eyes scanned around the room as if looking for traitors in the shadows.

"The boy," he hissed. "Have you forgotten about the boy?"

"The Trelawney boy, you mean? What about him?"

"That devil, Shrike, told us he was coming back from his other world, whatever that is. And we haven't heard a word from Shrike, not since he left for Runswick."

"It's only been a day or so, Jacob. Perhaps there is

nothing to report."

"And perhaps Shrike is playing a clever game, and has taken the money and run," Jacob spat back. "He is costing us a pretty penny, so he'd better deliver. I'd slit his gizzard myself if I found out he was cheating us."

"So what should we do?"

Jacob considered for a moment. "We wait, for a day at least. If we have not heard from Shrike by tomorrow, we will go to him. We can't get any further with Matilda until we have her daughter safely under our control."

"And Trelawney?"

"If we have Matilda, and Princess Gaia, then Trelawney and Cummerbund will be reluctant to do anything that puts them in danger. It may even be easier to capture the other folk that associate with Cummerbund - you know, the young pretty doctor and the coach driver. They are a weak, sentimental bunch, the lot of them. They will cave in as soon as we make any kind of threat against them."

"Yes, Uncle, I like the sound of that plan. Very much indeed. I was going to deal with those two insolent, unnatural women at some point."

Oliver stopped to skewer a hunk of meat from the plate in front of him. He twirled it round in front of his face, increasing his anticipation of the feast. Then he looked back to Jacob.

"It would give me great pleasure to do it sooner rather than later. Why do we have to wait? Why can't we just go and do it now? Why can't we skewer them, eh?"

"I don't want to walk into a trap. Shrike has not let us down so far. Let us give him a chance to send us a letter outlining what he has found out. If we don't get that by the end of the day tomorrow, then we will go and stay with our old friend at Mulgrave Hall."

A twisted smile crept across Oliver's face. "Lord Mulgrave, eh? And will he put his money where his mouth is this time, do you think? He scuttled away and made sure he was nowhere near the fallout from the failed bomb plot at Christmas. I don't trust him as far as I can throw him. Still, at least we will drink some fine wines from his cellar while we are there and we won't have to skulk in the shadows, like we do here. And we might get some decent food."

He brought the skewer closer to his face as if inspecting it, before suddenly snatching at the lump of meat with bared teeth and chewing it ferociously, with the juice dribbling down his chin.

*

Shrike held up the pebble to the light and revolved it slowly in his fingers. He was baffled. To him it was a plain stone, nothing more, but he knew that in the right hands, it was a powerful weapon. After all, he had watched the old man and the Princess, Gaia or Clara, or whatever it was she was called, do extraordinary things with it when it glowed with that sapphire light. All those hours of watching them go about their business in Kings Manor must have been worth something, surely?

He put down the stone and turned his attention to his pocket watch. It was time to make a move, but what sort of move and to what purpose was less clear. He glanced around the small room he had been allocated. The letter he had handed over to Mulgrave when he first arrived had obviously done the trick because his Lordship was falling over himself trying to be hospitable, insisting he lodge in one of the Hall's flagship rooms. Goodness knows what Jacob had put in the letter, but it had convinced his Lordship that he, Shrike, was a key player in their plan. It had taken Shrike some time to politely insist on a small room on the ground floor, away from the main entrance. He took a deal of trouble in making sure he was both polite and credible. He knew from bitter experience that fine Lords and Ladies were quick to take offence, especially from someone they thought would be more at home in the gutter. And Shrike was certain that, for the moment, Lord Mulgrave was someone who he needed to keep sweet. When the business was concluded, well, that would be a different story and old Lord M better watch out.

And the room was perfect for the time being. A door into the main house, another that opened onto the yard by the stables, it felt like accommodation that was meant for the chief stable lad: private, modest and convenient for the job. It meant that he could slip in and out of the estate without being spotted.

But what now? It was clear to him that he had to gain the trust of Grace and the Princess, because that would make it a little easier when he finally made his move against them. He'd seen what the Princess could do after spying on her lessons, and he would have to move very carefully with her. One wrong move and she would defend herself with the full range of strange powers she possessed. Any one of them was more than Shrike could withstand.

But the girl, Grace? She was a different matter. He hadn't quite worked out how she could be the sister of this mysterious boy, Tom, they had all talked about. Nor why she was here in Yngerlande, while he was in some other strange land. He would have to be careful while he found out more, but the more he thought about it, the more he became convinced that Grace held the key to this.

She was an odd character, a rather pretty girl who seemed clouded in sadness. She didn't seem to have any friends and clearly missed her brother. He couldn't work out what her place was at The Rectory, or how she fitted into the bigger picture. And that, thought Shrike, is the way in. She is terribly lonely, looking for someone who understood her and who would listen and be interested in her.

"After all," he muttered, "there is no-one on this earth who knows more about loneliness than me."

It was a thought that was a mere fact, a blunt statement of truth, rather than a lament. Shrike had long ago abandoned feeling sorry for himself as a way of being.

That, he thought, was weakness, and more importantly, it wasn't very helpful. And always, Shrike looked to see what to do next in terms of what was in his own best interests. It was the one true lesson his life had taught him. Look after yourself, because no-one else will.

If he could get her to trust him, and better still, to feel sorry for him, then he was halfway there. His mind raced as the germ of an idea took root and began to grow. And with it, his expression of distant concentration began to soften and his features broke into a grin. It would take longer than he had thought and he'd need a bit of luck, but it could work. He just needed to get down there and get the lie of the land before he jumped in. He'd have to wing it a bit and be ready to take advantage of whatever opportunity arose, but he was good at that. His quick wit had always got him out of trouble in the past.

There was one fly in the ointment, though. Jacob and Oliver. They would be champing at the bit, eager for news of his mission in Runswick. If he knew them, they would come charging in too soon, desperate for an update. The first thing he should do, before making his way to The Rectory, was quickly pen a letter outlining his progress. He would need to reassure them while telling them that he needed a bit more time to reel in the girl. As for the Trelawney boy, the one they were clearly most worried about, he would just say that he had been mentioned, but there was no sign that he was here or even on his way. That should calm them down a bit.

He sat at his desk and, pulling a sheet of parchment from his makeshift desk, dashed off his news, his quill scratching its spidery trail of black ink over the paper without pause. Once he had blotted the ink, he folded and sealed it so that they could be reassured that it was genuinely from him. He slipped into the main house and left it on a silver salver along with a collection of other letters to be delivered that day.

Just before he left, he checked his appearance in the

looking glass in his room. His clothes were tidy and clean: tight knee breeches and stockings, leather shoes with silver buckles, a blue frock coat with a white linen scarf at his neck all topped off with a tricorn hat. It was important that he looked both respectable but not too fancy to make his tale seem credible. He made sure he had left nothing incriminating lying around in his room, and with a final glance in the mirror, and a straightening of his hat, he went out into the stable yard, locking his door behind him.

It was still early, but the stable boys would be up and about tending to the horses even at this hour. He crept to the stall where he had left his horse and saddled up. Then, whispering and stroking the horse by the nose, he led it out into the yard. He swung himself into the saddle and walked the horse out the yard until they joined the main driveway. As soon as he was out of sight of the Hall, even from the highest of its many windows, he spurred the horse on and broke into a gallop. There was a lot still to do and the day was yet young. Time to get on with it.

SHRIKE IN THE SHADOWS

Della checked the saddle and bridle of her horse, and slung her bags over its back as it stamped on the cobbles of The Rectory's stable yard. She turned to Amelia.

"Be careful while I'm gone. Silas is away and there's no telling when he'll be back. After what he told us earlier I'm uneasy about leaving you here. I can always stay, if you prefer."

Amelia smiled at her. "No, no, you must go. They won't be able to find another driver at such short notice, and anyway, I know you love driving that coach over the moors. We shall be fine here. And I would not be at all surprised if Grandfather returns this evening with Mary in tow, just in time for dinner. Between us, Elizabeth, Grace, Clara and I will be safe and well. 'Tis you that should be careful. It's a lonely road over the moors to York. Highwaymen have been known to stop and rob folk at gunpoint, you know."

Della laughed. "Yes, I know that very well, because they have tried that with me before now." She winked. "They soon realised that was a mistake, though, and spent many a long night in York castle dungeons for their pains afterwards."

Amelia looked horrified. "You never told me about that!"

Della laughed. "Some things it's better not to know about. Now, look after yourself and everyone else, of course, Doctor Comfort! I'll be back before you know it."

They embraced with a kiss, and then Della broke away

and leaped into the saddle.

"Come then, Jet," she said, stroking the horse's ears, "a good gallop over the Moors will do us both the world of good."

She flicked the reins and spurred the horse' flanks. Jet broke into a trot and they disappeared round the stone gate post, on to the road ahead.

Amelia watched them go, a cloud of dust rising above the stone wall of the Rectory, tracking their progress.

"Has Della left for Whitby, then?"

Amelia spun round to see Grace and Clara in the doorway.

"Yes," Amelia replied. "She has to be in Whitby by noon for her shift. She's the driver for the coach to York today."

"Will she stay overnight?" Clara asked.

"She wasn't sure. They may ask her to do the return coach tonight, if they're short of drivers."

"And what about you, Amelia?" asked Grace. "What are you doing today?"

"I'm working in the lab this morning, preparing potions with Elizabeth and then I have to visit some patients in the village this afternoon."

Grace looked a little flustered. "Oh, don't you want me to come along with you?"

Grace had been working with Amelia, training to be a doctor, ever since she had arrived from England. Silas had thought she would need some purpose to help her settle into Yngerlande, and he had been right. It was one of the few consolations she had found in her new life there.

"Silas asked me to go alone. He thought it would be nice for you and Clara to spend some time together, away from your lessons."

Clara interjected. "And, as ever, Silas is right. It will be lovely. We have the whole day, Grace. What shall we do?"

"We could go down to the beach this morning and have a picnic and a walk along the cliffs and the shore,"

Grace replied. "What do you think?"

"Perfect! And then we can be back in time to see what Silas has discovered. He's bound to be back from Mulgrave Hall by then."

"Well, that's settled," said Amelia. "Let's go in and get ready. We'll need to tell Elizabeth and she'll help you prepare your picnic. I just need to get my doctor's bag ready and saddle up my horse."

They turned back to the house from the yard, leaving it bathed in the early morning sunshine. The door closed and from just within the canopy of the trees that bordered the Rectory garden, a figure stirred.

In the shadows of the trees, Shrike stroked his chin. He retreated further into the wood to the clearing where he had tied his horse. He stroked the horse's head and shared his thoughts in a low voice, as the breeze rustled through the overhanging trees.

"Well, well! So the Reverend has gone to Mulgrave Hall, has he? If anyone can enter the dungeon and release the prisoners it will be him. But he might find it harder than he bargained for, when he gets there. There'll be more guards around, if I'm not mistaken, after my little intervention earlier. And everyone seems to have read the script. The coach driver woman has gone to Whitby and will be away for at least a couple of days in York. The beautiful lady doctor is visiting the sick, like a good doctor should, and will be occupied for most of the day with her potions and cures. And the two young girls, the magical maidens, will be out and about on their own this morning."

He paused, his face a picture of concentration, bending his head to the horse's muzzle. He lay his head against the horse's neck and muttered out loud as he struggled to settle on the best way to proceed.

"I've got to split them up somehow. Get everyone out of the house, so that it's empty when those two girls return. And if we can make sure the old man knows they are prisoners as well, then he will not be able to fight back, for fear of what we might do to them."

A smile suddenly broke out on his face, and he slapped the horse's flank in triumph.

"Yes, of course, that's it! But…"

He stopped mid-thought as he rummaged around in his waistcoat for his watch. He flipped open the case. Yes, he had just about enough time.

"Come on, Silver, old girl, time for you to stretch your legs. We need to fly like the wind to get back here in time."

He hauled himself up into the saddle and picked his way through the trees as quietly as he could before he reached the road that led back to the moors. As soon as he was at a safe distance, he spurred his horse on and galloped off, clouds of dust rising in his wake.

*

Matilda paced up and down the room, stopping occasionally to look through the window to the grounds of Belton Hall far below. Behind her lay the remnants of the breakfast she had picked at. She had had a troubled night with little sleep, as she brooded on the plans her captor had explained to her the night before.

So far, she had been treated well, but that might change at any time. She did not believe a word of his story, of course. The minute Oliver had taken the throne, she and Princess Gaia would disappear. No doubt they would be taken to some kind of nunnery or large country house, somewhere in the middle of nowhere, where no-one could check up on them. The story would be put about that she and Gaia were being well treated and that Gaia was receiving the best medical care to "cure" her of her "witchcraft", but a few months later there would be some tragic "accident" and both of them would be dead.

Oh yes, there would be a respectable funeral, and then everyone would forget, too frightened of asking too many questions of the new King and his regime. And the minute they had got rid of them, then it would start. New laws would be passed, forbidding people of colour and women from holding high office. Rich, powerful friends of Oliver and Jacob, all white men no doubt, would be rewarded for their support by being given new estates and positions in the Government. Paintings of the old world that showed people of colour in positions of power would disappear. They would be barred from voting, and from "professional" jobs, and then from education. Women would be encouraged to stay at home and be mothers and housewives because it was more "natural", and then eventually, they would be compelled to fulfil those roles, whether they wanted to or not.

And before you knew it, it would be as if it had always been like that, and could not be any other way.

She shuddered at the thought. Her grandparents had talked to her about what they called "the bad old days". She had thought that that had been just old people's talk and that those days had gone forever. Obviously, the world had moved on and was getting steadily better as the years rolled by. It had never occurred to her that what had been won could be lost again. She shook her head and thought bitterly, "Truly, the battle for fairness is never over. Never."

She knew exactly what was coming and she was furious at herself for letting this happen. But all was not lost. That was why she had to keep trying to get to sleep at night and to eat properly, just so that she was ready when the time came for her to act. Until then she just had to be watchful, and look for any weakness, because she knew for certain that she would have to escape on her own. No-one was coming to rescue her, like in a fairy story. Of that, she was sure.

She looked outside again. On the neatly clipped lawn she saw patrolling soldiers appear periodically, as if they were circling the building. They were not her redcoats, by the look of them, who seemed to have completely disappeared. What had happened to them? Were they all part of this terrible plot as well? Had she imagined the loyalty of all of her servants and people? The thought of that pricked a tear in her eye, but before she had a chance to weep, there was a knock on the door. She gritted her teeth and hurriedly pulled herself together. Her pride would not allow her to let her captors see her in distress. She was determined not to give them that satisfaction.

The door opened without anyone waiting for permission to enter. Matilda smiled ruefully. So much for her status as Queen. A small head with stubby black locks poked nervously round the side of the door. She caught sight of Matilda and immediately flew into a panic that saw her mixing a bow, a curtsy and opening the door. "Yer Majesty. I've…er… come fer t' dishes, ma'am. Er… Yer Majesty."

Matilda smiled at her. "Come in, child, I won't bite."

The girl shuffled in, head bowed, and shut the door behind her. She fidgeted uncomfortably, shifting from foot to foot, paralysed by nerves.

"What's your name, girl?"

It was a question that seemed to cause her much consternation. Eventually, looking over her shoulder and around the rest of the room, she stuttered, "Daisy, Yer Majesty." As soon as she had managed to deliver this piece of information, she cast her eyes to the floor, as if her own shoes were objects of fascination and surprise to her. Matilda looked her up and down. Although she was young, she was, Matilda noticed, fairly tall and well-built.

Matilda smiled again. "Now, Daisy, come and sit by me, and tell me all about yourself."

She patted the cushion of the seat next to her and waited until Daisy had sat herself down and regained control of her own breathing. While she did so, smiling encouragement and nodding all the while, her eyes, glittering with concentration, found themselves continually returning to the large bunch of keys that hung loosely from Daisy's belt. She broke off just once to look her squarely in the eye. It was with some satisfaction that she realised that Daisy was exactly the same height and build as her. With her heart pounding, she spoke again.

"Carry on, my dear. I want to hear all about your family. Do they live nearby?"

SHRIKE PULLS THE STRINGS

Silas appeared in the darkness of the lowest corridor, with a faint popping sound and the merest glow of light from the spinning multi-coloured balls. He held up his hand and with a click of his fingers, the balls leapt up to his hand and he put them back in his leather pouch, drawing the string tight. He slid his way down the passage, until he was outside the door of a cell. He peered through the grille, his eyes straining in the darkness to focus. It was empty, so he moved along to the next door. And there, on the far side of the gloomy dungeon were two figures. One was clearly Mary Carruthers. He smiled as he caught sight of her face, grim set and determined. It would take a lot to defeat Mary. There was someone else there, slumped in the shadows opposite her. That must be Frederick Marlborough, judging by what Mary had said when they had last spoken. His head lolled around on his shoulders and he looked barely conscious.

He looked back both ways down the passage. To his right was total blackness. To the left, the faint, yellow flicker of a candle. That would be the guard, he reckoned. He moved like a cat, hardly breathing, until he turned the corner and saw a door slightly ajar, with the light faintly staining the floor and walls of the corridor. It was damp and cold, and in the light of the candle, he could see the gleam of moisture trickling down the crumbling stone walls.

Through the gap he could see the guard, sitting at a narrow table. He rummaged in his cloak and drew out his

Sounding Stone. Then he bent down and picked up a tiny pebble from the floor. Watching the guard carefully, he threw the pebble a few feet to the other side of his room. The guard sprang up. He reached for his pistol as he shouted, "Who's that? Show yourself, or I'll shoot."

He rushed to the open doorway, a lamp and pistol in hand. As he did so, Silas moved like lightning. He held the Sounding Stone in front of him, which suddenly glowed blue, flooding the passage with a brilliant luminous sapphire light. The guard gasped as Silas thrust it into his face. His other hand was firmly placed over the guard's heart and Silas simply said, "Sleep!"

For the guard, it was both a command and a gift. His angry face melted into blankness and his whole body subsided, still standing, but like lifeless clay. Silas gently propelled him back into his little room and manipulated his limp body so that he sat at his table, upright but zombified. He quickly went back down the corridor to the grille of Mary's cell. The noise of the earlier commotion had brought her to the door, scanning the corridor left and right as far as she could through the opening.

Silas brought his face to the grille.

"Mary? Are you alright? 'Tis Silas, Mary. All will be well now."

Mary gasped in relief. She seemed to deflate like a punctured balloon, as if she had been holding herself steady to survive.

"Oh, Silas! Thank goodness you're here. I don't think Frederick can last much longer without any treatment."

"Step back from the door, Mary."

She did as he had asked and immediately, with a burst of vivid blue light and a whoosh of sucking air, his body decomposed into a trillion particles and slid through the fabric of the door, to reappear and reassemble on the other side. He shivered and then urgently scanned the room. Marlborough was still slumped in the corner, unaware of what had just been happening.

Mary noticed his concern. "Marlborough has been most cruelly used, Silas. He needs some help, as soon as we can get it to him."

"I thought as much. This should keep him safe for a few hours more until we can get him out of this dreadful place."

He pulled a small glass bottle out of his coat pocket, unstoppered it, and poured the contents into Marlborough's open mouth. Immediately, he coughed and spluttered, and sat up as if an electric shock had gone through him. Silas placed both hands on his shoulders and brought his face level.

"Listen, we don't have much time. The potion I've given you is a temporary stimulant, but we need to get you to a doctor as soon as we can. But before we do that, we need to quickly go through what happened to you." He glanced at Mary. "To both of you. Marlborough, you first."

Marlborough's voice was weak as he began speaking, but steadily grew stronger as the potion worked its effect on him.

"I was placed near the King's Manor in York, on the instructions of the Queen, to keep an eye on Princess Gaia. Although Her Majesty was grateful for your role in saving her at Christmas, she wanted to be sure of your intentions. Do you understand?"

"Of course. And very sensible too. It's exactly what I would have done in her position. It was all arranged very quickly after the Christmas Ball, so it made sense of her to keep an eye on me and her daughter. After all, I could be anybody. So what happened?"

"I had a network of spies who had you both watched constantly. And I myself was able to watch at times. I sent back reports that she had nothing to worry about, and that Princess Gaia was thriving under your care. But then…"

He broke off, gripped by a coughing fit. Silas waited patiently for it to pass.

"And then..?" Silas gently nudged him to continue.

"I received a note from someone who claimed he had information vital to the Princess' safety. I was to meet him in The Kings Arms in York and to go alone. I was surprised when we met. He was a young man, barely more than a boy. Face as white as a sheet and a shock of red hair. He began to talk to me about what he had discovered, and then the next thing I knew, I was waking up, in chains and gagged in a room somewhere."

Mary interrupted him. "The same boy that was here yesterday? The boy that took the stone?"

Marlborough nodded. "Yes, it was him."

"We'll deal with one thing at a time, Mary. It's vital I hear Marlborough's tale first," said Silas. He turned back to him.

"It was not a prison then? Not here?"

He shook his head.

"No, I was brought here later. And it wasn't a cell, it was a comfortable room. The shutters on the windows were never opened so I couldn't see where I was, but I could hear the sounds of activity on the street and it sounded to me like I was in a house in the town. I was interrogated about what I knew and what my loyalty was to the Queen. I think he hoped to buy me, but when I made it clear that I would never betray her, well, that's when the violence started. He forced me to write letters and they used my personal seal to make them look genuine. The red-haired boy also practised until he could do my handwriting. He obviously thought that I wasn't going to survive the torture they had planned and it was too useful to have the Queen receive my letters. She trusts me absolutely, you see. I have been in her service for years, and now I have…"

He broke down and began to sob quietly.

"Now I have betrayed her and the Princess."

Silas leaned across and laid a comforting hand on Marlborough's shoulder.

"Don't reproach yourself, Sir. You have endured

terrible treatment, more than anyone could bear. And now, you still have a chance to get your revenge and to serve the Queen again."

Marlborough sat up, suddenly alert.

"How, Sir? Tell me how and I will gladly do it."

"Tell me - what was in the letters you wrote? And how many more did the boy himself write? In short, did you get any idea of the final instructions to the Queen?"

Marlborough racked his brains. "First it was details about overhearing you, at Kings Manor, talking to your accomplices, about imprisoning the Princess. Then, that you were working with the people behind the Christmas plot - Oliver and Jacob were the names mentioned. There was a complicated story about how your rescue of the Queen, and the prevention of the explosion at The Assembly Rooms, was all a set up, to allow you to get close to the girl."

He shuddered at the memory. "By that time, I couldn't write any more - I was too weak and my handwriting would have caused suspicion, and so the boy did it. He used the same parchment, and my seal, and his handwriting by then was exactly the same as mine, or near enough, at any rate. He read them aloud when he had finished each one. I think he did it to torture me with what was being planned. The last of them told the Queen that it was vital that she come north to rescue the Princess and to arrest you and your accomplices. She was to bring a small guard of redcoats, and the letter said she was to stay overnight at Belton Hall, with Sir John Brownlow, who had been sworn to secrecy."

Silas held up his hand to stop him. "When was that, Marlborough? It is important that you are precise."

He thought for a second. "Two days ago. It was the last letter I saw him do."

"Two days ago, you say. Then she may now be at Belton Hall."

Marlborough interjected, "I cannot believe that Sir

John is involved. He was always a great supporter of Queen Matilda. He would not betray her."

"Perhaps, like you, he had no choice. And, Mary, what of you? How were you imprisoned here?"

"I was in York, as we agreed. I tracked down Oliver and Jacob. Lord Mulgrave has installed them in Fairfax house by the prison, in secret."

Silas snorted. "The prison! He has more of a sense of humour than I gave him credit for. And you were caught?"

"Yes, I took a risk and tried to find out the details of what they were planning, but I was discovered."

"Have they harmed you in any way? You look remarkably well under the circumstances."

She shook her head. "Thankfully, there was too much going on, though I am sure they will return to question me further, particularly after your visit to the jailer."

"And the red-headed boy? He has been here as well?"

Mary's face fell. "I don't know how to tell you, Silas. He knew all about the Sounding Stones. And he had been watching you teaching Clara her lessons at Kings Manor. He knows of her powers."

"I knew it!" he exclaimed. "I was certain we were being watched, but I could never detect anyone. I scanned the room with the stone, but it never picked up any signs of human presence in the room. And it never fails - if there is someone there, it will find them. But with him there was no sign. I don't understand it."

"But, I hardly dare tell you the worst, Silas. The stone. He has my stone! He threatened to slit poor Marlborough's throat if I didn't hand it over. I told him it was worthless to him, but he knows some of what it can do. I'm sorry, I…"

Her voice faltered as she thought once again of what had been taken from her. Silas leaped in.

"All will be well, Mary, never fear. As you say, he can do nothing with the stone and we will retrieve it, one way or another."

His voice was even and confident, but the smile in his eyes faded as he spoke. The loss of Mary's stone was a terrible blow, there was no getting away from that.

"There is one ray of hope, though, Silas. He spoke of Mulgrave, Oliver and Jacob. He clearly knows they are not to be trusted and even if he started off working for them, he made it very clear that he was actually working for himself. He said he'd have to get rid of them before they got rid of him."

Mary shuddered as she remembered him.

"There was something chilling about him, Silas. It was as if he had never known warmth or friendship or happiness. He had an evil air that surrounded him. And he made it clear that killing was nothing to him."

"And is he still here, at Mulgrave Hall? Do they know he plans to betray them as well?"

Mary shook her head. "I don't know, I'm sorry."

"And who is he? Do you even know his name? Or, at least, the name he goes by? Because at the moment, he is a complete mystery."

"No, I don't. The only thing I do know is that he is dangerous. Deadly dangerous."

*

Shrike sealed his letter to Mulgrave and then bent down by the side of his bed. Using his knife, he prised up a loose section of one of the floorboards and then a second. He thrust his hand into the gap and felt around the space below. His fingers strained and then finally closed around the thing he was searching for. Carefully, he pulled it out. It was a wooden box, which he laid gently on top of his bed and inserted a key into the lock. It turned smoothly and Shrike opened the hinged lid to inspect the contents. Inside, nestled on a fat pillow of lamb's wool were six spheres the size and shape of apples. Holding his breath, he removed four of them and laid them down onto the soft cover of his bed and locked the remaining two in the casket.

Then he returned to the hole in the floorboards and stretched his hand through it to find a second box, exactly the same as the first. Thank goodness he had paid the Apothecary for a spare. It had cost him a pretty penny more, and it was dear enough anyway, but now he could take the others with him. He had no idea when he would be able to return to Mulgrave Hall and he was sure that these precious trinkets would come in very handy in the aftermath of his plan. It was a long shot and he would need as many weapons of surprise as he could get.

A bead of sweat had appeared on his forehead. With nerves of steel and a steady hand, he carefully placed the four remaining globes into their carrying case and turned the key in the lock. The minute he had locked the casket he breathed out in relief. He could relax now the mysterious spheres were safe.

But not for long. He had to get back to The Rectory as quickly as he could if his plan stood any chance of working, and he needed one last conversation before the gallop back. He went to the door of his room, opened it and looked out onto the stable yard. One of the stable lads was pushing a wheelbarrow and a shovel towards the stables.

"Hey! You lad. Come here, I've a job for you." Shrike bellowed the instruction at the top of his voice. The boy leaped out of his skin, and his barrow overturned, spilling manure all over the yard. The boy looked up, petrified. Shrike smiled to himself. He knew that the stable boys thought him the devil and crept around in fear of their lives when he was about. It was a useful weapon to have.

"Me, sir?" he stammered.

"Yes, you boy. Can you see anyone else around? Come here, lad, quick as you can."

The boy scrambled as close to Shrike as he dared.

"Sir?"

"Get me Timpson, lad. Tell him it's urgent. Understand?"

"Yes, sir. Timpson, sir."

The boy stood rooted to the spot. Shrike glared at him in silence, enjoying the boy's evident discomfort.

"Now, boy, now!" he bellowed.

The boy turned and ran in the direction of the house, relieved to be making distance between himself and Shrike. Shrike called after him. "A coin for you, lad, if he's here within a minute. And a slice of your liver for me, if he's not."

By the time Timpson appeared at his door, Shrike was ready to leave, his precious cargo safely stowed in his leather satchel. He left no time for pleasantries and instead handed over the two letters on top of the box he had prepared earlier.

"Hand this to his Lordship immediately, Mr Timpson, if you please. The box does not have a key. It is open. Don't bang it, or knock it at all, if you value your life. Or that of his Lordship."

Shrike paused and smiled as he noted Timpson's expression flicker slightly. He knew that Timpson was calculating whether it would be worth losing his own life if it meant Mulgrave died as well. For all of Mulgrave's servants, but particularly those that were black, that decision would be a close call, such was their hatred of their master.

Shrike also knew that Timpson was an intelligent man, and that it would take him only a second to reject the temptation. He reached out a hand to take the box with the parchment on top.

"Two hands, Mr Timpson, please. Two hands."

Timpson followed his instructions, bowed, and moved carefully towards the door. When he was at the threshold, Shrike called him.

"Oh, and Timpson? Place the box in the middle of the table, out of reach of anyone, and hand both letters directly to his Lordship. And leave the room as fast as you can."

Shrike watched him go, satisfied he had done everything he could do at the Hall. He carefully shouldered his satchel and walked steadily into the stable yard. The boy was still there, expectantly, holding Shrike's horse. He sprang up into the saddle, and with a flick of the reins, wheeled the horse around towards the gate. He looked back at the boy, whose face was a mixture of fear and admiration. Flicking a gold coin at him, he said, "Well done, lad. I'll have your liver next time." With that he spurred the horse out through the gate and onto the open road. The boy's eyes lit up as he held his treasure, and watched Shrike disappear in a cloud of dust.

THE WOODEN BOX

Mulgrave belched loudly, pushing his plate away and leaning back in his chair, his eyes half closed in contentment. Immediately, one servant sprang forward to remove the plate, a second refilled his coffee cup, while a third hovered anxiously, in case his Lordship had not, after all, completely finished eating.

Breakfast was Mulgrave's favourite meal of the day. He spent at least an hour over it, staring out onto the immaculately clipped lawns, while he methodically worked his way through successive mounds of food and drink and planned how he would spend his day. He never felt that a breakfast that finished without some casual humiliation of one of his army of servants was a good omen for the day to come. He needed to smell their fear, to remind himself that he was master of everyone and everything he surveyed. And, of course, it was good for them to be reminded at the beginning of each day exactly who was in charge. The daily reminder of their essential worthlessness was, he felt, uncommonly kind of him. It stopped them getting ideas and that saved a lot of unnecessary unpleasantness later. And there was nothing Mulgrave hated more than ideas, especially ideas in the wrong heads.

Ideas. That reminded him, suddenly, of the task at hand. He clicked his fingers and the gaggle of servants sprang into action, noiselessly clearing the table of all signs of breakfast. A fresh pot of coffee and a bowl of sugared almonds was placed at his right hand. Mulgrave surveyed the table, nodded and grunted and then clicked his fingers again. A crisp newspaper and a silver salver piled high with the first letters of the day was placed at his left hand. He picked up the copy of The Leeds Intelligencer, frowned and tossed it aside. It was the London paper he wanted, for the gossip from the Court, and to scan for the coded messages his spies would often place in the advertisements. Had any rumours started about Matilda, he wondered? Any allusions to the "unusual" Princess Gaia? He would have to wait until the latest editions arrived on the mail coach in York.

He turned his attention instead to the pile of letters on the dish, throwing each of them aside, until he found the one he was interested in. A sly smile spread across his bloated red face, and his cold piggy eyes glittered. He muttered under his breath.

"Ha! Now what does young Master Shrike have to say for himself, I wonder? And, more to the point, can I believe a word of it?"

He sliced through the red wax seal with his knife and eagerly unfolded the papers. As he read, his expression changed to one of intense seriousness. Once he had got to the end, he quickly scanned the papers again, occasionally stopping to stare up at the portraits of his ancestors that lined the walls of the room. Heavy oil paintings in ornate gilt frames, showing a series of men who looked like him: overweight, red-faced, dressed in silks and lace and velvet, decorated with gold, silver and an array of exotic jewellery. These were men who were exceedingly rich, exceedingly powerful and exceedingly privileged, and the current Lord Mulgrave was determined to outdo all of them.

A timid knock came at the door, which opened to reveal a middle-aged black servant with greying hair and a lined face. He waited in the doorway, a small wooden box in his hands.

"Forgive me, my Lord, but I have an urgent message from Master Shrike."

"Shrike? What more does he want? I've just ploughed

through his last letter. What is it now?"

"Begging your pardon, my Lord, but he was most insistent that this box be laid down on the table and that it should not be touched by anyone before you have read his letters."

"Shrike giving me orders now, is he? By God that young man is insolent. He goes too far."

Mulgrave sighed.

"Very well, Timpson, the letter if you please."

Timpson eased his way into the room, carrying the casket out in front of him as if it were precious and delicate. He laid it gently on the table and then passed the letter to Mulgrave. Mulgrave sighed again, and breaking the seal on the note, began to read. As he read, his eyes glanced nervously to the wooden casket Timpson had placed so carefully on the dining table. When he got to the end of the letter, he laid it to one side, and stared again at the casket, deep in thought.

Suddenly he bellowed, "Writing paper! And pen and ink. And my seal. Now, you morons! Now!"

The gaggle of servants lining the room jumped into action, falling over themselves to obey Mulgrave's orders, while taking care not to make eye contact or draw attention to themselves in any way. Once the writing equipment had been laid out in front of him, Mulgrave turned his attention back to the staff in the room.

"Now, get out, all of you. I'm sick of the sight of your ugly faces. Go to your normal stations and await further instructions. I have work to do."

They filed out of the room without further question. As they reached the door, Mulgrave bellowed at them.

"And woe betide the wretch who is not at his station, alert and ready, when I call. Today is not the day to make such a mistake, believe me! And, Timpson? I have one more task for you if you can manage it, you dolt!"

Timpson detached himself from the scrum of departing servants and stepped forward.

"My Lord?"

"Get me Captain Frobisher. I need him immediately, you understand. Immediately."

Timpson hesitated, and allowed a faint frown to crease his forehead.

"Captain Frobisher, my Lord?"

"Are you deaf as well as stupid, you cretin? Yes, Captain Frobisher, that's what I said. Have you grasped it now? Or do you need me to say it again? Dear God, you people are the very limit."

Timpson bowed and considered his next move very carefully. One more annoyance might well be too much for Mulgrave, a man he both detested and despised for his stupidity and vulgar greed. But his fear trumped both of those emotions and he did not care to feel again the lash of the whip, or experience the darkness of the dungeons without food. Both of those things had happened to him, as they had to nearly all the black servants at the Hall, and Timpson had learned how to survive the cruelty of Mulgrave's rule.

"Very good, my Lord," he said.

He turned to go.

"Timpson!" Mulgrave bellowed.

He turned to see Mulgrave holding a letter between his fingertips high above his head.

"My Lord?" he breathed.

"Get a rider to deliver this to The Rectory in Runswick immediately. Our fastest horse, mind you."

Timpson oozed forward and took the letter from Mulgrave's fingers, his head bowed.

"Thank you, my Lord."

Then, raging inside, he slipped away to get Frobisher before Mulgrave had an opportunity to find fault again.

Mulgrave watched him go for a moment, narrowing his eyes, before reaching for the quill and parchment. He dipped the quill into an inkwell and began to write, occasionally stopping to consult a well-thumbed booklet at his right hand. This was the code book that he used for all his letters to Oliver. He was a cautious man and he knew that he would be for the gallows if any of his letters were to be discovered written in plain English. He patted the little booklet and smiled. It was an inconvenience, to be sure, and Mulgrave was not used to being kept waiting, but it was an inconvenience that might well save his life one day.

Your Majesty,

There is news of the greatest importance from North Yorkshire. Our friend Shrike has removed the Princess and the young girl Grace Trelawney from the protection of the Reverend Cummerbund. He has also put into motion a plot to ensure that all the others from the Rectory are safely under lock and key here at Mulgrave Hall. I have taken steps to neutralise Cummerbund, Marlborough and the old woman, Carruthers. The same will be done with the rest of Cummerbund's crew from the Rectory. If he can see with his own eyes that these people are in danger if he makes any attempt to use his magical powers, then we are safe.

I humbly advise Your Majesty to remain at Fairfax house for the time being, until our plans fall into place. Then, when the time is right, we will proceed to Belton Hall to make sure the imposter Matilda has no choice but to step down from the throne to look after her daughter, leaving the way clear for you to be crowned. This will, of course, be seen as you saving the nation at a time of great danger and uncertainty.

Be patient for a few more days. Your time has come.

I remain your humble servant,

Mulgrave.

He read it a couple of times, checking his coding was correct. He had addressed it to Oliver, but thankfully, he knew it would be read by Oliver's uncle, Jacob. Jacob, a man with a formidable brain, could be relied upon to stop

Oliver acting impulsively. If it were down to Oliver, he would ride immediately to Mulgrave Hall in full view, acting like the returning King, and the whole thing could come tumbling down like a pack of cards.

And surprising Cummerbund and overpowering him down in the dungeons would be a tricky task to accomplish. He must have no time at all to react, but above all, Frobisher and his men must be able to get their hands on his magical blue stone. According to Shrike, without it, his powers were severely diminished. The Stone was the key.

Satisfied, he dried the ink, folded the parchment tightly and dripped molten wax on it to seal it, impressing his crest into it as it cooled. As he laid it down on the table, there was a quiet knock on the door. He looked up, remembering that all the servants had been dismissed.

"Enter," he called.

The door opened and a tall, well-built man in military uniform, with a sword at his side, strode into the room. He bowed.

"My Lord, you sent for me?"

"Frobisher, excellent. Come in, close the door behind you, and listen carefully. There's something I need you to do."

MORE PRISONERS

Amelia stared at the rider still sweating outside the front door of the rectory, holding the reins of his horse.

"And Lord Mulgrave has been taken ill, you say?"

"Yes, ma'am. Very ill."

"Can his own physician not attend him?"

"His Lordship's doctor is away in York, ma'am. He particularly requested you attend him, ma'am. Your reputation is growing, he said. He has a terrible fever, ma'am. Beg pardon."

The rider, nothing more than a boy, averted his eyes.

She thought for a moment and then decided. Grabbing her medical bag, she called back into the house, "Elizabeth, we have a patient to visit. Gray, get the carriage ready."

*

Less than an hour later, Gray brought the carriage to a standstill in front of the main entrance to Mulgrave Hall and steadied the horse while Amelia and Elizabeth stepped down onto the gravel driveway. A servant stepped up to greet them.

"I was asked to examine Lord Mulgrave. Could you show us to him, please?" she said.

The servant bowed. "Of course, Doctor. Please, follow me. I'll take you both to him directly."

"And our driver, Gray?" interjected Elizabeth. "He may have to wait for some time, depending on how serious his Lordship's illness is. Could you find somewhere for him to wait and arrange some refreshments for him, please?"

"Certainly, madam," the servant replied. "Arthur will take good care of him, rest assured."

He nodded in the direction of the carriage, where Gray was being led away, and a ghost of a smile passed across his lips.

"Now, if you'd like to follow me, ladies. Shall I take your bag, Doctor?"

He indicated the leather medical bag in Amelia's hand. She shook her head and clutched it close to her side.

"No need. My medical bag never leaves my side, sir. The contents are both valuable and extremely dangerous in the wrong hands."

The servant bowed again.

"Very good, Doctor. Now, this way, if you please."

He swept through the doorway into the grand hallway. Amelia had not been there since that night just before Christmas, and she was not particularly pleased to be going back. The servant led the way down corridors lined with oil paintings, stuffed animal heads and suits of armour. It was a gloomy place, Mulgrave Hall, full of shadows and secrets.

"I shouldn't like to get stuck here for very long," Elizabeth whispered as they scurried along the passage, "and certainly not after dark."

"No," agreed Amelia, "but hopefully, he is not seriously ill. You know what these aristocrats are like. It doesn't take much for them to think they're dying, when all they've got is a bit of a headache. We'll be finished before you know it."

"And then we can get back to The Rectory. I don't like leaving Grace and Clara on their own, particularly when Silas is still out and about."

"He's probably already back with Mary, having afternoon tea in the garden," replied Amelia.

The servant had come to a halt in front of a door at the end of the corridor. He turned to them.

"His Lordship is in here, Doctor."

He turned the handle and pushed the door which opened into a large, well-lit sitting room. Holding the door, he gestured to them to enter, and Amelia led the way, beginning to open her medical bag as she did so. To her surprise, there, standing right in front of her, was Lord Mulgrave, a picture of health with a beaming smile spread across his face.

"Your Lordship," Amelia stammered. "I thought you were unwell. I don't understand."

"No, my dear," he replied. "It's not me that is unwell. It's you."

Two men emerged from the shadows of the doorway, one seizing Amelia, the other Elizabeth. One hand held their arms tight while the other covered each of their faces with a damp pad. The last thing they both heard, as they slipped into unconsciousness, was the sound of a distant explosion, somewhere far below them, and the grating sound of Mulgrave's cackling laughter.

*

Earlier, Frobisher, with Mulgrave's instructions ringing in his ears, had carried the strange wooden casket from the breakfast table down the staircase that led to the dungeons below, his hands shaking and his fingers slick with sweat. At a safe distance behind him, were four of Mulgrave's personal soldiers. They crept into the darkness, lit only by flickering candles set into the dripping walls. Frobisher led them into a room at the top of the final flight of stairs, and set the box down carefully on a small table in the middle of the room. He turned and gestured to the four men, his finger held up against his lips. They gathered around him and watched as he opened the box and removed one of the balls that lay cushioned on their lambswool packing.

In a hoarse whisper, he repeated his instructions to his men. "Now, you all follow me down to the dungeon. In silence, mind you. We need as much time as surprise will grant us. Stay behind me until I give the word.

Understood? Now, lads, masks on and keep them on until I say otherwise."

They all, Frobisher included, tied bandanas over their faces to cover their noses and mouths and began to creep forward along the final corridor. Through the gloom, Frobisher could make out a light coming from the door to one of the cells and the faint noise of voices. He turned back to his men and gestured for them to stay put, out of sight of the door.

At the threshold of the door he stopped, then, taking a deep breath, he pushed it open and stepped inside. The three figures in the room stood frozen in shock, mouths open in mid conversation. Silas' hand moved slowly and smoothly to the pocket of his frock coat.

"Good morning, Reverend. I'm afraid you are trespassing here, as well you know. I'm going to have to arrest you for that, I'm afraid."

Silas smiled at him, his cool demeanour in stark contrast to the horror and panic on Marlborough's face. Mary Carruthers eyed the corridor behind him in silence.

"Now, I don't think that would be a good idea, do you? Many people have tried, all of them better than you and your master, and they have failed." His hand emerged from his pocket holding the Sounding Stone, which began to glow blue as he held it up, weakly at first but growing in strength all the time.

Frobisher, his heart beating fit to burst through his chest, matched Silas' smile.

"Not this time, old man," he said and in some swift movement he dashed the two balls to the ground at their feet. They shattered like glass and dense, yellow smoke streamed from the shards on the floor, thicker and thicker until the cell was full of choking fumes. Frobisher replaced his mask around his nose and mouth and stepped backwards out of the cell door. Silas, summoning all of his strength, lunged for him through the smoke, but the door was closing and Silas crashed against it.

"Now, men," Frobisher cried, "hold the door. It will only take a few more seconds. And keep your masks on."

They sprang forward and pushed forward with all their weight against the cell door. Immediately there was another crash against it from the inside, but weaker this time.

"Just a few seconds more," cried Frobisher.

They waited in position, listening for any signs of life on the other side and then, Frobisher silently motioned for them to step back from the door. Cautiously, he opened it a fraction. A few wisps of yellowish fumes threaded their way out into the corridor and died in the gloomy corners of the passageway. He pulled the door wider to let more fresh air into the cell, and then stood aside for the soldiers to enter. A minute later they dragged the three prisoners out one by one and clapped their hands and feet in iron manacles. Frobisher went straight to the unconscious figure of Silas, who was still clutching the Sounding Stone in his hand. He knelt and prised his fingers away from the stone one by one, until finally he was able to wrench it from his hand. He placed the stone safely in his pocket and turned back to the guards.

"Place them in three separate cells. Keep them chained, but make sure they have fully recovered from the fumes. Check on them every hour. And be careful. The Cummerbund fellow is a cunning chap, even without his stone."

He turned and strode down the corridor, the stone safely stowed in his pocket. As he made his way to the stairs leading to the main house, his fingers closed around the stone. He turned a corner in the passage, and then stopped abruptly by the sole candle that lit the way. With a glance in either direction, he brought the stone out of his pocket and examined it in the flickering light. Turning it round in his fingers, it appeared to be a rather ordinary, plain pebble from the beach. He shook his head, bewildered.

"So, this is what all the fuss was about. Well, let's hope Mulgrave is satisfied. For all our sakes."

*

Matilda crept to the locked door of her apartments at Belton Hall and crouched down, her ear to the keyhole. After a minute she rose, satisfied that the corridor outside was still empty. There wasn't much time left. Soon, another set of servants would arrive to see to her needs, and there were still things she must settle.

She turned her gaze back inside the room. At the far end, tucked away in the corner next to a tray full of dishes, was Daisy, her dark eyes wide with fear. Matilda scurried back to her, a warm smile, radiating warmth and reassurance

"It's alright, Daisy, there's no-one there, it must just have been the wind."

Daisy squirmed in her seat. "But, ma'am, I must go. If I am caught here, I will lose my job. I should have been back in the kitchen by now."

"No, Daisy, wait. You have been very brave to stay and listen to what I had to say. But I need you to be even braver now. You know that people like you and your family have a terrible future in front of them if I am removed from the throne. The grandson of the old mad King will return. He despises anyone who is not like him and his kind. We will not be treated kindly. Your family will not be treated kindly."

"But, Ma'am, I dare not. If I am caught I'll be imprisoned, probably even tortured, until I tell what I know. And…" She broke off into a shuddering sob. "And so will my family."

Matilda looked around wildly. "Shh!" she implored. "You must be quiet, or someone will come."

She laid her hand gently on Daisy's arm and began to gently stroke it.

"We've been through this. If we do it properly, you will be seen as the victim in this, not the villain. But it must be done tomorrow night. You must come tomorrow as usual, dressed just as you are now. And believe me, my child, you will be rewarded for your service to your Queen. Very well rewarded. Your family will never want for money ever again. And your father, Daisy. Think about your father's condition. My personal physician will take charge of his treatment."

Daisy, calmer now, thought for a moment. She nodded. "I am decided. I will do it, Your Majesty. It is a terrible thing they have done to you. And their plan for the Princess is downright cruel and wicked."

She stood up and collected the tray of crockery, and gave a small bow.

"I'll come back later this evening."

"With everything we discussed?"

"Everything, I promise. But now I have to go."

She went to the door and unlocked it.

Matilda watched her from the far end of the room, suddenly overcome with foreboding.

"Godspeed, child. Until tonight."

Daisy did not meet her eyes. She opened the door, took up the tray and once in the corridor closed it quietly. A few seconds later the familiar sound of the key turning in the lock was the cue for Matilda to begin her steady pacing up and down her apartment again. It was going to be a long night.

THIS CHARMING MAN

Shrike took one last look through his eyeglass, just to make sure. Far below him, on the beach, the tiny figures of Grace and Clara stirred. They stood up and stretched and then began to collect up all of their things and pack their bags. He lowered the telescope and, collapsing it, slid it into his pocket.

"At last," he muttered. "Time to perform."

He untethered Silver and swung himself up into the saddle. With a flick of the reins and click of his tongue, he encouraged the horse to turn away from the cliff and into a trot down the grassy cliff top towards the road leading to the hills above the beach and The Rectory. The sun was still high in the sky and beat down strongly. Even up on the top of the cliff there was barely a breath of wind, and far out into the North Sea, the waves were still and calm.

He had been watching them closely for the last hour or so, with little or no shade up on the cliff, so the breeze as he cantered along was a welcome relief. His linen shirt was soaked in sweat and in the wind, it chilled his skin and awakened his senses. As he picked his way down the track leading to the road, he pondered his plan once again. As he went over it in his mind, he grimaced. It would involve a bit of pain, but nothing he wasn't used to, and the prize would be worth it. He pictured all the main players, Oliver, Jacob, Lord Mulgrave, all of whom were expecting him to play his part. He played out his plan in his mind's eye and saw their incredulous faces, a mixture of disbelief, fury and admiration. Oh yes, he thought, as he dipped down into a little copse of trees that straddled the road, it would definitely be worth it.

Five minutes later, he led his horse into the entrance to the Rectory. He tied the reins to the hitching post at the side of the house and quickly scanned the grounds, walking round the building and peering into every window he passed. Everything was just as it had been left a few hours earlier.

Stooping down, he picked up a sizeable rock from the side of one of the flower borders. He weighed it in the palm of his hand before finally making his mind up. He took a deep breath and gritted his teeth. Then, raising the stone high above his head, he brought it crashing down on the side of his forehead.

He cried out in agony, and then clamped his lips together to silence himself. He sank to his knees for a moment, digging his fingernails into the palms of his hands as waves of jagged pain washed over him. After thirty seconds or so, he forced himself to sit up and breathe through the pain. He knew that it would pass, because pain was something he was familiar with. He also knew it was necessary, if his plan was going to work. Tentatively, he raised his hand to his forehead and gently touched the spot that hurt the most. He winced as he made contact and instinctively pulled his hand away. His fingers were covered in bright, scarlet blood. He smiled. "That should do it," he muttered.

He crouched down in front of the main door and strained his ears to listen for sounds of any approach. The curve of the driveway would give him enough cover, he thought, but only just. For a minute or so, all he could hear was the far distant sounds of the sea, and the haunting cries of gulls as they wheeled overhead, from the beach to the clifftop, constantly searching for food. And then, as his legs began to ache from the position he held, there was a new sound. A sound of approaching footsteps and casual conversation.

Immediately, Shrike lay down on the gravel, his body twisted as if he had just fallen awkwardly. He waited, rehearsing his lines over and over in his head. The footsteps came nearer and then, as the voices turned into the drive, the sound changed as boots crunched over the loose stones underfoot.

"Do you think Silas is back yet?" came one of the voices.

"Let's hope so–"

The reply was cut off as they noticed the body lying crumpled in front of the steps to the Rectory door.

"What on earth is that?" asked Grace

"It looks like a… no, it can't be…"

"It's a body, Clara. A body…"

She stopped and rushed forward. Clara called after her, "Grace, be careful! It could be a trap."

Grace ignored her and rushed towards the stricken figure of Shrike, his body twisted on the ground, his tricorn hat a few feet away from his body. She fell to her knees and pulled the body by the shoulder. He was heavy and it took her a second attempt with both hands to turn the figure onto his back. As she did so, she gasped in shock as she saw the bloody gash on his forehead. She turned back to Clara.

"He's injured, Clara, there's blood everywhere. We need to get him inside, quickly."

She bent down towards him and pushed his hair away from his forehead to get a better look at his wound. At that moment, Shrike, with perfect timing, opened his eyes, blinked a few times and groaned, clutching his wounded head.

"Aargh!" he groaned. "Where are they? You must be careful, Miss."

He grabbed hold of Grace's hand and held it tight.

"Who do you mean? There's no need to be scared, it's just me and Clara here."

"But they'll be back, Miss, you can be sure of that."

Clara had hung back a little, watching and listening carefully. Now, she chose to intervene.

"Let's get you sat up, young man, and see to your head. Grace, go and get him some water, and then we can dress his wound and hear his story."

She hurried off for the water, while Clara helped him to stand up. He seemed a little unsteady on his feet and she had to support him as she led him through the door into the house. Shrike made sure that his legs gave way once or twice so that he had to stop and lean heavily on her. He was careful not to overplay his hand though. He had the distinct impression that this one was much more careful than the other girl, Grace. He could tell by the way she looked at him narrowly and the cool, sceptical tone of voice. She was suspicious, of that he was certain.

She led him to sit at the large kitchen table, while Grace gave him a glass of water and began to clean his wound with a cloth and some of Amelia's herbal infusions. He winced as she dabbed at the gash in his head.

"This is a nasty wound, young man. How did you get it?"

"And why were you lying on the ground in front of our house? What's your name, for a start? We can't keep calling you "young man".

"My name's Shrike, Miss," he began.

"Shrike? That's an unusual name. But what's your first name? And what brings you here?"

"Shrike is my first name and my last name and my only name, Miss. Just Shrike, that's me."

"Well then, Shrike, tell us your story, if you please. What happened? And who are you?" asked Clara, eager to get to the bottom of their mystery guest.

"I came on an errand from Mulgrave Hall, I..."

"Mulgrave Hall! But that's where... "

Clara immediately placed a hand on Grace's arm and flashed a warning look at her. As far as she was concerned, it was better to give away as little as possible to this newcomer.

"Go on, Shrike. From Mulgrave Hall, you say?" Clara interrupted.

"Yes, I was sent there for the summer to continue my apprenticeship."

"Your apprenticeship? In what? Why would Lord Mulgrave take an interest in you?" asked Clara.

Shrike permitted himself a wry smile.

"A good question, Miss. As you have guessed, I am not from a fine family and must make my own way in the world, but his Lordship has made it his business to help me on the journey, so to speak. I am learning the workings of a great country house. Previously, I was in York, learning different aspects of his Lordship's affairs. I like to think that I have some talent and that Lord Mulgrave values my abilities."

Clara frowned. "But Mulgrave could have anyone he wanted to do his work. Why you? It doesn't make sense."

Shrike smiled smoothly. He had been expecting his story to be challenged so he was ready for it.

"I have wondered the same thing many times, believe me. I've finally come to the conclusion that Mulgrave is a good man, with an interest in helping others less fortunate than himself. His reputation is undeserved, from my experience. Although, after what's just happened…"

Clara snorted. "A good man? Now I know that there is more to this than you are making out. Mulgrave is a scoundrel, pure and simple."

Now it was Grace's turn to interrupt.

"Clara, look at his injuries. This is not the time to interrogate him. We need to treat him and then we can get to the bottom of his story."

Shrike turned to her and held her hand, squeezing it as if overcome with gratitude. He looked her straight in the eye. "Thank you, Grace, your concern is very touching."

His hand lingered, holding on to hers for a little longer than it needed to. Grace, a little confused, stared into his eyes and then shook herself free of the feeling that had suddenly overwhelmed her.

"Now," she said briskly, "let's finish off this dressing, shall we?"

She finished cleaning away the blood and then bandaged an absorbent pad to the wound. She stood back to check her handiwork. It was Clara who delivered the verdict.

"Not bad, Grace. Your apprenticeship with Amelia is obviously working."

She turned her attention back to Shrike who had endured Grace's pulling and prodding with just the occasional gasp of pain.

"So, Master Shrike, let's leave my opinion of Lord Mulgrave to one side for a moment. What exactly were you doing here at The Rectory? And how did you get this injury?"

"I overheard the instructions that were given to a group of men at Mulgrave Hall. There were about eight of them, but I didn't recognise them. They took a carriage with them. One of them drove it and the others escorted them on horseback. I didn't like what I'd heard so I followed them at a distance. I saw them turn into the drive here. They hammered on the door and one by one they overpowered the people inside."

"What? Which people?" Grace's voice quivered in fear.

"I don't know, Grace. A young woman with blonde hair. Very pretty. And an older lady. Oh, and a servant, I think."

"Amelia, Elizabeth and Gray, by the sound of it," muttered Clara. "What happened then?"

"There was an argument. The men asked where the others were and they grabbed hold of the people and gagged them and tied their hands and bundled them into the carriage."

"And you just stood there in hiding and watched, did you?" Clara asked scornfully. "Why didn't you do anything?"

"I tried, Miss, I really did. I came out of hiding and told them to stop. I said that Lord Mulgrave would not want this and that they would face the consequences if any harm came to these innocent people."

"Well, that obviously worked well, didn't it? Maybe you didn't try very hard, eh?" Clara could barely contain her anger.

Grace leaned across and laid her hand on Clara's arm.

"Shush, Clara, let him speak. It wasn't his fault."

Shrike hung his head.

"I'm sorry, Miss, I tried my best. But they just laughed at me and said it had been Mulgrave who had given the order. I grabbed the nearest one to pull him away from the older lady and that's when it happened?"

"When what happened?"

"One of the others hit me over the head with something and I don't remember anything else until now, when you woke me up. I'm sorry, I should have done more to help. It's my fault."

It was Grace's turn to take hold of his hand.

"No, Shrike, you couldn't have done more. It was very brave of you to try."

Clara took a step back and began to pace the kitchen as she thought, trying to make sense of Shrike's story. They watched her, waiting for her to speak. Shrike was on tenterhooks. He was confident that he'd won Grace over, but Clara was clearly struggling with his story. It all depended on her.

Finally, she stopped. She looked Shrike directly in the eye.

"Is there anything else you think you should tell us? Because we have some big decisions to make."

"Only that I think they will be back. They were expecting to find you two, and another woman. They will come back for you, I'm sure of it. We have to leave this place, and quickly."

Grace tightened her grip on Shrike's hand. She looked at Clara, fear in her voice as she spoke.

"So, what do we do now?"

DELLA ON THE TRAIL

Della jumped down lightly onto the cobbles of the stable yard of The Black Swan and handed the reins to the waiting ostlers. The team of horses stamped and snorted, their flanks steaming with sweat.

"Make sure these girls get a good feed and water. It's a hard ride over the moors in this heat," she said. "And take a look at the lead horse's hoof. She was dragging it a little over the last couple of miles."

She stretched, easing some life back into her arms and legs. It had been a long ride in the full sun and she needed a drink and a bite to eat before deciding what she was going to do next. Part of her was looking forward to a night in York. The beds at The Black Swan were comfortable, the food and ale good, and there were probably a few old faces to have a laugh and a chat with. But then again, she was wary of being away from Runswick when Silas had not returned and Mary Carruthers was still missing. There was definitely trouble in the air, she could sense it. First, she would have to check with the company if she was needed that evening to drive back to Whitby, or whether she was scheduled to do the return trip the next morning.

She hauled her saddle bag with her through the crowds that thronged the yard and made her way to the entrance to the inn. She shouldered open the door and strode into the noise and warmth of the crowded room, with its familiar smell of beer, food and pipe smoke. The lights from the lamps glittered on her spurs and her highly polished knee-high leather boots and the array of silver jewellery that she wore. The hum of conversation lowered and all eyes in the room turned on her. She smiled wryly at this. It was something she was used to. She knew she was considered beautiful. She had long, wavy jet-black hair, piercing green eyes, and flawless black skin. She also knew that she had a reputation of being a little challenging. The finest rider in all of the stage coach companies that operated across the north of Yngerlande, she was argumentative and refused to put up with any nonsense, from anyone.

So, as usual, she ignored the feeling of being judged by all the eyes that were upon her and strode to the bar, where a familiar face reassured her.

"Afternoon, Indira. I'll have a pint of your finest ale, if you please. And something to eat - I'm starving."

The figure behind the bar, a small woman with long greying hair, dressed in a sari of vivid electric colours, flashed a warm, beaming smile at her.

"Goodness me, it's Della Honeyfield. Were you driving the Whitby coach?"

"Yes, that was me. And I'm hot and sticky and I need that drink."

"And you shall have it, lass." She proceeded to pour from a wooden barrel on the counter. "So, will you be staying the night, or are you driving the evening coach back to Whitby?"

Della took a long drink from her flagon of beer, before setting it back down on the counter and sighing in contentment.

"Aah, I needed that. Now, staying the night? Well, I haven't decided yet, Indira. If I'm not on the return rota, I think I might. It's been a while since I had a night in York. Can I let you know later?"

"Of course, my lovely. It looks like we'll be full tonight, but we can always fit you in. Now, you go and get yourself a seat, and I'll bring over some food when I'm ready."

Della didn't need a second invitation to find a spot to put her feet up. She surveyed the room for a quiet corner to settle in, picked up her bag and drink and headed for a table in the corner. She looked around the room. The London coach had just got in and there were few free tables. It was the usual assortment of travellers: people up in York on business, well-to-do folk visiting relatives and one or two lone figures, nursing their drinks and eying the four corners of the room to see who they could strike up a conversation with later.

She sipped her drink, one eye on the main entrance, the other continuing to take in the people at the other tables. It all seemed very ordinary and above board. After all, there was no reason why it should be anything other than that. But after what Silas had said, she was on the lookout for trouble. Silas had made it clear that he was worried, and she would hate it if anything were to happen to Queen Matilda and Princess Gaia. The very thought of that name made her smile. When Della thought back to their first meeting last Christmas, she was very far from being a princess, just a young girl with a lot of spirit about her, someone after Della's own heart.

She was jolted out of her daydream by a clatter of plates and cutlery on her table, as Indira had returned with her food.

"There you are, lass. That will set you straight after your journey. It's the samosas, our speciality. Mary was quite taken with them, she was, when she had them."

Della stared at Indira, puzzled.

"Mary? Mary Carruthers? Have you seen her then?"

"Yes, my dear. She was in here a couple of days ago. Quite flustered she was. Not her usual chatty self, if you know what I mean. She didn't even finish her samosas, dear, and that's not like Mary. She had to go off quickly. Well, you know what she's like when she's got her teeth into something."

"But where, Indira? Where did she have to go?"

Indira frowned as she scoured her memory to recall what Mary had said. Della grabbed hold of her arm.

"Think, Indira, think! It's really important."

Finally, her face lit up.

"Fairfax house, that was it. Yes, she said something about two people. Let me see - Oliver and Jacob, yes, that was their names. And that she'd tracked them down to Fairfax House, near Clifford's Tower, and that she was heading over there to see for herself. Well, you should have seen her! She rushed out of here as if she were a twenty-year-old, she did."

Indira smiled at the memory, and then her smile faded.

"And I've not seen anything of her since then."

Her brow furrowed as the meaning of her own words sank in.

"You don't think anything has happened to her, do you? Should I have done something? I didn't think anything of it at the time."

Della stood up and took another gulp of her drink.

"No, Indira, I'm sure you did the right thing. There's really nothing the matter with her. But I am just going to pay a visit to Fairfax house, just to check. You take my bag and keep it behind the bar. I'll be back for it later."

"But, but…what about your samosas, Della? No-one has ever left one of my samosas before…"

By this time Della was halfway to the door. She called back to Indira, "Save them - I'll have 'em later." And then she disappeared through the door without waiting for a reply.

Indira shook her head and looked from the plate to Della's bag and then the door and back.

"Well. That's a waste of some good samosas, that is."

Still grumbling, she cleared the table and made her way back behind the bar. As she did so, two men who had been sitting behind Della, separated by a partition with small window panes in it, stood up. They took a quick look around the partition at the table where Della had been sitting, then they shared a look, and headed straight for the door.

By the time they reached the street, Della was just disappearing around the corner of Coney Street, headed for Spurriergate. The two men followed her at a distance, taking care not to be seen and not to lose sight of her. It was the middle of the afternoon now and the sun was high in a cloudless blue sky, beating relentlessly down on the crowds of people going about their business. Della dodged in amongst them, threading her way through the shoppers and the carriages and street traders. The two men were having a job keeping her in their sights. At the end of Spurriergate, with the bulk of Clifford's Tower looming above the rooftops, the shorter man stopped to catch his breath, and his bigger companion almost ran into him.

"Dear Lord, she can move like the wind, this she-devil," he gasped, mopping the sweat from his forehead with a grubby handkerchief.

"Well, we better not lose her," replied his companion. "'Twas a stroke of luck that we came across her like we did, but let's not make a mess of our opportunity. I reckon there will be more than a few gold sovereigns for this from the Masters, if we pull it off."

"Aye, happen you're right. And I don't think we need to worry too much about losing her. It's pretty clear where she's headed. But still, we need to be sure where she parks herself when she gets there, eh? After all, she's probably not going to knock on the front door."

He set off again, his companion following close behind, just as Della disappeared from sight. Dodging a line of carriages, they scurried across the road and turned the same corner that Della had. Immediately, they both stopped short. In front of them were the wide open spaces surrounding the tower where the town jail was situated on top of a large grassy mound, between the two rivers, the Foss and the Ouse, both sparkling in the sun. There were fewer people on the street here, and fewer places to hide.

The two men stared at the scene in front of them, and then back at each other.

Della, so distinctive in her appearance, so easy to spot in a crowd, had completely disappeared.

INTO THE LION'S DEN

The bow windows of Mrs Spelman's bookshop were crammed with volumes of all shapes and sizes. Behind the bottle green door, every available inch of floor space seemed to be taken up with precarious towers of books. There was a pathway of sorts that wound across the floor between the mountains of books, ending at a large walnut desk at the back of the shop. Behind that was a plain door leading to some kind of meeting room, and to the left, a rickety set of stairs that disappeared on its way round a corner leading, presumably, to more floors and more books.

Mrs Spelman herself, a small middle-aged woman with ivory white skin and a neat, greying bob of hair, surveyed the floor in front of her and sighed theatrically. Some of the towers of books were in a state of collapse and books were strewn across the floor, blocking any easy passage through the shop. Then, suddenly, she sat up and stared out of the shop window into the street. The green mound of Clifford's Tower was clearly visible, as were two men who, in a state of some confusion, were staring wildly around them.

She leaned back slightly, and from the corner of her mouth, said, "Try not to make a scene, Della, and don't make it too obvious, but are they the men that were following you?"

From behind her, a crumpled figure stirred and carefully lifted their head from behind the desk to peer through the window.

"Yes, that's them," she muttered.

"How positively ghastly, sweetie. No wonder you ran away from those two ugly brutes! But really, my dear, there was no need to mess up my books," drawled Mrs Spelman, "You have no idea how long it took me to arrange them like that."

"I think I probably do, actually," retorted Della, "but thanks, Jacinthe, you saved my bacon."

Jacinthe Spelman stood up as the two men moved away in the direction of the Tower.

"I think, my dear, it's safe for you to come out now. Your two admirers have moved on. Why don't I shut the shop and we can go into the back and have a nice cup of tea? Hmm?"

"A quick one, Jacinthe. I've got stuff to do."

"Evidently. Just give me a second."

She locked the door and turned the sign round so that it read "closed". Then she pulled down the blinds and showed Della through the door at the back. She bustled around with a kettle and teapot before Della cut in.

"Sorry, Jacinthe, let's forget the tea. I'm in a hurry."

Jacinthe flashed her a look of disapproval and put the teapot down with a bang.

"Please yourself. It's not as if I've just rescued you or anything."

Della immediately regretted being so sharp. "Sorry, Jacinthe, you were brilliant, honestly, but I've really got to make a move."

"Not until you tell me what's going on."

Della hesitated before finally making up her mind. She needed Jacinthe's help if she was going to get anything done that day.

"There's stuff happening. Silas and Mary are in trouble. Silas thinks that the mad old king's men are making another move. I think that Oliver and his uncle, Jacob, are in Fairfax house, plotting. Mary went there on their trail, apparently, and she's not been seen since. I just need to see with my own eyes, and try to find out what they're planning."

Jacinthe raised her eyebrows. "And how are you going to do that, with those two heavies looking out for you? Yes, you managed to give them the slip this time, but they will be watching Fairfax House like hawks. There's no way you'll be able to get in without being spotted."

Della shrugged. "I don't know, but I haven't got much choice, have I?"

Jacinthe thought for a moment. Finally, she asked the question.

"Have you ever wanted to be a man, Della?"

*

When she slipped out of Spelman's Books fifteen minutes later, the transformation was complete. A young black man, with a white powdered wig and a neckerchief of brilliant white silk, looking for all the world like a respectable attorney or man of business, would pass unremarked in these crowded York streets. As she crossed the road, she caught sight of her reflection in the window of the shop opposite.

"Hmm. Not bad, even if I do say so myself. Now, all I have to do is learn to do that funny walk men have."

Self-consciously, and all too aware of her hips, she continued down the street, keeping her eyes alert for the two men who had been on her tail. She stopped at the corner and, pretending to look in a shop window, quickly scanned the road ahead. There was Fairfax house, a magnificent new town house, dominating the street. She cracked a secret smile and then, almost immediately, suppressed it. There were her two "friends", sheepishly approaching the grand front door.

"Going to report to Oliver and Jacob, I'll bet. Let's see if I can sneak a look."

She waited until they had gone in, and when the front door closed, she slipped round to the side of the house, and, looking quickly all around her, scrambled over the high wall surrounding the gardens. She jumped down, hidden amongst the bushes. Using them as cover, she inched towards the house and the large french window that faced onto a sweeping lawn. Luckily, the windows were thrown wide open to encourage a cooling breeze through the house on such a sweltering July day. She risked a quick peek around the edge of the window frame, before jerking her head back and sinking to the floor hidden in the bushes.

It was them alright! She'd never forget Oliver's sneering, haughty expression, as if it were painful to him to have to put up with lesser human beings, and Jacob's sour, scarred face, that always looked as if he had indigestion. She'd just managed to catch a glimpse of the two men who had been following her, handing over a sealed letter to Oliver. From her hiding place, Della could only hear snatches of the conversation as the four men moved around the room. Damn, if only she could get closer.

She had managed to hide herself in the middle of a large rhododendron bush that grew along the wall of the house and which had been shaped to hug the window frame. She scanned the inside of the bush quickly. A strong branch forked out from the main stem, and projected diagonally upwards towards the window pane itself. She hauled herself up the trunk and onto the rogue branch, inching carefully along it so that her head was right next to the glass, but she was still able to keep hidden in the foliage. Once in position, she was able to settle, clinging to the structure of interconnecting branches, and listen.

The four men were engaged in an excited discussion. Oliver was waving the letter around in front of him. It was open and the pages flapped, revealing neat handwriting in black ink.

"It's from Shrike, as we thought," said Oliver.

"Well?" demanded Jacob, irritably. "What does he say?"

Oliver scanned the pages. "He says that all is going to

plan and that everything is in place…"

He flicked through it, already bored by the effort. "And there's more dreary details here about this and that. Heavens, he is a dull young man, Master Shrike, droning on and on."

Jacob could contain his impatience no longer. He snatched the letter from Oliver.

"For goodness sake, Oliver, you are like a silly child. Give it here."

Oliver began to protest, but Jacob silenced him with an imperious wave of the hand while he read the letter, frowning.

"Yes, good. He says he needs a little more time to reel in Matilda's strange witch of a daughter, but that it should be done in a couple more days. Mulgrave has the old man, the Carruthers woman and Marlborough. Shrike himself has engineered the capture of Doctor Comfort and the housekeeper woman from The Rectory, along with their manservant, and they too are under lock and key at Mulgrave Hall."

Oliver sniggered. "Goodness me, those cells will start to get a little crowded. Everyone, it seems, is captured. How marvellous! This is such fun, Uncle. It's all going so well."

Jacob considered carefully. "Too well, if you ask me. And what about the Trelawney boy, any news of him, I wonder?"

He went back to the letter and read on. At the mention of Thomas Trelawney, the blood had drained from Oliver's face. He held on to Jacob's sleeve.

A triumphant smile broke out on Jacob's face. "Yes! He says that it had been planned to summon the boy from his devilish land, wherever it is, but because they are all safely imprisoned away from The Rectory, no-one else has the powers to do it. Excellent!"

Oliver let out an elongated sigh of relief and sank down into a chair. A faint smile eventually took hold on his face and he closed his eyes. Jacob slapped him on the shoulder.

"You see? I do believe that everything is beginning to fall into place, Oliver. We just need to wait a little longer for Shrike to deal with the girl."

The two men were still there, silent witnesses to the impact of their news. The smaller man, a middle-aged black man with thinning, greying hair, stepped forward and coughed discreetly.

Jacob, noticing them again as if for the first time, barked with irritation. "Well, what is it? Waiting for payment, no doubt. Well…"

"Beg pardon, my Lord, but there is another matter."

Outside, gripping on to the bush for dear life, Della's ears pricked up. She leant forward so that she could catch every word he was about to say.

"What matter? Out with it, man."

"If it please you, my Lord, we came across the coach driver in The Black Swan in Coney Street. She was just off the Whitby coach. We overheard her talking to the Landlady about Mary Carruthers. She shot off as soon as she heard of it and we followed her. She was heading here, my Lord, we are sure of it."

Throughout this conversation, Oliver and Jacob had exchanged glances. Outside, Della moved a little closer, her knuckles pale with the effort of clinging on.

"It's the Honeyfield woman. The partner of Doctor Comfort. She was a thorn in our sides last time. A remarkable woman and not to be underestimated."

Oliver shook his head. "What is wrong with these people? Do they never learn when to give up? "

Jacob turned back to the messenger. "So where is she now? What did you do, man? Speak!"

He hung his head. "We followed her, my Lord, but then she gave us the slip. But we felt sure you would want to know, so we came straight away."

Oliver exploded in rage. "You lost her? Dear God, man, what on earth do we pay you for, you miserable worms? And you seriously expect payment? I'll…"

The men never found out what Oliver was planning to do to them because just at that moment, there came a terrible ripping sound and a crash from directly outside the window. There, directly in front of them, was the crumpled figure of Della, covered in branches and torn leaves. In a flash, Jacob opened the french windows and all four of them dashed outside and pounced on her as she thrashed around, trying to free herself.

They dragged her unceremoniously into the room and surrounded her. Up until that moment, her disguise had held up very well and Jacob addressed the figure as if it were a man.

"Well, Sir, explain yourself! What on earth are you doing skulking around our gardens? Spying? Speak, or you'll find yourself before the magistrate, even with your fine silks and wig."

He stared at the bedraggled figure accusingly, waiting for answers, when he suddenly stopped. Della's white powdered periwig had slipped to one side and was perched on her head at a jaunty angle. A stray, long black wave of her hair escaped and hung over her shoulder. In a flash, he reached out his hand and whipped the wig from her head. Her whole head of hair, a cascade of jet -black waves, fell over her shoulders.

The two men burst out simultaneously. "That's her, my Lords, that's the one we saw. It's a woman, my Lord."

Jacob cast a withering look in their direction.

"Really? You astound me. Now, bind her hands and feet and take her upstairs. We'll deal with Miss Honeyfield later." He smirked at her. "Won't we, Della?"

The sound of her protests was muffled by a gag, as struggling in vain against her captors, she was bundled out of the room and up the stairs.

A LOOK OF LOVE

The late afternoon sun streamed through the windows of Silas' study at The Rectory. Grace and Clara sat on either side of the great leather-topped desk. Sheets of parchment with broken seals lay in front of them. Silas' hastily written letters of instruction had been read and reread many times. The letters had made it clear that, in an emergency, Clara was to use her newly practised powers to summon Thomas from England, and that between them, they should use their combined powers to foil the plot against Clara's mother, Queen Matilda.

Clara, in particular, had been very wary about reading them while Shrike was there, and even more unwilling to discuss it with him. But Shrike was persuasive and persistent. And Grace was more ready to listen to what he had to say.

"But why shouldn't we summon Thomas? Silas made it clear that is what we should do. And, to be blunt, Master Shrike, we know an awful lot more about Silas than we know about you," Clara asked again.

"Of course, I understand your loyalty to Silas. And you're right, you don't know me at all. But look again at what the letters say - call for Thomas in an emergency. This is not yet an emergency. I will go back to Mulgrave Hall and snoop around a little. We need to know whether they are all there: those I saw being taken earlier, and the others: Silas and Mary Carruthers. I can use my influence to find out what his Lordship intends to do."

"That does sound like a sensible way forward, Clara.

Better we know their intentions, surely, before getting Thomas here," said Grace hesitantly.

"I thought you would want your brother to be here, and as soon as possible. I don't know why you've changed your tune suddenly." Clara looked at Grace with narrow, appraising eyes.

"I do want him here, obviously I do," Grace snapped back angrily. She hesitated, instantly regretting her outburst. In a more soothing voice, she continued, "It's just that nothing will be lost if we just wait a little while. Let us see what Shrike comes back with. And if he is not back by the end of the day, we will do what Silas has asked."

Shrike had been watching and listening carefully. He did not want to seem as if he was pushing for the delay. Nothing would be more certain to push Clara into outright opposition, so he had been biding his time. He just had to wait a little longer.

Finally, Clara relented. "Yes, alright. We will wait. But make haste, Shrike. We need to know everything by midnight at the latest. And if you are not back, we will do what Silas asked of us."

Shrike stood up to gather his things in readiness for the ride to Mulgrave Hall. As he did so, he deliberately winced as if in pain and brought his hand to his wounded forehead. Immediately, Grace sprang up and went to him, taking his hand in hers.

"You must be careful, Shrike. The wound is not yet healed, and you may have concussion. Don't overexert yourself, and be back as soon as you safely can."

He smiled warmly at her. "Thank you for your concern. But you may both be in danger. I will do what needs to be done."

With that, he released her hand and went to his horse, still tethered to the hitching post at the front of the house. Grace watched him go. Clara watched Grace and her fears grew. Her face was aglow with a look of concern and sympathy. Perhaps, even, a look of love.At the end of the curving driveway, he turned and waved goodbye to them. With a flick of the reins and a jabbing of his spurs, his horse broke into a canter, and he was gone.

THROUGH THE WINDOW

Della made her wrists as thin and flat as possible as she tried yet again to squeeze them through the iron manacles. Still, she could not force her hands free, and she slumped back in her chair, wincing in pain. One thing was certain - this was her best chance of escape. Oliver and Jacob were dining out, stuffing their faces with fine food and wine, and they would not trouble themselves with her for some time yet. Della had noted that they had left in plain clothes of a dull colour, with collars high covering their faces. Things were clearly still not settled then and they were being careful to stay under cover, for the time being at least.

In the room with her was just one guard who was clearly rather lazy. He had not bothered to bind her feet, nor make sure the manacles securing her hands were attached to anything. If she could just get the handcuffs open or off her wrists somehow, she would be able to give them the slip. But if Oliver and Jacob finished their dinner, and came back the worse for drink, then everything would be so much more dangerous for her, and her chances of escape would have gone.

The guard sat opposite her, slumped in his chair, snoring. She could see the key to her handcuffs clipped to his belt, rising and falling with his regular, deep breathing. She looked down at the chain that bound both wrists together and her mind began to work furiously. If she could just get him close enough, off his guard, she might have a chance. Finally, she took a deep breath and decided.

She called out across the room, loud enough to wake him, but not too loud to alert any of the other servants or guards in the house. She knew that there was at least one other, but she had no idea where he was. He could be in the room next door for all she knew.

"Hey," she called out, "hey, mister. Wake up, I've got something for you."

The man stirred, and after a second, sat bolt upright, playing the part of a guard to perfection. He knew Oliver and Jacob did not take kindly to lackeys such as himself falling asleep on the job. He blinked, and instinctively reached for his keys. As soon as he located them, clipped to his belt, he seemed to relax, confident that he was still in control. Della watched him closely.

"What did you say? What is it that you want?" he barked at her.

"I need some water," she replied. "I'm parched."

He grunted contemptuously.

"It's not a bloody hotel, you know. You can manage until their lordships return."

"Please," she begged, "just a mouthful. Look" - she gestured with her chains at the table in front of him - "just a bit from your jug there."

He glanced down at the pitcher of water, shook his head, and poured some grudgingly into a wooden cup, grumbling all the while. He brought it over to her.

"Here, take this and then let's have some peace and quiet."

He leaned towards her with it. Just at that moment she cried out, pointing behind him with her chained hands. He spun round, fists clenched, and Della saw her chance. She leaped from the chair and wrapped the chain connecting her handcuffs around his throat. Before he could move, she twisted the chain tight against his windpipe. His hands flew to his neck and he frantically tried to get a grip on her hands or the chain itself. Della was ready for him, kicking his legs from under him so that he crashed to the floor with Della on top of him. This sudden, uncontrolled fall tightened the chain around his throat even more. No matter how much he thrashed around Della was able to hold the chain fast, and his breath began to come in horrible rasping wheezes. She felt his hands begin to fall away from her, and all his strength ebbed from his body. She held on for one last second, and then relaxing her grip, she hauled him upright and crashed his head down on the side of the table. His body fell lifeless onto the floor in front of her and lay still.

She fell back, panting in fear and exhaustion. Looking over at the body of the man, she was gripped with the terror that she had gone too far and killed him. She had been in a lot of scrapes over the years, but she had never actually harmed anyone. She looked down at her hands and saw to her distress that they were shaking uncontrollably.

She muttered to herself, "Come on, Della, get a grip. You have to look at him, just in case."

She gritted her teeth and turned the man over. There was a nasty cut and bruise on his head, but he was still breathing.

"Thank god," she sighed. "He's alive. Now, let's get out of these chains and get out of here, before anyone comes."

She found the keys on his belt and, looking anxiously towards the door all the while, tried several in her handcuffs before one finally turned in the lock. They fell from her and she rubbed her wrists, massaging some life back into them. Then she sat her jailer up in a seat and gagged him, locking the handcuffs she had just escaped from onto his wrists, fastening him to the table leg. Her final precaution was to lock the door from the inside.

"That might buy me a bit of time. I'll need every extra minute I can get," she thought.

Taking a final glance around the room, she opened the window and hoisted herself onto the window ledge. It was dark now, and it was a cloudless night, with a half-moon casting the garden in a ghostly, silvery light. There was a short drop onto a smaller roof below and from there she was able to make her way down, clinging onto the shrubbery, until her feet finally stood firmly on solid ground. Just as she clambered to the top of the same section of the garden wall she had climbed earlier, there came a sound of a carriage drawing up on the cobbles outside Fairfax house. She crouched down, thankful that the top of the wall was cloaked in shadows.

Then she heard the voices from the street. It was Oliver and Jacob, and a couple of other men's voices she did not recognise. They were clearly a little drunk, laughing and rather too loud.

"Now let's deal with that insolent coach driver," one said.

She did not wait for the reply. As soon as she heard the slam of the front door she dropped down into the alley, and ran off in the direction of the Black Swan, through the moonlit streets.

A NOD AND A WINK

Silas stirred painfully and opened his eyes. Whatever the fumes had been from the two bombs that had rolled over the prison floor, they had been powerful and effective. They had all lost consciousness almost immediately and now Silas was aware of a powerful stabbing pain that jagged across his forehead every time he tried to move. Thankfully it was gloomy when he woke up, and he was able to squint into the shadows without too much inconvenience. He awoke expecting to still be in the dark and damp dungeon, but it appeared that he had been moved. It was not one of the finest rooms of Mulgrave Hall, but it was a great improvement on the cell.

He was sitting on a chair, his legs and hands manacled in heavy chains. Instinctively, he raised his hands and tried to feel the pocket of his frock coat, patting it a couple of times before trying the other side. Frantically, he tried again.

"Looking for something, Reverend?"

The voice was mocking and superior. Silas jerked his head in the direction of the voice. Standing opposite him was the smirking figure of Lord Mulgrave. He was pink faced, with a sheen of sweat glittering on his forehead underneath his periwig. The light from the candle flashed in his piggy little eyes that were buried deep in folds of plump skin.

"You!" Silas exclaimed. "You've tried this before and it didn't work the last time."

"But it will this time, believe me, Reverend."

He held out his hand. Nestled in his palm was a small, plain pebble.

"My stone!" Silas gasped. "But how did you…"

He stopped and shook his head.

"Of course! That's why you used those stun bombs. So that I wouldn't have a chance to use the stone against your men."

"Very good, Cummerbund. You got there in the end. And, speaking of the end, let's get down to business, shall we?"

Mulgrave gestured to two servants who had been waiting in the shadows. He snapped his fingers.

"Candles."

The two men each lit a taper from the candle in front of Silas and then moved away, their figures ghostly in their own halo of yellow flickering light. One by one, they found the other candles in the room and lit them. Each candle brought to a life another pale spirit, each one shackled like Silas, but unlike him each was gagged. One by one they emerged from the gloom and each one was a fresh blow to Silas' heart. Mary. Marlborough. Elizabeth. Gray. Amelia.

Mulgrave snapped his fingers again and the two servants slid back into the darkness. Whether they were still in the room, or merely concealed in the shadows, Silas could not tell.

"Well," Mulgrave pronounced with an oily smile, "this is very nice, isn't it? A reunion of all the old traitors."

Silas bit his tongue. He wasn't going to play Mulgrave's little game and ask questions. He was content to wait, knowing that Mulgrave would say what he had to say before long. But inside, he was burning to know what had happened to Grace, Princess Gaia and Della. Why weren't they there? He hoped that, somehow, they had got away and were hiding together somewhere, planning their next move. The only other possibility was too awful to contemplate.

Mulgrave shifted from foot to foot and his smile froze and began to fade in the face of Silas' unexpected silence. His wig was hot, his scalp itched, and his emerald green waistcoat was a little too tight, its buttons straining against his bulging belly. It had been some time since he had eaten and he wanted this business over and done with so that he could retreat to his comfortable drawing room and nibble some delicacies to tide him over until dinner. Finally, he could wait no longer.

"But enough of these games. Let's get down to business, shall we? We've collected your ragtag army of friends and associates to ensure you don't do anything silly. We know of your strange powers and we know your little pebble here magnifies them somehow."

He stopped and held up the Sounding Stone, turning it round between his thumb and forefinger.

"Strange, isn't it? It looks so ordinary, so plain. And yet, in the right hands, it is a rare thing of beauty. And…"

At this he paused and turned once again to Silas.

"And of power."

Silas spoke for the first time.

"But in your hands, my Lord, it is just an ordinary pebble. As I am sure you have discovered."

"Oh, yes of course, and that is rather disappointing. But at the very least, it is not in your hands and that is the main thing."

"Tell me, my Lord, how is it that you know of the Sounding Stone?"

Mulgrave took another look at the small, grey pebble in his hand, and then slipped it inside the pocket of his coat.

"Yes, you are quite right, Cummerbund. It is time to move on. And your question will let us do just that. I know about your tricksy little pebble because of this remarkable young man here."

He gestured behind him and from the shadows stepped Shrike, his red spiky hair, green flashing eyes and pale skin almost luminous in the pools of yellow light cast by the arrangement of candles. His bandage had been removed, leaving a livid gash at his temple.

From behind their gags, gasps of shock could be heard from the other captives. From Marlborough, the sound was of fear.

"May, I present my associate, Master Shrike. You have him to thank for everything."

Shrike gave a little bow at this introduction before standing to attention again.

Silas studied this newcomer carefully.

"You look very familiar, Master Shrike. Have I seen you somewhere before?"

Shrike smiled politely. "Oh, yes, Reverend. I was always in attendance at Kings Manor, at your sessions with the young Princess. Gaia or Clara, I can never remember what her name is. I saw you frequently. But you didn't see me, not really. Except perhaps when I was clearing away your plates and glasses."

Silas began to speak again, but was stopped by Shrike's raised hand.

"No, don't apologise, I'm used to being ignored. And it was very instructive, seeing you use your Sounding Stone. And seeing the girl get rather good at everything you taught her. It's a shame in many ways."

Silas was puzzled. "A shame? In what way?"

"Well, that she will never get to use those skills. Such a waste of your time…"

It was Silas' turn to interrupt. "What do you mean? What have you done to her? If you have harmed her in any way, I'll–"

"You'll do nothing. Or at any rate, nothing that we don't want you to."

Shrike's voice had taken on a harder edge.

"No, they are both safe and well and waiting for me to return. They think I'm on their side, you see. I'm very good at that, even if I do say so myself. They think I've come here to snoop around and find out what has happened to you all, and that when I get back to the rectory, that we are going to make a plan to come and rescue you all."

Shrike began to laugh, a harsh unfeeling cackle that grated through the air. His shoulders shook and he wiped tears from his eyes.

"Oh dear, forgive me, Reverend, but it always amuses me to think how stupid most people are. They continue to believe in fairy tales, long, long after childhood is over."

He recovered himself and continued. "Let's cut to the chase. Queen Matilda is held securely at Belton Hall. You are all here and will be joined shortly by the Princess and Grace. You no longer have your Sounding Stones, and are much less powerful without them, and you know that if you don't cooperate, we will begin to dispose of everybody here, in front of you, one by one."

Shrike was pacing up and down methodically, like an actor striding across the stage, while he continued.

"Matilda will be forced to abdicate the throne and officially hand it over to King Oliver, on the grounds that her daughter, Princess Gaia, has been possessed by dark powers and has been practising witchcraft. They will be sent to a religious house, a nunnery, if you will, where they will commit to living the rest of their lives in quiet obscurity, devoting their lives to God. And King Oliver can begin to rule Yngerlande as it should be ruled, for the benefit of the rich and powerful. White men will be centre stage once again, and everyone else will be subservient. People of other races, women, unnaturals, will all be back in their proper place and Yngerlande can be great again."

Silas had been listening intently throughout Shrike's speech, stroking his chin thoughtfully.

"Well, all that makes perfect sense and is more or less what I had expected. Except for the last bit"

"Which bit?" asked Shrike, puzzled.

"Well, what's in it for you, Master Shrike? I don't believe for a moment that you believe all of that tosh about restoring power to the old rich families so that things can go back to the way they were before. You weren't here in the bad old days. They are long gone, thank goodness. I can't think of one good reason why you would want Oliver as King. Or why you are working for someone as useless as his Lordship here."

Even in the shadows, it was obvious that Mulgrave had gone a shade of purple in fury at Silas' casual disrespect. He spluttered, "Have a care, Cummerbund. Keep a civil tongue in your head, or I'll slice it off myself."

Silas dismissed him with a wave of his hands, rattling the heavy chains as he did so. He continued, "Of course, you will be paid for your work, but you would be paid no matter who was in charge. You are obviously a very talented young man. Why hitch your star to the losing side?"

Shrike's face had lost its smirk. His eyes narrowed and his mouth flattened into a straight line.

"You don't need to waste any of your time thinking about me. Take my advice and spend it thinking about how to save your friends."

He stepped away into the half shadows where Mulgrave had been standing watching the proceedings. Then he took Mulgrave's arm and turned him to face away from the prisoners and spoke to him in a low voice. Silas strained against his chains to lean forward in a vain attempt to listen to their conversation. Even Mulgrave seemed to struggle to hear Shrike, because he moved closer to him and bent his head towards Shrike's lips, with his arm around his shoulder.

After a moment, they separated and turned back to face the semicircle of captives. Mulgrave's face carried an enormous smile. Shrike took a step towards Silas.

"One more thing, Reverend. You may be hoping that your friend, the Trelawney boy, is on his way to rescue you all."

Silas froze at the mention of Thomas' name. Shrike

continued.

"Well, I'm sorry, he's not. I don't think the Princess will be taking any notice of the instructions you left. They're waiting for me to return before they do anything else."

Shrike beamed again and pulled out his pocket watch.

"And they won't have to wait much longer."

Silas' face fell. It seemed as if their last hope had been dashed. If Tom was not coming to save them, they were finished, surely? He struggled to keep a brave face as he processed this news. Shrike stepped within touching distance of him, and stared at him in an intimidating way, moving his head forward until it was just a few inches from his.

"Sorry to disappoint."

A surge of anger flared up in Silas, and his fists clenched instinctively, even though they were weighed down by his iron handcuffs. And then he saw it. Shrike was holding the Sounding Stone directly in front of him, between his forefinger and thumb. No one else could see it.

Silas was baffled. He began to stutter, "Wha…?" but stopped as Shrike enclosed the stone in his fist and slipped it back in his pocket. Shrike stepped back a little, and winked at Silas before immediately turning on his heel and leaving the room, Lord Mulgrave at his side.

TIME FOR THOMAS

Grace peered anxiously out of the front window of The Rectory into the moonlit garden. They had left a lamp burning at the gate so that they could keep an eye on anyone who came up the drive. Nothing. She turned back into the room and paced around for a while, wringing her hands together. Almost immediately, she returned to the window and looked out again. Behind her, the grandfather clock ticked loudly.

"Grace, come away from the window and sit down. He will not return quicker because you are watching for him. We must talk about what we are going to do." Underneath Clara's concern, there was a faint note of disapproval, of irritation almost.

Grace turned. "We've talked and talked, Clara. We just have to wait now."

She came and sat at the table, opposite Clara. Clara reached out and took her hand.

"Grace, we don't know anything at all about Shrike. He could be anyone. He could be working for Mulgrave, or Oliver. You need to be careful. He seems to have cast some sort of spell on you."

Grace snatched her hand away. "Don't be ridiculous, Clara. Yes, he was nice to me. You can't possibly imagine how much I've missed having friends of my own age. He didn't treat me like some kind of freak. You are too suspicious - there are nice people in the world, you know."

She got up suddenly.

"I'm going to the end of the drive to keep a lookout. I need some fresh air to clear my head."

Clara watched her go. There was no point trying to convince her. Grace had obviously made her mind up that Shrike was just what he seemed. Clara shook her head. So Grace thought that she, Clara, couldn't possibly understand what it was like to be alone and for people to think she was a "freak". Clara knew it wasn't Grace's fault, but it was hard to take, given the fact that she was the one in danger. She was the one who could be accused of being a witch. What was it Grace had said earlier? "The thing is, I can't die because I'm dead already."

Well Clara could die and so could her mother, the Queen of Yngerlande.

She looked out of the window and saw Grace lit up in the lamp on the perimeter wall of the Rectory, waiting patiently for Shrike to arrive. Her mind was made up. She crept out of the room and made her way to Silas' study, his desk illuminated by a single candle. In the light it cast, she could see the sheet of parchment from Silas lying on the desktop. It was time to follow Silas' instructions. It was time to summon Thomas Trelawney.

*

Shrike spurred on Silver as he galloped across the top of the moors. It was a still, sticky night, and the breeze of the gallop was cooling. In the half-moon, the heather of the moors was a ghostly pale purple, and there was a sweet scent of wild honeysuckle in the air. Far off to the east, he could see the white breaking waves of the North Sea. Buried deep in his coat pocket was the Sounding Stone, and in his saddle bag, safely stowed, were the remaining stun bombs. He felt a sudden rush of happiness wash over him, and he pulled on the reins to bring Silver to a juddering halt.

There were the lights of The Rectory, with the tiny pinpricks of light from the houses of Runswick below that. He stopped for a moment, just to breathe in the sweet air and drink in the sights of this newly beautiful world. He felt that he was on the edge of everything turning out as he had planned it, on the edge of an entirely new life. In the warm still night air, and the silvery light of the moon, with the far sound of the sea, powerful and restless from the horizon, he laughed. It was an exultant laugh, a laugh of pure, unadulterated joy.

Still wallowing in his feelings of invincibility, he whispered to his horse, "Come on, Silver. Time for us to seize the prize, old girl." With a click of his tongue, and a jab of his spurs, he pushed the horse into a gentle canter down the lane that led to The Rectory.

*

Mulgrave walked over to the window of his study, his lips pursed. Damn that Shrike boy. Insolent and far too cocky. He needed taking down a peg or two, Mulgrave was sure of that. And he couldn't be trusted, he was doubly sure of that. He wanted to believe that Shrike would return with the Princess and Grace Trelawney, as they had agreed. As soon as he had them under lock and key, he could contact Oliver and Jacob and then nothing could stop their plan. Not even the wretched Trelawney boy or the old fool wizard in his cells below. But nothing with Shrike was straightforward. Dealing with him was like standing on shifting sands. And sometimes Mulgrave had caught him looking at him with a strange expression on his face. It was almost as if Shrike knew him. And there were times, in certain lights, when he did remind Mulgrave of someone, but he could never put his finger on who.

He shook his head to drive these ideas from his mind. Down on the gravel below, in the gathering dusk, he noted with satisfaction the group of riders preparing to leave for The Rectory in Runswick Bay. He watched them mount up and canter away down the long drive out of the estate. He smiled, a cunning, calculating smile. That would keep Shrike on his toes. He may be a clever, devious young man, but who was he, really? No match for a peer of the realm, from one of Yngerlande's oldest families. A guttersnipe like Shrike, from the slums of York? No - keep him on his toes and keep him in his place, that was the way to deal with him. He wouldn't have to worry about Shrike for too much longer.

*

Silas sat alone in the darkness of his cell. As soon as Mulgrave and Shrike had left, all the prisoners had been returned, one by one, into single cells, deep in the dark, damp bowels of Mulgrave Hall. He had turned it over and over in his mind, but still he could make no sense of it. Why did Shrike secretly reveal to him that he had stolen the Sounding Stone from Mulgrave's pocket? What game was he playing? Whose side was he on? And, most importantly, what was his plan now?

He peered into the darkness. It would be no problem for Silas to get out, even without his Stone, but they had been very cunning. They knew that Silas could not do anything that might endanger the others, so he would simply have to watch and wait, until an opportunity to act presented itself.

As he sat and examined everything he knew about the boy Shrike, one thing became increasingly clear. It was vital that Clara had followed his instructions in his letter. It was plain who they must turn to now. Thomas Trelawney was the only person who could unlock this situation before tragedy struck. It was time for The Friend to return.

II

THE FRIEND AND THE GHOST.
England, The Present Day

Tom sat at his desk, a few random exercise books scattered across the top, just in case one of his parents came in and he could hurriedly pretend to be doing some homework. His room was in darkness, except for the light from his mobile and the narrow cone of light cast by the lamp.

He'd been brooding about the fight at school, the severe dressing down he'd endured from Banksy, his stupid headteacher, and the embarrassment of his parents being summoned to his office, as if they had been the ones in trouble. The very first day back at school. It wasn't even September yet, and already he'd messed things up. The worst thing was Banksy trying to be sensitive and understanding, dancing around the fact that Grace, his sister, had been killed by a car the year before. Poor old Banksy! He was much more suited to being horrible to kids and enforcing petty rules than being nice.

His parents had been horrified, of course, and the inevitable result was more whispered conversations that were quickly silenced with a strained smile whenever he happened to walk into a room where they were. Even as he thought this, a wave of guilt swept over him. He knew it was just love and care and fear, all tumbling around together, ever since Grace's accident. And he loved them, obviously. It was just that, sometimes, he wished they could just treat him normally and stop worrying so much.

There were times when he wished that he could escape.

Just disappear and leave all of it behind. He would give anything to see Grace again, to return to Yngerlande, just for an hour or two, to talk to her about things. And Clara, of course. He had never met anyone he felt more connected to than her, but as the days had passed since he and Dan had returned, it had become harder and harder to believe that it had all happened, that it wasn't just a fantastic story.

He sighed. Every night he sat at his desk, or lay on his bed staring at the Stone, waiting for something to happen. Watching and waiting. But nothing ever happened. Sometimes he felt like throwing it in the bin, forgetting all about Yngerlande, so that he could concentrate on his real life, here and now. He reached across to his phone to check the time. It was 1.15am. That was it, he thought, time to go to sleep, otherwise he'd feel even worse in the morning.

Suddenly, the phone vibrated in his hand and the familiar ping of an incoming message broke the silence. He was taken aback. Who on earth would be messaging him at this time of night? He peered at the screen and read the message.

You still up, bro? I overheard my Mum and Dad talking about you getting suspended from school today. What happened? You OK?

He smiled. It was from Dan. At least there was someone who he could still trust. He rattled off his reply, thumbs a blur of speed.

Why r u up so late? Everything OK with you?

I'm fine, man. The question was about you. WHAT HAPPENED?

I just got into a fight with some knuckle dragger at school. He was talking about Grace and I just lost it and punched him. Stupid thing to do. I'm excluded for three days.

Good for you. Sounds like he deserved it!

Tom shook his head and typed his reply. He knew that

Dan was trying to be supportive and it was nice to have someone who always backed him up, but he was wrong about this.

Nah. He's a moron, but that's no excuse. I shoulda just ignored him. Now, I get in trouble and Mum and Dad are on my back, worrying about me all over again. And I'll have to deal with Stupid Boy when I go back to school. Nightmare.

He waited, watching the gently pulsing dots, followed by the reassuring message, "Dan is typing…"

Do you ever think about what we did at Christmas? In Yngerlande, I mean. It was cool wasn't it?

Tom frowned.

I think about it a lot. But why are you thinking about it now? What's happened?

Nothing. I just look at that Sounding Stone and wonder if it'll ever go blue. Do you think we'll ever go back?

Dunno. I wish we could though. It was nicer there than here. Sometimes I feel I don't wanna be here.

There was another pause, before Dan typed his reply. In the gap Tom thought about what Dan had said. He had never thought before that Dan was looking at his Stone as well, waiting for another adventure. He had assumed that he had just stuffed it away in a drawer and forgotten about it. His cousin was not the sort of person to spend time thinking about stuff. He was a doer, not a thinker or a worrier, someone who always had something on the go.

You're freaking me out now, bro. What do you mean, not want to be here?

I wanna see Grace. And Clara. And have an adventure, just to get away from all of this crap.

Again, there was a pause, with pulsing dots. Dan's message, when it did come through, was something of a surprise to Tom. It was simply two emojis - one of a smiley face and the other of a big red heart.

He typed back, a little too self-conscious.

What do u mean?

Clara!

And then Dan repeated the heart emoji, only this time it pulsed.

Dan didn't give him time to reply before messaging again.

Clara! That's a relief. Now this all makes sense.

Tom felt himself going red and was relieved this exchange was being done via WhatsApp, not face to face. He grimaced and jabbed his message back.

Ha Ha. But, as usual, you're wrong. It's not like that at all. But enough - time for sleep.

Message tomorrow, lover boy?

Yeah. Night, loser.

He sat back in his chair, half annoyed and half amused by his cousin. There was something about Dan that meant you couldn't be seriously fed up with him for long. He smiled and was just about to come out of the app, when his eye was caught by a change in the light in the room and his ear picked up the faintest of vibrations in the air. He looked more closely and gulped silently. Picking up his phone again, hardly daring to breathe, he managed to type one word.

Wait…

There, at the back of his desk, the grey mottled pebble had begun to glow with a brilliant blue light. The Sounding Stone, for the first time since he had returned from Yngerlande, was about to transmit a message, and Tom was bathed in a deep blue wash of colour.

MESSAGES IN THE NIGHT

There was a crackle of electricity in the air of his room, as the Sounding Stone pulsed its energy across two worlds. Tom didn't have to worry about disturbing his parents or the neighbours. He knew from his experience of the Stone the Christmas before, that time in his house was frozen and would be until the stone turned back into an ordinary pebble. No-one in his house, nor anyone passing in the street below, would be aware of anything strange happening.

His heart raced as the blue light pooled around him and the hairs on the back of his neck stood up. A voice came through, at first as if from a great distance, crackling and faint, but then as clear as if it were in the same room.

"Tom? Tom, speak if you're there. It's me, Clara."

At the sound of her voice, a trail of stars began to fizz around him, twining their way around his limbs like bindweed choking another plant. Beautiful. Natural. Deadly.

"Clara?! I didn't expect it to be you. I thought it would be Silas. It's wonderful to hear your voice."

He was submerged in a tidal wave of emotion that he struggled to contain. He was saved by the urgency of Clara's situation. She cut in.

"Tom, listen, I haven't got much time. We are all in terrible danger here. We need you. You and Dan, if possible."

"But what's happened? And Grace … How is Grace?"

He listened intently as Clara told him the story as quickly as she could. By the time she had got to the end, his expression had changed from delight to huge anxiety and then finally, one of grim determination. He had a million questions to ask, but had to bite his tongue as she raced through her story. He was just about to find out more when Clara's voice changed. She still seemed to be racing against time, but now there was a note of fear in her voice.

"Thomas, I must go. Read the letter, Tom. Read the letter." Her voice faded and swirled away like water down a drain. The blue light was sucked into the stone, leaving a humble pebble on his desk.

"Clara! Clara, what do you mean? What letter? Clara!"

But there was only silence in response. He sat frozen at his desk. Through his open window, the warm still air of a sultry August night carried pollen heavy scents of summer. He could see cars parked outside in the street lamps, the same stars in the jet-black sky. A cat, eyes like neon slits, padded across the front gardens and disappeared between two houses. It all seemed so ordinary. He couldn't match it up with what had just happened.

"Come on, Tom," he berated himself, "just think. You can't just sit here like a lemon. What did Clara tell you to do?"

Daniel! That was it - he had to contact Dan. He glanced down at his computer screen. Dan was still there, but judging by the last few messages he had sent, each one more frustrated than the last, he was furious. The last couple of messages were typed in raging block capitals. In bold.

Tom took the plunge and messaged back. Within a minute he was rattling the keyboard, with messages going back and forth as Tom told Dan the story of his exchange with Clara. He had obviously done a good job because by the last couple of messages, Dan had reverted to lower case.

You sure about this?

Course I am, man. Clara told me, it's from Silas. Hold

your Sounding Stone.

But what about my Mum and Dad? How long will I be? Last time, I couldn't survive in Yngerlande for more than a day.

This is different. You've got a Sounding Stone now. We can both be there as long as it takes.

And we don't need the grandfather clock?

No, the Stone takes care of it all. Now, shut up and concentrate.

Rude….

Ready, steady…now.

Thomas held on to his Stone as the cursor on his screen flashed next to his last message. He took a deep breath, brought the Stone to his lips, and lightly kissed it. Blue light flooded the room, and small ordinary sounds - the humming of the hard drive, the gurgle and creaking of water in the household pipes, and the far distant hum of traffic - all disappeared to be replaced by a suffocating blanket of silence. Almost immediately, the blue light was sucked away, leaving thick darkness and Thomas found himself blindly groping in front of him, his hands waving desperately trying to find some familiar bearings.

Back in England, in Thomas' room, all was in darkness. A figure was huddled under the duvet of the bed, snoring rhythmically. The clock on Thomas' bedside table had stopped, and everything was frozen in time.

BAD NEWS

Grace's heart began to race the second she heard the sound of horse's hooves galloping down the lane towards her. In the half moonlight, the distinctive shock of spiky red hair immediately identified the rider as Shrike. The horse scrambled to a halt as Shrike saw her waiting, pulled on the reins and leaped out of the saddle in one flowing movement. She ran to him and gave him a hug out of relief. Then she stepped back, slightly embarrassed.

"Well? What news?"

Shrike, as ever, was calculating the different elements of his response. He was delighted that Grace felt something for him. It was something to file away and use when needed in the future.

"The news is bad." His face was grim and serious.

Grace looked horrified. "But Silas and the others are all well, aren't they?"

"Yes, for the moment. But it's us that are not safe. We have to leave as soon as we can."

"Leave? But why?"

"Mulgrave's thugs will be here any minute. There isn't a moment to lose. Where is Clara?"

"Indoors. Come on, let's go in and you can tell us both everything."

She turned without waiting for an answer, and shouted up at the house, "Clara, it's Shrike, he's back. We have to leave, right now." She scrambled back to the front door as Shrike led his horse to the hitching post.

Up in Silas' study, Clara froze as she heard Grace's

voice. She did not have much time. The Sounding Stone's blue light stained every aspect of the room and she had to finish her link with Thomas before Grace caught sight of it. Grabbing the Stone from the desktop, she hissed, "Thomas, I must go. Read the letter, Tom. Read the letter."

The blue light was suddenly sucked away and Clara was left in the gloom of the study that was lit by a single candle. She scrabbled around on the desktop for a sheet of parchment and a quill. Dipping the quill in the ink pot she began to write as quickly as she could, keeping her ears sharply trained on noises outside. She must not be surprised, either by Shrike or Grace, while she was still writing.

From the passage outside came Grace's voice. "Clara! Where are you? We must talk. Shrike has news and we don't have much time. Clara!"

Clara put down the quill, and hastily rearranged things on the desk.

"I'm coming!" she cried. "Just a minute."

She took a quick final glance at the study, before slipping into the corridor and shutting the door. She made her way to the kitchen. Sitting on either side of the table were Grace and Shrike. Shrike's saddle bag was carefully draped over the back of his chair. Shrike looked up at the sound of her entry.

"At last! Clara, we have to leave. Right now," he said.

"What do you mean? Why the hurry? What's happened?" Clara demanded.

"It was a difficult visit to Mulgrave Hall. I only just managed to get out. It's clear now that Lord Mulgrave has been up to no good all along, plotting against you and the Queen."

"You don't say," muttered Clara sarcastically. "We told you that before you left, Shrike. So, at least now you believe us."

He hung his head and when he spoke, his voice was a

little lower. "I'm sorry I doubted you. It's just that he had been good to me in the past."

Clara cut in. "Let's not worry about the past. What exactly happened? What did you find out? And why is there such a rush all of a sudden?"

Shrike continued, "They have your friends all there, locked up in separate cells, down in the dungeons beneath the Hall. Cummerbund, the Doctor, Mrs Carruthers, all of them. Cummerbund can't escape or use his powers because he knows they will hurt the others if he tries anything. I think..."

He hesitated, eyeing both of them as if he could not bear to go on. Underneath, Shrike was hugely enjoying his own performance. He had already convinced Grace. The challenge was to do the same with Clara.

"What? Come on, Shrike, spit it out," Clara demanded.

"I think he would stop at nothing to get what he wants. He would kill them, I am sure of it."

Grace gasped out loud and brought her hand over her face in horror.

"No! He can't, surely? What can we do?"

"Well, the first thing we have to do is get out of here. His men are on their way to get you. We've got to leave. Find somewhere where we can regroup and plan what to do next."

"How do they know we're here?" Clara asked sharply. "That was you, wasn't it, Shrike? How can we possibly trust you? We don't know anything about you."

"Yes, it was me. I had to keep them thinking I was on their side. And you can trust me because I'm here, warning you. If I was your enemy, I would just have stayed at Mulgrave Hall and let his lordship's thugs do the rest, wouldn't I? I'm taking a big risk here."

Clara stopped, brow furrowed, mouth set, watching Shrike's expression. Finally, she decided. "Yes, alright, we can't just wait around to be captured. But where should we go?"

"What about Mary Carruther's cottage? We might be able to get a message to Silas from there."

"No," interrupted Shrike, "it's the first place they will look after here."

"And we can't go anywhere down in the village. We can't put all of our neighbours in danger," said Grace.

They were silent, racking their brains for what to do next. The sound of the clock ticking reminded them that Mulgrave's men would be getting closer with every tick.

"Look, if we don't go in the next five minutes, we might as well start to barricade the house and get some guns loaded," said Grace, a note of desperation in her voice.

The three of them looked from one to the other and back again. Clara was just about to reveal that she had contacted Thomas, as Silas had taught her, when Shrike suddenly broke the silence.

"I know somewhere we can go. Somewhere safe."

"Well why on earth didn't you say so then? Why are we wasting time hanging around here waiting to be caught," Clara burst out in frustration.

Grace reached out and laid her hand on his arm. She sensed that he needed reassurance rather than Clara's hectoring. "Where is it, Shrike? And what's the problem."

He smiled back at her in response.

"It's up on the moors. Near White Water Falls. No-one knows about it except me. But we only have my horse. It's impossible. Unless we can get more horses in the village."

Grace and Clara exchanged urgent glances. Grace turned to Shrike.

"We can go through the tunnels."

She saw the baffled expression on his face. She laid out a map on the table in front of him and pointed.

"Look, The Rectory is here. There's a network of tunnels that smugglers have used for years. They go down to Hob Hole, at the foot of the cliffs in Runswick, but they also go here."

She slid her finger along the map to the middle of the moors.

"We know them, you see. We've been through them before."

Shrike's face lit up.

"The place I know is just a couple of miles from this point. Come on. We've got to go, right away."

"Let me just put some food and drink in a bag first. We may be glad of it later," said Clara. She grabbed a backpack and stuffed it with bread and cheese from the larder as she frantically tried to think of an excuse to go back to Silas' study. She was desperate to talk to Thomas again before they left.

Suddenly, her thoughts were interrupted. From outside came the sound of horse's hooves, and then muffled shouts of men. They all froze.

"Shh!" hissed Grace. "We'll have to creep out of the kitchen door into the garden. If we go through the bushes and keep the wall in touching distance, we'll get to the old outhouse at the back of the garden. The shrubbery will give us enough cover. Come on."

They slipped out of the door and Shrike, who was bringing up the rear, closed it as quietly as he could. He followed Grace and Clara, holding tight to his saddle bag, as they plunged into the thick undergrowth by the garden wall. They stumbled along in the darkness, tripping over protruding roots and tangles of brambles. At one point they had to freeze and hold their breath when they heard men's voices on the other side of the wall, waiting for orders. They gestured to each other with fingers held on lips, and waited stock still, only a foot away from Mulgrave's men. Suddenly, there came a shout from the house. The first men had broken in and found the house empty.

"Hey! Check the garden you lot. We'll try upstairs."

The men out in the lane began to move towards the entrance of The Rectory and Grace decided they had to get to the outhouse, no matter what noise they made. They scrambled through the shrubbery, snapping twigs and rustling bushes, before making a dash for the door to the outhouse which was shaded from the half moonlight by two overhanging oak trees.

"Hey! What was that?" One of the men shouted. "There's someone in the garden, down by the shed."

The three of them dashed through the door, closing it firmly behind them and barricading it from the inside. Grace led them to the corner where there was a trapdoor that led to the tunnels. She pulled it open and gestured frantically to the other two to go through. No sooner had Shrike's head disappeared than Grace followed, closing the door as quietly as she could. All they could do was hope that in the darkness of the shed, the trapdoor would be well camouflaged and they would not be followed. Grace dropped down the last couple of steps into the arms of Shrike and Clara. They huddled together in the darkness, hardly daring to breathe. The sound of the men's boots on the floor of the shed above them was deafening. All three of them waited for the inevitable, and were prepared to run blindly along the inky black tunnels.

But nothing came. There were a few more shouts from above and the sound of boxes being ransacked and cupboards being opened. Several pairs of boots could be heard directly above the trap door, but then came a louder shout.

"Hey, you lot. There's somebody in the house. Come on, all of you, let's get 'em."

The footsteps thundered away over the floorboards towards The Rectory, and the three of them were left in the cool, damp darkness of the tunnels.

NIGHT RIDE

The streets were emptier now, though there was still the odd person making their way home at the end of the day. Della had sprinted the minute her boots had hit the cobbles below Fairfax house and had not looked back. She had ignored the occasional puzzled looks cast in her direction and those who looked soon lost interest. A young man running at night through the streets of York was not so unusual. Now her lungs began to burn and her legs ache, but still she would not stop. Just a few minutes more and she'd be safe. Finally, she darted down an alley that led from Coney Street to the river, and in the deep shadows under the eaves of the jumble of buildings that crowded in on her, she stopped, hands on her knees, her chest heaving as she fought to catch her breath.

She was pretty sure she hadn't been followed. For one thing, it would have been impossible for anyone to keep up with her without making a tremendous clatter on the cobbles. But it was only a matter of time. When they discovered her gone, they would come after her. And they would come back to The Black Swan, because that's where they had first spotted her.

Her breathing came easier now and with that relief came the possibility of thinking straight. She avoided the main entrance to the coaching inn and went down to the alley that led to the river. She knew that she could find a way in from this back alley, a way that would allow her to sneak in and out without being seen.

She crept along the alley until she came to the rear wall

of the inn's courtyard. In one corner was a door that was used by the stable boys and kitchen staff and occasionally to take deliveries from the river, which was less than twenty yards away. She tried the handle, more in hope than expectation, and was not surprised when it didn't turn. She cursed under her breath. Indira was meticulous when it came to security.

She looked up at the walls while she thought what to do next. She reckoned she could probably get over the wall, if she could find a first foot hold, but it was a long drop to the cobbles below and it would make a noise that would wake the dead. Her eyes travelled upwards until she saw it. A window, larger than the rest, with a balcony overlooking the river. That was Indira's bedroom, she was sure of it. She remembered her boasting about how lovely it was to have an evening glass of wine watching the boats ply up and down the Ouse on a summer's evening. That must be it.

She double checked. All of the other windows with a view of the river were smaller. None of them had a balcony. Yes, this was definitely Indira's room. She scrambled around on the ground and took up a handful of pebbles and grit. Looking all around her, she aimed at the window with her first pebble. She was a good shot and the tiny stone struck the windowpane with a musical plink.

She waited, hiding by the wall in the shadows. Nothing. Surely Indira had not gone to bed already? It was still early, not much after ten o'clock. She tried again and once more struck the window with ping. Still nothing.

"Come on, Indira, wake up. You can't be that tired, you've got too many servants to run around and do your work for you," Della muttered.

She was just about to have a third attempt when a light showed through the glass, and a figure appeared, holding up a lamp and wrapping a dressing gown around herself. She opened the window and peered out into the darkness.

"Indira! Indira!" hissed Della. "Down here."

She stepped out of the shadows.

Indira leaned forward and stared.

"Della, is that you?"

"Yes, it's me. I need your help, Indira."

"Again? Saints preserve us, I'm getting too old for this, Della. And so are you, my girl. What mischief are you involved in this time?"

"Better you don't know, Indira. Trust me, these people are dangerous. But listen - I'm in a hurry and I've got to go now, but I need your help." As Della whispered hoarsely, she continued to look around, her eyes flicking left and right from the shadows.

"Okay, Della, just wait. I'll be right down."

She disappeared from the window and Della was left fidgeting nervously in the lane. Then she heard footsteps on the cobbles on the other side of the wall and the sound of a key being turned in the lock of the door. It opened a crack, and Indira poked her head through the gap.

"Della! Come in, girl, and let me lock up again. York is full of cutthroats and thieves at this time of night."

She stepped aside a couple of inches and beckoned to Della to squeeze through the gap. Indira scanned the alley in both directions before shutting the door and locking it again. The courtyard was empty, half in darkness, with the opposite side dimly lit from a couple of lanterns that burned through the night. She took Della by the shoulders.

"What's happened to you, girl? Where's all your jewellery and finery? And what's happened to your hair? You look like a man. What have you been up to?"

"It was Jacinthe's idea. Nearly worked too. I had a spot of bother at Fairfax house with some of Lord Mulgrave's people who have taken the house for the summer, and I'm afraid that Silas might be in trouble. I've got to get back to The Rectory to check all is well."

"Jacinthe, eh? I might have guessed she'd be involved. And what now? And quick, the Manchester coach is due in the next ten minutes. I'd rather have you out of sight before that gets in. The inn will be teeming with people when that happens."

Della looked her squarely in the face. "I need a horse, Indira. Your best mount no less. And I need you to replace me as driver on tomorrow's coach. I have to ride to Runswick and The Rectory tonight and as quick as I can. This is not a job for one of your old nags. And I'd rather not be followed. It's a wild and lonely ride over the moors at this time of night. The perfect place for an ambush."

Indira thought for a moment.

"Wait here. I'll be five minutes. And don't move - you need to stay out of sight."

She turned and scurried across the courtyard to the stables. A couple of minutes passed before she returned.

"My best horse is saddled and waiting for you. There's just one more thing. Follow me."

Della knew better than to ask questions. She followed in Indira's wake as she slipped into the pub and climbed the stairs to her rooms. Once inside, she locked the door behind them and gestured to Della to sit down at her dressing table. Della looked in the mirror and watched Indira's quick fingers nimbly fiddle with a bowl of hair grips. After a minute, her luxuriant dark hair had disappeared again, clipped tight against her skull. Indira leaned down into a drawer and pulled out a grey powdered wig, complete with pigtail. She fitted the wig and then completed the look by jamming a tricorn hat on Della's head.

She stood back to admire her handiwork.

"Not bad. You look roguishly handsome as a man. Be careful not to walk through the inn. You'll have all the girls making eyes at you."

Della winked at her. "Come on, Indira, I'm used to that. But, seriously, that's very good. A man I will be."

"It's important that no one sees a beautiful young woman ride out tonight. Just in case your 'friends' ask."

She leaned over and gave Della a hug.

"The horse is ready for you. There's food and water in the saddle bags. And you'll need these."

From another drawer, Indira drew a pair of pistols and a pouch of powder and handed them over.

"Now go. And be careful."

Della took the pistols from her.

"Thanks, Indira. For everything."

She slipped out into the corridor and down to the stables. Indira closed the door and went out onto her balcony overlooking the courtyard. After a minute, the shadowy figure of a fine-looking young man, riding an equally magnificent snowy white horse, left the stable and picked their way steadily to the main entrance to the inn. The figure looked cautiously both ways down Coney Street, and then, with a flick of the reins, broke into a trot eastwards. Della's night ride had begun.

RETURN TO YNGERLANDE

Tom's arms flailed blindly around him in the pitch blackness. First, his left hand scraped against a wall of some kind. Then his right hand suddenly sliced through an icy cloud. The shock was like swimming in a warm sea and out of the blue coming across a cold current. He froze and turned to look at his hand, the hairs on his neck standing upright.

In the thick darkness, his hand was visible, having stopped in the middle of the silvery, shimmering form that had appeared by his side. It was Daniel! Tom jumped out of his skin and screamed.

Dan, his body a fume of grey mist that was luminous in the dark, also gave a sudden start, and gasped out loud, but then recovered himself.

"Tom! Good to see you." He gave a wry smile. "In every possible way."

Tom was recovering from the shock, his heart still racing. For a second, he couldn't speak.

"Hey, Tom, it really is good to see you, but it's not that good." He looked down at Tom's arm.

"Uh?" asked Tom, baffled.

"Your hand, man. I reckon it's resting on my liver at the moment."

Tom followed Dan's eyes and saw his hand resting in the middle of Dan's translucent body.

Horrified, he pulled it out immediately. "Sorry, man. I didn't realise."

"No problem, bro. It's an easy mistake to make. So,"

he continued, "here we are again. You've even got the usual fancy dress on."

By this time they were both becoming accustomed to the dark. Tom looked down at his body, and through the gloom could just make out his strange clothing: knee breeches, buckled shoes, frock coat, white linen shirt. He reached for his head to find, as expected, a tricorn hat. Then he looked across at Dan. He glowed a luminous silvery grey, still dressed in jeans, t-shirt and trainers. He was also slightly translucent. Tom could see through him to the stone wall behind him. He hovered a few inches off the ground and his body pulsed and shimmered. As he bounced in a gentle, soothing rhythm, his locks did the same. Dan was very particular about his hair.

"So, you're still here as a ghost, just like last time," said Tom.

"But where is here, exactly? Are we in the passage from the grandfather clock? And where does it lead? Silas' study, maybe?"

"Dunno," replied Tom, "but there's an easy way to find out. Come on."

He turned and began to walk deeper into the gloom of the passage. Dan slid along beside him, keeping an eye out for any sign of the end of the passage or a door of some sort.

"What are we gonna do if there's someone waiting for us at the other end? Someone bad, I mean," asked Dan. "And where have Clara and Grace gone?"

"I reckon you're gonna have to slide in first like a ghost, just to see what's going on. I'll hang around in the clock until you come back and report."

"And then what?" Dan replied. "Do we try to meet up with the girls? Or should we make our way to Mulgrave Hall to rescue Silas and everyone? And who exactly is this Shrike guy?"

Tom shook his head. "Dunno," he said again. "All I know is that Clara said there was a letter in the study.

Maybe that will give us some answers. Come on. The sooner we get there, the sooner we'll know."

They made their way along the passage in the darkness. Tom kept the fingers of his hand in contact with the wall to keep him walking in the right direction. It was eerily familiar and just before they reached the end, they both began to slow down, anticipating the door. They stopped at the same moment and exchanged a look.

"This feels like the end, doesn't it?" asked Dan.

"Yeah," Tom replied, "I'm sure we're at the door of the clock here." He had instinctively lowered his voice, even though he knew from his experiences the Christmas before that once the door was closed nobody on the other side would be able to hear them, no matter how loudly they shouted.

He stretched out his hand in front of him. His fingertips lightly brushed against a smooth wooden surface.

"That's it. That's the door," he announced. He looked across at the silvery figure of Dan. "Do you know what to do?"

"Of course," he replied, before doing a series of ghostly somersaults. "I'll slide through the door, stay invisible, and check out the study and the rest of the Rectory. If anyone's there, I'll hang around and earwig to get an idea of what's going on."

As if in celebration, he twisted himself into a corkscrew shape, and spun around like an electric drill.

"Will you stop doing that!" Tom exclaimed. "This is dangerous. We can't afford to make a mistake. You've got to concentrate to stay invisible, remember."

Dan immediately stopped spinning and reverted to a static, shimmering form.

"Yeah, sorry, Tom. Got a bit overexcited. I'd forgotten how cool this was. I'll concentrate,

promise."

"Don't be too long in there. I don't want to be stuck

here in the dark wondering what's happening."

Dan took a deep breath and took a step towards the door.

"And Dan," Tom called.

Dan stopped abruptly, inches in front of the door. "Yeah? What is it?"

"Be careful in there, man. Remember last time. Some of these people are dangerous."

Dan grinned back at him. "Don't worry, I'll be back before you know it"

He turned and walked straight at the door. His smoky form sliced through it, taking its silvery luminescence with it. The passage was once again plunged into darkness as Dan disappeared. Thomas, his heart hammering at his chest, was completely alone.

*

Matilda pulled her rough shawl tighter around her shoulders and closed the door behind her. She fumbled with the bunch of keys at her side, praying that her trembling hands would be able to lock the door without drawing any attention to herself. After a few scrapes and clinks, she managed to turn the key, and with her head down, turned to go down the corridor towards the staircase. Daisy had explained in some detail, over and over again, what her routine was when leaving the room at the end of the day. Daisy, who, at that moment, was gagged and bound in one of the cupboards in Matilda's suite of rooms.

"You finished for the day then?"

She froze. Daisy said no-one ever spoke to her. What was she to do? She must remain calm. She forced herself to half turn, and from behind her shawl and cap, she mumbled, "Yes, Sir, at last. Good night to you."

She turned again.

"Good night."

She carried on down the corridor, certain that, at any minute, rough hands would grab her and haul her back.

She could barely breathe and her heart was pounding. All she could concentrate on was putting one foot in front of the other, on completing the next step and then the one after that. She found herself at the foot of the stairs. Following Daisy's instructions, she turned towards the back of the house and the kitchens. Daisy had explained, over and over, that those servants who did not live downstairs in the grand house, who came in from the village and returned each day, would use the rear door from the kitchen. The Lords and Ladies would not want their lives to be spoiled by the sight of the common folk coming to and fro, using the same entrance as their betters.

The corridor got progressively darker and quieter before reaching the stairs down to the basement, but to her horror, once she got to the bottom, it was even brighter and busier than the grand hallway above. There was a frantic bustle of activity as servants came and went in all directions, but principally, in and out of the kitchen, which was the heart of this under stairs world. There was chatter as well. Casual greetings and farewells were exchanged back and forth. It was just as Daisy had explained, but still came as a shock to Matilda, whose nerves were stretched to breaking point.

She knew that there would be a gathering in the kitchen of the staff that were leaving. There it was their custom to have a final drink and something to eat before boarding the wagon that took them back to the village. It was also a time for gossip and any last-minute arrangements or changes for the next day. Daisy had stressed to her that she must not go in there because they would all notice if she did not take part in the idle chatter, as usual. Instead, she should take her chance to slip out into the yard through the door in the passage leading to the kitchen.

Matilda's eyes darted this way and that as she made her way along the corridor, checking the others and hanging back, waiting for the opportunity to disappear through the door outside. Her head was covered by her shawl, her breathing shallow and perspiration stood out on her forehead as she edged towards her decision. A quick look both ways told her that at last the coast was clear. She sprang towards the door, opened it with trembling, sweating hands, and dashed out into the dark courtyard.

The next part of Daisy's instructions had puzzled her. "Wait until the others come out to the cart and join them at the back as they pass. Don't be surprised at what happens after that, Your Majesty. You have more friends in the Hall than you realise."

She shrank against the wall, hidden in deepest shadows, and scanned the courtyard. All was quiet, except for the distant buzz of conversation coming from the kitchen. What on earth could Daisy have meant? At that precise moment in time, she felt utterly friendless. But then the door slammed open, swinging on its hinges, banging back against the walls a couple of times, and loud, raucous conversation poured out into the yard, along with the yellow lights.

The first stirrings of hope in Matilda's heart were stamped out almost before she was aware of them. The first group to come out were Redcoats, muskets at the ready, grim-faced, and serious. She put her head down in the shadows to avoid eye contact as they marched past her. Then the servants followed them out, chatting as they always did at the end of their work. Matilda let them pass her and begin to board the cart. What must she do? She couldn't just let them leave without her, but if she made her move at the wrong time, in front of the Redcoats, everything would be lost. She was rescued from her agony of indecision by the young girl at the back of the group. Short and plump, with mousy brown hair, she barely looked fourteen. "There you are, Daisy," she began breezily. "Come on, don't hang around. Come and sit at the back with me."

Matilda stared at her with desperate eyes, unable to

speak. The girl smiled and nodded in encouragement. She took Matilda's hand and led her to the step at the back of the cart. Inside, there were about fifteen people, who each in their turn, turned to flash Matilda an encouraging smile. They said nothing out of the ordinary, though, taking care to keep their conversation light and natural. Outside the cart, the Redcoats watched them all get in, with muskets drawn and mouths firmly set.

The cart set off, pulled by two Shire horses, built for strength, not speed. It rumbled along the driveway to the main entrance that led to the road. Reaching the entrance, it stopped by the gatehouse where two more redcoats were on duty. They gave a cursory glance inside the cart and waved it on.

"Off you go," called the redcoat at the back, "safe journey. Goodnight."

"Goodnight," came the chorus from the cart. Inside, Matilda and her companion gave each other a look and breathed heavy sighs of relief, as the cart set off again through the gate and on to the road. Then, without warning, there was a volley of musket shots from the direction of the house, followed by frenzied shouts and the thunderous noise of horses galloping along the driveway towards them.

"Halt! Stop that cart."

The driver pulled the cart up on the road that skirted the estate. On the other side was thick woodland. As they scrambled down, the girl whispered to Matilda, "When we are down on the road, you must run for the woods. We will stop them."

"But…" Matilda stammered.

"No," said the girl, firmly. "We will stop them. You must flee, with all speed."

The knot of servants gathered themselves at the woodland edge of the road. Even in the darkness, it was clear that the forest was thick. Once anyone had got in there in the dark, it would not be easy to find them. The redcoats approached, rifles drawn.

"Hands up, all of you," the captain of the troop commanded. "Don't move, and don't do anything reckless. If you have nothing to hide, you have nothing to fear, but be warned. My men have strict orders to shoot if necessary."

The servants all walked towards the redcoats, their arms above their heads.

"Now!" the girl hissed. Matilda looked blankly at her.

"Now, Your Majesty, the woods!"

She gave her a little push and Matilda, once she had started to move, sprinted as quickly as she could towards the edge of the forest. As she ran, she held a picture of Gaia firmly in her mind's eye.

The Captain saw her dash away. "Stop, or we'll shoot! Men, take aim."

The rest of the servants turned and began to rush towards the woods, so that the soldiers could not possibly have a clear view of Matilda as she dashed to the forest.

"She's getting away, Captain," shouted one of the men.

He looked over the heads of the crowd of servants. Matilda was receding into the distance, her figure blurring against the black backdrop of the woods. In a panic, the Captain gave the order. "Shoot! Shoot, you dogs, or I'll have you all horse whipped."

A volley of shots rang through the night air, causing a flurry of birds to take to the wing from the treetops in a cacophony of flapping and cawing. Then came another, more horrific sound. A sound of screaming and moaning. A sound of agony and despair. And then there was silence.

A LETTER FROM CLARA

Dan gasped as his body passed through the door of the grandfather clock. For a moment he was gripped by an icy cloud that made his heart race until he arrived on the other side. He remembered from the last time he had visited Yngerlande how to maximise his concentration to make sure he remained invisible. But he was in luck. He materialised inside the familiar room of Silas' study. It was just as he remembered from all those months ago. Wood panelled, with a candle on the desk that was almost burned down to a stub, the flame guttering in a pool of wax.

He slid over to the desk to make sure the flame was safely extinguished. No matter what calamity Silas was in the middle of, he certainly would not be pleased if The Rectory burned to the ground. He was just about to reach over to the candle when, in its flickering light, he saw two parchment letters laid out in the centre of the desk. He could see, even upside down, that one was addressed to Tom. It was Silas' handwriting. He gulped. They were important, he was certain of that. Trembling, he reached out to gather them up and then froze, his hand shaking, his heart hammering against his chest. There were footsteps outside in the corridor. And voices.

Without a second thought, he zoomed to the door on the other side of the room and silently turned the key in the lock. Whoever they were, the locked door would delay them for a minute or two. He was just in time. No sooner had he finished turning the key when the handle began to turn and then rattle as the door wouldn't open.

"It's locked." Dan heard the muffled voices through the thick oaken door. Another voice came. "Maybe there's someone in there."

"Stand aside. We'll soon find out"

Dan jumped in shock as the first heavy blow sounded on the door. Standing to one side, he watched as more strikes bludgeoned the old wood which began to tear and splinter under the assault. There was a final, violent crash and the door burst open, with wood splinters flying everywhere, ripping against the frame. Two men eased into the study warily, the first holding a pistol high in front of him, the second a lantern that illuminated their faces as they stepped over the shards of torn wood into the room. Dan, floating invisibly in the corner, watched them keenly. They both looked young men in their twenties. The first was a white man, tall and slim, with oily, jet black hair that fell on his shoulders and a wispy pointed beard. The second, holding the lantern, a muscular black man with tightly cropped hair, was clean shaven and had a pair of pistols tucked into his belt.

Dan smiled invisibly as both men shivered when their bodies detected the icy chill of his ghost-like state.

"Dear Lord, it's like an ice box in here."

The other man drew his pistol from his belt and gestured to the other to be quiet. With his other hand he scanned the room with his lantern.

"Nobody. I could have sworn there was someone in here. I could just feel it."

The other man scoffed. "Well, clearly there isn't. Remind me not to rely on your feelings in the future. I'd like to live a long and prosperous life."

His companion shook his head. "Well, you've got no chance of doing that in your line of work. It's only a matter of time before his Lordship slits your throat for you. The trick is to get out with enough money before he decides to do that."

"If we go back to Mulgrave Hall with nothing for him,

he might just do it there and then. They've obviously fled, those two girls. And not long ago, from what I can see."

He moved towards the desk and felt the candle. "Still warm, see. Check all the doors and paintings in this room. Cummerbund is a devious old cove, no matter that no one has a bad word to say about him round these parts. I wouldn't be surprised if this house was riddled with secret tunnels."

They both began to circle the room, using their fingertips on the edges of the paintings. Dan had to flatten himself partly into the wall as they stumbled around the room looking for any hidden openings. He followed them round the room to make sure he could overhear their conversation, but he was beginning to get tired. This was the first time for months that he had been a ghost in Yngerlande, and although he loved it, it took a lot of concentration. He dug his fingernails into his palms and thought, "Come on you two, there isn't anyone here. Don't hang around, it's time for you to go back to Mulgrave Hall."

It was as if they had heard him. They did a brief double check of every room, but it was clear to Dan that their hearts weren't really in it. They had already made up their minds. He followed them finally to the front door of The Rectory, taking care to keep out of their way so they didn't accidentally walk through him. It was there, in front of the open door, that Dan heard their final snippet of conversation. And they had left the most intriguing detail till last.

The man with the beard pronounced the search over.

"No, they've definitely gone. There's no point staying here any longer. We'll have to go back to the Hall and face the music, I reckon."

"You said that about the two girls. But what about Shrike? Is he with them, do you think?"

Dan froze. Shrike? That was the man with Clara and Grace. the one no-one trusted. He slid a little closer, trying to hang on to their every word.

"Shrike? He will be where he always is, doing what he always does."

The other man frowned. "What's that then?"

"Hidden in plain sight, making sure he comes out on top, that's where Shrike'll be. He's a devil in human form, that one. He gives me the creeps. I dunno why his Lordship keeps him on. He's more trouble than he's worth, if you ask me."

"Well, no one did ask you, did they? Tell you what, when we get back you can let his Lordship know your considered opinion. How about that? I'm sure he'll be delighted. He might even give you another purse of silver, eh?"

"Very funny, Jeremiah. But you mark my words, that Shrike's a deep one, and no mistake. I wouldn't trust him as far as I could throw him."

They continued their conversation as they went out and onto the gravel driveway. Dan, bobbing invisibly in the doorway, watched as they mounted their horses and rode off. He breathed a sigh of relief. At last, he could rematerialise and relax. His silvery figure fumed in the night air and then he zoomed through the corridors and rooms back to Silas' study. He slid through the heavy wooden door and went straight to the grandfather clock. Tapping on the door, he bent down and hissed, "Tom! Tom, it's me. You can come out now."

Immediately, the door swung open, and Tom stepped into the room.

"At last! I thought you were never going to come back. What the hell have you been doing?" Tom blurted out.

Dan gave him a look. "Finding stuff out, man, just like we agreed. I haven't just been messing about."

"Sorry, bro." Tom said. "It's just hard waiting in the dark in silence. So, what happened?"

"No problem, man. It was a success. The two guys - old Mulgrave's men- searched the house but couldn't find anything. They reckon Grace and Clara have legged it. And, even better, I found this."

Dan fumbled in the pocket of his jacket and pulled out the two letters he had discovered on Silas' desk. He handed them over to Tom. They both went across to Silas' desk, spread the sheet open and lit the lantern. He shaded the light, just in case there was still anyone lurking outside and bent over the writing.

It had obviously been written in a hurry. The writing was scrawled with the occasional ink blot. It was from Clara.

Dearest Thomas,

I leave this letter for you in haste. We have to go before Mulgrave's men discover us. They already have Silas and everyone you care for under lock and key at the Hall. My mother is also arrested and they are just waiting to kidnap me so that they can force my mother to hand over the crown to Oliver. They plan to denounce me as a witch. We will leave through the tunnels to a hiding place they do not know about, up on the Moors. You must follow, if you can. I will try to leave a trail for you to follow. We are in the hands of Shrike, who tells us he knows a safe place, and there we must plan our next moves.

I do not trust him, but your sister has fallen under his spell. I will watch over her, but we need you, otherwise we are lost. My powers are much stronger than when we were last together, but I cannot do this alone, especially now Silas is captured. Obviously, he could escape without a second thought but he is afraid of what they will do to the others.

Come soon. I long to see you again.

Your friend,

Clara

Hunched over the letter in a pool of flickering light, Tom and Dan looked at each other, their faces etched with worry. Even Dan, who was normally irrepressible, looked subdued.

"All of them," he said, "all of them under arrest. Even the Queen. This is bad, Tom."

"And who's this Shrike dude?" asked Tom. "I don't like the sound of him. Clara is obviously very suspicious of him."

"I heard the two guys in the house just now talking about him," said Dan. "They weren't sure of him either. It was almost as if they weren't sure which side he was on. But Tom…"

He hesitated, unsure of whether to go on.

"What? Spit it out, man."

"They were sure about one thing. They said that he was, what was it again. Yeah, that's it, they said he was "the devil in human form". I don't like it, Tom, he sounds crazy."

"And my sister and Clara are in the middle of the Moors alone with him."

There was a pause. The edges of the night crept in at the windows and in the thickening darkness outside of the lantern's cone of light, they sat and thought about what was in front of them. The silence grew, hand in hand with darkness, punctuated only by the clock ticking.

Finally, Tom spoke, "We'll have to follow them through the tunnels. We'll take a lantern and some matches with us, and some water." He looked directly into Dan's eyes. "Are you up for this? It's bound to be dangerous."

Dan smiled. "Course I am. I didn't have much on anyway. Double Science and PHSE, that's all. I'd rather be in a tunnel in Magic Land, pursued by bears and wolves than that."

"Good man. I knew I could rely on you. Come on. I'll put the lantern out until we get inside the tunnel. It's in the outhouse in the garden, remember?"

"What about the other letter? The one from Silas?"

"No time, I'll read it later. We've got to get going."

When the flame of the lantern was blown out, the

room and corridors were flooded with an inky blackness and they felt their way down the corridor to the back door. Outside, even though it was dark, the air was still heavy with July warmth, and there was a sweet smell of honeysuckle in the garden. In front of the old outhouse, they stopped and listened, just in case anyone was lying in wait. There was nothing - no horses or voices in the lane, just the distant sound of gulls and the waves breaking on rocks far away down by the cliffs. Satisfied, Thomas reached for the handle of the shed door. Just as his fingers closed on the handle, the unmistakable sound of an approaching horse shattered the night's silence. Tom and Dan looked at each other in panic, paralysed by this unexpected turn of events. The horse screeched to a halt on the gravel. Finally, Tom shook himself into action. He rattled open the door, and they both crashed through as it swung open, sending tins and tools scattering everywhere. He managed to reach out and close it, his heart hammering against his chest. In the dusty gloom of the shed, Tom signalled to Dan, his finger over his mouth, for silence. Thirty seconds later, footsteps approached and stopped directly outside the door.

WHITE WATER FALLS

The light of the lantern swung to and fro as they walked, casting grotesque shadows on the rough stone walls. They walked in single file: Shrike at the head, then Grace with Clara bringing up the rear. Every now and then Clara turned and peered back down the tunnel, just in case. Tom was still in England as far as she knew, and there would be no Mary Carruthers to come to their rescue. Mary was under lock and key, just like Amelia, Elizabeth and Silas. And her mother. With a sudden, guilty start, Clara realised she hadn't thought of her mother for several hours now. But she was imprisoned as well, and she would know that Kings and Queens had been killed in the past by ambitious traitors with an eye on the throne.

Her heart sank. Everything seemed hopeless. Without Silas, how could they possibly defeat Oliver and his supporters? She looked ahead. Shrike pressed on into the darkness. He was silent and there was a sense of urgency about him. Clara watched him closely. There was something about him that she couldn't quite put her finger on. She wasn't sure what it was, but it disturbed her. Even more disturbing was the fact that Grace seemed to be completely taken in by him. If there should come a point where she had to choose between Shrike and Clara, she wasn't certain which way Grace would jump.

They had been walking up a gentle slope for some time now, and the air in the tunnel seemed fresher than before. Surely, they would reach the end soon. As if in answer to her thoughts, Shrike stopped abruptly.

"I think we've got to the end of the tunnel. Clara, you've been here before, haven't you? Come and look at this. Is this the right place? How do we get out?"

Clara pushed past Grace, her hand trailing along the side walls which were knotted with gnarled tree roots.

"Hold your lantern up higher, so I can see," she instructed Shrike impatiently. He did as she said and Clara inspected the ending in the swaying light. It was a wooden slatted door with an iron handle and latch.

"Yes, this is it. We came through here last Christmas. It was covered in ivy and bindweed and it took us a while to hack our way through it. But it won't have all grown back since, so we should be able to get out pretty easily."

She reached for the latch and turned it. It was a little stiff but eventually it moved and she pulled on the door. There was some resistance at first and then, with one last heave she was able to force it open, the door edges ripping through the few remaining strands of vegetation. A warm breeze billowed through the open door, and they could all see the velvet black sky and a scattering of stars.

They slipped through the door and found themselves on the edges of woodland. To their left, higher up, was a road. To their right, the woods thickened and stretched away as far as they could see.

"So," said Grace, "what now? Where exactly are you taking us, Shrike?"

"Well, that depends on where exactly we are," he replied. He fumbled in his saddle bag and pulled out a folded sheet of parchment. He sat down and spread the sheet open, smoothing it out on the dry carpet of leaves that covered the ground.

"Come and have a look at the map and show me where we are."

Grace and Clara both knelt down beside him. The map showed the outskirts of York in the bottom left-hand corner, stretching up to Runswick Bay in the top right. It was old and creased, with notes inked in and certain locations circled. Clara traced a line from the village to the moors, using the location of Mary Carruthers' cottage to guide her. Using the woods and the road, she found their rough location and pointed it out to Shrike.

"This is where we've come out - just on the edge of these woods, here."

While she was doing that, she took as long as she could and scrutinised the map without making it obvious that that's what she was doing. South of their position, deeper into the moors, she noticed that a circle had been drawn around one particular spot. It was labelled "Hard Crag Towers" and within the circle was a drawing of an old house, set deep within a thick forest, with several high, crenelated towers. Next to it, she noticed, was a waterfall that fed into a river that snaked through the forest and over the moors to the sea.

Shrike pointed to Hard Crag on the map.

"This is where we're going. Good, it's closer than I thought."

"What's Hard Crag, Shrike? And how do you know it?" Grace asked him.

Shrike stood up and folded the map as he did so. He glanced around the spot where they had come out of the tunnels and put the map back in his saddle bag.

"It's an old house I know. No one goes there anymore - it's abandoned. But I've got a key."

A frown passed over Clara's face.

"Abandoned? Why? And how come you've got a key?"

Shrike flashed a dazzling smile at her. "Don't worry, Clara, we'll be safe there. We can rest and eat and then we can decide what we're going to do. But we need to get a move on. Come on, it's this way."

"Wait a minute, Shrike," said Clara. "Who else knows about this place? Will Mulgrave and his cronies think to look for us there? How do we know they're not there already, waiting for us. This could all be some elaborate trap for all we know."

There was a pause. In the silence that followed, the sense of being in the middle of the wild, miles from anywhere or anyone, grew. The leaves in the canopy overhead rustled in the warm breeze. In the distance, there was the sound of running water, as if from a stream, followed by the mournful hoot of an owl, out hunting for its dinner.

Shrike's eyes darted this way and that. He opened his mouth to answer Clara's question but before he could utter a word, the sounds of the night forest were interrupted by galloping hooves crashing through the undergrowth. From the bank of bushes to their right, a deer, tongue lolling, eyes staring, came crashing towards them. It careered past them and dived back into the undergrowth to their left.

All three of them instinctively fell to their knees, cowering in shock. Each of them looked from one to the other and back again. Then, in close pursuit, a huge grey wolf burst into the clearing, followed by six more. They ran steadily, calmly in comparison to the deer, but all the more frightening for that. There was a relentless determination about them and their pursuit, as if they all knew that it was only a matter of time before they caught up with the desperate hind. And then, as quickly as they had appeared, they were gone again and the clearing was still and quiet once more.

Grace breathed again. "Come on, Clara, we haven't got time to discuss all of this. We're in the middle of a forest that's crawling with wolves. Hard Crag Towers sounds just fine to me. Lead the way, Shrike."

She and Shrike got to their feet. Clara got up and followed them. She would keep her objections under wraps for the time being. Shrike plunged into the depths of the forest, away from the road. Within minutes the forest canopy had closed above them, and they were trudging in thick darkness. There was a half-moon, which occasionally cast its light through gaps in the tree cover, but for the most part they were walking in heavy gloom.

They walked in silence. No-one seemed inclined to pick up the conversation about Hard Crag Towers. Grace trusted Shrike. Clara was biding her time thinking. Shrike was concentrating on the trail in front of him. He had his story ready if he were asked again, but he wasn't going to volunteer it himself. There was plenty of time for that later.

They pressed on, through brambles that whipped back in their faces, lacerating hands. After a while, a new sound gradually broke through the silence. It was running water, rushing through rocks, gurgling and fizzing, getting louder as they walked towards it. Clara had also noticed they had been walking up a gentle slope, and the woodland was now punctuated with great limestone rocks that made the trail harder to navigate in the darkness. Without warning, the trail suddenly took them into a clearing in the woods, and they found themselves on the bank of a rushing, foaming river that surged over rocks on the riverbed, producing a torrent of white water.

The sight took their breath away. They came to an immediate halt and each of them took a minute to take in the scene. The far bank was twenty yards away and the moonlit river looked like a formidable obstacle to cross. One slip on the gleaming, jagged rocks would cast any traveller into the rushing water, where survival would be more a matter of luck than skill. Then to their left, rose an even more impressive sight. A great, sheer cliff face rose sixty yards or more into the sky, covered by a shimmering curtain of white water that sent spray high into the night air.

Grace put her hand to her mouth and gasped.

"Oh, my word!" she managed to say. "It's magnificent. I had no idea this was here."

Clara too was almost lost for words. Her eyes sparkled in the face of such a sight.

"Yes, it's beautiful," she said at last, "but a little

frightening at the same time."

She turned to look at Shrike.

"So where do we go from here? We must be nearly there by now."

Shrike smiled. He seemed unaffected by this new, spectacular sight, as if had seen it many times before. He opened his mouth to speak when a new sound ripped through the air, cutting across the hiss and rumble of the rapids and the tumbling sheet of water.

A wolf cry. High and mournful, the howl jagged across the night sky and sent a chill down everyone's spine. Then, before any of them could react, the cry of the lone wolf was joined by others. Soon, the night air was a cacophony of howls. A wolf pack, and a fearsomely large one at that.

Grace instinctively grabbed hold of Shrike. He put his arm around her shoulder and hugged her to him tightly, his brain ticking over like a reptile. Over her shoulder, his eyes met Clara's, and there was a flash of icy recognition that passed between them. He half turned, to break the spell.

Grace cried out, "Wolves! Lots of them by the sound of it."

"Let's hope they caught up with that deer," replied Clara coolly, "this will be a lot worse if they're hungry."

"Come on," said Shrike. "Whether they're hungry or not, we need to get away from here. Follow me."

He released Grace and quickly climbed upwards towards the waterfall. Grace and Clara followed him, puzzled.

"Where are you taking us, Shrike?" asked Clara. "We can't possibly climb up there."

Shrike turned. "No, of course not. Just follow me and check your footholds and your grip."

He clambered over a series of rocks perilously close to the edge of the churning water. The rocks were greasily smeared with lichen and treacherous underfoot, and more than once one of them slipped and had to cling to the rock by their fingertips. They went in single file, Grace behind Shrike and then Clara. Grace glanced up at one point and saw that Shrike was hard up against a sheer wall of rock, right next to the outer edge of the curtain of rushing water. She looked down to check her foothold and when she looked again, Shrike had disappeared.

She screamed his name in a blind panic, fearing he had slipped over the side.

"Shrike! Where are you?" she called, just as she had reached the wall where he had been a moment before.

"Here, Grace. All is well, my dear."

His voice was calm and, as she looked to her right, she could see that he had slipped in behind the curtain of water to a narrow shelf of rock projecting from the main face of the cliff. He smiled and held out his hand, pulling her into the safety of the niche. He pulled her to his other side and moved along to help Clara clamber to this secret shelf.

She had just reached the top, and exactly as Grace had done, she looked to her right and spotted the recess behind the waterfall. Shrike reached out his hand and she stretched hers up until their hands met. Just as they made contact, her foot slipped on the greasy outcrop of rock she had planted it on, and she fell. Behind Shrike, Grace gasped in fear. Clara cried out, a strangled cry, and saw her legs and feet dangling fifty feet or so above the jagged rocks below. Shrike gripped her hand firmly and began to pull her upwards towards him.

"Hold on, Clara, I've got you. Stay calm. All will be well."

But then, in terrible slow motion, their grip began to lessen and their hands, sodden in the spray from the waterfall began to slip and slide inexorably towards release. Clara scrabbled around wildly in terror, her legs swaying against the rock wall. Shrike, his face contorted in concentration, maintained his grip, digging in his nails, and then leaned out over the terrifying vertical descent of spume and limestone. He lunged with his other hand and grabbed hold of her tunic.

For a dizzying moment they teetered on the edge, swaying as Shrike fought to dig in his heels and push back against the downward momentum. Grace, behind Shrike on the ledge, was transfixed with fear, her hand covering her mouth as she watched them, powerless. There was a terrible moment when Shrike and Clara's eyes met. Clara pleaded with him silently. This, she knew, was the moment that he could let her slip without suspicion. The moment seemed to last an eternity. Then Shrike roared as he summoned all his strength, and hauled her with brute force back onto the shelf. They both fell backwards, crashing against the craggy limestone wall of the cliff and lay there exhausted and gasping for air. All three of them embraced. Grace began to sob. "I thought…I thought..."

Clara reached out a hand to her. "I know. I thought so too. But all is well, Grace. All is well."

Shrike sat up and peered over the side. Through a gap in the curtain of surging water, they could clearly see the near bank of the torrent they had just left. A pack of wolves burst into the space. At the water's edge they stopped, and raising their heads, they sniffed the air and set up a tremendous cacophony of howls. They detected human scent, but could not locate humans, and their frustration echoed through the warm still air of the forest.

Up above, from the safety of their shelf, the three of them observed the pack below, howling, scrabbling, searching. Eventually, they admitted defeat. The leader of the pack sent up a fearsome howl, and then broke into a trot, back down into the forest, followed by his pack.

Shrike watched them go. He turned to Grace and Clara. Clara was massaging the palm of her hand where Shrike's fingernails had gouged bloody trenches. Grace embraced her, evidently still in shock. They both looked up at him, in awe and fear and cautious admiration.

"Well," he said evenly, "we need to get a move on if

we're going to get to Hard Crag Towers. The next bit should be easier. Just ten minutes now. Come on."

Shrike and Grace went on ahead. Clara was alone when she reached the end of the ledge. She quickly looked all around, and then, when she knew that she could not be seen, she closed her eyes and gripped the rocks behind the sheet of tumbling water. Her face was etched with the effort of concentration, and she had to steady herself for a second when she relaxed. She looked back at the entrance to the rock shelf and allowed herself a moment of satisfaction. There, only visible to her and Tom, was a single star, where she had shed it, lighting the way forward.

SHOTS IN THE DARK

Earlier, Della spurred on her horse for the final stretch over the moors. When she had last stopped, to let the horse drink from a stream, she could smell the salty sea air on the warm breeze. Only another twenty minutes or so and she should be at The Rectory. But what would she find there? She had a nagging feeling in the pit of her stomach that something terrible had happened, and that she would be walking into a situation that she had no power to put right. When she had left, all had been well. Silas was on a mission to Mulgrave Hall to rescue Mary Carruthers, Grace and Clara were set for an afternoon of walking and picnicking, and Amelia had her medical rounds to do. But without Silas, The Rectory was unprotected and an easy target for anyone with weapons and determination.

She shivered at the thought. Then she pulled herself together. Fear wouldn't do anyone any good in this situation. She would just have to make sure that she dismounted before The Rectory so that she could creep up on anyone who might be there without alerting them to her presence. And then what? She put the question out of her mind because she knew, in the back of her mind, that she did not have a convincing answer to that last question. That would have to wait until she got there.

She jumped back up into the saddle and spurred her horse into a canter that quickly turned into a gallop. She had covered the wildest bits of the Moors already. She had passed on the other side of a valley to a herd of steedhorns as they grazed, and was sure that, as she skirted a woodland near White Water Falls, she had caught a glimpse of the shaggy outline of a brown bear as it shuffled back under cover. Now, as she thundered over the brow of a hill, with the North Sea flat and calm under the thin moonlit sky to her right, and the high bare rocks of the moorlands to her left, her blood ran cold as the peace of the night was shattered by the howl of a wolf.

Then there was a tremendous yammering of the pack, far off deep into the forest, accompanied by the agonising death whimpers of whichever wretched creature the pack had caught. It was a chilling sound, but neither Della nor her horse faltered this time. The sooner she reached The Rectory the better. She rode like the wind for another fifteen minutes until she reached the cliff top road above Runswick Bay.

It was late, about one in the morning judging by the position of the moon in the sky. No-one would be abroad in Runswick at this hour. The fishermen would be enjoying another hour or two in their beds before they had to put to sea for the mackerel shoals, and the farmers would also have a few more hours of sleep before they had to tend to their animals. The only person who she might encounter at this hour in Runswick would be Silas, who often walked out in the dead of night to think and to watch, as he put it.

Where was he? And was he safe? Her mind had wrestled with this during the whole wild ride from York, once she was clear of the city and confident that she wasn't being followed. And the more she thought, the more afraid she became. She galloped hard, all the way to The Rectory, despite the danger of being heard, and leaped from the horse the second it had crunched the gravel at the entrance.

She reached down to her belt and pulled out the two pistols that Indira had given her back in York. As quietly as she could, she cocked the trigger of each one, and slipped through the gate in the shadow of the high walls. From her hiding place she could see the door to the main house was wide open, and the house was in complete darkness. Her heart hammered against her chest. She could hardly bear to think what she might find in there, but she knew that whatever it might be, she had no choice but to go and see.

Just as she was about to take her first steps towards the door, an action that would necessitate her leaving the shadows, she heard a muffled crash away to her right, at the back of the garden. She froze. Then, she turned to look and caught a glimpse of a light. There was someone in the outhouse! She stepped out from the shrubbery and raced to the door, silent as a shadow. As she did so, she had a fleeting sight of the figure inside the shed. It brought her crashing to a halt, her breathing unsteady, her pulse racing. She shook her head, not believing the evidence of her own eyes. There was only one way to find out.

Raising both pistols in the air, she kicked at the door of the shed with her leather riding boot. The door clattered open, slamming violently against the inside wall of the shed. Framed in the light of their torch, was Thomas, frozen in shock and disbelief. Della's face slid from grim determination to a half smile, as she began to believe the evidence of her own eyes, and she started to lower the pistols. "Thomas…?" she muttered.

Just then, the ghostly form of Daniel materialised in front of her, a silvery glimmer of watery fog.

She screamed, a blood curdling, high pitched slash of a scream. Then came another noise, a deafening double explosion that cut across the scream and smothered it into silence. She looked down at her hands and her worst fears were confirmed. She had pulled the trigger of both pistols, aiming directly at Thomas.

Time stood still as Thomas watched the whole thing unfold. The blood in his veins turned to ice as he tracked the two heavy lead balls of shot arrow towards him through the clouds of choking smoke produced by the guns. In a blur, his hands flicked up in front of him and tightened into fists.

The smoke cleared and Della saw Tom standing in front of her, his fists held high as if protecting himself. She dropped both pistols and put her hands to her face in horror, as she waited for Tom's lifeless body to drop to the floor. Then, in disbelief, she saw Tom take a step towards her, his hands held out in front of him. He opened his fists and looked down at his hands, a great beaming smile spreading across his face. In the palm of each hand lay a red-hot piece of lead shot.

"That wasn't very friendly, Della. I thought you'd be pleased to see us again," he said.

"What," she stammered, "you caught the bullets? How could you, that's not..."

Her voice trailed off. She shook her head and began to smile as well.

"Not possible? You should know me better than that, Della."

She jumped forward into his arms with a delighted squeal and they hugged. Finally, she pulled away from him and looked him in the eyes.

"Oh, Thomas, it's so good to see you again. You don't know how much we need you."

She stopped suddenly, as if something had just occurred to her. "But it was Master Daniel as well, wasn't it? The ghost is back as well? Sorry, that's why I shot. I'm not used to ghosts appearing in front of me."

Dan, who had been keeping out of the way, invisible, judged the coast was now clear and popped back into view.

"I can't deny it, Della," he said, smirking. "Sorry, I didn't mean to frighten you earlier. Well, obviously, I did, but that's because I didn't know it was you. I'd give you a hug, but..." He looked down at his shimmering form and shrugged his shoulders. "You know..."

All three of them laughed.

But then the seriousness of their situation pushed its way to the front again, and the laughter died away.

"Listen," said Tom, "we've got to get a move on and there's a lot to say to each other. Just follow us, and we'll talk while we walk, ok?"

He moved back to the corner of the shed, towards the trapdoor.

Della looked puzzled. "Walk where? We're in the shed, Master Thomas."

He pulled up the trapdoor with a flourish.

"The tunnels, Della, the tunnels. After all, we had so much fun down here last time, didn't we?"

Without waiting for an answer, he and Dan disappeared down the ladder into the darkness. Della shook her head, laughed quietly to herself and followed them. The trapdoor closed with a gentle click and the shed, and The Rectory, were left in darkness and silence at last.

THE SINGLE STAR

For the first fifteen minutes after they had left the waterfall behind, they had walked through dense woodland, with Shrike striding confidently out in front. Then, without warning, they emerged from the forest onto a rough gravel track which skirted the forest to their left and right. Straight ahead of them, looming out of the thin moonlight, was a high stone wall, crumbling and covered in ivy and lichen.

"This is it," announced Shrike. "We've just got to climb over the wall and we're almost done."

Grace looked up at the towering wall in front of her. It was about ten feet high and when she reached over to gauge how stable it was, the stone crumbled in her hands. It seemed to be held together by the lattice of clinging ivy that covered it.

"You sure about this, Shrike?" she asked. "Looks a little tricky to me."

He smiled at her. "Don't worry, I know the best place to climb."

"You've done it a lot then?" asked Clara, a little too eagerly.

"Many times. I know this place all too well."

He moved a little way down the track, following the wall as it curved around before giving way to a tall, rusted set of iron gates that were heavily padlocked.

"I don't suppose you have a key for these, do you?" enquired Grace.

"No such luck," laughed Shrike in reply. "No-one's

been through those gates for years. Even if we had a key, the padlock is probably rusted shut permanently now. No, there are firm hand holds in the wall just beyond it. Look, just here."

He pointed at the next section of the wall.

"I'll shin up first. Watch where I put my hands and feet, and when I get to the top, I'll direct you."

He stretched both hands up to his first handholds, took a grip and hauled himself up. Then he repeated the action three or four times. Within seconds he had reached the top and he swung his legs over so that he could straddle the wall comfortably. Grace went next, with Shrike's encouragement, and she too reached the top, scrabbling to keep a tight grip on the clinging ivy as well as the fissures in the surface of the stone.

Clara watched her ascend unevenly from down below. She just had enough time. She caught hold of a protruding rock to steady herself and then slipped into a trance-like state for a second or two. When she opened her eyes, she stumbled against the wall and looked back and forth along its length. Just next to the rusting gate, half hidden by a tangle of ivy, she caught sight of an old weather-stained sign, screwed firmly into the stone work. She reached across and pulled the greenery to one side, exposing the lettering, fading, but still legible. "Hard Crag Towers. Home for Children with…"

She couldn't read the rest. Just as she was about to pull away more of ivy, Shrike shouted down from above her.

"Your turn, Miss Clara. Quickly now, we need to get inside."

She looked up at him and their eyes met for a second. He held her gaze and his eyes flashed in the moonlight, his mouth set in a twisted line of determination. There was some kind of struggle going on between them. Clara knew that he knew what she had seen, and he wanted to drag her attention away from it, if he could. The moment was less than a second and then it was over. He held down his hand for her.

"Clara, we need to make a move."

She shook herself.

"Sorry, I was miles away."

She sprang up the wall, finding the handholds and footholds with ease. Like a cat, she was at the top of the wall in an instant and found herself sitting beside Shrike, straddling the summit.

"Very impressive, Clara. You don't need me at all," he said smoothly, smiling at her.

She looked over his shoulder, into the grounds of Hard Crag. Below her was Grace, also staring out towards the house. In the weak moonlight, she could see that the grounds formed a natural amphitheatre, with the house sitting squarely in the centre at the lowest point. She supposed that was why they hadn't caught sight of the house up until this last moment, and why it wasn't somewhere they were familiar with. All of the houses that had been established up on the top of this high moorland usually occupied prominent positions on the highest ground so that the fine families that lived there had commanding views of the wild countryside, and everyone else could see just how splendid their houses were.

Hard Crag was different somehow. It was nestled deep in this extensive hollow, surrounded by thick woodland, almost as if it were trying to hide from view. It was completely in darkness - evidently there was no one at home, whatever kind of home it was - but set against the lighter moonlit sky, it was a jumble of crenelated peaked towers like the fairy tale home of a witch or dark magician. The sight of it sent a shiver down Clara's spine and she turned away to look back over the moors and forest, back the way she had come.

The view was of a solid wall of darkness, the edge of the forest blending into one solid mass. And then, almost imperceptibly at first, came a flash of starlight. She rubbed her eyes and looked again. Yes! There it was again!

Growing stronger this time, the star shone brighter and then multiplied into a trail of fizzing, sparking stars. Her heart leaped for joy. It was working.

She carefully rearranged her face to adopt a blank expression and then jumped down to join Grace, immediately followed by Shrike. The three of them stood together, their eyes drawn to the crumbling pile ahead of them.

It was Grace who spoke first.

"You sure about this, Shrike? Looks a frightening, evil sort of place to me. Gives me the heeby jeebies."

"Evil? No, Grace. It's just a house, just stone and mortar. Don't worry, houses aren't evil."

He smiled at them both.

"I'll lead the way. I know a way in. Then we'll be safe and we can get something to eat and drink."

Both Grace and Clara suddenly realised how hungry and tired they were. They hadn't eaten for hours, and the journey and the worry for their friends had left them exhausted. They stumbled wearily after Shrike as he pressed on through the bushes towards the house. As they did so, they could not see the strange, twisted smile that played across his face, nor hear the words he murmured under his breath.

"No, Clara, it's never the houses that are evil, or to be feared. It's the people in them you need to be worried about."

*

By the time Tom, Dan and Della had reached the end of the tunnel they had all shared what they knew of the story. Della by this stage had unpinned her hair and replaced her jewellery, now that her man's disguise no longer served any purpose. Tom had listened to the whole of Della's story. Now was the time for questions.

"What I don't understand, though, is how come you don't know who Shrike is? From Clara's letter, he has played a great role in all of this."

"I have no idea who he is, Thomas. But I suppose he must have arrived after I had left to drive the coach to York," she replied.

Tom frowned in the darkness.

"You don't think he waited until everyone had gone, do you? Like, he was watching the house?"

Della thought for a moment. "Well, that's the only explanation, I suppose." She shivered. "But that's a bit creepy, the idea we were being watched and nobody knew. He must be very good at making himself invisible."

At that moment, Dan did a triple somersault over their heads.

"Very good. But not as good as me," he said, before resuming his position walking next to them.

Della smiled. "No, Daniel, of course not. No-one is as good as the ghost at keeping invisible."

Tom interrupted, impatient. "But from Clara's letter, it sounds like he's convinced Grace much more than Clara."

He suddenly stopped in the tunnel and turned to Della, laying his hand on her arm.

"You've been with Grace since Christmas. How has she been, Della? I worry about her."

"Of course you do. She is quiet and withdrawn. She enjoys The Rectory and loves everyone there, but for a young girl, she does still brood on what she has missed out."

"So," Tom continued hesitantly, "she could be carried away if she met someone her age who was interested in her."

Della nodded. "Yes, I think that's very possible. Everyone needs love, Tom."

Dan chose that moment to execute an even more complicated corkscrew twirl in the air.

"If you're gonna talk about Leurve, I'm going straight back down the tunnel back home. Come on, we've reached the end. I'll go through and check what's on the other side. Although, if I remember it right from Christmas, it comes out on the edge of the forest, just near Mary Carruthers' place."

He didn't wait for an answer, but slid through the wooden door and the tangle of old brambles, into the world outside. Waiting in the gloom on the other side of the door, Della and Tom jumped out their skin as the silence of the tunnel was shattered by a howling and yammering from the other side. They looked at each other in alarm, but almost immediately the shimmering, luminous figure of Dan slid back through the entrance.

"What the hell was that, man?" Tom demanded. "Sounded like something was being ripped to shreds out there."

"Well spotted. Wolves. And a deer by the look of it. Or what was left of it at any rate. They were a bit put out by a ghost appearing in the middle of their dinner. They really do have disgusting table manners when you get up close," replied Dan.

Della looked aghast. "Did you just materialise in the middle of them eating?" she asked.

"Yeah! It was awesome. But don't worry - once they had got over the shock, they hauled the carcass deeper into the woods. It'll be safe enough for us."

Tom looked sceptical. "How do you know? It kind of depends which way we have to go, doesn't it?"

Della cut through their bickering.

"Alright, boys, let's go and have a look, shall we? Follow me."

She forced the door open and stepped tentatively out into the woods, looking all around her for any sign of a lurking wolf looking for a second course.

"Come on out, the coast is clear."

Once out, they all gathered at the entrance. The sky was still dark although there were the first stirrings of light away over in the Eastern sky. At their feet, on the fringes of the wood, was a bloody trail where the wolves had dragged the remainder of their dinner into the depths of the forest.

Della looked all around her. "I can barely recognise it," she said. "Last Christmas there was a couple of feet of snow, and we were all freezing to death. We were lucky to survive it." She looked back at Tom. "So, which way do we go?"

Tom had been worrying about this ever since they had entered the tunnel back at The Rectory. He had no idea which direction the others would have taken. He looked off to his right, into the gloom of the woods.

"I'm pretty sure that that's the way we took last time. And Mary's cottage is down that way, remember."

Della shook her head. "But if Shrike is taking them somewhere he knows, it won't be to Mary's cottage, surely? It could be anywhere. Didn't the letter from Clara give you any clues?"

Tom's face dropped. "Not really - just that she would try to leave some signs, whatever that means."

Dan zoomed back into view, after a quick slither around the trees in the forest.

"Sounds like Hansel and Gretel. Maybe she's dropped some breadcrumbs for us to follow."

Tom was silent, staring past Dan back towards the road. His face was creased with disbelief.

"Come on, Tom, I was only joking," said Dan.

Tom pushed past him, and strode off away from the trees. Della and Dan exchanged glances.

He turned back, a triumphant smile answering their fears.

"She has left breadcrumbs! But only I can see them. Come on, follow me."

Della shook her head. "I've got no idea what you're talking about Tom, but it worked last time, so, against my better judgement, I'm going to trust you. If you can see breadcrumbs, who am I to argue?"

He set off into the darkness with a stride full of confidence. Only he could see it, but it was unmistakable to him. There, on a lone ash tree that flanked the road, was a single, brilliant star, its silver light winking at him like a silent alarm.

They walked on, following Tom as he picked his way through the wild landscape. They forded streams, skirted woodlands and scrambled over boulders. Each time he thought he'd lost the trail, another lone star called out to him, showing him which direction to take. Sometimes the star was left on a tree trunk, sometimes a rock, but always it made the choice of direction clear.

Like Shrike, Grace and Clara before them, they heard the sound of water at White Water Falls before they saw it. In the moonlight, the spray above it sparkled with millions of points of refracted light, with the torrent below crashing over jagged boulders as the river raced relentlessly on towards the distant sea. All three stopped for a moment to take in the scene in front of them. Dan floated out above the crashing water for a better view, and then streamed back to dry land and the others.

"I love being a ghost." He grinned. "That's an amazing sight."

Della agreed. "That's White Water Falls," she said. "It's a bit of a local beauty spot, but not many people come out here. There are all kinds of tales about spirits walking abroad and ghouls and the like. Supposed to be a haunted house of some sort up on the moors here."

Tom pricked his ears up. "Haunted house? Do you think that's where Shrike might be headed? Where is it, exactly?"

Della jerked her head behind the waterfall. "Up yonder," she said. "On the other side of the bank, and then there's a bit of a climb to the high moors."

Tom surveyed the torrent of water a little more closely. "But how on earth can we cross to get up there? Dan could do it of course, but we all need to get across. Clara must have left another star somewhere."

He began to scour the rocks and bushes in the thin

moonlight. And then, without warning, he saw it. There was a flash to the side of the falls, marking the spot where Clara had left a starry trail. He edged along, the sheer drop barely an inch or two to his right.

"Careful," Della shouted in alarm, "it's a long way down there, you know. One slip and you're a dead man."

Tom turned back to face her. "It's alright, Della, there's a way through here - behind the water. Clara's left another sign. They've definitely been this way."

He reached up to the rocks above, and hauled himself up. Della followed him and a minute later, they had all navigated their way along the ledge, behind the curtain of water. They gathered at the other side and looked back the way they had come. It was a sobering sight. The spray from the waterfall rose into the night sky, the light from the half-moon transforming the droplets into a sparkling cloud. Down below, the rocks were jagged and jutted through the raging torrent. It was impossible to see the hidden track they had taken and there appeared to be no feasible way of crossing.

For Dan, it had been no different to sliding down a tiled corridor as a ghost, but he realised what a feat it had been for Tom and Della.

"Wherever this guy Shrike is taking them, he doesn't want to be easily found, does he? This place must be really well hidden."

"You're right," Tom agreed. "I've got a really bad feeling about this. I don't like the sound of this guy at all."

"Can you spot any more stars?" asked Della. "We should just follow the trail and get to them as soon as possible. Then we can work out what to do about Shrike."

Tom scanned their surroundings and in seconds spotted what he was looking for.

"Yes, there it is," he said, pointing away beyond the rocky outcrop they had arrived at. "Good old Clara, I knew we could rely on her. Come on, just follow me."

He set off towards the single star he had seen, with Della and Dan following closely behind.

HARD CRAG TOWERS

They pressed on towards the house, and, skirting the front, they followed Shrike who was headed for the back of the building.

"Why not the front?" asked Clara.

"There's another way," he replied. "Some of the building is derelict. There's only a few rooms I use, and they're at the back. You'll see when we get in."

They continued in silence, with Shrike leading them. They had already had to pick their way through tangles of bushes, and over cracked and broken paths. It seemed that when the house was first built, there had been neat gravel paths and extensive borders and ornamental shrubs, but that was quite clearly a long time ago. Now the borders were thickets of brambles and bindweed, pressing right up against the crumbling walls of the building and spilling out onto the paths and the old lawns. What was probably once a neatly mowed lawn was now swaying, knee-high grasses and nettles, and it was hard work pushing their way through it. More than once, a snaking branch of springy brambles would viciously whip back into the face of the person just behind. By the time they got to the brick wall at the back of the house, both Grace and Clara had livid scratches across their faces, and their hands and wrists were bloody and sore.

Even so, Clara noticed that Shrike knew the route like the back of his hand, and that, although they made their way through a mass of overgrown bushes, they seemed to be proceeding down a corridor where it was more easily passable than everywhere else around them. This route had been used many times before, and recently at that.

She looked up at the wall that towered above them. It was several floors high, and all the windows she could see were boarded up with old splintered planks of wood. The brambles and ivy they had battled through covered much of the surface of the wall, as if they were squeezing the life out of the building. She cricked her neck to try to see the top of the house, and she just caught a glimpse of some of the towers, noting that there were some windows that were not covered with planks. Presumably, whoever had tried to secure the house had reckoned that no one would be able to get through windows that high.

Just as she did so, something dark and leathery brushed past her face and hair. With a scream, she stopped and frantically waved her arms around her head, desperately trying to protect herself against whatever horrible creature was weaving around her again and again.

"Urghh," she called out, "what's that?"

Shrike pushed past Grace and grabbed Clara's arms roughly.

"Sshh!" he hissed. "We don't want the whole world to know we're here. It's just a bat. It's harmless. The house is full of their roosts. They're harmless."

Grace looked nervously at the sight of Shrike pinning Clara's wrists to her side.

"Shrike, that's enough. Let her go, there's no need to grab hold of her like that."

His face froze for a second as he processed Grace's disapproval, before it softened and his calculating instincts reasserted control. He let go of Clara, and touched her arm gently.

"I'm so sorry, Clara, I didn't mean to hurt you. We just need to be quiet here and I knew exactly what it was."

Clara rubbed her wrists ruefully. "That's alright," she said, "but why do we need to be quiet? The house is empty, surely."

He nodded. "Yes, the house is. But you never know what could be waiting in the grounds. It's force of habit, being silent."

Clara and Grace exchanged a glance.

Shrike continued. "Look up. Can you see them now?"

They all stared upwards. Silhouetted against the pale sky, slightly silvered by the moon, was a churning black cloud of fluttering shapes, like oversized moths. Just the sight of them brought on involuntary shivers and Clara shook her hair and scratched at her head. She shuddered again.

"If that's supposed to reassure me, Shrike, it's not working. I keep thinking they're going to get tangled up in my hair."

Shrike snorted, "No, they are far too clever for that. But to make you both feel better, let's get inside the house."

He fumbled inside a pocket and pulled out a large rusty iron key. To their surprise he moved towards the ivy-clad wall and inserted the key between the twining growths. With a smooth turn and a pull, a door opened outwards, with the ivy cladding swinging with it. It was a perfect piece of camouflage. The vegetation appeared to cover the whole wall, but on closer inspection it became clear that none of the shoots that clung to the walls crossed the join between the door and the wall.

They crossed the threshold into a pitch-black interior which had a cold, damp edge to it, even on this sultry August night. Shrike closed the door behind them and reached for the shelf just inside the doorway. There was a repeated clash of steel on flint, and suddenly the darkness fled from a flare of light. The spark from the tinder box caught on the kindling, followed by the warm flood of light as Shrike expertly managed to light the lamp that was there waiting for him.

The yellow flame dispelled the darkness, pushing it back into the corners. He held it high in front of him, and the shadows danced grotesquely across the walls and floor like a crazy puppet show. Their eyes slowly adjusted to the gloom and the sudden, flickering flashes of lamp light. Gradually, they began to piece together a picture of the room they were in. It was spacious, with a high ceiling, and a stone floor. There were hooks hanging down from the ceiling, and on one side of the room, a vast black cooking range, still with some ancient pans in place on the hob. Much of the walls were taken up with cupboards and some of the doors hung open, revealing neat piles of crockery within.

Even in the badly lit night, they could see it was enormous, a kitchen made to service hundreds of people rather than simply the needs of a rich family. Before they could ask any questions, Shrike put down his lamp, turned back to the door and locked it. Grace and Clara exchanged glances.

"Why are you locking us in, Shrike?" asked Grace uneasily. "You don't need to do that, surely?"

"The last thing we need is to spend the night worrying about someone walking straight through the door and murdering us in our beds. It's the only way in, you see."

His earnest smile was meant to disarm them, and Grace, always looking for a reason to trust him, returned it. Encouraged, he continued.

"Come on, we all need to eat and drink. And talk. Follow me, but be careful. Some of the floorboards are missing."

He moved out of the old kitchen into the corridor, the lantern held high out in front of him so they could all see the way forward. The others followed. As usual, Clara brought up the rear. Passing through the doorway into the hall, she muttered under her breath. "The only way in? That means it's also the only way out. And guess who's got the only key?"

SHADOWS AND COBWEBS

They picked their way through darkened corridors and up flights of stairs, the light from Shrike's lamp swaying to and fro across the walls. In the sweep of the light, strange objects leaped out at them, before disappearing back into the darkness. An oil painting of a startled swan, shelves full of dusty books, and, terrifyingly, a stuffed bear towering on its hind legs, its teeth gleaming in a snarling jaw. Both Grace and Clara cried out and grabbed each other in fear as the lamp picked out this fearsome creature ready to attack them.

Shrike turned calmly back to them, hearing their cries. He held his lamp high and steady so they could see the beast for what it really was: a shabby, stuffed creature trapped in a glass case, forever harmless.

"You see, Ladies? There is nothing to be afraid of here, except your own imagination, and the darkness. The light of day will always banish such fears." He smiled warmly at them.

Clara scowled at him. "Ladies? Don't think for a moment, Master Shrike, that we are silly girls afraid of our own shadows. Your only advantage here is that you have been here before and we have not. We have seen and done things in this world that would freeze the marrow in your bones, young man."

His smile disappeared and his eyes narrowed as he surveyed them. When he spoke, his voice had an icy edge.

"Oh, I'm sure you have. And you will almost certainly have to do so again, before this adventure is over. You will just have to hope that I can match you, eh?"

There was almost a crackle in the air, as Shrike and Clara held each other's gaze in a battle of wills. But then, Clara looked beyond the bear and in the steady light cast by Shrike's lamp, caught a glimpse of one of the rooms off the corridor through an open door. Intrigued, she went to the door, pushed it further open and took a step into the room. There were rows of desks, each one with a chair behind it and a sunken inkwell in the corner. She scanned the walls. There were shelves of books and a large blackboard still with the chalky ghosts of old lessons on it.

"Why," said Grace with some surprise, "it's a classroom."

She turned back to Shrike, whose smile had faded. "Was this a school once then?"

Shrike beckoned her out of the room.

"Come, Miss Clara, we must eat and rest. It's not far now."

They climbed more stairs and in the light of the lamp the corridor became narrower, the walls crowding in upon them. The higher they went, the more dilapidated the building became. There were no surprises looming out of the lamplight up here, just thick cobwebs and crumbling plaster on the walls. As they turned a corner on one landing, they passed in front of a window that looked out onto the grounds. Shrike strode past it, but Grace and Clara paused. The window was broken and the warm night air trickled through the gap. It faced the way they had entered the grounds, across a half moonlit lawn, fading away in the distance to the walls and the beginning of the forest.

They stood side by side at the window and leaned forward to get a better view. Away to their left they could just make out an indistinct mass near the far walls. It was hard in the gloom to tell exactly what it was. A collection of bushes swaying in the wind perhaps? Or the crumbled bricks and stones of a ruined outbuilding. They both peered through the night air, straining their eyes until something definite came into focus.

It was Grace who spoke first. "Is that a…?" She hesitated. "No, it can't be, surely."

Clara continued. "It is. It's a herd of steedhorns, sleeping. Goodness, I've never seen so many in one place before."

She called out to Shrike who had continued his steady progress along the corridor.

"Shrike, did you know there's a herd of steedhorns out here in the grounds?"

He turned, distracted.

"Hmm. Steedhorns? Oh yes, they use the grounds for safety. There's plenty for them to graze on, and hunters don't know they're here. So they're quite safe." He smiled. "Well, at least until we need some meat to eat."

Grace looked aghast. "You mean you hunt them, Shrike? For food? Such beautiful creatures - how could you?"

"It's amazing what people will do if it means they survive. Even a kind-hearted soul like yourself, Miss Grace," he replied coolly.

"We call them unicorns in my world, Shrike. People don't think they exist, that they're just in fairy stories."

Shrike considered for a moment. "We have much to discuss, all three of us. And we can do that now when we eat. And you can tell me all about "your world" as you call it. But come, we are here now."

He moved towards a door leading off the corridor. Grace followed close behind him. Back at the window, Clara lingered to take one last look outside. The steedhorns were still lying down asleep. She looked away to her right, to where they had entered the grounds from the forest earlier. Suddenly her heart leaped. In the darkness, just by the walls, a light flared. She gasped. A fizzing fountain of stars leaped into the night air, swirling and twining around themselves in an upward spiral. But, she knew, only she could see it. To anyone else this was just a blank vista of darkness.

"Thomas!" she whispered. "He is here at last."

"Miss Clara," Shrike called from further ahead. "Don't hang back - the corridors are dangerous in the dark."

She looked into the darkness. Holding the lamp high to illuminate the way, Shrike's face shone out of the gloom, pale and luminous, his red hair aflame in the lamplight.

"Coming!" Clara called back. She made her way to where Shrike and Grace had stopped, her heart still silently singing at what she had seen beyond the wall of the grounds. Shrike turned to the door, another large key in his hand. With a pull of the handle and a twist of the key, the door creaked open. He went in and ushered the girls in as well.

"We'll be safe here," he said.

They looked around the room, and a gasp escaped Grace's lips.

"Oh!" she breathed, looking all around her. "It's huge."

The wall opposite the door was a bank of windows that allowed the half-moon to cast a cold silvery light in the room, such that the lamp was almost not needed. It was a long rectangular room with a high ceiling. Along the other wall, opposite the windows, was a neat row of beds, each with a side table. The beds were little more than cheap wooden frames, each with a thin, stained mattress. There were a few, close to the door, that had meagre pillows and blankets.

Grace and Clara took it all in silently. There were a few drab oil paintings of landscapes on the walls, hanging askew and covered in cobwebs. The ceiling and the corners of the walls were also festooned in cobwebs, and dust was piled high in the corners. A couple of the windows were cracked and lying in a pool of moonlight at the far end, the body of a crow, once glossy jet black, but now a crumpled grey, lay lifeless on the floor.

Clara shuddered. "This used to be a dormitory of some

sort, didn't it? Shrike, it really is time to do some explaining. What is this place? Why have you got keys? Why is it abandoned and derelict? Who else knows about it?"

"All in good time, I promise. Let's eat first. We'll all need our strength in the next day or so and we might not be able to eat quite so easily again."

He laid his saddle bag that he had been carrying so carefully on their journey on to the first bed, nearest the door, and then rummaged for his keys again. He selected one from the bunch, and unlocked the cupboard in the side table. Bending down, he pulled out a half-eaten loaf of bread, a hunk of cheese and a stoppered bottle.

Grace and Clara watched him closely while he prepared. The table and spaces around that first bed showed all the signs of having been used before. There was a notebook on top of the side table, and a metal cup and plate. There was also an ancient cracked mirror and just inside the cupboard they could see two or three well-thumbed books. The other beds in the room seemed untouched in comparison. The bedside tables were covered in dust, and the cupboard doors were splintered and hanging loosely their broken hinges, revealing bare shelves inside. The whole scene looked as if Shrike had been here many times before, but always on his own. His was the only bed that had been used.

There was a fireplace set into the middle of one of the walls, and a pile of logs and kindling neatly stacked by the side. The logs, and the ash and cinders in the grate, showed the fire had been recently lit. Shrike saw them look hopefully at the fireplace.

"No fire tonight, I'm afraid," he said apologetically. "It would be good to have something hot to eat - a nice cut of steedhorn, perhaps, but we can't risk it, not when Mulgrave's men are out looking for us. They might see the smoke."

He cleared a space on the next bed and laid out the

food, as if it were a table. Then he opened a large cupboard in the far corner of the room and got extra plates and cups for Grace and Clara. Finally, he opened the bottle and poured three drinks.

"What's that?" Clara asked suspiciously.

"Small beer," he replied. "It's the only drink that won't go off if it's stored for a long time. It's very weak, and it's a lot healthier than water."

Grace and Clara looked at the food and drink spread out in front of them. Suddenly, they realised just how hungry they were. They each tore off a piece of bread and cheese and devoured it as if it might be their last. Silence fell on the silvered, shadowy room as they each ate their fill.

*

The trail of stars carefully left by Clara led them steadily to the grounds of Hard Crag. Tom retraced their steps and found the entrance the others had used half an hour earlier.

"This is where we go in," he said.

As usual, it was much easier for Dan. His ghostly form zoomed over the high stone wall to check what awaited them on the other side. For Della and Tom, it involved some shinning up a ten feet tall crumbling stone wall. Eventually they reached the top, with scraped knuckles and aching muscles, and were able to jump down on the other side comfortably.

In front of them stood the impressive bulk of the house, all in darkness in the hollow of the grounds. Tom looked up at one of the towers at the corner of the building. His heart skipped a jump, as he saw the rising spiral of stars, splitting the night sky in front of them.

"Clara!" he said.

Della looked at him, puzzled.

"Can you see her? Is Grace there as well?"

He shook his head. "I don't know, but I'm sure they will be together. I can just see her stars, and I guess that she can probably see mine." He noticed Della's expression. "No, I don't know what they are, either. I just know we both have them."

Della looked up at the imposing dark bulk of the building in front of them, rising out of a sea of weeds, bushes, brambles and ivy all clinging to it, as if trying to bring the building down and strangle it. Her eyes strayed to the top of the house where Tom had pointed. Suddenly she froze and caught her breath.

"Look!" she hissed. "Up there, where you saw the stars. There's a light, I'm sure of it."

All three of them looked up. Sure enough, a thin, feeble smudge of light lit the black window frame. Silhouetted against it was a figure, looking out into the darkness. It was impossible at that distance to tell who it was.

Immediately, Tom looked to Dan.

"Can you get up there, Dan, and have a quick look? It would be good to know what we're getting ourselves into."

"You think that's a good idea? She'd absolutely freak out if I just zoomed through the walls three stories up."

"I'm not exactly sure what "freak out" means, but I can guess. He's right," Della agreed. "Maybe we should all get in and then Dan can do his thing while we creep around in the shadows. We don't want to let Shrike know we're here. We still don't know whose side he's on."

Tom thought for a moment. "Yes, that's what we'll do. Between us, we should manage it. But we must slip in without a noise."

He headed off again, following the trail of stars Clara had left, towards the house. After a minute or two, they arrived at the small door at the side of the house that Shrike and the others had used. Della tried the handle. It was locked. She tried it again. First giving it a rattle, and then, as quietly as she could, a push with her shoulder.

"Damn!" she exclaimed. "It's locked. We'll have to find another way in."

"They must have come in this way," Tom said. "The

trail of stars is quite clear here. That means that Shrike must have a key and he's locked them all in."

He shook his head. "I don't like it. We need to get in here to see that they're all right. But we've got to do it without making any noise. The last thing we want is to alert Shrike."

"Leave it to me," said Dan, his wispy outline rippling like smoke from a candle. "I've been dying to do a bit of ghosting."

He didn't wait for an answer, but slipped through the solid door in an instant.

Della and Tom waited anxiously outside in the dark. In the silence of the night, their ears sharpened to the sounds that were imperceptible before. The hoot of an owl. The creak of the breeze in the timbers of the house. A rustling in the thick undergrowth that had pressed up against the building. And then, just as it seemed that they could not bear the waiting any longer, a fume of silvery smoke leaked through the heavy wooden door, and Dan reassembled himself in front of them. He bobbed and grinned, looking very pleased with himself.

"Well?" demanded Tom. "You look pleased with yourself. Come on, spit it out? What did you find?"

"And more importantly, can we get in?" added Della with some impatience.

By way of celebration, Dan suddenly rocketed into the sky and then plunged back to earth, tumbling head over heels like a gymnast. By the time he returned to where they were standing, he had slowed and came to a graceful landing. His smile was even wider than normal.

"Dan, you are so annoying when you're pleased with yourself. Just tell us, man. What happened?"

He made a conscious effort to straighten his face and then continued.

"It's a right mess in there. Pitch black, full of rubbish and cobwebs and whatnot. Some of the floorboards are missing, and I got the feeling that there's plenty of mice and rats scuttling around. Feels like it's been empty for years. But the door opens into the old kitchen and I found a window that's broken. If you reach in through the hole in the glass, you can pull the handle and open it. It's big enough for you to climb through. Come on, I'll show you."

He drifted along the side of the house to a window that was almost completely covered in ivy. Tom and Della followed him. A minute later they were inside, after Della's leather riding gauntlets had made short work of the shards of glass left in the broken window pane. To Tom's relief, in the darkness, the trail of stars Clara had left for him to follow were clearly visible. They were definitely on the right track.

"Listen, you're both going to have to follow me. Stay close - we can't risk having a light and the floorboards are treacherous. We can't talk, except whispers in an emergency. When the star trail runs out, you'll have to do your ghost thing again, Dan. But be careful. We can't assume that Shrike is Mr Nice Guy."

They nodded and then set off into the dark depths of the house. Gradually their eyes got accustomed to the light, and they made steady progress, picking their way past piles of rubbish, broken furniture and loose floorboards. After a few minutes, and several flights of stairs, Tom slowed to a halt, raising his arm to warn Della and Dan who were close behind. He turned and raised his finger to his lips, and then jabbed it forward, pointing to a door just ahead of them along the corridor. They crept along and huddled together just outside the door.

In the stillness of the house, the sound of conversation from the other side of the door came through, low but perfectly clear. They settled for a moment, aware of every creak of the floorboards and every gust of wind outside. For a second or two, until their ears had attuned to the quiet, they heard their own careful breathing and the thumping of their hearts.

*

On the other side of the door, Grace and Clara sat on one of the beds, surrounded by the remnants of their meal. On the bed next to them was Shrike.

"What I still don't understand is how you know about this place. You've obviously stayed here before. You've got a cupboard with your stuff in it. The food is a bit stale but not rotting or anything, so you must be a frequent visitor here. And you've got a key and seem to be able to find your way around the building blindfold." Clara paused for breath. Shrike maintained his silence, judging what he could say in response and what he still needed to be cagey about.

Grace took up the questions.

"What is this place, Shrike? And why does no-one seem to know anything about it? It's well hidden, and the top of the moor is wild and desolate, but the locals always know everything. I've not been here long, but no one has ever mentioned a house like this by White Water Falls."

She hesitated.

"Was it some kind of school? Must have been a very long time ago if it was. The place obviously hasn't been used for years."

Finally, Shrike responded. "Yes, it was a school, I think, but it's been left abandoned for years. I just came across it by chance, when I was doing some work up on the moors for Lord Mulgrave. The boundary of his estate is not far from here. I came in to have a look, expecting to find at least one groundsman or someone guarding it, but there was no-one. It was completely deserted. So I broke in to have a look around and I thought it would be good to have as my little secret. Somewhere I could go and escape whenever I wanted to be on my own to think, away from the people at Mulgrave Hall. I always felt like I was being watched there."

Grace nodded. "I can understand that. Sometimes you need to get away from everyone."

Shrike and Grace exchanged a quick smile. Clara felt a pang of guilt, watching her. She sounded so sad. She must have felt totally abandoned when she arrived in Yngerlande knowing nothing and no-one. No wonder Thomas had asked her to keep an eye out for her, to be her friend. And really, when she thought about it, she had failed in that.

Shrike continued. "I mentioned it to some of the lads at Mulgrave Hall, and one or two of the pubs round and about, but whenever I did, there was an awkward silence and folk changed the subject. The most I ever got out of them was the idea that something terrible had happened here and that it had been closed down, years ago. The tale was that the house was cursed or haunted or something and that none of the locals would go near the place, not even in daylight. Well, that made it perfect for me. I knew I could stay here undisturbed. So, bit by bit, I moved some of my stuff up here."

He shifted awkwardly on his bed. "So, now you know. And I must ask you not to tell anyone else. I don't want to lose this as a hiding place."

Clara had been listening intently, holding Shrike in a steady, sceptical gaze.

"Alright, so that's how you know about this place. And I understand having to leave The Rectory, in case Mulgrave's men came back for us. But what now? What's your plan? If you really are on our side, like you say, how exactly are we going to release Silas and all of our friends from Mulgrave Hall? Not to mention my mother."

Shrike thought for a moment, weighing up all his options. Finally, he spoke.

"They are expecting me to return, and to make some arrangement to bring you to them. They can't do anything without you. So, we have some leverage there. I'll pretend to negotiate with them, for as much money as I can carry. They think that I am working for them, but they don't really trust me."

"They're not the only ones," said Clara drily.

Shrike held up his hands. "Alright, Clara. I know you don't like me. That's not a problem, I'm used to not being liked. You're the daughter of a Queen. All of your life you've had servants at your beck and call. Fine clothes, the best education, money and power. You can't possibly understand the life of someone like me. What it's like to have nothing. Not knowing where you're going to sleep each night, or when your next meal might come along. Having to live on your wits and learning to trust no-one. That's the main thing I've learned. In the end, all of us are on our own. You cannot rely on anyone but yourself, because everyone else is on the make. Friends are a luxury that people like me can't afford."

He stopped, apparently overcome with bitterness, a pained expression on his face.

Grace stepped towards him and laid her hand on his arm. "I can understand that, Shrike. I know what you're feeling."

He took her hand and squeezed it.

"Thank you for that, Grace. I think you do understand, I really do."

Then he let go and turned to Clara.

"I'm going back to Mulgrave Hall to cheat them. I'll go on my own, and work out a way of forcing them to release your friends. It's too dangerous for you two to go. If you turn up there, they have enough soldiers to capture you. Then you'll be in the dungeons with the rest of your friends, and before you know it, Clara, your mother will have been deposed, and the two of you will be dispatched to a nunnery while Oliver becomes King."

He stopped, his eyes gleaming and determined.

"And some time later, when he is safely on the throne, and he has soldiers in every town of Yngerlande, the pair of you will simply disappear, never to be seen again. Is that what you really want to happen?"

"No, of course not," Clara snapped back, "but it's also

too dangerous for us to stay here. What do you expect us to do? Just wait here for Mulgrave's soldiers to come for us, while you are left there laughing at us? We're not as stupid as you seem to think."

"But Clara," Grace interjected, "that doesn't make sense. Shrike could have just made us stay at The Rectory if all he wanted was to hand us over. You're not being fair to him."

"No, Grace, you're blinded by him, because you think he's your friend. Your first true friend. But he isn't. The reason he's brought us here is because here he still has control over us. We are his bargaining chips. If we had waited at The Rectory, the soldiers would have just captured us and taken us back to Mulgrave Hall. Shrike would have been left with nothing. Don't you see, this way he gets the money. And they will pay a fortune for us, because without us, Oliver can't easily become King."

Shrike stood up from his bed, and reached for his saddle bag. His face had gone very still, save for his eyes that darted back and forth around the darkened room. Just at that moment there was a blur of movement and noise and action. The door to the passage slammed open, banging against the side wall, and through the gap strode Della, two flintlock pistols in her hands. Her dark hair streamed behind her, and the lights from the lamp sparkled on her silver and jet jewellery, and the barrels of her pistols. Shrike shrank back in alarm.

"Take your hands off those bags," Della shouted. "Step into the middle of the room, quickly now! And show me your hands. Now! Hands in the air."

Shrike had recovered his poise by this time. He had quickly appraised the situation, and saw that he had no choice. Slowly, deliberately, he moved away from the bed into the middle of the room with his hands high in the air. But his sense of coming to terms with a new situation lasted only a second. First, the ghostly figure of Dan appeared directly in front of him, as a shimmering fume of silvery smoke, gently pulsing.

Shrike dropped his hands and jumped out of his skin, a gasp of fear escaping his habitual, cool demeanour. Then, before he had a chance to understand what was happening, from the open doorway came a steadily thickening stream of stars. Everyone in the room could see them this time. They stared at the door as the stream turned into a torrent, and then turned their heads, as the stars rushed in to meet a second stream, this time of blue stars that poured from the frozen figure of Clara. The twin streams met in a whirlwind, intertwining in a raging, spitting surge of energy that produced a great rush of wind that blew through the room, breaking the windows and out into the night.

The wind disappeared as quickly as it had sprung up, and in the silent stillness that it left behind, the stars were also suddenly sucked away, and they were all left open mouthed, staring at the space where the twin streams had combined. It was Clara that broke the silence.

"Hello, Thomas," she said simply. "What took you so long?"

STARS AND STONES

There had been a flurry of hugs and greetings, and tears had been shed. Throughout it all, Shrike had stood apart, watching carefully, desperately trying to make sense of the extraordinary theatre he had just witnessed. Ghosts, guns and a spectacular display of cosmic energy of incredible power had not been part of his plan. He would have to rethink, and quickly. He knew, even in the midst of this outpouring of emotion, that shortly, probably in the next minute, all of that would evaporate and some hard questions would be asked. It was essential that he had ready answers.

But even as his reptilian brain whirred furiously, grappling with this dilemma, another part of him, a part he hardly recognised, was both baffled and entranced by the genuine display of emotion that was being played out in front of him. He was gripped by jealousy and had never more acutely felt the outsider. He watched, fascinated as Thomas and Grace, brother and sister separated by death, finally let go of each other, tears streaming down their cheeks. He supposed this was love, but he wasn't sure. It was something he had often heard of, never felt and assumed was simply a fairy story. Perhaps, he thought, it really did exist.

But for now, he had more pressing things to deal with. After her initial reunion with Grace and Clara, Della had kept her pistols aimed at Shrike's head, just to stop him entertaining ideas of making a run for it. Daniel shimmered palely in the gloom, with occasional swoops around the dormitory, just to make sure Shrike didn't get too comfortable. And if all that wasn't enough, Shrike's mind kept going back to the mind-boggling display of stars that had erupted on Tom and Clara's reunion. Like everything else, it was totally inexplicable by any normal standards, but Shrike knew that of all the wonders he had just witnessed, the chemistry between those two was the most significant, the most powerful. In short, the most to be feared.

Tom stepped away from Grace and turned to Shrike, who stood facing the others who were arrayed in front of him in a semicircle, blocking any escape.

"So, Shrike, if that's your name, let's cut to the chase. There is a lot to do and time is short," he said.

"Shrike is my name," he replied, with a touch of defiance in his voice, "but you have the advantage of me there. I don't know who you are, or your companions, and I don't know why you feel you must point guns in my face. It's not very friendly."

Tom smiled and nodded to Della.

"It's a fair point. I think you can put them away now, Della. They've served their purpose, keeping him quiet until he worked out who was in charge."

She returned the nod and lowered her guns.

Thomas began again.

"My name is Thomas Trelawney, from England. Grace here is my sister, and Della is a friend to Silas Cummerbund and all at The Rectory."

Shrike nodded at Dan who was quietly shimmering like a candle flame, a foot or two off the ground.

"And the ghost?"

Tom laughed. "You seem very calm, Shrike. Do you believe in ghosts, then?"

"I did not until now. But I trust my own eyes and believe them. It's what other people tell me that I don't believe."

"Dan is my cousin, also from England. But here in

Yngerlande, in your land, he can only appear in ghostly form. But as to belief, you are going to have to trust what I say, no matter how hard it is for you. It will be your only chance of getting out of this alive."

Shrike snorted. "You don't know me very well, do you? There is nothing that can keep me held down for long. Nothing."

"We'll see about that later. But for now, we need a plan, and the one you just outlined won't do. You can't go to Mulgrave Hall on your own, because we don't trust you. We will have to come with you. Dan can remain invisible, so that bit is easy. And as you've seen, Grace and I have certain powers that will allow us to release Silas and the others, and then rescue the Queen."

"But are you sure about these powers, as you call them? I spent the summer in York, in Kings Manor, watching Cummerbund and the Princess here practising her powers."

Clara looked dumbfounded. "What?! You were there? But how? We did not see you."

Shrike smiled. "Yes, I was there. And no, you never saw me. Or at least, you weren't aware of who I was. You should think about that very carefully."

Grace looked at first surprised and then very upset. Her eyes sparkled with the beginning of tears.

"But, Shrike, why were you spying on them if you have good intentions towards us? I don't understand. That's not what you told me before."

His voice softened. "Grace, you must trust me. I know it looks bad, and yes, I was working for Lord Mulgrave. But I did tell you that, right when we first met. And now I've seen what he is planning, I will work against him. He thinks I'm his servant. That could be very useful when we finally get to Mulgrave Hall. I've told you the truth."

Grace fell silent, trying to take in what Shrike had just said.

Tom interjected. "But why is it important that you saw

Clara in training? How does that change anything?"

"The Princess is good, very good. And I watched her powers grow and her control of them increase. But she has not used them since, when she has had ample opportunity to do so. I don't think she has full control of them. I think she doubts herself. To be blunt, she cannot be relied upon, particularly in a crisis."

Tom looked across at Clara.

"What do you think, Clara? Can you control your powers?"

She shook her head. "I could with Silas. There were all kinds of things I could do at Kings Manor. But since he has been away, nothing works any more, apart from little, trifling things. I have tried. All the way from The Rectory, through the tunnels and over the moors to here, but none of my spells have worked. I'm sorry, Tom."

She hung her head and looked down at her feet. There was silence in the old dormitory. It was Shrike who broke it.

"So, you see, Master Thomas, your plan is over before it begins. Clara can't use her powers reliably enough to defeat Oliver and Jacob. The only plan still on the table is mine. I will go alone to Mulgrave Hall."

"That really won't be necessary. Look!" said Tom, in triumph.

He fumbled inside the pocket of his frock coat, and pulled out his closed fist, which he showed to everyone in the room. Slowly, his fingers opened, one by one, revealing a pebble already beginning to glow the deepest blue.

"The Sounding Stone!" breathed Grace. "I didn't know you had one."

"A gift from Silas," he replied.

He held the stone high in the air on his palm, and its blue light filled every corner of the dormitory. Then, from the pocket of Clara's coat, another blue light, this time with a tinge of green, began to leak. Slowly at first, but then as a raging flood, the light surged from her pocket and combined with the light coming from the stone in Tom's hand, sliding and twining until the two lights were completely commingled.

Clara gasped, unsure what was happening. Her face was garishly illuminated in the light that seemed at its strongest between her chest and chin.

"But where is it coming from?" she managed to ask at last.

Della stepped towards her, a frown creasing her face. She reached out towards Clara's chest, sending ripples of blue green light cascading over the walls that produced crazily dancing shadows of jagged, elongated shapes.

"It's coming from your heart, Clara. Your heart."

Clara reached down and put her hand inside her shirt. She fumbled for a moment, as if wrestling with a particularly difficult button, and then managed to pull out her hand. She opened her hand and there, in the middle of her palm, lay another Sounding Stone. The second she opened her hand to show them, the explosion of stars from both her and Thomas began again. It raged around them, accompanied by a howling wind that scoured the walls of the dormitory, knocking pictures from the walls and overturning furniture. They all had to grab hold of something to stay on their feet, such was the power of this sudden typhoon. Their hair streamed in the wind and their features were contorted in the struggle to stay upright.

All except Tom and Clara. They stood perfectly still and calm, untroubled by the great forces swirling around them. And then, in a second, the light and the stars and the winds surged out of all the windows, ripping open the locked door at the end of the dorm, and they dispersed into the night air. An eerie, still silence descended on them, blanketing everything and everyone in the room.

The others, one by one, let go of whatever they were holding on to and began to recover themselves, straightening their hair and brushing down their clothes in an attempt to catch their breath and make sense of what had just happened.

"Hell's teeth!" whispered Shrike. "What was that? There is some powerful magic at work here."

Clara looked down at her hand, the Sounding Stone by now transformed back into a humble pebble.

"It's my Stone! Silas gave it to me, just before he left for Mulgrave Hall. I sewed it into a hidden pocket in my shirt, just above my heart. I had forgotten all about it, until now." She smiled. "Silas knew we would need it and here it is."

"The two Stones work together to multiply their power," explained Tom. "With the two of them, you will be able to use all of the powers you worked on with Silas, and even more, probably."

He turned to Shrike. "So, you see, Shrike, our plan is the only thing that can work. And now you've seen what power we can control, I'm sure you will want to be on our side."

Shrike's eyes, glittering in the light of the half-moon outside, glanced imperceptibly to his saddle bag, still lying on the floor by the bed. A stroke of luck, he thought to himself, that it hadn't been hanging up on the peg because it would have been blown all over the dorm, with catastrophic consequences.

"Yes indeed," he said finally, "that was very impressive."

Grace surveyed the wreckage of the room.

"Just a minute," she said, "where's Dan?"

They all cast their eyes around every corner of the dorm. His shimmering form was nowhere to be seen amongst the debris from the explosive events that had just occurred: broken furniture, window glass, overturned beds.

"Master Daniel!" called Della. There was no answer, just the sound of the summer breeze a little louder, now many of the windows were smashed.

"Dan! Come on, man, this is no time for messing

about! Where are you? Show yourself!"

Again, nothing stirred.

The tone of Tom's voice changed now.

"Dan, you're starting to worry me now. Are you alright?"

The room was darker now than before. Their one lamp had been smashed in the roaring wind that had passed through and the only light was from the half-moon outside. But then, they all became aware of millions of pinpricks of light all over the walls, ceiling and floor of the dorm. The light intensified, and the tiny brilliant beacons began to shuffle together, converging on one spot in the middle of the room.

They all stared as the dots of light grew, taking on a definite shape in front of them. What more could possibly happen? As the shape gradually came into focus, their bemusement changed, first to disbelief and then mild amusement. Finally, as they could no longer doubt the evidence in front of their own eyes, Tom burst out laughing. There in front of him was the shimmering figure of Dan, in his usual ghostly form. Except that it wasn't quite his usual form. The reassembling of the pinpricks of light had not quite gone to plan. Dan's nose was firmly attached to his bottom and his head was tucked underneath his arm. The final indignity was that his dreadlocks had attached themselves to his chin, leaving him resembling nothing more than a giant, dying sunflower.

The others joined in Tom's laughter. Even Shrike abandoned his usual sarcastic smirk for a wide smile of disbelief. Deep within the head of the sunflower, Dan's mouth was set in a grim straight line.

"It's really not very funny," he hissed between gritted teeth. "Not very funny at all."

"Look on the bright side, Dan, that wind could have blown you all over the grounds and woods outside," said Tom, struggling to get his giggles under control.

"Sometimes I wish I'd never ever walked through that grandfather clock with you. Just give me a second. I'll have another go to straighten myself out."

His face creased with effort needed to reassemble his particles, as if he were lifting an enormously heavy object. Gradually his shape began to shift in front of them until he had completed the task.

"How do I look?" he asked.

"Back to your beautiful best, Master Daniel," replied Della, her face lit up with a smile.

To celebrate, he zoomed to the ceiling and back again, doing several somersaults on the way.

When he landed, he gave a little bow, like a gymnast completing a particularly difficult routine. Pleased with himself, he proclaimed, "Come on then, there's no point hanging around. Let's get on with it."

There was no time for a reply. The door at the end of the dormitory that had been ripped open by the power of the Stones, suddenly blew open again, slamming against the wall with a tremendous crash. In the dormitory, they all jumped out of their skins, their nerves jangling. The door slowed down, swinging gently to a halt, its hinges creaking eerily until all that could be heard was a growing sound of the wind out into the night.

They relaxed after the initial shock. They all looked around at each other, one to the other, to share their sense of relief.

"What's in–" began Thomas.

He got no further. From the darkness of the newly opened room came new sounds. First, the hooting of a single owl, joined by more and more, until there was a crescendo of owls all hooting together. Then came a snuffling and shuffling and the sound of heavy steps coming towards the gaping doorway.

They all looked at each other, gripped with fear, and then looked to Shrike.

"What the hell is that?" demanded Clara.

THE MENAGERIE

"We won't find out by hanging around out here. We need to go and take a look," said Dan breezily.

Tom snorted. "That's easy for you to say, Ghost Boy. Whatever is in there won't even see you, so you're safe. Not the same for the rest of us."

Della stepped forward. "We should all go in together, then. Better to face it like that."

"But what's in there, Shrike? You must know?" asked Grace.

They all turned to look at Shrike who was standing at the back of the group. He was cowering against the wall, his face disfigured by a look of sick horror.

"I don't know," he stammered, his voice breaking. "I can't go in there. You can't make me."

They had never heard Shrike speak like this before. His voice, normally so weary and cynical, was quivering with emotion. Grace stepped forward and reached out her hand to touch his cheek. He flinched, like a whipped dog expecting another blow from its cruel master. She stroked his cheek and spoke soothingly to him.

"It's alright, Shrike, you don't have to go in."

Frowns and raised eyebrows shot round the group. Then Tom intervened.

"Grace, you stay put here and keep an eye on him, ok? We'll go and look." He turned to the others. "Ready? Come on."

Cautiously, he stepped towards the open doorway, the others right behind him. Then, with a final look behind him, he stepped over the threshold. It was noticeably lighter inside and colder. There was a cool breeze on his face. Despite this, there was a sharp, pungent smell in the air, harsh and chemical. He looked up and found himself looking directly at the velvet black night sky, studded with stars and drifting clouds. The light from the half-moon, just visible at the edge of the jagged hole in the roof, cast a soft silvery light into the space. He took another step inside and immediately at the far end, there was a rustling and a scratching sound, accompanied by the soft clearing of many throats. He looked that way and saw immediately just how big the room was. It was like a football pitch and seemed to run the entire length of the house. He narrowed his eyes to try to see what was making the noises, but that end of the room was shrouded in deep shadow.

The room was derelict, like many of the others in the house, but this was worse. They couldn't tell how long the room had been open to the elements, but the damage was already considerable. The walls were stained and in sections the plaster was crumbling away. There were a few standing pools of water collected on the floor and the boards underneath were warped and blackened.

Tom could make out a strange variety of furniture spread around the walls, but it wasn't obvious what the purpose of each item was. He took a step forward to the nearest one and began to examine it closely. Behind him came Della, Clara and Dan, who all began to fan out to investigate the cavernous room. Tom reached towards the bench in front of him.

"Is that…?" he began and then stopped abruptly. "Hey, come and look at this. This isn't just an attic room, it's more like…like a prison."

In his hand he held a set of chains and leather restraints that were connected to a large horizontal pair of wooden beams.

"Aren't they the stocks?" asked Dan. "You know, those things that were used in the olden days. You stuck your head and wrists in the holes and then you were locked up. People could come and throw rotten fruit at you. We did it in History."

Tom looked more carefully at the old wooden surface that was rough and splintered.

"I think rotten fruit would be the least of your problems if you were stuck in these bad boys," he said. "Look - I think this is blood. Old and dried maybe, but still blood."

"And look over there," said Clara, pointing at the wall between a pair of tall wooden cabinets, "stuffed animals. There are stuffed Steedwings there."

They all swung round to take a look. It was true. There were two magnificent Steedwings, tall and powerful, their brilliant glossy white coats covering toned muscles. Their shaggy manes hung down from squat, lean necks and their huge wings were neatly folded by their flanks. They were half in shadows and half in moonlight. The light made their coats glow out of the darkness.

They stared in admiration at these exotic creatures, their mouths hanging open in awe.

"Wait a minute," stammered Della. "No, they can't be, surely… They, they're real…"

As they looked, the Steedwing furthest away pawed its hoof on the floorboard. Its companion whinnied, and suddenly shook its mane, as if it were troubled by a fly.

"What the…?" started Dan.

Then the first Steedwing took a step towards them, as if they had both decided on something.

All of them, except for Clara, took a few paces back towards the door.

"Whoa, I don't like this," said Tom. "This is not good at all."

While the others clustered together in fear, Clara walked towards them, clicking her tongue. They came to meet her.

"Clara!" began Della. "I'm not sure this is a good idea."

Tom reached for her arm. "No, it's alright, look. Remember last Christmas, when we were stuck up on the Moors?"

The Steedwings towered over her. She held out her hands to them and they both knelt at her feet, allowing her to stroke their heads, ears and mane. One at a time, she nuzzled their heads and began to whisper into their ears, in a language that none of the others could recognise. The Steedwings whinnied with pleasure. After a moment, she stepped back and invited the others to take her place, so that the Steedwings could get their measure. After a moment or two of stroking, whispering and snuffling, the introductions seemed to have been completed, although the animals were, at first, a little disconcerted by Daniel the ghost.

Then, they all drew back and began to talk in lower voices.

"What was that cool language you were using, Clara?" asked Dan. "When you were talking to the Steedwings?"

She looked puzzled. "Was I talking in a different language? I don't know what it was. I didn't even know I was doing it, it just sort of happens. They seem to know who and what I am. It's strange, because I don't know myself. Anyway, they are at peace with us."

"But what are they doing here? How did they get in? Do they live here? Seems weird, huge animals like them living in a top floor flat."

Clara frowned. "What's a top floor flat?"

It was Dan's turn to frown. "It's a…oh, never mind. It's an England thing."

Della looked up. "I suppose they started coming in when the roof collapsed. The hole's big enough. Maybe it's safer for them up here, where nobody comes, than being out on the high moor. People hunt Steedhorns. And a Steedwing would be worth something. Most folk think they are extinct."

"Don't look now," said Tom, "but they're not the only

things that have moved in."

He silently pointed upwards, to the ceiling directly above their heads. It was in the corner of the room space, away from the gaping hole in the middle of the ceiling. At first it appeared to be an uneven black mass, but as their eyes focused, they all saw what it was.

Della shuddered and her hand flew to her face. "Uurggh! Are they…"

"Bats," confirmed Tom, "hundreds of them."

Now they had been identified, it became easier to spot them. It was a colony of roosting bats, all hanging upside down from the rafters, strange, angular parcels, like black leather stretched around twigs. Suddenly a handful of them dropped and flitted around their heads, swooping and plunging and clicking. They all dropped to their knees, scrabbling in the hair with clawing hands, as if they were afraid that a bat would get tangled up with them. But as quickly as it had happened, the individual bats dispersed, and with papery fluttering and squeaks, they rose out of the broken roof and into the warm night air.

They watched them go, each of them still wanting to scratch at their skin.

"That's what the smell is," said Tom, "their urine is like ammonia. Nasty stuff. They must have gone hunting. Maybe they go out at different times in groups."

"Long as they don't hunt humans," said Dan, "they can go out whenever they like, as far as I'm concerned. Pretty creepy though."

"They're harmless," said Clara, "and we need to investigate the rest of this room, just in case."

She set off to walk to the far end of the cavernous space, leaving the Steedwings and the bat colony behind. The others followed, picking their way carefully over and around the debris that covered the floorboards. They reasoned that the floorboards must be safe if they could take the weight of the two enormous Steedwings, so their attention was focused on the walls and the ceiling. They stopped occasionally to linger by a strange piece of equipment or furniture. There were several metal cages, with chains and handcuffs fastened to the bars, and at some places in the walls, metal contraptions that were shaped like a human being, were secured by strong bolts.

They looked at each other, with expressions of disbelief and a growing sense of horror.

"I think some terrible things have gone on in this room," said Della, shaking her head, and holding a heavy chain with a spike at the end of it. She got no further with her speculation. There was a sudden whoosh of wing beats above them, and silhouetted against the half-moon in the room hole, was an enormous snowy owl that swooped through the space, a limp rat hanging from its beak. Its flight, almost silent now, banked steeply upwards and the owl landed on a cross beam at the far end of the room, directly opposite the bat colony.

Their eyes followed the smooth and silent flight path of the owl to its destination. There was one more surprise waiting for them. There were a set of multiple beams set across the roof space, and roosting there, silent and impassive, were ten or more other owls. They gripped the beams equal distances apart, and sat in the shadows like a row of ancient statues that had been carved long ago. The latest arrival gripped the rat in one set of razor-sharp talons, and began to tear its flesh in strips with its powerful beak.

It was an eerie scene, Steedwings, bats and owls, frozen in the shadows and moonlight, surrounded by broken and rotting furniture. They stood in silence for a moment, waiting for the next surprise.

"It comes to something," said Dan, bobbing like a boat at sea, "when I'm the least weird thing in the room."

The laughter broke the tension and they all felt able to move forward with a plan again.

"I'm just gonna do a quick whizz round to check there are no more horrors waiting for us. It'll just save time."

"Good idea," agreed Tom. "Then we should go back in and lock this door again, just in case the Steedwings change their minds about us. It's time to ask Shrike some more questions."

Dan didn't need to be asked twice. Within seconds he had zoomed around every nook and cranny of the massive room. He even drifted out through the ceiling hole to check what was on the roof. And then he was back, bobbing and looking pleased with himself.

"It's all clear out there. Come on, let's get out of here."

"Yeah, you're right. Time to nail down this plan with Shrike," agreed Tom.

They turned back to the entrance to the room and picked their way past puddles and broken equipment. At the open doorway, Clara shouted out, "Hey, Grace, you should have seen the strange animals in this room. They were…"

She stopped as she crossed the threshold and didn't finish her sentence. The dormitory was empty. Grace and Shrike, who minutes earlier had seemed distraught, had both vanished.

SECRETS AND LIES

She had been grateful when the others had gone into the far room, leaving her alone with Shrike. "To keep an eye on him", they had said, as if he were some kind of criminal. Why couldn't they see? It seemed perfectly obvious to Grace that Shrike was much misunderstood, and that nobody was willing to give him a chance. He was the first person she had met in Yngerlande that seemed genuinely interested in her. Since she had died in England and been given a second chance at life in Yngerlande, she had struggled to adapt. She felt guilty even thinking about it, never mind saying it out loud. The others were very kind, and had been very good to her, but it wasn't like having your own, proper friends.

And so, when Shrike had seemed concerned about her, and asked her questions, and seemed to understand loneliness and suffering, it was like a breath of fresh air. There is nothing more powerful than the feeling of connection with another person, and Grace was dizzy with the feeling. After so many months of sadness, this was blissfully unfamiliar.

The others went off on their adventure in the next room. It seemed appropriate somehow. She looked across at Shrike, still cowering in the corner.

"What happened in that room, Shrike? Why is this house important to you? It's not just a good hiding place, is it? Something happened here, something you can't bear to think about, and yet you keep coming here, by the look of this dorm."

She paused and looked around. Amid the rotting plaster, blackened floorboards and broken furniture, Shrike had carved out a little place that was his. A desk, of sorts. Books and notebooks. Food and drink. The cold, sad remnants of a fire, that ultimate symbol of homeliness, lingered in the grate, forensic evidence of previous lonely nights spent here at Hard Crag. What was it all about?

Shrike hesitated. He was still struggling with whatever dark fears haunted him about the room at the end of the dorm. Finally, with a conscious act of will, he stirred himself.

"You're right. This is a fearful place to me. But I have never spoken of it, not to anyone. I feel that, perhaps, I could speak of it to you and you might understand. But not now, not with the others. They are suspicious of me. I don't blame them. I would be in their place. But then, I have always been suspicious about everyone I meet."

He paused, lost in thought for a moment, and then turned his piercing green eyes on Grace.

"Except for you," he said, lowering his voice. "I don't know why."

"Listen, Shrike, we haven't got much time. The others will be back in a minute. What do you plan to do? You should listen to Tom. I hear what you say about trust, but surely you can see that we are more reliable than Oliver and Jacob. Not to mention Lord Mulgrave."

Shrike hesitated, his eyes flicking this way and that, but always lingering on the broken door to the adjoining room.

"I can't explain in here, with that door open. I stay in here because the door is always locked. To be so close, but safe on the other side of the door, helps me think I am winning, bit by bit. But not with the door open."

"Winning what, Shrike? Tell me." She took his hand in hers. It was shaking. "I can't help you if you won't tell me."

He squeezed her hand. "Come with me, just for a minute, and I'll tell you."

"Where to?"

"Come, I'll show you."

He stood and helped her to her feet, picking up one of the flickering candles with his other hand.

"It's just through here."

He led her through the door into the darkness of the corridor, holding the candle high in front of him to light the way. He turned in the direction away from the room that was so terrifying to him and stopped a few yards later in front of another door. He turned the handle and ushered Grace inside.

"It's alright, we'll be safe in here," he said, following her in and shutting the door behind them. Grace gasped as she took in her surroundings, revealed little by little in the light cast by the candle. Shelves, floor to ceiling, emerged from the surrounding darkness, crammed with books.

"Is this some kind of library?" she asked, peering into the gloom beyond the flickering candle.

"No," replied Shrike, holding the candle up high, "it's just a book cupboard, like a store room. I used to hide in here sometimes, in the corner, and read."

He led her to the end of the shelf and turned a corner, where there were a couple of chairs hidden behind some dusty boxes. He led her to them and they sat, facing each other.

"I have never told anyone this," he began. "You must swear to me you will not say anything to anyone."

She took his hand again.

"Not a word. I promise."

*

When Grace and Shrike finally returned to the dormitory, they met a hostile reaction.

"Where have you two been?" Tom asked irritably. "We've been worried sick about you. We've looked everywhere."

"You didn't look very hard," replied Shrike. "We were just along the corridor, talking." Grace saw Tom's fists clench at Shrike's reply. Her voice was calm and reassuring in response.

"We were just talking, Tom. There's nothing to worry about."

Tom went to open his mouth in reply, but thought better of it. His stance relaxed, his fists unclenched.

"Alright," he conceded, "you're here now. Sit down and listen. We've got a lot to talk about, and some big decisions to make."

They settled down, each perched on the edge of a bed, and began.

They went over it several times before it was decided and agreed. Finally, with a smudge of light appearing on the horizon, over the tops of the trees that separated High Crag from the moors, they called it a day.

Tom surveyed the ranks of beds lined up in the dormitory.

"What do you think, Shrike?" he asked. "Are those beds OK to sleep on?"

"My bed is the only one that has been used for years," he answered. "But the rest are dry at least. I'd sleep on them, rather than in them, if you know what I mean."

Tom nodded. "Well, we should all get a couple of hours of sleep if we can. We need to make an early start tomorrow and we'll need our wits about us if the plan is going to work."

What he didn't say was that, whatever the state of the beds, it was essential that they would all be in the same room. The last thing they needed was for Shrike to get cold feet, and suddenly disappear in the middle of the night. They each chose one of the beds in the row. Thomas and Della took hold of the bed next to Shrike, one at each end, and dragged it so that it was blocking the door.

"No offence, Shrike, but we don't want anyone coming in through that door during the night. Or out, for that matter."

They each settled down for the night and the lamp was extinguished. The darkness in the room was total and sudden. As each of them lay back on their separate bed, the swirling, pulsing blackness sent a chill down their spines. Their worst fears, nightmares from childhood perhaps, stories of shapeless ghouls and wraiths that lay in wait for the innocent and careless, pricked their minds relentlessly.

The sleeplessness these fears provoked lasted just long enough for each person to face their own private demons. Della lay awake, gripped by a terror of something happening to Amelia. She pictured her, alone and afraid, deep in the dungeons at Mulgrave Hall. Whatever else happened the next day she would do what she had to, to ensure that Amelia was unharmed.

Grace tossed and turned uncomfortably next to her. She was gripped with her own fear. Coming soon would be a choice to be made, a choice so fundamental, so profound, that she struggled to face it. But face it she must, eventually.

Clara grappled with interlocking worries. Could she carry out her part of the plan they had discussed and agreed? Was she capable of it? What if she couldn't manage it after all, just as Shrike had implied? How long would Thomas stay in Yngerlande? What did her feelings for him mean, anyway? It wasn't love, or not as she understood it, but something even bigger than that. His presence helped her to accept and embrace her difference. Her powers became not the tricks of a freak, but gifts to be proud of. She felt, in a way, that she was the mirror image of Grace. Not dead, but still bereft and alone without Tom. And looming over all of that, was the awful possibility that her mother would be killed. It was a troubled time before sleep finally took her.

For Thomas and Dan, the time was taken up not with their personal fears, but with a pressing conversation, in hoarse whispers, at the far end of the door. Dan waxed and waned palely, like a flickering candle flame next to Thomas who was perched on the end of one of the beds.

"I don't think that I will need to sleep in this ghostly state, the same way that I don't need to eat," he began, "but I'm worried."

"Worried?" Tom raised his eyebrows. "That's not like you. What are you worried about?"

"Last time we were in Yngerlande, we both had to return to England after a few hours. It was like recharging our batteries. Remember? And by now we should be feeling tired. Washed out, you know? Why is it different this time? Can we stay indefinitely?"

Tom looked back across the dorm, half in deep shadow, half illuminated by the moon. He could see the outline of the others lying still on their own beds, some gently rising and falling with the steady breathing of sleep upon them. He reached into his pocket and brought out his Sounding Stone.

"I think it's this," he said, holding it in the palm of his hand. It lay there unchanged, a plain pebble from Runswick beach. "Because we came here when the Stones called us, we can stay longer."

He shook his head, unsure, and replaced the Stone in his pocket.

"At least, I think so. I dunno. Sometimes I think that I don't know anything anymore."

Dan bobbed around him.

"Listen, man. You need to trust your instincts here. In Yngerlande you're like a different person. You're in charge. You know what to do. You're the leader. Don't question it, just go with it. The plan will work, I'm sure it will."

Thomas lowered his voice even further.

"And what about Shrike? I don't trust him. And I'm worried about Grace. She believes in him. And she's desperate for someone to believe in."

"Don't worry. Everything will be fine. She will be fine. I think you need to sleep. I'll just bob around here for a bit. At least I can keep an eye on him, while everyone is asleep."

There was nothing else to do. Tom settled down in the bed across the door next to Shrike, and after a few moments of anxious worrying, he too succumbed to sleep.

In the bed next to him, Shrike lay still in the shadows. He hadn't overheard Tom's conversation with Dan - they were too far away for that, but he could guess what they might be saying about him. To the casual observer, he was fast asleep, his heavy regular breathing only just this side of a snore. Time passed, and each of them sank into sleep in the darkened room. While the others slept, Shrike brooded. Normally he could fall asleep anywhere and at any time, but on this night he was troubled. He had never spoken honestly to anyone, not since he was a little boy, a long, long time ago. And yet, just an hour or so before, he had revealed all his secrets to Grace, someone he barely knew. Well, nearly all of them. A couple of days ago that would have been part of his usual scheming, but now? It nagged at him like a toothache, this strange feeling he didn't recognise and couldn't identify.

After everything that had happened that day, the one image he could not shake from his mind was not of ghosts, or tunnels or the strange powerful magic between Grace and Thomas. As he drifted into sleep, the one thing that troubled him was the memory of Grace holding his hand while they had talked.

A STRANGE GATHERING

An hour or so later, they were all roused by Tom. Stretching their aching bones and fighting the desire to go back to sleep, they hauled themselves out of bed and began their preparations.

After five minutes, they congregated at the door of the dormitory.

"You lead the way, Shrike," said Tom. "You know the house best."

They went into the corridor and retraced their steps from the day before. In daylight, it was less scary somehow, though the full extent of the dilapidation of the building was clear to see. The corridors and stairs were choked with dust and cobwebs, such that they could see their trail from the day before. Finally, they reached the ground floor and the door that led into the kitchen. Shrike pulled out his key and let them all out, before turning back to lock it again.

It was a cooler start to the day. A breeze blew from the north, and the leaves of the trees rustled. There was a chill to the wind and some of the leaves were just beginning to turn golden brown and red. Soon, it would be autumn. They walked around to the front of the house, picking their way through overgrown grasses and brambles that were sodden with dew. Clara moved to the front and went on until they had emerged from the tangle of vegetation and found themselves on what used to be a wide, sweeping lawn leading from the house down to the perimeters of the estate. She held up her hand to signal them all to stop.

She reached for the small horn she kept clipped to her belt.

"You should all cover your ears," she said to them. Immediately, everyone except Shrike held their hands tight over their ears. Shrike stared at them, his expression a mixture of bewilderment and contempt. Clara looked at him, raising her eyebrows. She shrugged.

"No? Oh well."

She brought the horn to her lips and blew. The sound was immense, and cut through the pounding rain and rumbling thunder. Shrike fell to the ground, clasping his ears as if he had been shot. Thankfully, it only lasted a second or two before it rumbled away, like thunder, leaving a silence that seemed even more oppressive than the strange sound it had replaced.

Shrike scrambled to his feet, staring at Clara.

"What the hell was that?" he asked. It was Clara's turn to shrug. There were more pressing things to attend to than Shrike.

First, the herd of steedhorns that were quietly grazing by the wall separating the grounds of Hard Crag from the wilderness beyond, raised their heads from the grass. Slowly at first, but then with steadily increasing speed they moved as a herd towards the house. It wasn't a stampede, more like a response to an urgent summons. Then from the sky came a fluttering, like wind through a field of wheat. Above their heads came a grey cloud, swirling and swooping in formation. It came for the roof, swerved around the house and then plummeted.

Everyone below ducked for cover and instinctively covered their heads, but just before they struck, the cloud dissolved into the separate forms of owls, just as the herd of steedhorns came to a halt before them, standing in orderly ranks in a semicircle. The owls gracefully arrested their flight, raised their talons, and settled gently, one owl on the back of each steedhorn.

Before anyone had time to comment on this strange

spectacle, the sky was full once again. This time it was black, as hundreds of bats descended from their roost at the top of the building, to settle one at a time, on the steedhorns. The audience was now settled in their seats for the entrance of the star attractions.

They waited for a minute, all eyes fixed towards the sky. Della looked across at Clara.

"Are you sure this is going to work?" she asked.

"I'm not sure of anything," Clara replied, "things just sort of happen."

"It worked last time, remember? Just be patient and have some faith," said Tom.

Shrike scoffed. "Faith! If I'd known all this was based on faith, I would have gone with their lordships. Enough of these fairy tales, we must make a start and set out for Mulgrave Hall, before..."

He got no further with his suggestion. A wind suddenly sprang up out of the stillness, leaving their hair streaming behind them. The woods surrounding Hard Crag set up a moaning, waving, rustling, with individual trees straining to stay upright and the entire canopy above the trunks bucked and reared like an ocean on a storm. They each struggled to stay upright on their feet when, as quickly as it had come, the wind dropped and an unearthly quiet settled upon them all. From between the clouds, three tiny white forms appeared, speeding towards them. As they approached, they emerged into focus. Three blindingly white Steedwings, their great snowy wings beating with an easy power, came towards them in a V-shaped formation. They swung round, their wings stirring a secondary wind around those who were stood waiting on the ground, as they gently came to a rest in between the animal audience and their passengers.

They stood snorting and pawing at the ground with their hooves. Clara walked forward to the central Steedwing and stroked its muzzle, bending her head towards it. She whispered in its ear while stroking its muzzle and then stepped back.

Turning to the others, she said, "Time for us to leave. I suggest that, Tom, you go with Shrike."

Tom nodded. A thin smile flickered on Shrike's face.

"You want me to get on one of these beasts? Are you mad?"

"We haven't got time to travel another way," replied Clara. "We must get to Mulgrave Hall as soon as we can, and the Steedwings will save us hours. We are privileged they will carry us. It is not a favour they grant lightly."

"And we've done it before. Or the others have at any rate," said Grace, a reassuring smile on her face.

Shrike's expression barely softened. "I suppose in the circumstances I have little choice," he said grudgingly.

"None at all," Clara replied. "Grace, you come with me. Master Ghost, you can attach yourself somehow to Della and her mount. I'm not sure how it works for such as you."

Dan grinned. "Me neither. Only one way to find out though."

Clara turned back to the Steedwings and began clicking her tongue in a hypnotic, soothing rhythm. They snorted, and then kneeled on their front legs. Giant creatures that they were, this was enough to allow the others to clamber on board. Once set, the Steedwings gently got back up and stood tall. From the lead beast, Clara turned back to them all.

"Everyone ready?" she called. "Hold tight."

Without further warning, each creature launched itself in the air with a spring from their legs and powerful beating of their wings, their massive muscles rippling under their snowy white hide. After four or five strokes of their wings, they were high above the roof of Hard Crag. Looking down, over the shoulder of each of the Steedwings, they could see the crumbling brickwork and rotting gutters disappear into the distance as they climbed ever higher into the sky. After a minute or two of steady climbing, they passed through the wispy cloud layer and wheeled round to head eastwards towards the coast.

The ride was over very quickly. The familiar coastline of Runswick Bay came into view, with its sheer, jagged cliffs, pockmarked with entrances to caves and tunnels. The Steedwings swung out over the North Sea, glassy and calm below, before continuing the circle to approach the land above the village. They could make out The Crab and Lobster nestled in the curve of the cliffs, and then, up above, the stately roof of The Rectory.

All three Steedwings began their descent, coming to a graceful halt in the Rectory garden. They dismounted and Clara went to each one to stroke their muzzles and whisper into their ears. Within a minute, they had taken to the skies again, and flew off back in the direction of Hard Crag.

"Come on, let's quickly check The Rectory and the stables," Tom said.

They discovered that The Rectory was just as they had left it. Luckily there had been enough fodder left in the stables for the horses to have fed and watered since they had been gone. Shrike walked over to one horse at the far side of the stable and caressed its head. He turned back to the others.

"Silver is here," he said. "But this is not where I left her. Someone has been here alright. We need to check the house."

They did just that. Della, pistols in hand, slipped through the open front door and crept, room by room, to the kitchen. She emerged after a minute, smiling, pistols stowed away and a piece of parchment in her hands.

"Good old Nathan. He checked on us when no one had been down to The Crab and Lobster for a few days."

She passed the letter to Tom who read it aloud.

Dear Reverend. I hope you will forgive the liberty, but I came to check to see that all was well at The Rectory. I am worried about what I found - the house open, no-one at home, strange horses wandering the grounds, and strange folk asking questions at The Crab. I have stabled and fed the horses and closed the doors. I will return every day, just to keep an eye on things.

Your friend,

Nat

"Hopefully, we'll be able to thank him properly when all of this is done," said Tom.

"Whenever that is," said Shrike, his cold eyes flicking over each of them in turn.

"Well, the sooner we get started, the sooner we'll be back," replied Tom. "Let's get on with it."

They quickly ate and drank, not knowing when they'd be able to do so again. As they had agreed, one of them was to remain at The Rectory. The others boarded the carriage, with Della taking the reins and Shrike sitting next to her. With a flick of the reins, the carriage moved off, out of the driveway and into the lane. The plan had begun.

SHRIKE MAKES A PROPOSAL

The carriage crunched to a halt in front of the Hall and two servants scurried out to take care of the horses. Della, hands on the reins, shooed them away while Shrike carefully disembarked, holding a pistol and a leather satchel, which he, with some deliberation, placed over his shoulder.

"Leave the horses. Miss Honeyfield will sit with the carriage," Shrike began, in a voice of cold determination. He stroked his pistol as he spoke. "Tell his Lordship that Shrike is here as promised. There are a couple of things we need to get straight before I come inside. I'll wait here."

There was a pause as both servants looked at each other in a panic.

"Now, if you please," he barked.

The two jumped out of their skins and then hurried away, leaving Shrike holding the horse's bridle. Dan took the opportunity to slide out of the carriage up to him. In a low voice, checking first that they were completely alone, he said, "Remember, Shrike. Let's stick to the plan."

Shrike nodded, scowling. The Hall had far too many windows, and someone, somewhere, would be watching them, he was sure of that. They had come too far to make such an obvious mistake. He turned away, in a performance meant to convey impatience. Dan got the message, but hung around anyway, invisible, just in case.

They had little time to wait. The imposing front doors opened and Lord Mulgrave waddled out.

Under his grey periwig, he scowled and sweated, his red

face expressing his distaste for having been made to greet his visitors outside. Mulgrave was not a man used to walking anywhere, nor to responding to the request of others, and he was on the verge of a furious explosion of rage. The assorted servants that trailed in his wake looked nervous. They had all witnessed his temper before and could recognise the signs.

"Shrike," he bellowed, "this had better be good. You take liberties, young man, that would see most people needing to visit their doctor. I am not accustomed to taking orders, or meeting carriages like a damned ostler."

Shrike bowed, a sly smirk on his face.

"Your Lordship, my apologies. Your servants have obviously misrepresented me. I would not dream of issuing orders. But I did think that you would want to have a conversation alone, before we go in the house."

"Go in the house? You presume too much, you insolent dog," Mulgrave barked back at him. "My house receives Kings, Master Shrike, not guttersnipes such as you."

Unperturbed, Shrike continued, "I know your lordship is terribly proud that Oliver and Jacob are at this moment planting their royal backsides on your finest silk-covered furniture, but you do not really want them to hear this conversation first. And at the moment, they are only really Royal in their imaginations. And yours, of course."

Mulgrave's face turned a darker shade of crimson and he almost shook with fury. Before he could either speak or explode, Shrike beckoned him with a contemptuous crook of his finger, to take a look through the carriage window.

"I'd take a look inside and then tell your army of servants to go back inside. This chat is not for the likes of them."

Intrigued, Mulgrave stepped forward and peered through the windows of the carriage. His eyes adjusted to the shadows inside. He frowned as the two figures came into focus. Princess Gaia and the insolent Trelawney girl were inside, both chained, looking defeated and afraid. His frown rearranged itself into a wide beaming smile as he turned back to Shrike.

"You have them, Shrike, just as you said. Well done, young man, well done indeed. Oliver and Jacob will be delighted. Let's get them inside and deliver the good news."

Shrike held up his hand. "Not so fast, your Lordship. I have them, you're quite right about that, but you don't. And you won't, unless you do as you're told."

"What do you mean, Shrike? Don't trifle with me. We had an agreement, so don't think about going back on it now."

"Things have changed. I have something you want. Something you need desperately. If you can't deliver it, Oliver and Jacob will be furious. They can't succeed without the two people inside this carriage, so my terms have increased."

"Ah! So that's it, is it? I might have known it would just be a question of money with you, Shrike. After all, you're just a worthless nobody from the streets of York. Well, more money is not out of the question."

He stopped and his gaze took in the carriage before returning to rest once again on Shrike. His cold brain was ticking methodically, calculating his advantage. His eyes narrowed as an idea occurred to him.

"But have a care, Shrike. Why shouldn't my men just take the prisoners now? You are on your own and unprotected. My house is full of armed men trained to do my bidding. Don't you think you might just have made a little mistake, eh?"

Shrike sidled up to Mulgrave and lowered his voice. "All of your servants and soldiers hate you with a passion. They would like nothing more than an opportunity to see you bleeding in the dirt. Trust me, my Lord, they have told me so many times."

Mulgrave's face fell. He looked around the gathered

servants and soldiers, their eyes hard, their faces set. Shrike chose his moment.

"Send them all inside. Then we can do business. This is for your ears only, my Lord."

There was a momentary struggle between his instinctive dislike of being told what to do, his fear and his greed. Fear and greed won. He turned back to the house and called, "Inside, all of you. Now!"

The gaggle of servants slipped away, grateful to be out of the firing line. He turned back to Shrike.

"Go on, Master Shrike. Make your proposal. But be careful. There are two very powerful men inside. Your offer will need to be enticing." He thought for a second. "And deniable," he added.

Shrike took Mulgrave by the elbow and ushered him further away from the carriage as he spoke.

"Whatever the offer is, it will only work if you back me up with Oliver and Jacob. That is why we are having this conversation here. I will hand over the Princess and the Trelawney girl, in exchange for a substantial quantity of gold sovereigns and the release of the other prisoners."

"What are the prisoners to you?" Mulgrave asked sharply. "Are you getting soft? I would have expected you to leave them to their fate. And they will be reluctant to agree. I know that Oliver, in particular, has been looking forward to taking his revenge on the beautiful doctor and her partner, that infernal coach driver girl over there."

Mulgrave glanced back at the carriage, where, out of earshot, Della waited patiently in the driving seat, her hands loosely holding the reins. Shrike followed his eyes, lowered his voice, and winked.

"I expect you to use your powers of persuasion then. The Doctor and her partner are meaningless in the grand scheme of things. And once Oliver is King, he can do what he wants. You know where they all live."

"And do you include the Reverend Cummerbund in the release? They will never agree to that. He is a very dangerous man, if man he is. His powers are mysterious."

"Yes, I do. His powers are nothing without his stone. And without the others. The boy Trelawney has not come to their rescue, as they had hoped. On his own, he is a mere conjurer, doing party tricks."

Mulgrave considered for a moment. "And the money?"

Shrike rummaged deep in a pocket and brought out a folded piece of parchment. He handed it to Mulgrave, who jammed a monocle into his left eye, opened the letter and scanned it quickly. He burst out laughing and his monocle fell to the ground.

"Are you mad?" he spluttered. "This is a fortune."

"Does he want to be King?" asked Shrike coolly. "He has a choice."

"But they will not have that amount of money with them. He never carries money, not even a shilling. Kings expect ordinary people to deal with that kind of business."

"But you do. And he will be very grateful. He will remember who made it all possible. And that person could be you."

Mulgrave's eyes shifted left and right. Sweat was trickling down his ruddy cheeks now, and he mopped his face with his silk handkerchief.

"The money can be arranged," he said finally. "And the prisoners can be released. After all, they are nobodies."

He stopped, looked around and lowered his voice.

"Apart from Cummerbund. They will never agree to releasing him."

Shrike smiled. "Then we will not tell them that part of the plan. We can arrange for him to "escape" sometime later, and you can blame one of your idiot jailers."

Mulgrave hesitated again. He was in an agony of indecision and shifted nervously from foot to foot.

"It's time to decide. You must take me up to meet His Majesty and I will put all of this to them. They will argue and you will back me up and they will agree. If they do not, and the prisoners do not appear at your front door,

Della will drive like the wind, with the Princess and the girl in the carriage, and their plan is doomed forever."

He let Mulgrave think on that picture for a moment before beginning again.

"But instead, you will take me to your study where your safe is, to collect the money. Then we will escort the prisoners to the carriage and they will change places with the Princess and the Trelawney girl. I will load the chest of gold and we will drive away with the prisoners. And then you, your Lordship, will have the exquisite pleasure of delivering the Princess and the girl to the future King. I can picture the scene now."

Evidently, so could Mulgrave. A smile of pure pleasure spread across his face.

"And Cummerbund?"

"Bring him to the meeting and let me speak to him. All will be well."

"Yes, indeed," smirked Mulgrave, picturing a future of luxury and influence at the right hand of the King. "Very well."

A SAFE FULL OF SECRETS

Mulgrave turned and waddled back across the gravel to the Hall with Shrike at his side.

Dan came behind. He slipped through the great oaken doors and caught sight of the two men disappearing round the corner of the massive staircase that dominated the entrance hall. He slid up behind them and tracked them up to the first floor until they reached the entrance to his study. Mulgrave threw open the doors and beckoned Shrike to follow.

The study was wood panelled and well-lit, with scores of candles lighting every part of the room, including a huge candelabra suspended from the middle of the ceiling. There were thick Persian rugs on top of polished oak floorboards, and the walls were hung with tapestries and oil paintings.

"So, your Lordship, the sovereigns if you please," began Shrike. "Then we can get this thing over with."

Mulgrave scowled. Parting with money was painful to him. Parting with this amount of money was unbearable. His eyes glittered with intent as he turned over Shrike's proposal. "Shrike may think he has outwitted me, but once Oliver is King, he won't be able to hide for long. And then all of the gold will come back to me, where it belongs," he thought to himself.

That settled it. He turned back to Shrike.

"Very well, Master Shrike, you shall have your money."

He waddled over to the far wall where there was a life-size portrait of one of Mulgrave's distant ancestors. He ran his hand down one side of the frame. There was a faint click and the portrait swung away from the wall to reveal an iron safe door, slightly smaller than the portrait, but still considerable. A fully grown man could walk into it and stand upright.

Through the open door, Shrike could see shelves containing leather money bags, a weighing scale, and various chests. There was also a collection of rolled parchments, tied with red ribbons, or sealed with wax. These were clearly valuable documents of various kinds.

Mulgrave walked in, opened a chest and began to fill it with leather bags. He shivered and rubbed his hands together. "Hell's teeth," he exclaimed. "It's like an ice house inside this cupboard."

Once again, he began to shift the bags. From the chinking sound, they contained coins. Shrike moved alongside Mulgrave.

"May I?" he asked.

"Suspicious cove, ain't you, Sirrah? Don't you trust me, a peer of the realm?"

"Forgive me, your Lordship, but you have taught me well. The nobility of this godforsaken country are the least trustworthy of all. Begging your Lordship's pardon, of course."

He opened the first bag and took out a gold sovereign. He held it up to the candle light and then bit into it. Satisfied, he threw it back, tied the bag and threw it back into the chest. While he was doing all of this, his eyes carefully scrutinised the papers and parchments on the nearest shelf, but like a common stage magician, his actions distracted the attention of the audience. He was confident that Mulgrave had not noticed his interest in anything other than the money.

When Mulgrave had stuffed the chest to the brim with money bags, he gestured to Shrike.

"Bring that out to my desk. Then two of the servants will take it down to the hall, ready to load into your carriage. I hope you don't mind, but this cupboard needs to be securely locked before anyone else comes into the room. It's for my eyes only, you understand."

Shrike hauled the chest to the desk and then swung it up onto the desktop. While he was struggling with the chest, Mulgrave quickly went back to the safe. He closed the door, did a random selection of numbers on the lock and then pulled the portrait back closed. He stood back, a satisfied smile on his face. The wall presented its customary ordinary face to the world, disguising the riches behind it.

"Perfect," he proclaimed. "Now," he said, turning back to Shrike. "Let us take tea with the King."

"What a treat! Lead the way, my Lord," said Shrike. He followed Mulgrave, turning to glance behind him. Momentarily, he gave a thumbs up sign, to all intents and purposes to thin air. Invisibly, Daniel hovered behind him, grinning. He had, of course, been present throughout, and had made very sure he could see Mulgrave, and his hands, at all times. "And now," he thought, "I'm the only other person in the world who knows the combination to Lord Mulgrave's safe. Being a ghost certainly does have some advantages."

*

There were two armed guards stationed outside the drawing room. As Mulgrave approached, with Shrike just behind him, they uncrossed their pikes that barred entrance, and knocked discreetly on the doors. Immediately the guards on the inside opened the doors, swinging them inwards.

Shrike nodded approvingly.

"Hmm, your security is admirable," he said. "It would take a lot to get unauthorised access here."

"Of course," replied Mulgrave, "there is a lot at stake." He lowered his voice and continued, "Try not to be quite as insolent as you usually are, Shrike. This is the King after all."

"Not yet," Shrike replied. "There's still a chance you'll mess it all up."

He saw Mulgrave's face: a mixture of horror and fury. "Calm down. I'll be my most polite and all will be well. Really, Mulgrave, you need to relax a little."

Mulgrave composed himself and walked into the room with Shrike beside him. Oliver was lounging on a red velvet chair eating grapes. Jacob stood by a window staring out at the driveway that led to the Hall. He turned at Mulgrave's entrance, his perpetual scowl fixed to his face. He was a tall, thin angular man, and the scar on his cheek added to the impression of a man suspicious and cynical about the world who was quick to lose his temper.

Mulgrave bowed low. "Your Majesty," he intoned.

Shrike's greeting was less fawning. "Masters," was all he managed, with a stiff nod of the head.

"Well?" Oliver drawled, as if he were bored with the whole business. "Have you got the young chickens with you? This has gone on long enough."

"And why, Shrike, you insufferable oik, were we kept waiting for your letter?" Jacob interrupted with a flash of anger. "Why do we have to follow you out here, to the back of beyond, as if we are common tradesmen pursuing a debt?"

Shrike contained his irritation and turned on his easy charm, casting a radiant smile at both men.

"Patience, gentlemen. This has been a difficult task, even for such as I. I judged it better to secure the prize, rather than write letters. And of course, I succeeded."

Oliver sat up, all pretence at indifference abandoned.

"You have the Princess? Here?" He could barely contain his excitement.

Shrike nodded, with a faint smirk.

"Do you hear that, Uncle? Everything falls into place. At last! I will be King. And all of the damage that has been done to our great country can be swept away and put right. A toast, gentlemen, a toast to the future under King

Oliver."

He scrambled up out of his seat and scurried around to pour glasses of wine for the four of them. Jacob, still scowling, stepped across and laid a hand on Oliver's arm.

"One moment." He turned to Shrike. "Forgive my suspicions, but I have a feeling that our nasty little friend here has more to say before we get our hands on Princess Gaia. Am I right, Master Shrike?"

"As ever, Jacob. I have the means for you to take the crown. That's worth a lot more than we agreed. It's worth everything, actually, so the price has gone up. His Lordship here, a clever man, has agreed and because he is your loyal servant, he has provided me with the gold. We have also agreed to the second of my terms. All the prisoners who are currently locked in the dungeons far below us will be released. They are no longer of any value to you. I will escort them from the cells to my carriage, and we will swap them and the gold for Princess Gaia and the young Trelawney girl. Then we will depart, and I hope, never see you again."

There was a pause. Oliver and Jacob exchanged looks.

"Master Shrike," said Jacob, "You have done very well. But, pray, give us a moment. We need to consider your proposal. Mulgrave, escort him out to the corridor if you please and then return. We need to clarify a few things."

Mulgrave raised an eyebrow as if he were about to protest at being treated like a common servant, but he bit his tongue, and ushered Shrike to the door. As he closed the door with Shrike in the corridor, he whispered to Mulgrave, "A moment, no more. They will take the bait, I am sure of it."

Shrike nodded. As Mulgrave turned his back and re-entered the room, Shrike caught Daniel's eye, as he hovered palely by the entrance. He winked, unseen by anyone else, and Dan drifted away to float next to Oliver and Jacob to eavesdrop on their conversation. The last thing they needed now was some kind of attempt at a double cross.

"… but letting them all go, Jacob? That would be madness. We can't agree to that, surely?"

Jacob rubbed his chin while he considered. "They can all go except Cummerbund. He's far too dangerous, even without his damned magic pebble, or whatever it is. He stays in the cells for the time being. When you're safely installed as King, he can be got rid of."

"And what about the money, Uncle? He is twisting our arms up behind our backs. It's a fortune."

Jacob laughed and shook his head. "He's a rogue, young Shrike. He reminds me of myself. He knows we need what he's got so he's driving a hard bargain. Good for him! And while our loyal friend, Lord Mulgrave here, is stumping up the money, what do we have to worry about, eh?"

At this, Mulgrave gave a slight bow of acknowledgement.

Jacob continued, "He's happy to do it, because he will be expecting his reward when you're safely on the throne, Oliver. And he'll get it. And so will that villain, Shrike. Just like Cummerbund, and the other prisoners, as soon as the time is right, they will disappear. We'll make sure of that."

Mulgrave, bowing and scraping, plucked up the courage to ask a question.

"So," he stammered, blinking, "you are happy to proceed on those terms, then? All released but Cummerbund, and the gold loaded into Shrike's carriage."

Jacob looked quizzically at him, an eyebrow raised. "Happy? Oh, believe me, Mulgrave, we're positively ecstatic. Bring him back in, tell him the glad news, and let us have a toast to Yngerlande's future."

Oliver giggled. "I'm so happy, I'll even pour the wine."

He bustled around with the bottle and four fine crystal glasses, while Mulgrave waddled to the door to admit Shrike. Oliver called out to him, "Come in, come in, Shrike, my dear fellow. After consideration of your terms, we have an agreement. And to celebrate, let us drink a toast."

Glasses of wine were passed around. They stood in a circle with their glasses held high.

"A toast," Oliver began again, "to Making Yngerlande Great Again."

Jacob and Mulgrave beamed as they chorused, "Making Yngerlande Great Again!"

Next to them, Shrike, with a knowing, half smile, and in a lower voice, said merely, "Yngerlande." They all chinked their glasses together in fellowship and took a sip of their wine.

"I must make haste, your lordships," said Shrike. "There is a lot to do. If you would be so good as to have a servant direct me to the dungeons, with a key, then we can release the prisoners and take them to my carriage outside. After that, it will be just a matter of swapping our prisoners for yours, as it were. I suggest you have some of your armed men escort us from the hall."

Mulgrave beamed at him, still flushed from too much red wine and too much success. He could not stop his mind from drifting off into fantasising about his future life as the man who had enabled Oliver to become King. The thought of it made him quite dizzy.

"Of course, Shrike, my good man. Allow me."

He barked at one of the guards on duty just inside the room.

"You there! Escort Master Shrike down to the dungeons immediately. He must have whatever he needs, understand. And then inform me when he is ready to depart."

The guard bowed silently, opened the doors and said to Shrike, "This way, sir."

Shrike, bowing first to the three men in the drawing room, followed him out, with the ghostly figure of Dan at his side. They paced behind the guard as he strode through the hallways and down several staircases on their way to the cells. As they went, Shrike's sharp eyes took in as much information as possible: entrances and exits, where the servants were positioned, how many armed guards and soldiers there were. Daniel and he didn't risk trying to communicate - they would be alone soon enough.

It didn't take long for Shrike, with the authority of Mulgrave's servant beside him, to convince the guards to hand over their keys, and go for a break and a bite to eat up in the kitchen. There was much back slapping and hand shaking. Clearly, Shrike had charmed these men, as he had done so many others before. As they left, they turned back to him.

"You're a pal, Shrike," said Jem, the older of the two, "we owe you a drink in return."

The two men left in high spirits, looking forward to this unexpected break.

Back in their room, Daniel appeared, having been an invisible ghostly presence throughout the last conversation.

"You're very persuasive, Shrike. And you seem to know everyone."

"It's always very useful, having contacts. You never know when you're going to need them. But now, we need to get on with this. I've got to get back to Mulgrave's study without being seen. I need you, Master Ghost, to go ahead of me to check the coast is clear. If you see someone up ahead, come back and warn me. But don't materialise again, that would be too dangerous."

Dan nodded. "I'll just touch your hand and whisper. If you feel an icy chill, you'll know you've gotta hide. Ok?"

He hovered in front of Shrike, shimmering and pulsing like candle light through mist.

"But why do we need to go to his study? Shouldn't we just get on with releasing everyone?" he asked.

"Trust me," replied Shrike. "We need some backup, just in case. But we need to get going. You lead the way."

Dan shot off down the corridor, invisible to all. As he

went, he thought, ruefully, "Trust you, Shrike? That's not as easy as you might think."

He was careful, as they progressed through corridors and flights of stairs, to double check up ahead, and in the many shadowy corners. The Hall was full of servants and soldiers. It was just as full of nooks and crannies, and old, towering pieces of furniture that provided the perfect hiding place for anyone who needed to stay hidden. They managed to get to the study without being interrupted, after a couple of close calls.

With a quick look both ways down the corridor, Shrike tried the door, and when it opened, he slipped through the gap and closed it gently, making sure there was no click to draw anyone's attention.

Dan, feeling the familiar shiver through his veins as he slid through the solid oak door, joined him. Shrike was already making his way to the portrait on the wall. He reached for the frame, and slid his fingers along it until he felt the catch. Within seconds the portrait had swung back, revealing the imposing bulk of the safe door. He turned to Dan, floating behind him.

"The combination. Quick, we haven't got much time."

Dan told him. "But I still don't see why you need it."

"Later, Master Ghost, when we have more time." His fingers were already turning the dial of the lock back and forth according to the numbers Dan had given him. All of the barrels fell into place and the door swung open easily with a gentle tug on the handle. He strode in, past bags of gold and jewels, and made straight for the shelf of documents. He rifled through a collection of scrolled parchments, flicking his eyes over the tag on each one. Roll after roll were examined and then discarded, until finally he let out a cry of triumph.

"Yes, at last," he breathed and kissed the seal on the parchment. He reached for the next one in line, and had the same reaction. Quick as a flash, he tucked both parchment scrolls inside his frock coat and patted them down. Then he turned to Daniel, bobbing and baffled beside him.

"Easier than I thought," he said, a huge smile on his face. "Come on, let's not push our luck. We need to lock up and get out of here. It's time to release your friends."

Dan didn't argue. He slipped out through the door to check the corridor. It was deserted. Shrike redid the combination, clicked the portrait back into place, and slipped back out to rejoin Dan. He closed the door behind him and they set off the way they had come, back down to the dungeons.

Behind him, Mulgrave's study slumbered. Candle light sparkled on the silver. The fragrance of freshly cut flowers perfumed the air. The grandfather clock ticked reassuringly against the silence. The room was as it had always been. No sign of its most recent visitors remained, and that secret would be hidden until the next time Lord Mulgrave entered his safe room, looking for a very particular pair of documents.

THE BEST LAID PLANS

When they got back to the dungeons, they double checked the guards' room, but it was deserted, a single lamp illuminating their discarded playing cards in the middle of the table.

"Good," muttered Shrike to Daniel, "I thought that pair wouldn't drag themselves away from a hot pie and a flagon of ale. They would just get in the way if they were here. But we must be quick. The sooner we're away from here the better."

"What do you think, Shrike? I reckon we should speak to Silas first, before we go to the others," said Dan.

Shrike agreed. "I'll start with Cummerbund. While I'm doing that, why don't you slip into each cell individually, just to prepare them for what's going to happen shortly. It will be a shock and they need time to adjust themselves to the prospect of freedom."

"Makes sense, I suppose. If you're not here when I've finished, I'll find you in Silas' cell."

He turned and slid through the door of the first cell. It took ten minutes or so for them to see everyone and reassure them and then Shrike unlocked each cell and the prisoners gathered together. There were hugs and kisses and handshakes all round before Shrike led them up the stairs and along corridors to the main entrance to the Hall, where Daniel slipped once again into invisibility. They were a strange, bedraggled band on their way to freedom, walking through the perfumed passageways of Mulgrave Hall under the watchful eyes of armed guards.

Waiting outside with the carriage was Della. She had been pacing up and down, crunching the gravel ever since Shrike and Dan had left them. She caught sight of Amelia at the head of the procession and ran to meet her.

"Della!" cried Amelia and dashed out of line.

They hugged briefly and the tears came thick and fast. Della held her off and looked closely at her face.

"Are you alright? Have they hurt you?"

"I'm fine, really. But Marlborough is not. We need to get somewhere safe where I can treat him."

"Of course. You all need to get inside and we are to go directly to The Rectory and wait for Silas there."

She ushered them all inside the empty carriage, secured the doors, and with a flick of the reins, set off down the driveway to the main gate. After a minute, they turned on to the road leading out towards the moors, and were lost to sight.

At a window on the first floor, three figures had watched every second of this scene play out below them. Under their watchful eye, Shrike beckoned to the others, chained and waiting in the shrubbery. They had deliberately kept out of sight of the released prisoners, but now it was their turn. Feeling the eyes of Oliver, Jacob and Mulgrave fixed intently on him from above, Shrike played his part to perfection. He led the prisoners roughly to the door of the Hall, and pulled them by their shackles over the threshold. The great door swung shut behind them. Mulgrave Hall held them now.

*

Silas sat in his cell enveloped in darkness, waiting for the next stage of the plan to unfold. It was fraught with danger and much of it depended on Shrike. He turned over and over in his mind what Shrike had revealed, and still he could not be sure. Pure evil, that's what Mary Carruthers had said about him, and she was a good judge of character. But then, so was Silas and he just couldn't decide how far to trust Shrike. If only he could have retrieved the

Sounding Stone from him, then he, and everyone else, would be safe. He just had to wait a little longer, just until he was certain that the others were safely out of Mulgrave Hall and on their way to The Rectory. Then, and only then, would he make his move.

His thoughts were interrupted by the harsh sound of the key in the lock. The door swung open to reveal the two guards silhouetted against the half-light in the corridor.

"You're to come upstairs with us," said the first. "Lord Mulgrave's orders. But first, put your hands out in front of you. And no funny business."

Silas did as he was told and the second man put his wrists into shackles.

"This way, if you please. Quickly! The high ups don't like to be kept waiting."

Silas nodded, and the three men, Silas sandwiched between the two guards, marched out into the passageway.

*

Shrike led the way, occasionally glancing behind him to check he was not marching ahead of Princess Gaia and Grace. They followed, their chained hands out in front of them, stony faced and silent. At the door to the Drawing Room, the two guards stood aside to open the doors and announce their arrival.

Shrike ushered his two prisoners to take their place by his side where Oliver, Jacob and Mulgrave could see them clearly. Oliver was in a state of high excitement. Everything he had dreamed of, through all his years of exile, was on the verge of coming true. Even his uncle, the usually dour-faced Jacob, looked less irritable than usual, as he slowly registered the significance of what was happening in front of him.

"Well, well, well - Princess Gaia and the Trelawney girl," said Jacob, struggling to contain his delight, "welcome to Mulgrave Hall. You've no idea how long we have waited for this moment."

The Princess and Grace remained silent. There seemed

little point in arguing with them in this situation. They would simply wait and listen.

Oliver on the other hand, had controlled himself for as long as he could. He burst out laughing at the sight in front of him.

"Ha!" he exclaimed in triumph. "Not like you people not to fight back. But then perhaps you realise that you're beaten, and you're about to go back to your rightful place in society. If you're lucky that is. None of your unnatural witchcraft is going to save you now. The old man Cummerbund is stripped of his powers, so don't expect him to come to your rescue. And the boy Trelawney, well, he is nowhere to be seen. Perhaps he was too busy?"

He walked up to the Princess and held her chin. "Or maybe he just doesn't love you anymore."

'Where is my mother, the Queen?"

Oliver gave a twisted smile. "She's never really been the Queen, let's be honest. And now everyone will know that. And they'll know all about you and your dark arts. So the people won't come to your rescue either. They hate nothing more than a witch. And they will be delighted when the speeches are made and the truth comes out, that I, Oliver II, am their new King."

"Where is she?" Gaia repeated.

"She has been a guest at Belton Hall, and is probably on her way to Kings Manor in York as we speak. We thought it fitting for my coronation to take place in York, the ancient northern seat of the Kingdom, to bind the country together as one. Of course, there will be a second ceremony in London at St James' Palace, and once we've done that, I'll never set foot in the north again if I can help it. Nasty, cold, godforsaken place, the north. Full of peasants and terrible food."

"Oliver," broke in Jacob gently, "we need to make friends before we throw around insults. Hold your tongue at least until this is all settled."

There was a knock at the door, and Silas was delivered

by the two prison guards, who ushered him into the room and left, backing out of the room bowing and scraping.

He looked entirely unaffected by his time in the cells. His eyes glittered with life and intensity under his grey hair and pigtail, and he stood tall, his chained hands held out in front of him. He surveyed the room, his gaze falling on each of those present in turn. He gave a nod to Shrike and then turned his attention to Princess Gaia and Grace. His expression changed from a smile of pleasure, through a frown of puzzlement, finishing with a final smile of quiet satisfaction. For the first time in several days, he felt confident about the outcome of this extraordinary situation. Almost immediately, he resumed the blank expression he had been wearing when he entered the room. Like a poker player, his objective was to give nothing away to his opponents.

Oliver turned away from Princess Gaia and welcomed the new arrival.

"Ah, Cummerbund. Good. Now we are all assembled together, we can move forward. In a moment, you will go back to the cells. Tomorrow, we will ride to York with the Princess here, to be reunited with her mother. We have no further need of you, or of you either." At this point, Oliver gestured towards Grace. "You will both be held here until we conclude our business in York and assume the crown. The girl and her mother will go to a nunnery."

"And then what, Oliver? Once you are King, what do you plan to do with us all?" Silas' voice was steady and even, as if he were asking what was for tea later, a mere, casual interest in what was planned.

"Oh, I haven't decided that yet. I might keep you as my personal conjurer and bring you out to do party tricks after dessert." He smiled and idly picked up an apple from the bowl in front of him. "Or, I might not."

He took a bite from the apple and the crunch echoed around the room. He chewed on it and then threw the remainder into the small fire that was burning in the hearth.

"The whole point of being King, Cummerbund, is that I can do whatever I want. With whoever I want."

Silas nodded. The others watched in silence. Looks flashed around the room, between Princess Gaia, Grace and Shrike. A bead of sweat formed at the back of Shrike's neck and suddenly rolled down his spine, a chill shiver. It was simply a question of timing now.

Gaia broke the silence. She turned to Grace, just as they had planned.

"Then we must say goodbye. But first, a final hug."

They moved towards each other, face to face, and held their chained hands out to each other. They pulled together and embraced. Jacob scowled at them. "That's enough of that nonsense. We've–"

There was suddenly a shout from outside, at the front of the Hall, that cut through the scenario in the drawing room. More voices joined in, and then the sound of a single horse galloping furiously up the drive towards the house, thundered through the air. Oliver and Jacob hurried to the window overlooking the main entrance. A jet-black horse, its flanks soaked in sweat, careered to a halt, sending a spray of gravel everywhere. The rider leaped from the horse, his tricorn hat sent flying into the air. He ran to the footmen at the door, frantically waving a scroll of parchment in front of him. They scanned it quickly, saw the seal and the rider snatched it back from them and dashed inside the house. Jacob hauled up the sash window.

"What the devil is going on?" spluttered Jacob. "Hi, you there," he shouted down at one of the footmen. "What on earth is all this commotion? Who was the rider?"

The footman, ashen-faced in terror, managed to croak back in reply, "Begging your pardon, Sir, 'twas a messenger from the South. It's the Queen, Sir…"

They turned away from the window, utterly perplexed.

"The South? The Queen… What can this be..?"

He was cut off by the sound of someone running towards them in the corridor outside, followed by harsh warnings shouted by the guards. The door burst open and the rider, red-faced and perspiring, ran forward, the scroll pointing at Oliver in his outstretched hand.

Oliver snatched the scroll, broke the seal and unrolled it with trembling fingers. His eyes scanned the sheet quickly, his lips moving as he formed the words.

"Well?" demanded Jacob. "Spit it out, man."

Oliver sank down into his chair, still holding the parchment in one hand. His mouth hung open loosely, he looked from side to side as if searching for an explanation. Finally, as if he had suddenly realised there were others in the room, he looked up.

"It's the Queen," he stammered. "She's dead."

SHRIKE ON THE EDGE

Clara and Grace stepped back from their embrace. The distraction had allowed them to unlock their manacles as they had planned, but they kept them on, as if they were still chained. Grace stumbled a little and Clara had to stoop to support her.

Oliver and Jacob were oblivious to everything else in the room, apart from the shocking news they had just received.

"But how..." Jacob started, "I mean what happened?"

"Trying to escape, apparently. They found her gone from her apartments at Belton Hall. She'd forced one of the maids to give her the keys... I don't know, it's not clear from the letter."

"But she is dead, yes? That much is clear, at any rate?"

"Oh, yes," Oliver replied, "quite dead."

A strangled sob came from the two young women in chains. Everyone looked across at them, but it was hard to tell which of them had cried out.

"Damnation, this changes everything," said Jacob, slamming his fist down onto the table in front of him. "We need to go to York now. With the Princess. Send word to all of our people across the country. We will need all of the soldiers promised us. We will have to announce her death straight away. It will be proclaimed around the country that Matilda is dead."

He eyed Princess Gaia closely.

"That Matilda is dead," he continued, "at the hands of her daughter, the witch..."

There were murmurs of shock and outrage from the prisoners in the room.

Jacob raised his voice, "At the hands of her daughter the witch, who will be put on trial."

Oliver smiled. "Actually, Uncle, this might have worked out rather well for us in the end, don't you agree?"

"But why would Oliver become King? On what authority?" Silas stepped forward and asked the question with a quiet insistence.

Jacob laughed. "Old man, we have thought of everything, don't you see? We have a signed declaration from Matilda naming Oliver as her successor. And, of course, we have our secret weapon right here, don't we, Master Shrike?"

Shrike made a stiff little bow of acknowledgement. His face wore a strained half smile.

"What do you mean?" demanded Silas. "Why is Shrike your secret weapon?"

"Shrike has many talents. One of them is the fact that he's a master forger. A few minutes of study of someone's handwriting and he can produce a copy that the person themself would accept as genuine. It's the work of an hour at most for him to produce a confession from the Princess that she is responsible for the Queen's death. It's quite delicious."

Oliver broke off this point, an irrepressible bubble of giggling stopping him from continuing. He managed to compose himself and went on.

"Because now, of course, we don't even have to deal with the pressing problem of what to do with the Queen and her daughter. The Queen has dealt with herself. The daughter will now be dealt with by the Law."

He stopped again and looked directly at Silas.

"Now, we only have to deal with you, Reverend. Just you. Oh, and your friends of course."

There was a chill that went around the room, despite the gently flickering fire. Jacob gathered a few papers from the table by the window.

"We'll go to York now, with the girl," he said. "Shrike, you will stay on here and finish things off. Everyone, do you understand?"

Shrike swallowed. Now a bead of sweat erupted on his forehead. He licked his lips and made to speak, but stopped abruptly and wiped the sweat just before it began to roll down his cheek. His fists clenched, knuckles a deathly white as he tried again.

"Everyone?" he managed to say. It came out as a dying croak.

Jacob stared at him, a frown growing on his face. The others in the room looked around at each other, from one to the other, not quite believing what they were hearing.

"Shrike?" Jacob repeated, his voice rising with an edge of steel to it.

"Everyone?" Shrike asked again. "Even the Trelawney girl?"

"Everyone. Now is not the time to waver, Shrike. It must be everyone, or we will never be safe. They are nothing to you."

There was a terrible pause in the room, and Shrike teetered on the edge of a precipice. He looked around the room, one face at a time, registering their silent shock. He finished by looking directly at Oliver and Jacob.

"No, you are right. Now is not the time to waver. But it is you who are nothing to me."

With a lightning movement of his right hand, he pulled something from the pocket of his jacket and threw it to Silas, who caught it in one hand and held it aloft. Blue light flooded from it, filling the room with a luminous glow.

"Now!" he shouted at the chained figures next to him. Princess Gaia and Grace stepped forward and held their hands high in the air above their heads. The chains fell from them, crashing on the floorboards with a crunch, and when they held hands, there was a deafening crack like a bolt of thunder. A fountain of pearly white stars erupted from their entwined hands. It shot up to the ceiling and sent tendrils down to all four corners of the room, swirling and twisting in a crazy, joyful reunion.

Oliver and Jacob cowered on the floor, aghast at what they had witnessed. The two figures in front of them gradually emerged from the pulsing blanket of stars that surrounded them. The stars formed a curtain, pulled back to reveal the action, like those at either side of a stage. The figures of Princess Gaia and Grace seemed to melt. Both Oliver and Jacob stared, rubbing their eyes, as if they were uncertain that they could be relied upon.

The figure of Princess Gaia lost her black, short locks. The hair grew longer and lighter. The face began to stretch and the skin paled. The figure grew taller and broader in the shoulders. Next to them the second figure also stretched and reformed like plasticine. Grace lost her pale skin and straight hair. Her features remoulded themselves. Eyes turned from blue to brown. The brown eyes were sparkling and there were tears streaming down her cheeks. There was a final, ecstatic flourish of a volcano of fizzing stars, before they all died away, and a dull, even quiet descended on the room.

Standing in front of them were two very familiar figures. Where the Princess had stood was now Thomas Trelawney, a quizzical smile on his face. Next to him, the girl who had been Grace, was returned to her real form, Clara, or the real Princess Gaia. Her eyes brimmed with tears.

Silas, the Sounding Stone still bursting with blue light, stepped forward.

"Thomas, my boy, and Princess, I can't tell you how pleased I am to see you here with us."

Oliver and Jacob cowered on the floor.

"What black magic is this?" stammered Jacob. "Where has that wretched Trelawney boy come from? Where have the others gone? What has happened?"

Thomas answered him. "Quite simple, Jacob. Shape

shifting. It's an ancient skill to take the form of another human being. Clara and I both have the skill. We knew we had to have some kind of disguise to get anywhere near Mulgrave Hall without being stopped."

Shrike cut across them. "But where is your sister? Where is Grace?"

"Grace is at The Rectory, waiting for us all to return," replied Tom. "Della is on her way now, with the released prisoners in the carriage."

Shrike took his time to digest everything that had just happened. His eyes flicked from side to side as his reptilian brain whirred silently.

"Shrike," Jacob began, desperate to urge him to follow orders.

"Master Shrike," interrupted Silas, stepping forward, "there is a choice to be made. I think you can see who will win here. There's no point in choosing the wrong side."

Before he had a chance to answer, Oliver lunged forward without warning and grabbed Mulgrave. Before anyone else could move, he had Mulgrave's arm twisted up around his back with one hand, and held a knife to Mulgrave's throat with another.

"Don't move!" he barked. "If anyone steps out of line, His Lordship here will have his throat slit. Understand? That damn Thomas Trelawney boy won't win this time, despite his devilish powers."

Silas held out both hands appealingly. "Stand aside everyone. There will be no blood shed today."

Everyone froze. Oliver inched Mulgrave towards the door, a step at a time, with Jacob joining them, his eyes constantly circling the room to guard against anyone not taking instructions from Silas. Mulgrave stumbled forward, sweat streaming down his cheeks, his free hand held up in front of him, as if he were asking for mercy. He snivelled and sobbed, great choking gasps that prevented him from speaking.

"I beg of you," he finally managed to say. "Have I not

always been a loyal servant? Why are you doing this, my Lord?"

Oliver stopped in his tracks, and jerked Mulgrave back, sending a stab of pain through his arm. He cried out in agony. Oliver hugged him close and laid the edge of his knife against his throat. He gently increased the pressure until the edge of the blade sliced the skin and a red line of blood welled up.

"Shut up, you miserable toad. Shut up, do you hear me? Any more from you and you will not live to see the other side of this door. Nod your head if you understand me, but not another word."

The others watched on, aghast at what was unfolding in front of them. They hardly dared breathe, never mind move. Shrike, on the other hand, saw that all the attention was on the knife pressing against the folds of skin on Mulgrave's neck. He reached inside the leather satchel he'd been carrying since they had left Hard Crag, his eyes fixed on the drama that was unfolding in front of him. He moved with the ease of the seasoned pickpocket, his actions barely creating the faintest stir of molecules in the air. Before even he was aware of it, he had found one of his remaining stun bombs, and had thrown it at Oliver's feet.

There was a deafening explosion and the room was filled with thick, choking smoke. The calm of a moment earlier was shattered. Shouts came from all sides of the room through the dense, mustardy fog. Blurred figures loomed out of the gloom and then receded again, each one unrecognisable. Suddenly, the smoke took on a blue tinge that grew steadily in strength, illuminating the distinctive figure of Silas, who held the Sounding Stone aloft in an attempt to disperse the fumes. Jacob saw his chance. He leaped for the stone, grabbing it from Silas' grip and knocking him to the ground in the process. As soon as he had the stone in his grip, the blue light drained away and the room was once again submerged in darkness.

Shrike, his brain ice cold, peered through the gloom to the spot where Oliver had had Mulgrave in his grip. He saw a sudden movement towards the door and pounced, grabbing hold of the first thing he came into contact with. There was a cry, a stumble, a volley of curses, and a slipping away. Shrike's fingers scrabbled wildly to keep hold of the sleeve he had managed to grasp. He pulled the body towards him and reached with his other hand to hold him down. Just as he was about to drag him away, there was a shout and Shrike felt a sickening blow to the head. As he sank to the floor, he could dimly see Oliver and Jacob slip through the door into the corridor beyond, and out of the corner of his eye, he caught a glimpse of the first flames licking at the curtains. It was the last thing he saw before everything went black and he fell away into unconsciousness.

FIRE AND FLOOD

They all began to stir at about the same time. The smoke had cleared and a few minutes of breathing the clean air blew away the fog in their heads. One by one, they got to their feet unsteadily and surveyed the room, heads pounding, mouths dry. The room was a picture of total chaos. Overturned chairs were scattered around, there were broken glasses and a strange selection of fruit sprayed around the carpet in front of the fireplace. Silas, already conscious, was standing in the middle of the devastation, frowning and repeatedly patting down his pockets as if searching for something.

As they tried to make sense of this incongruous scene, they slowly became aware of an unfamiliar sound: a growing crackle and then a rush of wind turning to a roar. Their bemusement was over almost as soon as it registered with them, as there was a great surging whoosh of wind, and a sheet of flame leaped to the ceiling from the curtains of the main window.

"Oh my God," shouted Tom in disbelief. "Fire!" He turned to Shrike in disbelief. "Why the hell did you throw that stun bomb in here? This was bound to happen."

They squared up to each other. "Should I have just stood by while Oliver and Jacob got away with Mulgrave as their prisoner?" Shrike snapped.

"Well, they got away anyway," Tom answered. "That doesn't matter now. We've got to put this fire out."

He looked frantically round the room and saw a half full jug of water on the table. He seized it and dashed the contents against the sheet of flame that was now the curtains. There was a hissing and fizzing as the intense heat battled with the water, but there wasn't enough of it to make a difference. They would have needed two hundred such jugs of water to stem the flames. The fire was so intense that Tom had to shield his face to stop himself being scorched.

"It's no good," said Shrike, "we'll never put it out now. We've got to get out of here, before it's too late."

He ran to the door and scrabbled with the handle. He rattled it back and forth with increasing violence, but it wouldn't budge. He turned back to face the others. "It's locked," he said, "we're tra…"

He trailed off as he caught sight of the bulky figure of Lord Mulgrave lying face down behind one of the sofas.

"Look," he continued, his voice beginning to tremble, "it's Mulgrave."

The others rushed around to where Shrike was pointing. Silas got there first. He bent down and gently rolled the body over. Gasps of horror came, as they saw the ugly red slash across his throat, and the steadily thickening pool of blood spreading in a dark stain across the floorboards.

"It must have been Oliver," said Clara, "he was the one who had the knife against his throat. How awful."

"But an accident, surely," said Tom. "He wouldn't just murder him in cold blood, would he?"

Shrike bent down next to Silas. He put out his hand and laid it gently on Mulgrave's cheek. His breath caught in a series of gulps and he blinked rapidly as he took in Mulgrave's face. If not for the jagged, bloody gash across his throat, he would have looked strangely peaceful, as if he were taking time out in a snatched sleep. For a fleeting moment, a satisfied smile flickered across Shrike's face.

The others watched him, unsettled by his uneasy response. And then he seemed to shake himself free of his first instinctive reaction. His face hardened into its usual blank mask, minus any sign of humanity, even including the perpetual sneer of half mocking he habitually wore. His mouth was set in a thin, straight line and he seemed to prepare himself. Finally, he broke the silence and answered the question.

"Clearly, Oliver will do anything to become King," he said, grim-faced. "We all need to be very careful from now on."

Dan, who had frantically zoomed around the room earlier, bobbing and weaving through the choking fumes of the stun bomb, lit up in a quivering shadow of luminescence, to catch everyone's attention.

"We all need to be very careful right now, or we're gonna be toast. Burned toast. Look."

He pointed back towards the window. The whole wall was a sheet of raging orange fire now and the room, clear of fumes a few minutes earlier, was filling up with black smoke. Flames leaped up from the curtains and began to travel across the ceiling above them, causing globules of paint to fizz and blister, before falling to the rug below.

"Come on, quickly! Follow me. We've got to get this door open," interjected Silas, raising his voice.

Clara looked down at the still, bulky figure of Mulgrave on the floor. In the raging chaos that was engulfing the room, the body was eerily quiet and unmoving.

"What about him?" she asked.

"There's nothing we can do for him now. Leave him. We must look to save ourselves now."

Silas turned away towards the door. As the others followed, there was a tremendous crash and the air was full of sparks and smoke. They all fell to the floor, cowering in shock, and looked back. There was a jagged hole in the ceiling above the tower of flames. Below was the rubble of plaster and wooden laths that had collapsed from above.

Tom turned to Clara. "Come on," he said, holding out his hand, "we don't have much time."

He hauled her to her feet and they both approached

the locked door. Holding hands, they both stared at the door handle, their faces contorted in concentration. Stars fizzed along their arms through their clasped hands, spiralled around their bodies, before funnelling towards the handle. The others were sandwiched between the growing wall of flames and the intense bank of heat it was throwing out, and the spectacular display of fireworks that Tom and Clara were generating.

"Hurry! Or we're all done for," shouted Shrike, his face steaming with sweat and blackened with ash and soot.

The stars intensified and then, slowly at first, the handle began to turn. Through the thickening smoke, they could just make out the bar of the lock, just visible in the gap, begin to turn. With one last effort, Tom and Clara forced it completely open. Silas rushed forward and grabbed the handle, and with a quick twisting motion opened the door. The flames drew a hurricane blast of wind from the corridor into the room, and the flames at the far end roared into even greater strength.

They all collapsed through the open door and fell into the corridor gasping for breath. The only one who was not affected, of course, was Dan. He could not survive the fire, but it had much less effect on him than the others. He was able to slide through the walls and doors to protect himself from the worst effects of the flames, and to do so in a calm and measured way. Now he hovered above the others, who were still trying to catch their breath and come to terms with their narrow escape. Dan bobbed above them, gently trying to rouse them to move.

"Come on, you lot. You can't lie there all day. You might have escaped the fire in that room, but it'll be all over this corridor in five minutes. We've got to get outside and away."

Slowly the others dragged themselves to their feet. There were scorched hands, and singed hair, and the after effects of a little smoke inhalation, but no serious damage had been done. By now, all of the servants were aware of the spreading fire. The corridors were full of them carrying buckets of water desperately trying to extinguish the flames. They were outside the Hall as well, attacking the fire from both directions. But there was no sign of Oliver or Jacob.

Silas called them all together.

"We must get back to The Rectory to plan our next move. Oliver and Jacob will be heading for York and Kings Manor, if I know anything about them. They will want to proclaim Oliver's claim to the throne and start spreading false stories about the Queen and the Princess here."

They all looked at Clara. For the first time, the reality of the situation hit them. Clara's mother, Queen Matilda, was dead. Clara felt all of their eyes upon her. She trembled and her eyes stung. Tom moved towards her and took her hand. She smiled at him gratefully, but then shook it off and recovered her poise. Now was not the time to break down.

"Silas is right," she said, with only the slightest quiver in her voice, "we can do nothing for the dead. It's the living we must protect now. Oliver and Jacob have to be stopped, however we have to do it."

Silas agreed. "You all go out onto the lawns and summon the Steedwings. There are things I must do. Go to Runswick. I will meet you there."

Tom frowned. "Are you sure, Silas? What more do you have to do here?"

"Yes, Thomas, I am sure."

He looked down the corridor which was filling with black acrid smoke.

"Quickly! Go now, before it's too late."

They scrambled down the corridor and raced down the stairs to the gardens. Silas watched them go and turned back to the drawing room that was now a raging inferno. He checked all of his pockets one last time and shook his head.

"Damn!" he cried. "My Sounding Stone. I must have dropped it in the chaos." He faced the wall of heat at the doorway, took a deep breath, and strode into the room that was now a nightmare of blistered walls, billowing smoke and brutal flames. Calmly, seemingly unaffected by the intense conflagration, he searched the floor and retraced his steps of earlier, looking under tables and at the bottom of bookcases. He even checked beneath Mulgrave's body.

"Nothing!" he whispered. He stopped, suddenly struck by the return of his memory. "Of course. It was Jacob that grabbed it and knocked me out."

Mind made up, he turned back to leave. Everyone had evacuated now, and the fire was spreading through the house uncontrollably. Without warning, cutting through the terrible sound of the flames and the wind, came a shuddering and groaning from above, and before he could take another step, an entire section of the ceiling crashed down from above like a flaming meteor, blocking the way to the corridor. The flames were so intense that they beat him back, and he was surrounded by choking, toxic smoke and a narrowing circle of fire.

He was trapped.

The others had scrambled down the stairs and out into the grounds, joining a growing tide of people who streamed out of the house and away to safety. They burst from the main entrance, reddened eyes stinging, lungs painfully labouring for air, and staggered down the steps to the green clipped lawn that sloped down from the house and skirted the lake. A gentle breeze, perfumed by freshly mown grass, brought them some comfort after the horrors of the house, and they collapsed onto the lawn, exhausted by their ordeal.

The lawn and the gravel paths that circled the house were strewn with scores of people. They stood and stared in shock at the fearful spectacle of the great house that loomed up in front of them. Their faces were smudged with soot and for many of them, trails of tears were smeared against their grubby cheeks. A few desultory conversations sprang up as they tried to make sense of it. Others, largely the younger, fitter men, had made a human chain from the lake, and were frantically trying to control the blaze, passing buckets of water up to the front of the house, to be thrown ineffectually against the raging inferno.

In the fresh air, their heads began to gradually clear. It was Tom who noticed it first. He looked up at the blackened window of the drawing room, and to his horror saw a dreadful scene unfold before him.

"Silas!" he screamed in disbelief. The others followed the direction of his shaking, pointing finger. Through the billowing smoke at the window, they could all see the familiar, angular figure of Silas desperately trying to smash the glass of the window. He lifted a chair high above his head and was just about to bring it crashing through the glass, when there was a rumbling sound like an earthquake and the ceiling of the room collapsed entirely, sending sprays of sparks and smoke high into the air. The collapse continued and the whole floor came down like a deck of cards, crushing the room below. There were screams from some of the escapees who were sitting too close to the building, and they surged across the lawn to get as far away from the house as possible.

Tom, Clara, Shrike and Dan stood stock still, frozen in fear and disbelief. Dan's ghostly form surged away from them towards the house, but even he was defeated by the intense heat from the inferno that roared in front of them. He beat a hasty retreat and retired to the others.

"It's no good," he gasped, "it's impossible to get any closer. No-one can survive that much fire."

They looked from one to the other, horror and sadness etched on their faces in equal measure. In a final, theatrical flourish, the dark clouds above were caught by a deathly, silvery sheen as a jagged bolt of lightning arrowed from the clouds to the roof of the Hall. A second later, the air was split by a crack of thunder directly above them, like a shot from a cannon, and the first fat drops of rain began to fall. Within seconds, the sky was a sheet of torrential rain, and the second bolt lightning came to be followed by wave after wave of other strikes. The storm had arrived.

ESCAPE

The rain came down in sheets from a darkened sky that had turned the late afternoon summer's day into an unnatural twilight full of menace.

Tom grabbed Clara's wrist, not noticing her eyes glittering with tears

"You must summon the Steedwings, Clara. We've got to get out of here and back to Runswick as soon as we can."

She wiped her eyes and nodded. "We need to move away from the crowds. Come on."

Following her, they ran across the lawn, their footsteps already sending up a squelching spray. When she judged they were far enough away from the Hall, and out of the trees, she brought the small silver horn clipped to her belt up to her lips.

"Cover your ears," she instructed. They did not need telling twice. She blew and the same deafening, unearthly sound filled the air. All around the grounds of the Hall, the people who had escaped from the fire and were now huddled together drenched, turned their attention away from the flames for the first time and stared up at the sky, trying to locate the source of the sound. As they stared, a new sound began, the sound of the crowd gasping in wonder and disbelief. They pointed to a gap in the clouds above them.

Two brilliant, white Steedwings soared through the clouds, then turned and banked and began to glide down to the sodden lawns below. The sun coming through the same gap in the clouds, turned the rain spattered wings and coats of the flying beasts into a dazzling display, and they had to shield their eyes as they came down to earth.

They landed a little way from Clara and the others. She called to them in a language that nobody else recognised. The lead Steedwing folded its great wings, sending spray all around, and trotted up to her. The horse towered over Clara, and had to bend down so that she could stroke its muzzle, and whisper in its ear. It whinnied softly and lowered itself onto its knees so that she could clamber aboard. Its partner did the same and they climbed up, Clara and Shrike on one Steedwing and Tom and Dan on the other.

"Hold on tight," she called to the others. "Let's go."

She whispered in the ear of her mount, softly stroking its mane and ears. After they had all clambered on, both Steedwings got to their feet and began to gallop across the lawns. With a great spring from the ground, they unfolded their wings and leaped into the air, their massively powerful wings beating to create a surging updraft of air. They soared as their wings continued to flap with a smooth, regular action.

Tom glanced down at the scene they had just left. The blackened hulk of Mulgrave Hall belched smoke into the air, and the gloom of the skies was partly lit up by the dying sheets of flame that still fitfully leaped from the wreckage. The thunderstorm was beginning to bring the fire under control. But his view of it, and the crowds of people scattered about the grounds of the Hall, only lasted a moment. The wind sent their hair streaming behind them and the rain lashed down from the thick dark clouds. It was only when they reached the clouds that they levelled off, and they could take a breath. But they could not relax. Seconds later, a great crack of thunder and lightning battered the air around them. The Steedwings did not turn a hair, continuing their powerful flight through the sheets of rain, jagged lightning bolts and explosive cracks of thunder.

The flight was quick. They soon began to bank smoothly to the left as the Steedwings descended through the clouds. When they broke through, the familiar sight of the coast at Runswick Bay, and The Rectory, standing prominently on the cliffs above, greeted them. A minute later, the Steedwings had come to a graceful halt in the walled garden of The Rectory. All four of them slid down to the ground, exhausted after their flight. It had stopped raining by this time but they were all drenched and frozen to the bone. Clara went to both Steedwings, whispering her thanks and then stood back. There was a flurry of whinnies and snorts, and a show of hooves pawing the ground before they leaped into the air once more. In seconds they had disappeared, arcing through the clouds back in the direction of the Moors.

Before they had time to gather their wits after such a challenging journey, the back door of The Rectory opened a crack, and a hand appeared, beckoning them in, accompanied by a hoarse whisper.

"Come on! Get inside, quickly, before you all catch your death of cold."

They did not need telling twice. Squelching over the sodden lawn, they dashed for the door, tumbling inside as it was opened wider in welcome. When the last of them had crossed the threshold, it shut behind them, leaving the garden growing ever darker in its watchfulness.

*

It was a sombre gathering that sat around the large deal table in The Rectory kitchen later. Darkness had fallen and the room was lit by lamps and the flickering from the small fire opposite the cooking range. The four who had made the storm flight from Mulgrave Hall had finally got themselves warm and almost dry, apart from Daniel, whose ghostly form had felt nothing of the lashing rain and biting cold.

The storm had rolled away over the cliffs to the north and east, and was fizzling out somewhere over the wild

North Sea. An occasional distant crump of thunder echoed back to them, now safe and warm indoors, as a reminder of the violence of the earlier storm they had ridden through. No such reminder was needed of the real storm they were in the middle of at that moment.

Elizabeth Somerville had sought comfort in preparing something to eat for everyone, but they had all approached it with more gratitude than appetite, as the reality of the previous few hours began to sink in for all of them. After a tearful reunion, with hugs and reconnections between friends who had not seen each other for the last few days, they finally faced the barely believable reality of death. And not just any death. Queen Matilda's death had been confirmed and Clara had been inconsolable once the adrenaline of the last few hours had ebbed away. She would never see her mother again. There was so much she wished she had said to her, so much she wished she had done. When she had cried herself dry, she gave a final, cathartic sigh that racked her whole body, and drying her eyes, she said to all around the table, "Well, enough of that. For my mother's sake and in her memory, we must move forward. We must plan what to do next. But first a toast."

They all raised their glasses, whether full of wine or water, and looked to Clara for her lead.

"To the Queen," she said simply and held out her glass to chink against all the others.

But no one moved their glass. They fidgeted in their seats and a sense of awkwardness descended on the group. It was Mary Carruthers who broke the silence.

"But, Clara, my dear. That is you now, don't you see? You are the Queen now."

She looked dumbfounded, and looked from one to the other around the table in confusion.

Mary continued. "To Queen Gaia. Long live the Queen."

She touched her glass to clink with Clara's, and the

others joined in with the chorus. "Long live the Queen!"

But it was not a cry of celebration. In their subdued mood, it more resembled a judge's sentence from the dock. Clara's next question added more gloom.

"And what of Silas? He cannot be dead too, surely?"

"You saw that fire just like we did," replied Tom. "There was no way out of that room and the whole ceiling caved in just as we left. I think we have to prepare ourselves for the worst and plan what to do without Silas to help us."

Elizabeth looked across at him.

"Silas will find a way, I'm sure of it. He must. He cannot be..."

Her voice trailed off and she looked away. An awkwardness descended on the gathering as a strained silence grew around them. The only sounds were the occasional moans of wind from the dying storm in the trees, and the unstoppable ticking of the grandfather clock. And then Shrike spoke.

Up until this point, he had been silent, a stranger in a group of friends, who had nothing to contribute to their agonised speculations about death. When he finally spoke, his voice cutting across the silence, it felt like nails scratched down a blackboard. All eyes turned to him.

"Forgive me, but that is enough now. We must decide what we are going to do, and soon. The redcoats will be swarming all over Runswick before too long and we cannot be found here. If any of us are arrested, we will never see the light of day again. Oliver and Jacob will see to that."

"What do you suggest?" asked Tom.

"We need to get to York before they do. If they put out the story about Clara being a witch then all is lost. And once Oliver is on the throne, it will be very difficult to overturn that. All of the army and the nobles will take the winning side. And without redcoats, we cannot hope to win."

"You forget, Shrike, that we have some powers between us. And we can finally use them without worrying about our friends in captivity," Clara replied.

"True enough, Your Majesty," Shrike said with a twisted smile, "but without the Cummerbund fellow, you are easily beatable."

"And what about you, Shrike?" said Della. "I still don't understand why you jumped ship at the end. After all, you've been working for them all along. And if you could have forged the confession, as Oliver explained, then why didn't you stick with them? You'd have been in the clear. It just doesn't make sense. And it certainly doesn't make us trust you."

Shrike's green eyes glittered in the candle light.

"The thing is, I wouldn't have been in the clear. Not with Oliver and Jacob. If everything goes to plan and Oliver becomes King, do you think they would just pay me my sack of gold and let me live a quiet life, happily ever after?"

He snorted at the idea. "No, of course they wouldn't. They would have me killed at the first opportunity, without a second thought. I would never be able to rest in peace and enjoy my gold. I'd always be looking over my shoulder, waiting for the silent dagger between the ribs. Whereas, you people…"

He paused and looked round the table at them, smiling.

"Forgive me, but you are an unlikely bunch of assassins. I've watched you closely. Quite frankly you are all too, too..." He struggled to find the right word, before finally settling on it. "...too nice, that's it, too nice to get rid of me. Some of you would think twice about sticking a knife in a potato to peel it. I've never come across that before. I decided, quite selfishly of course, that my chances of a long and happy life were better with you."

"So, you're saying that the fact that Oliver ordered you to kill us all, as soon as they had left to go to York, had nothing to do with it?"

Shrike shook his head. "No, of course it did. It forced me to make the choice and to act then. I knew Cummerbund needed his magic pebble, and with it, you would all be able to overpower them. And it would have worked if they hadn't grabbed Mulgrave."

Dan shimmered into view, bobbing and rippling, like a candle flame.

"But what about the papers you took from Mulgrave's safe? What was all that about? What were they and why are they so important?" he asked.

"That's my business, Master Ghost, not yours," he snapped in a flash of anger. He looked around the room and noted the puzzled faces of his companions. They had never seen Shrike lose his temper. No matter what the provocation, he had always been like a shard of ice. A cold heart and a blank mask, that was Shrike.

"But…" began Grace.

His voice softened. "We have no time for this, truly. We need to leave and we can't leave without a plan."

"He's right," said Clara. "We should split up to make it harder for them."

"We must use the Sisterhood," said Elizabeth. "We have people all over the country and we will need all of them if we are going to fight back. Mary, I suggest that you and I head to London. We can take a boat from Runswick and then pick up a ship from Whitby. If we hurry, we can go to Nat at the Crab tonight."

"By sea?" asked Mary, her eyebrows raised.

"Safer," replied Elizabeth, "especially if we go tonight. We can be in Tilbury in a few days time, if the winds are with us."

"And then on to Covent Garden. We can disappear for a while at Hester's."

"Exactly. Della, Amelia, you should go to York to Indira or Jacinthe. You must change your appearance, both of you. They will be looking for all of us, and two striking young women like you must not be seen together."

Amelia had a determined set to her jaw. "Well, if Della can dress up as a man, I'm sure I can too."

She took up her long blonde ringlets in one hand and held them up.

"And anyway, it was time for a new look. This hair can go."

"Good," nodded Elizabeth. "Can you ride there tonight?"

Della returned the nod. "If we keep to the moors and avoid the main coaching roads, we should be alright."

Elizabeth turned to Clara, Shrike and Grace. "And what of you? Where is the safest place for you to go?"

Shrike answered immediately. "We must return to Hard Crag. No one knows anything about it except me. It's the safest hideout I know."

A flash of concern passed across Tom's face.

"I don't like it," he said. "It's too dangerous. Can't you go with one of the other groups?"

Grace laughed. "Tom, you forget. Nothing is dangerous for me. I'm dead already, remember. It's the perfect place."

He looked at Clara. "What do you think? Will you be safe there?"

"I'll be as safe there as anywhere. But, what are we actually going to do? How are we going to fight back? I don't want to hide for the rest of my life."

They all looked from one to the other around the table. No one could bring themselves to say what they were all thinking. Without Silas, without The Watcher, how could they possibly win? It suddenly felt very daunting. A quiet fell upon them, an oppressive realisation that their world had changed in an instant, and that it would be a huge undertaking to try and recapture what they had lost.

Eventually, Mary broke the spell. "We will wait. Watch and wait. Some of us can communicate with our Sounding Stones. The others must be patient and wait for the call." She turned to Tom and Daniel. "You two must go back to

England now. You've already been here too long. Watch your Stones and wait for the call. When it comes, you will know what to do. And remember." She paused for a moment and was caught between a half smile and tears. "Remember, we need you. We can't do this without you."

Tom nodded. "We'll be ready. But, Mary, I feel bad about leaving you all in this mess. Especially without Silas."

"No, no, enough of that. Let's keep hold of our optimism, shall we? We're going to need it. Summer's over by the look of it, and we will need strength to get through the hard winter that's coming." She turned back to the others. "Now, we really need to get going. Half an hour to collect what we need. We need to clean up as well, so that there's no sign that we've been here, just in case. So, come on everyone, let's get to it."

They rose reluctantly from the table and set about the tasks at hand. As they cleared the table and ferried the dishes to the kitchen, each of them was preoccupied with the same, unspoken thought: when will we all sit together round this table again? It was a question that none of them dared dwell on for too long. Once the kitchen was clear, the different parties began to make their preparations: packing bags with the bare essentials, cutting hair, changing appearance, readying the horses. In amongst this activity, final conversations took place in snatched moments in private corners of the house. Some were of farewell, others of planning. Some were of love.

*

Amelia stood in front of the mirror in her room and examined her reflection. Her long golden hair was now a shoulder length bob, dyed black. She wore breeches, a linen shirt, silk scarf and dark blue frock coat, topped off by a tricorn hat.

Della came up behind her and put her arms around her.

"Perfect! Every inch the country gentleman," she exclaimed. "And what of me? Do I pass muster?"

Amelia considered Della's reflection. She too had transformed herself into the image of a regency gentleman. She turned and kissed Della lightly on the cheek.

"You'll do for me," she said.

"Even without my jewellery?"

"Even that. But we must be careful. Until Oliver is brought down and Clara is on the throne, we are in danger. These are dark days in front of us."

Della dropped her smile. Her face was serious and determined.

"That, my sweet, is why we must win this battle. We must."

*

Tom went to find Grace. He knocked lightly on her door and slipped inside when she answered.

"I've barely seen you since I've been back," he said. "I'm sorry. But I don't know whether that's my fault or yours."

"Both, probably," she replied. "And now you must go. Back to England and home."

Tom was submerged in a wave of guilt. Grace sounded so sad.

"It's just that, when we met up again at Hard Crag, you seemed to want to spend your time with Shrike."

Grace flashed him a look. She snapped back, "And you with Clara."

"The thing with Clara is different. We have a connection. There's nothing we can do about it," Tom replied, "it's just there."

Grace rolled her eyes. "That's nice for you," she said pointedly.

"Oh, Grace, come on," he snapped. "If we're gonna fight back against Oliver and Jacob, it will be through me and Clara. I'm not boasting, it's just a fact. And without Silas, it will be much harder."

"Do you think Silas is really gone? I can't imagine it."

"I saw him in the fire, remember? No one could have

survived that."

"But Silas isn't just anyone. He's The Watcher."

"I dunno. Maybe." He shuffled from foot to foot awkwardly.

"Listen, will you be alright with Shrike? Hard Crag's a pretty creepy place. And winter's coming."

She shook her head. "I know you don't like him. None of you do. But he's different to what you think. He's been very nice to me. You don't know how lonely I've been here. It's been nice to talk to someone of my own age who listens."

Tom reached out and took her hand. "I know it's hard for you. I'm pleased you have a friend, honestly. But be careful, that's all I ask."

She smiled. "Goodness me, Tom, how grown up you are. You suddenly seem much older, somehow."

"I feel much older. It's the responsibility, I guess."

He stopped and suddenly enveloped Grace in a hug. He held onto her for as long as he dared and then pushed her away.

"It's time to get going. Be careful. And use the Stone."

*

An hour later, The Rectory stood in darkness. The storm had long since passed, and the wind had dropped so that the stillness of the night was disturbed only by the occasional gust that shook the first leaves from the trees. Over the constant, distant sound of the sea below, came a new noise: horses' hooves clattering on the road that passed the house. One direction led down to the sea and the other upward to the wild moors. The horses wheeled into the drive from the road. There was twenty of them, a redcoat troop, and bringing up the rear was an open cart.

The leader of the troop jumped down from his horse and tethered it to the post. He turned to his men and called out, "Cover back and front. And check the outhouse at the back. You four…" He pointed at the men at the front of the troop. "You come with me. Pistols drawn, lads. These are desperate rogues, by all accounts."

He hammered on the front door with the butt of his pistol, and when there was no answer, indicated to one of the four to deal with the door. They entered The Rectory in a flurry of banging and shouting, lighting lamps as they went. The men that had been dispatched to the back of the house did the same, opening doors and examining any possible hiding place. But they found nothing.

The Captain knew after a minute or two that they were too late. The birds had flown the coop. The search carried on for another ten minutes, just to make sure, while his face grew ever more furious. He'd be blamed for sure. That's the way these things worked, he knew that.

"That's enough," he bellowed, "let's go down to The Crab. Then we'll start knocking a few heads together, and see who talks first."

The riders streamed out of the gate and made their way down to the harbour. As the ringing sound of their hooves died away, there was another moaning gust of wind, heavy with salt and the smell of the sea. In the moonlight, the leaves, tinged with brown and yellow, danced briefly until the wind died down and they settled gently on the sodden lawn. The Rectory stood deserted, waiting for the time when life and noise and bustle would return again.

A COLD WIND BLOWS

The weather had turned completely in the previous few days. The warmth of summer seemed a distant memory. With the breaking of the storm had come the breaking of the seasons. Skies were grey, the wind was chill and the mornings started with the first mists. For all of them, it felt like the beginning of something new, the turning of a page in a book.

In York, the streets were thronged with redcoats, on every corner, and in force at every gate in the city walls. There were crowds in the streets, all making their way through the jumble of ancient back alleys, all heading in the same direction, towards the Minster. The atmosphere, though, was not one of celebration. Instead, the air was full of fear and foreboding. Under the watchful eyes of the redcoats, there were whispered conversations, with eyes darting everywhere. Was it really true? Queen Matilda was dead, at the hands of her daughter, Princess Gaia, who had confessed to witchcraft and gone missing. On every street corner there were lurid posters offering a reward for information leading to the arrest of the Princess, or The Witch Traitor, as she had been dubbed.

And even more incredible, Oliver, the grandson of the old mad King from years ago, was named as Matilda's successor and was to be crowned in public today at York Minster, in a ceremony to be repeated at St James' Palace in London the following week. No one quite knew what to make of it, but no one, apart from those who had taken advantage of this unexpected holiday and were already a little the worse for wear with drink, dared voice their worries.

The crowd shuffled towards the Minster, which stood in the early autumn greyness, stately and aloof, a timeless symbol of things remaining the same, even through war, famine and disease. It had been there for the old, mad King, it had been there for Queen Matilda, and now it was ready to receive Oliver.

The first ranks of the crowd were admitted at the back. It was clear that there was barely any room left, and that thousands more would have to make do with gathering outside, straining to hear anything they could of the service, and waiting patiently for the King to leave at the end, so they could snatch a glimpse of the new sovereign.

Inside, amongst the lucky few who managed to squeeze in at the back, Della and Amelia craned their necks to get a better view of the proceedings.

"Any sign of them?" asked Amelia.

"Not yet, as far as I can see. Maybe they are keeping a low profile for a while, until the heat dies down."

"I was sure Silas would turn up. In disguise, maybe, but I thought he'd be here somewhere."

Della bent towards her to answer and then noticed a tubby, middle-aged, balding man staring at them. He looked away over her shoulder, and smiled and signalled to someone behind them. She wasn't sure. He was either a skilful spy or someone who had genuinely seen someone they knew in the crowd. She couldn't take the risk and pulled Amelia towards her.

"We need to be careful what we say. This crowd is full of Oliver's spies," she whispered.

Amelia nodded. "That's not all," she replied. "Look around - who do you see in this bit of the crowd?"

Della looked all around them, puzzled. "Nobody," she replied, "everybody. I don't know what you mean, it just looks normal to me."

Amelia shook her head. "Now look at the front, in the

posh seats."

She did and gradually, understanding broke out on her face. "There are no people of colour in the best seats. It's just white people. Where are all the other Lords and Ladies of colour?"

"They've got the back rows. Look, right there just in front of us."

She pointed ahead of them. There they sat, in all of their finery. They still had their silks and furs and jewellery. But their faces told another story. Expressions that veered from fear to fury. There was the occasional nervous glance, the touch of a wife's hand on a husband's arm.

Things had changed and this, they all knew, was only the start.

*

After a week at sea, the sight of London, spread out on both sides of the Thames, was a welcome one. They had seen the pall of smoke that hung over the city from miles away, and even that brought a smile to their faces after several days of being tossed on an angry North Sea. They had spent most of the journey down in their cabin, only venturing out on deck at night, when they could take no more of the incessant pitching and rolling of the ship. Even then, they kept their faces covered as well as they could and kept their voices low.

Now, the wind blew in their faces as their ship approached the Execution Dock at Wapping, each with a single leather hold-all at their feet. Once the ship was secured and the boarding plank lowered, they stepped gingerly onto the greasy cobbles of the dock, clutching their bags. Amid the unceasing bustle of the port, with goods from all four corners of the globe being unloaded and carted to the warehouses that lined this stretch of the river, one thing stood out, sending a shiver of fear through them. There were lines of redcoats, muskets over their shoulders, looking for anyone suspicious who might be about to disembark from the steady flow of ships that docked here during the day. Mary and Elizabeth exchanged a glance. Mary leaned over to Elizabeth as she pretended to fiddle with the straps of her bag.

"Remember our story," she whispered before turning away.

The shrill voice of the newsboy rang clear above the hubbub. "Read all about it! King Oliver crowned today. Ceremony at York Minster! God save the King!"

Mary and Elizabeth exchanged glances. Through the crowds, they caught a glimpse of the news boy's billboard. It confirmed his repeated cries: Oliver was to be crowned that day. Mary went over to the boy, flipped him a farthing and took his double-sided sheet of news. They poured over it for any scrap of information they might need later, having been starved of news in the previous week as the North Sea had battered and buffeted them for two hundred miles.

"It seems very quick. He is to be crowned today. It's only been a week," said Mary under her breath, her eyes darting everywhere over the crowds.

"Once he is confirmed as King, it will be harder to do anything about it. That's why they want to rush it through," Elizabeth replied.

"I wonder if Della and Amelia will be there to see it," said Mary. "It's agony not knowing where everyone is and if they are safe."

"That's why we must get to our lodgings as quickly as we can. If there are messages for us, they will have been sent there. We need to get there and take stock before we make our move."

She looked up to see a hansom cab coming their way, the horse's hooves clattering on the cobbles of the dockside. She raised her hand and shouted, "Hi there, driver!"

The driver yanked on the reins and the horse pulled up within a few yards of them. Elizabeth scrambled up to the driver, hauling her bag with her.

"Covent Garden, driver, please."

They both climbed up inside the cab, swinging their bags after them. The door slammed shut and the horse, encouraged by the driver's clucking tongue and flicking reins, trotted along the harbour side encore turning sharp right onto Wapping Wall. The cab faded into the distance, leaving Execution Dock behind, to be swallowed up by the great metropolis. London had them now.

*

"How much longer must we wait?" Clara's impatience, her frustration at their inaction, screamed from every word she said, every expression on her face.

"Like I said last time you asked - as long as it takes," Shrike replied bluntly. He continued to whittle another piece of wood, squatting down by the fireside. His blade flashed this way and that as he worked the wood, shaving, cutting, gouging and chopping to get the shape he wanted.

He looked up momentarily from the knife. His voice softened. "You must be patient, Clara. We are all waiting for a sign. It could come from London or from York. Or even from Runswick. If we make a move without it, we would just be committing suicide. They will be looking for us, you can be sure of that."

She turned away and paced, yet again, to the end of the room and the barred window. She clambered up onto the ledge and peered through the bars into the grounds of Hard Crag. Dusk was beginning to gather, the darkness clotting around the edge of the forest that crowded in on the wall of the estate, but she could still make out the herd of steedhorns doggedly cropping the grass. She thought, not for the first time, that a short blast on her horn would bring a Steedwing to carry her wherever she wanted to go. She shook her head. Not yet. Not yet.

Shrike interrupted her thoughts.

"If you need useful employment to distract you, why not go down with Grace and gather some more wood? We're running low and the cold is starting to bite."

Grace looked up.

"Yes, Clara, let's go. The walk will do us good," she said brightly. There was another reason to go, one she did not need to mention. They had to talk, Clara and her, about Shrike. And about Clara's mother, the Queen. Now they had both experienced death, they were linked more strongly, somehow. And yet they had not been able to bring themselves to have that conversation. Perhaps now was the time.

They gathered their coats and set off.

"Don't be long," cautioned Shrike, "it's getting dark and we need to lock the door. Just in case."

He watched them go, waiting until the door to the dormitory was firmly closed. He took up his knife again and with a few more deft strokes, finished his work on the pieces of wood, laying them down on the hearth. Then, with a quick glance all around him, he reached under his bed for his satchel. He rummaged deep inside it for a second before pulling out the documents he had retrieved a week ago in Lord Mulgrave's study. He unfolded them carefully, smoothing them out on the bed, and began to read them. As he did so, a smile grew steadily on his face. Finally, he patted them with satisfaction, and replaced them carefully in the satchel, before sliding it back underneath his bed.

The smile grew wider now. He picked up his three whittled pieces of wood and lined them up in a row on the hearth to the side of the grate. Three cleverly shaped little dolls stood in a row. As he put each one down, he recited their name softly under his breath.

"Princess Clara. Mistress Grace. And Lord Shrike."

And he began to laugh.

*

Tom stared across his desk at his Sounding Stone. It seemed as if he had done nothing but stare at it since he returned from Yngerlande, nearly a week ago now. He stretched and yawned and glanced at the time on his phone. Nearly 2 am. He really should get to bed and get some sleep, if only to stop his parents and teachers hassling him about how tired he looked. "Is everything alright, Tom," they would say. He would smile and nod, and say, "Yes, of course. Just got a bit of a bug, that's all." But all the while, in his head, he was screaming at them. No, of course I'm not alright.

He undressed and fell into bed, burrowing under the duvet to stop himself from looking, either at his phone, or at the Stone on his desk. In the darkness, he thought back to his journey back from Yngerlande.

It had been a bit of a scramble. The others had all left The Rectory while he and Dan had stayed a little longer. Dan hovered on guard in the Hall, with a view of the approach from the lane, just in case, while Tom searched Silas' study. He had wanted to sit there for a moment or two before making the journey back through the grandfather clock. He couldn't believe that Silas was really gone and felt sure that if he looked hard enough for it, a clue could be discovered amongst his things in the study. He had rifled through drawers, flicked through sheafs of papers, looked in boxes and envelopes and under ornaments, but there had been nothing.

And if Silas truly was dead, what did that mean for him and Yngerlande? He was The Friend after all, and everything he knew about this strange land, so familiar while being so different at the same time, he knew because of Silas. Without Silas, was he still The Friend? And if he was, who was The Watcher? He sat at the desk, one candle flickering to ward off the darkness, lost in thought.

And what of Grace and Clara? He felt guilty that he had not spent more time with his sister, but consoled himself that nothing terrible could happen to her. After all, as she had reminded him sadly, she was already dead, and anything after that must be a bonus. It was strange getting used to her in Yngerlande. Perhaps this was what people meant when they said, in the depths of his grief at her death, that time is a great healer and that eventually, the bereaved find a way to move on.

And Clara? Or Princess Gaia - Queen Gaia as he should call her now. Well, she wasn't dead and he did worry about her. Particularly in the company of Shrike, who he didn't trust an inch. How can I possibly leave them in his clutches?

He had had little time to ponder that question. Dan suddenly slid through the wall towards him hissing a warning.

"We've got to go. The Redcoats are back. Look"

Tom crept to the window, hardly daring to breathe, and had peered out, crouching down so he did not stand out from outside. There they were down below, a handful of redcoats, muskets primed.

"Sarge," whispered one of the voices, "there's a light in that room just above us."

Tom froze for a second and then, with a quick look towards Dan, darted to the grandfather clock. He yanked at the door, his heart hammering against his chest, but it was stuck. As he frantically pulled at the handle, he heard the front door downstairs open and footsteps come hammering up the stairs. With one last heave, the door of the clock slid open and Tom had thrown himself inside, slamming the door shut behind him. Dan slid through the heavy wood with ease. Tom lay back against the door and breathed a long and heavy sigh of relief. No matter how much they banged on the clock, Tom knew they would never be able to gain entry. They were safe.

But now, in the cool, still darkness of his room in England, what was that safety worth? He would give anything to go back, just to feel that he was helping. Anything must be better than this terrible waiting. He looked across one last time at his desk and the Sounding Stone, praying for a flash of blue light, but there was nothing.

He sighed and settled down, finally, to sleep. He'd start

again tomorrow.

*

The smell of smoke and ash still hung in the air, even though the fire had been extinguished completely several days ago. Mulgrave Hall was a sorry sight in the gathering gloom of late September dusk. The bulk of the house stood, just as before, a stately, solid building of sprawling magnificence, but a dark and ugly scar was slashed across it, where the fire had brought about a partial collapse of the middle section of the house. It had been the monumental thunderstorm, with its torrential rain, that had prevented total destruction. A violent conflagration matched by nature's own violence.

A handful of staff remained to look after what was left of the Hall. Many had lost their jobs, but some were kept on to keep the grounds and the ruin safe and secure. The ground floor was still habitable, apart from the central area, and work had begun on clearing the wreckage and beginning the process of repair. Lord Mulgrave's body, or what was left of it, had been recovered from the ruins and the funeral had already taken place, but the future of the house and the estate itself was much less clear. Try as they might, no one had yet managed to locate a copy of his will. With no surviving close relatives, ownership of his estate could not be decided. The executors were bracing themselves for a long legal fight, as people making claims came forward in the hope of getting their hands on some of the Mulgrave riches.

During the day, the Hall was a bustle of activity, as an army of workmen laboured to repair the fire damage and make the building watertight and weatherproof before the onset of winter. But as the sun dipped below the horizon, and darkness gathered around ruins, they left for home in the surrounding villages. The gates were locked and the estate stood alone under the night sky. It was deserted, save for one solitary night watchman, Clegg. His task was to keep the building secure against robbers. The Hall was full of valuables: priceless antiques, old oil paintings, gold and silver plate.

He had had to be on his guard at first, as there were a couple of attempts to break in by casual thieves trying their luck. But they stopped after a week or so and rumours began to fly around the neighbourhood. Strange lights and noises at night, unexplained bumps and the sound of footsteps on floorboards above, where no floorboards now stood, shadows in corridors. All of these featured in the stories that were being spread about Mulgrave Hall. The Haunted Hall as the locals now called it. Even Clegg, a man who was not given to flights of fancy, had had a disturbing encounter there, one night soon after taking the job. He mentioned it to no one, wanting to protect his reputation, but from that point on, he resolved to stay firmly put in his comfortable little room, sleeping in front of his cosy fire, rather than venture out on patrol after dark.

So there was no one who witnessed the stirring of the ashes and charred furniture, no one who saw the strange dancing lights playing on the blackened walls near the source of the fire, and no one who heard the faint echo of footsteps pacing the corridors of this desolate ruin.

No one noted these things, but they were there.

In his room, Clegg shivered. He got up from his easy chair to fetch another log for the fire and tossed it into the grate, sending sparks flying and shadows dancing on the walls. From outside, a sudden gust of wind moaned and rattled the windows. He peered through a gap in the curtains at the darkness outside. The first spray of rain splattered against the window, and the trees were like waves out on the North Sea, just a mile or two further east.

A cold wind was blowing across the Kingdom. The warm, bright days of summer were already a distant memory and it would get worse before it got better. Winter was on its way.

The End

The final part of the "Yngerlande Variations " trilogy, 'When Stars Collide", will follow shortly

ABOUT THE AUTHOR

Rob was an English teacher in London for many years, and now, when he's not writing, he trains new English teachers. "A Cold Wind Blows" is his second book for children and young adults.

Originally from Teesside, he became familiar with Runswick Bay, the North Yorkshire Moors and the city of York, first as a child and then as a student. His love of the history and geography of these locations can be seen on every page of The Watcher and The Friend series.

www.ingramcontent.com/pod-product-compliance
Lightning Source LLC
LaVergne TN
LVHW091106080826
845145LV00008B/1824